KT-563-393

To Hazel Osmond who had faith in me when I barely had faith in myself, George and Libby wouldn't exist if it wasn't for you.

She had groaned in embarrassment as he continued to eat his lasagne.

She watched him now as he picked up the last crumbs of his bacon sandwich, and smiled.

'Oh, I got you something,' George said, passing over the brown paper bag, before he started singing his own version of 'Twelve Days of Christmas'. *'Ten days before Christmas and my true love gave to me, a mug with a picture of the sea.'*

Libby smiled. He had started this twelve days of presents two days before when he had presented her with a Christmas pudding onesie complete with a hood with a holly leaf and huge red berries sewed to the top. The day before he had given her a big bag of rum and raisin fudge when they had been shopping in the town, her favourite sweets in the world. She quickly tore apart the paper bag and pulled out a mug that must have held at least a pint of tea. It was the tackiest thing she had ever seen. It had a picture of White Cliff Bay on the side but it wasn't tasteful, it was bright and garish in colour.

'And look what happens when you pour hot water in it.' George grabbed her tea and poured it inside. Straight away, lights started to flash all over the mug, including on the oversized lighthouse, and a tinny version of 'All I Want for Christmas Is You' drifted from some internal speakers.

Libby laughed. 'I love it,' she said, honestly.

'Now you have something to remember us by,' he said, glancing over at a few boxes in the hall and for a brief moment his face fell with disappointment before he slapped on a smile. 'How's the packing going?'

'There's not a lot to be honest. The flat came with its own furniture. There's a few books and things I've acquired over the last few months that I'll probably take to a charity shop. I don't really have stuff, I don't need it. I came with a suitcase of clothes and I'll probably leave the same way.'

'That's a bit sad, isn't it? To have no belongings other than the clothes on your back.'

Libby shrugged, happily. 'Happiness doesn't come from the things you own, it comes from experiences, the things you do, the places you go to, the people you meet. That's what fills your life, not material possessions.'

'And you've never been tempted to stay in all those beautiful places you've visited, you've never once found somewhere you could call home?'

She smiled. 'It doesn't work like that for me. I have to travel for work. Being an author means doing lots of research. Wherever my story is set I always immerse myself in that place, eat, drink, sleep, breathe it until the story is finished and I move on to the next place. I've always worked like that, I probably always will.'

Suddenly a noise from above them disturbed their conversation.

Squeak. Squeak. Squeak. Squeak. Squeak. SqueakSqueak, SqueakSqueak, SqueakSqueak, SqueakSqueak, SqueakSqueak, SqueakSqueak, SqueakSqueakBang.

They both looked up.

'Twice!?' she muttered. 'Seriously? Do they not have a TV in their flat?'

SqueakSqueak, SqueakSqueak, SqueakSqueakbang, SqueakSqueakBang, SqueakSqueakBang, SqueakSqueakBang, SqueakSqueakBang.

'Oh!'

SqueakSqueakBang.

'Oh!'

George chuckled. 'They really are loud, aren't they?'

She pulled a face.

8

'Well come on, Lib, we can give them a run for their money.' He stood up and pulled her towards her bedroom. Leaving her by the doorway he leaped onto her bed, jumping up and down on it like a trampoline. The bed made a satisfying squeaking sound and the headboard banged obligingly against the wall.

She laughed at him. 'Oh George,' she moaned loudly, from the doorway.

'How long do you think my penis is?' he hissed. 'Get over here.'

She ditched her dressing gown and walked over to the bed.

'Christ, Lib, we're only pretending, you don't have to get undressed.' He stopped bouncing long enough to help her up onto the bed. They both started bouncing again.

'Oh George,' she shouted, 'that feels so goooood.'

'Oh Libby,' he groaned.

'George, harder George. Oh God that's it George. GEORGE! Faster George.'

'Libby, Libby, OH Libby.' He started jumping faster.

'Spank me George, spank me.'

He spluttered with laughter.

'Oh.'

'OH.'

'Oh God.'

'OH.'

'OHHHHHHHHH,' moaned George, finally falling onto the bed exhausted. She fell down next to him.

'Oh George,' she called loudly, 'that was the best sex ever. You're amazing, big boy.'

'Why thank you, Miss Joseph, glad you enjoyed it.'

'No, you're supposed to say something nice about me.'

'Oh sorry, erm…' He thought carefully. 'Libby' he said loudly, 'you have great tits.'

'Is that it?'

'Well it's true, you do.'

'Pervert.' She smirked. 'I just said that was the best sex ever and all you can say is that I've got nice tits? Surely you can do better than that?'

He rolled his eyes. 'Libby,' he moaned loudly, 'and Candy my beauty, that was the best threesome I've ever had.'

She could barely talk for laughing. 'Great, now I'm some kind of sex-crazed porn star, excellent.'

'Glad to be of service.'

'And if they knew that Candy was that mannequin in your bedroom, they would be worried.'

He chuckled.

They lay in silence for a while to see if there was any reaction from the newlyweds. But there was none. Clearly they had been outdone.

Libby rolled onto her side, propping herself on her elbow to look at him. She smiled at the self-satisfied look on his face, as if they really had just had sex.

'Fancy a walk?' she said.

'Yeah of course.'

'Well get out my bedroom then so I can get dressed.'

'Aw, am I never going to get a repeat performance of your nudity?' he said as he walked out.

'Nope never.' She laughed as she closed the door behind him.

'That's a shame,' George said to the closed door, 'because I really rather enjoyed it.'

———

Despite it being the middle of winter, the sun was making a desperate attempt to warm up the windy shore. Great gusts tore at their clothes and whipped their hair around them as they walked along the almost deserted beach nestled in Silver Cove. The only other person there was Seb, throwing a ball into the surf for his beloved fat retriever Jack to collect. He waved at them as they walked.

George loved White Cliff Bay, with its tiny thatched cottages, the bigger townhouses, and the great Bubble and Froth, Seb's pub, with the best-tasting ale in the world. He especially loved the quieter part of Silver Cove where he and Libby lived. It literally consisted of one straight road with houses on one side looking out to sea. There was a pub, a small shop and that was it. A five-minute walk up the hill and over the headland led to the main town of White Cliff Bay with all the local amenities.

He and Libby crunched over the pebbles towards one of the many rock pools that had formed on the beach. She crouched down and carefully lifted one of the big rocks to see what was under it. A small pearly grey hermit crab scurried out in protest at being disturbed and a pale yellow starfish, its legs struck out at odd angles to its body, pulsated against the mossy rock face.

'I do love the starfish. They're so beautiful, like a little bit of magic washed up on the beach.' She put the rock down gently, and picked up another one.

He watched her with a smile, her dark hair streaming behind her like a banner, her large green eyes filled with a continual wonder at the varied sea life that ended up on Silver Cove beach every day.

'If you like starfish, you'll love the sunstar, now they're beautiful. I'll have to take you scuba diving one day, Lib, there's so much more beauty out there under the waves.'

She stood up. 'I'd love that. Would we find seahorses? I'd love to see one.'

'I doubt it – there are some breeds that live round Britain, but they're so shy and timid I doubt we would spot any. But there's loads of other things we would see, the visibility round here is quite spectacular.'

'But doesn't it take ages to learn?'

'I can teach you the basics, and I'd look after you. Besides, we wouldn't be going that deep, only six or eight metres, so if anything went wrong you could just come straight back up.'

'That would be so exciting, do you have the gear?'

'No but a mate of mine runs a dive shop in White Cliff Bay, he'd lend me what we need.'

'Be a bit cold though, would we wear wetsuits?'

'Are you kidding, in these waters? We would die. It'd have to be a drysuit, and a thermal undersuit and your clothes under that.'

She laughed. 'I'd look like a Michelin Man.'

'Yeah. It'll be better in the spring, warmer and the visibility is nicer too. If you stay until then I promise to take you.'

'Maybe I can come back and visit you when it's warmer.'

'That would be great,' George said, knowing in his heart that once she left at the end of the year he'd never see her again. They never spoke about that though. She insisted that they would stay in touch, but there were no friends in her life, no one she spoke to from her travels. When he had put his number in her phone all those months before he had been stunned to see her contacts list consisted of her agent and her publisher. It was easier to pretend they would still be friends than confront it, it was easier to ignore that when she left it would completely and utterly break his heart.

He carried on with the façade. 'You have to spit in the mask to stop it from steaming up too.'

Her face fell. 'Spit in my mask?'

He wiped a tiny splash of muddy water off her face, then quickly stuffed his hands in his pockets as he walked away from her. 'Yeah, and no matter if you get the best-fitting mask in the world, you always get a bit of water that seeps through, which means when you take the mask off you'll be left with a snotty residue across your face.'

She caught up with him, picking up a good-shaped pebble for skimming. 'I get the feeling scuba diving isn't the sexiest sport then?'

'No definitely not, still keen?' He turned to face her.

'Absolutely.'

He loved that about Libby: her spirit of adventure, her boundless energy. In fact he loved every little thing about her, and had been completely in love with her ever since he first set eyes on her.

Unrequited love, he was quite the expert. As it turned out even his ex-wife hadn't loved him.

Libby, of course, had no idea about his inappropriate feelings for her, how he loved her with everything he had.

He glanced over at her, her smile lighting up her face, her eyes reflecting the colour of the sea. It was about time he got over Libby. She just didn't see him that way. Nothing was ever going to happen there, she was leaving in just over two weeks. By the end of the year he was determined he would be over this silly little crush and he could watch her leave without her ripping out his heart on the way out.

—

They walked back towards the flats, a large old house that had long ago been converted into four separate apartments and given the rather original name of 'Sea View Court'.

George spotted a small van parked up outside. An older man was lifting a box out the back.

'Giselle?' the man called. 'Giselle? Where do you want this one to go?'

A blonde girl ran down the steps wearing leggings, which showed off her wonderful long legs, and a tiny knitted jumper, which showed off her tiny waist. George swallowed. Her hair was cut short with a long fringe that swept over her eyes, but it gleamed in the sun, like gold. Her eyes were huge, an amazing intense blue. She was the most beautiful woman he had ever seen. He knew without a doubt this was the woman he was going to marry. The easiest, quickest way to fall out of love with one unobtainable woman was fall in love with another.

'Oh thanks, Dad,' the blonde vision said, 'just put it in the lounge. I'll sort it out once it's all in.'

'Hey, do you want some help?' George asked, quickly leaving Libby's side.

'Oh, that'd be great, thanks.' Giselle broke into a heart-stopping smile.

'I'm George.' He held out his hand. 'I live at number two.'

'I'm Giselle, and I'm on top of you.' She tucked a strand of golden silk behind her ear. 'I'm moving into number four.'

He ignored the innuendo for the sake of future relations. 'Excellent.' He took the hand that was now extended towards him and shook it warmly, just as Libby arrived at the back of the van.

'Hi, I'm Libby, I live at number one, here let me take those,' she said, indicating the pile of books tucked under Giselle's arm and he watched her take them, and then she was gone. He wondered what they looked like standing there, him and Giselle, smiling at each other awkwardly. Well, Giselle was smiling awkwardly, he was grinning like a Cheshire cat. A Cheshire cat on Ecstasy.

For the next half an hour, they worked diligently between them to get all of Giselle's stuff into her flat on the second floor. There wasn't a lot, but what there was, he noticed, was very tasteful. There was also a lot of weird cooking paraphernalia which Libby found out was used for making different kinds of sweets for her online business.

Eventually, the van was empty and Giselle's dad left.

'Thank you so much,' Giselle said warmly, 'you've both been very kind. But now, well, I guess I better go and unpack. I'll see you around.'

She disappeared up the stairs and George stared after her in wonderment. He heard her flat door close and then quickly bundled Libby into her flat.

'George, what are you doing?'

'Oh Lib, she's beautiful.' He leaned against the inside of the door and sank to the floor.

'Yes she is, very.'

'Libby, I think I'm in love.'

She sat down next to him and gave him a playful nudge. 'Then go and ask her out.'

'Are you mad, have you seen me?'

She frowned. 'George, you're lovely.'

'Lovely is a polite way of saying fat.' He absently patted his belly.

'No, it's not, you're lovely and funny and incredibly attractive, ask her out.'

'No, I need to lose some weight first, and get a haircut, maybe some new clothes.'

'But then you won't be you any more. This is you, and you're perfect the way you are, anything else will just be a disguise. If she's going to fall in love with you, she needs to fall in love with the real you. You above anyone else should know the pitfalls of false advertising.'

Writing radio adverts for a living, George knew how to sell chocolate to the Easter bunny. If only he himself could be presented in such an appealing way.

'You're right, Lib, she should fall in love with the real me.' He looked down at himself, despondently.

'Hey! You're the loveliest, most wonderful, sweetest, kindest person I know; if she can't see that then she's blind.'

He kissed her head. 'Thanks Lib.'

She stood up and pulled him to his feet. 'Go on then, ask her.'

He paled. 'Now? No, I can't ask her now.'

'Yes you can.'

'Well what do I say?'

'You say, "Hi Giselle, I figured you might be tired after all this unpacking, do you fancy coming to the pub for something to eat? The Bubble and Froth does a mean steak and kidney pie."'

He nodded, yes he could do that. That was easy. Very casual, very simple. He opened the door and walked purposefully up the stairs and caught Libby doing a little giddy victory dance for him before she shut the door.

He climbed to the top of the first flight then hurried back down again, but before he reached the bottom stair he forced himself to turn around. He climbed four stairs this time, stopped, climbed one more stair then ran back to the safety of Libby's flat.

Her face fell as he came back in. 'What happened?'

'Yeah, I couldn't do it.'

'George!'

'Well what if she said no?'

'What if she didn't?'

He shrugged. 'Maybe I'll leave it a few days, you know, let her settle in.'

'Maybe you should get in now before someone else swoops in. Why don't you practise on me?'

'What?'

'Close your eyes and ask me out, imagine I'm a beautiful woman.'

George smiled wryly – he really didn't need to imagine that – but he closed his eyes anyway. He could still see her though, in his mind, looking pretty in her jeans and hoodie, and funky purple boots. She had a quirky style. When she was writing her romance stuff she always had at least one pen in her hair. And though the hoodie she wore today was an old grey one, she had pinned to it the most beautiful emerald sequinned flowered brooch. It matched her eyes exactly. Though this was not helping him to prepare for asking Giselle out.

He opened one eye and looked at her expectant face. When nothing was forthcoming, she rolled her eyes and ushered him out of the flat.

'Knock on my door and ask me out.'

'OK, role-play, I like it,' he grinned, 'though I'll get changed first, smarten myself up a bit.'

She shrugged. 'If it will make you feel more comfortable.'

———

As George disappeared back to his flat, Libby switched on her laptop and smiled at the tiny snowman that had been placed next to it the day before. George was clearly determined to Christmas-sify her, whether she liked it or not. The computer pinged to life and she opened up her current story, set in a rural seaside town at Christmas. Her publishers had expected it to be handed in months ago but for some reason this story had stagnated on her laptop. She had no desire to finish it and she didn't know why. She was famous for her romance stories, especially Christmas ones with snow, glitter, handsome heroes and gorgeously cosy love stories, but it was the romance parts she was having trouble with the most.

There was a knock on the door and she went to answer it, ready to be seduced.

George was standing there in a full tuxedo with black tie, and gleaming cufflinks. She nearly laughed except he looked so vulnerable.

He cleared his throat, straightened his shoulders, fixed her with a sultry stare. 'Hey little lady, fancy getting out of this hellhole and hitting some gin joints with me?'

She suppressed a laugh, but he had already seen the smirk.

'Too cheesy?'

'Very cheesy. Humphrey Bogart?'

'No, that was all me.'

'You're overthinking it.'

'What about the suit?'

'You look fantastic, really suave, really sexy, but a tiny bit overdressed for a pint down the Bubble.'

He arched an eyebrow. 'Sexy, eh?'

She smiled. 'Yes, if we were going to Royal Ascot together, I'd be proud to have you on my arm.'

'Right, I'll remember that next time I get offered free tickets for Royal Ascot. You can be my date.'

'Definitely, though you should know I'm a terrible loser and a really bad gambler.'

'I'll hold the purse strings that day then.'

She nodded. 'Probably wise.'

'Shall I try on something else?'

'Yes, please do.'

'Good, this collar is killing me.'

'I'm impressed that you can do up a bow tie though, it's not something many people can do.'

He took it off to show her it was a clip-on. She laughed, as she closed the door.

She walked back to the computer, her fingers hovering over a rather bland description of the sea. It wasn't just romance scenes that were taking a battering, all of her latest writing lacked sparkle. Because she had no enthusiasm for the romance, the rest of it hung limp and flaccid on the pages too.

There was another knock on the door just as she was poised to write something descriptive and wintery about the trees that lined the beach.

This time George was dressed in a black suit, with a black shirt and tie.

'Going to a funeral?'

'Right, of course,' he said, looking a little apologetic.

'How about something that shows your sporty side?'

'Right, OK.' He trudged off.

She closed the door again – not that it normally stopped George, but making him knock was all part of the role-play.

She went back to the computer, looked over the last paragraph she had written and sighed.

Another knock on her door. She doubled over with laughter when she opened it.

'What?' mumbled George, though she could see that he was trying not to laugh as well. He was dressed in a skin-tight wetsuit which accentuated every gorgeous curve of his strong body, with a mask and snorkel in his mouth and flippers on his feet.

'George, it's perfect,' she said, clapping her hands together, trying really hard to keep her eyes above his waist. 'Now let me see you manage the stairs in those things.'

He waddled carefully to the foot of the stairs and carefully placed his left flipper sideways on the step. With great effort he managed to put his right flipper sideways on the next one up, looking like a very bizarrely dressed Charlie Chaplin.

It was at this moment, as he struggled to move his left flipper up onto the third stair, that Giselle came running down the stairs towards him.

CHAPTER 2

Giselle stopped when she saw George, a shocked expression on her face. He quickly wrenched the snorkel out of his mouth. A thin string of saliva still connected it to his mouth and draped across his face like a rather attractive nose chain.

Libby snorted with laughter as Giselle, obviously deciding that ignoring this was the best tactic, tried to get past him, but the stairs were not quite wide enough to let this happen. George clearly wanted her to be gone almost as quick as she wanted to get away; there was something that actually looked like fear in her eyes. With some effort, he managed to turn sideways, though as his flippers were too long to fit on the steps this way, he had to stick one leg out. It struck Libby, as he held on to the banister with one hand, that he now looked like a scuba diver attempting to perform ballet. She wondered if Giselle would be impressed if he executed a pirouette. With just enough space for her to squeeze past, Giselle quickly ran out the main front door.

He pulled his mask off and looked after her sadly.

'It's OK, George,' Libby said, putting a hand on his arm, 'this will be something you can laugh about on your first date, it will be one of those funny things you can tell your grandchildren.' She pulled her sleeve over her hand and gently wiped the saliva off his face.

'I suppose,' he said, directing the words at his flippers.

Unable to bear seeing him so humiliated, she took his hand and led him back towards his flat. 'Come on, why don't I pick something from your wardrobe?' He flapped despondently after her and she shuddered with suppressed laughter.

While George got out of his wetsuit, she flicked through his clothes – he certainly had a unique style. There was nothing drab in here apart from the black funeral suit he had tried on moments before. And she liked his style – it matched his personality, loud and colourful. She smiled when she remembered how it had been mainly George's clothes that had led her to believe he was gay in the first place – a completely wrong stereotype anyway, seeing as most gay men dressed unbelievably well. She concentrated on finding something for him that made him look lovely and endearing.

'Ah, this shirt is perfect.' She selected a pale blue long-sleeved shirt, and held it up to George's chest. 'Yes, it brings out your tan. Wear it loose over jeans.' She flicked through his pile of jeans and picked out a dark blue pair. 'These, they're smart, and with the shirt you'll look casual but suave at the same time.'

He took the offending items. 'Are you sure? Just the shirt and jeans?'

She nodded.

'Tie?'

'No.'

'Right.'

'And what are you going to say? Ask me out,' she insisted.

He took a deep breath, closed his eyes for a second. 'Libby, would you like to go for a drink with me tonight?'

'Perfect,' she said. 'Except for one tiny detail.'

'What's that?'

'Make sure you get the name right.'

He grinned. 'Yes, of course, Giselle, Giselle, must remember, must remember.'

She looked round his room. It was perfectly tidy – another reason why she had thought he was gay. Perfectly tidy that was, apart from one thing.

'And you might, if the date gets as far as your bedroom, want to remove Candy.' She gestured at the mannequin in the corner. 'She's a bit freaky.'

'I can't get rid of Candy,' he protested, slinging a protective arm round the mannequin's shoulders. 'I'm still waiting for her to change.'

'Honey, you can wait all your bloody life, she is never going to change into Kim Cattrall from *Mannequin*.'

'I can hope. Besides, she looks after my ties.' He gestured towards Candy's arms, draped in his tie collection, like a very bizarre clothes rack.

'Anyway, stop trying to distract me. Are you going to ask Giselle out now?'

He sat down and sighed heavily. 'In a few days, I need to psyche myself up first. I'm not sure how to do the whole dating thing. I don't know what to do or what to say. I think I need to practise first. Me and Josie never really dated, we were just together and then we were married and now we're not. The divorce only came through earlier this year, just before you arrived, and well, I haven't had the heart to date anyone since. Josie put me down, she shattered my self-esteem and I'm only just picking up the pieces.'

She sat down next to him. 'I hate that she destroyed the confidence you have in yourself – you look at yourself now as if you're not good enough any more.'

'For the last two years of our marriage she went elsewhere for sex. I clearly wasn't good enough for her.'

'What did you see in her? She sounds vile.'

'As loath as I am to defend her, we had some really good years. She was a lot of fun when she was younger but so much of that disappeared after we had been married for a few years. I think she grew bored of me.'

'She was an idiot. Any woman would be lucky to go out with you, exactly as you are. You're sweet, funny, incredibly sexy. If I wasn't leaving I'd go out with you in a heartbeat.'

He stared at her. 'What?'

She swallowed. Where the hell did that come from? She rarely dated, she'd never had someone she could call her boyfriend and she had no desire to either.

Suddenly his phone erupted in his pocket. Fishing it out, he looked at the caller ID. 'Sorry, it's my mum.'

'No worries, I have to get on with some work anyway, send her my love.'

He answered it. 'Hey Mum, hang on a sec.' He covered the speaker. 'Pub tonight?'

She nodded.

'I'll see you at six.'

She left him chatting to his mum and headed over to her flat. She needed to make sure George was going to be OK when she left. She couldn't bear the thought of him being too scared to date anyone, either from the fear of getting hurt again or the fear that he wasn't good enough. She had to do something to show him how wonderful he was – but how would she change his mindset in just two weeks?

She sat down in front of the computer, staring at the screen with no enthusiasm for writing. She had struggled recently, in the last few months. She had never before had any kind of writer's block. But she had never thought about staying somewhere before and she wondered somehow if the two were linked. She had lived in some of the most beautiful places in the world but none had sucked her in like White Cliff Bay.

The weird thing was, Libby Joseph had almost been wiped from existence fourteen years before. Eve Loveheart, her pseudonym, had been a character in a little known children's book, one who had adventures and travelled the world, and at the time it seemed fitting that Libby would assume that identity. She'd even managed to get fake IDs with her new name, assuming that if her dad ever came looking for her she could never be traced. Every place she went she always gave her new name. While her publishers and agent knew her real name, no one else in the world was privy to it.

But on her first day in White Cliff Bay, when she had met George with his friendly eyes and huge smile, she had introduced herself as Libby Joseph without any thought. Maybe it had been the recent news of her dad's death, maybe it had just been George and subconsciously she had known that she could trust him, but it had been as if a shield had been lifted and she didn't have to hide any more. For the first time in a very long time, people were allowed to see the real her. It had felt a wonderful relief at the time, but now she wondered if not living behind the façade meant she had lost the character she became when she wrote. The one with sass and all the moves. The one that knew about mind-blowing sex and heart-warming love stories, when really she had no knowledge or experience of any of that. How many times could she write a love story with a happy ending when that had always passed her by?

Although she had been on a few dates over the years, there hadn't been anyone that had really grabbed her attention and she realised now that part of that was the men had probably dated Eve Loveheart not Libby Joseph. Writing devastatingly sexy heroes who were super romantic had ruined her for men. She wanted what she wrote about in her books and she wasn't going to settle for anything less. Unfortunately the perfect man didn't exist. The men she had dated had never held her hand or danced with her, they'd never made love surrounded by candles or in front of a log fire but, most importantly, there had been a complete lack of spark or even any fun. She never stayed anywhere long enough to develop any kind of serious relationships and truth be told she liked it that way. Well, that was until she had come to White Cliff Bay, when an inexplicable ache had settled in her heart. It was something she had never felt before and she was having trouble recognising what it was. Loneliness perhaps, or maybe an affection for the people and the town. A huge part of her wanted to stay to explore these feelings but she had never stayed anywhere before. The thought of staying in White Cliff Bay filled her with fear and joy all at the same time. But now, for the first time, she feared leaving almost as much too. Six months was always her limit before she moved on. She told herself or others it was to do with her work as an author but in reality there was so much more to it than that.

She stared at the story she was currently working on, *The Long Winter*, and flicked through to the bit she had written last. To say it lacked some of her usual sparkle would be an understatement.

She needed some romantic inspiration and right now she had none. She needed to date someone. If she was going to write as Libby Joseph and not Eve Loveheart, then she needed to date someone as Libby too. It didn't have to be anything serious, just a few dates to get her head back into the romance zone again. It would give her something to write about, the romantic gestures, the little looks.

Suddenly she had an idea and it might actually kill two birds with one stone. She smiled, pushed back from the keyboard and stood up. This could actually be a brilliant idea.

—

George's front door burst open, just as he'd got out the shower and was standing naked in his bedroom.

'George! George!' Libby called, running from his lounge towards his bedroom.

He threw himself across the bed and slammed the door, just as she was about to come in.

'Bloody hell, George, a second later and you'd have smashed my face in. Do you have a woman in there, is that what you're hiding?' She rattled the handle mischievously.

He quickly pulled on some clothes. 'Yes, we're having mad passionate sex, go away.'

'I can't, I have something brilliant to tell you, could you not stop just for a few minutes? Knowing your sexual prowess I'm sure she could do with a breather.'

He smirked as he pulled his t-shirt over his head and opened the door.

'OK, Libby Joseph, you have two minutes, but then I have to go back in there and finish what I've started.'

'I've had an idea. You should take *me* out on a date.'

His heart leapt. That *would* make sense. She loved talking to him, thought he was funny and sweet. It had only taken her six months to see that they were perfect for each other and now…

'Then you can practise what you would say to Giselle, what little anecdotes you could use on her to make her laugh. I can give you some advice on the things to do and avoid on a first date. We can help each other out. I need some romantic inspiration for my book and you need to practise dating again before you ask out Giselle. I want to help you – you deserve to have someone wonderful and I will be so happy if I leave here and you're with

27

Giselle. It can be my goodbye gift to you, get you back into the saddle again.'

He tried to hide the disappointment from his voice. 'Now, that is an excellent idea. You can be my guinea pig. Wait, does that mean I have to take you to some fancy restaurant?' He hated fancy restaurants. He never knew what to order, which fork to use first, which glass the red or white wine went in, and felt that the waiters knew as soon as you walked in that you weren't a regular to such establishments. They would always give you that look, the look you would give a piece of turd when you had accidentally stepped in it.

'Perhaps you should just take her to the Bubble and Froth,' she said. 'It's your favourite pub, she'd get to know what sort of things you like and you'd be more relaxed. Besides, if you take her somewhere posh it gives her false illusions about what sort of person you are.' She hesitated. 'But then again, George, taking her to a restaurant rather than your local *would* show that you're making a bit of an effort. So maybe a compromise? Oooh, how about that new Indian that's opened on the far side of White Cliff Bay on the road to Port Cardinal – The Cherry Tree? We could go there. Then it's not posh, but it's somewhere a bit special… plus,' she grinned, cheekily, 'I really fancy a curry.'

'OK, sounds good, and then after we can watch *Psycho*. I've just got a digitally remastered version of the original.'

'Ooh, I do love a good thriller. So tomorrow night?' Libby asked.

George nodded, unable to hide the grin from his face. He was going to take Libby out on a date. His day had suddenly got a lot better.

———

As they walked to the pub later that night Libby glanced over at George, trying to conceal her smile. He was wearing a green jumper with a huge reindeer face smiling out from the middle of it. He looked ridiculous but somehow utterly adorable. When he found a girlfriend she hoped with all her heart that it would be someone who would appreciate George exactly how he was, stupid jumpers, silly sense of humour and all his wonderful quirks.

He saw her smiling at him. 'You admiring my jumper?'

'I love it. It's so you.'

He smiled and as she looked away over the sea, she felt his hand slip into hers. She looked up at him in confusion, her heart stuttering with this sudden show of affection. They had an incredibly close relationship but it had never progressed to hand-holding before.

'If we're dating we probably should...' He gestured to their entwined hands, a look of mischief on his face.

She laughed but she didn't remove her hand from his and he didn't remove it either. There was something so incredibly sweet and natural about holding hands with her best friend. It had started to snow again, gentle flakes twisting and twirling in the night sky, and holding hands with this wonderful man under the snow made her smile and gave her the warm and fuzzies. The wind was up and the waves were crashing theatrically onto the beach, adding drama to the moment. She didn't need to imagine romantic moments; she could find real romance right here. Dating George was going to give her exactly what she needed.

As soon as they entered the pub, George peeled off to talk to Seb, the landlord, and spying her friend Amy sitting in the corner, Libby wandered over to sit with her.

The huge Christmas tree sparkled and glowed next to Amy's table with old-fashioned traditional decorations that matched beautifully with the simple Victorian-style décor of the pub.

Amy was reapplying a coat of deep red lipstick. She was so glamorous, Libby envied her. Even though Libby would always choose comfort over style when it came to clothes, she would love to have the confidence to dress as Amy did. Today, dressed in a fifties red and white flowered dress, with matching mile-high red stilettos, she looked gorgeous, her long black hair plaited with a flower at the end. But even when she worked behind the bar, she wore clothes like this.

Libby pulled at her hoodie self-consciously. 'You look gorgeous, as always.'

Amy sighed as she put her lipstick back in her bag. 'Well, at least you noticed.'

Amy's eyes slid over to the bar and Libby followed her gaze to Seb who was laughing with George and Sally, the other barmaid. Seemingly this corner of the room didn't even exist for him.

'Do you not think you might be barking up the wrong tree?' Libby watched how Seb was with Sally … was he flirting with her?

'No, he likes me, I know he does, he just doesn't want to show it. Especially not with Judith lurking around like a bad smell.'

'I like Judith.' Libby suddenly diverted her attention to stroke Jack, Seb's dog, who had come over to see if they had any food he could scrounge. 'You can't blame her for still feeling protective towards Seb, for still keeping an eye on her son-in-law even though…'

'…Her daughter's been dead five years,' Amy said with a groan. 'I know, I know, don't keep reminding me.' She took the last swig of her drink before saying in a quieter voice, 'Have you any idea how hard this is for me too – I've not only got to fight my way past a dead wife to get to him, but also the dead wife's mother.'

'Judith's bound to be extra critical about any woman who she thinks is going to take her daughter's place.'

Amy sighed, pulling Jack's ears fondly. 'She's certainly extra critical of me.'

'Well, you did set fire to her shed at your barbeque in the summer.'

'I've paid for a new one, but the dislike set in before that.'

'Oh yes, "Gnome Gate".' Libby giggled.

'It's not funny.'

'It so is.'

Amy's nephew, Charlie, had come to stay last summer, a twelve-year-old whirlwind of clumsiness, practical jokes and big freckly grins. He thought Judith's gnomes next door were hilarious. Over the week that he'd stayed, he had moved several of them into provocative sexual positions. One poor gnome, bending down to get a frog from a pond, had suddenly found that another of the male gnomes had snuck up behind him and taken a shine to him. Judith had been horrified. Not the best way to impress Judith, especially when it seemed Amy had to get past her to get to Seb. Since Marie's death five years before, Judith had taken it upon herself to look out for him and rumour had it no one was good enough to replace her little girl.

Amy sighed. 'I don't know, Lib, maybe it's too complicated. Maybe I should just go out with someone nice and sweet instead.'

'You don't want nice and sweet, Amy, you want passion and love and complications. Nice and sweet would bore you.'

George appeared then, passing Libby her pint of cider and Amy her glass of red wine, before sitting down next to Amy, awkwardly arranging his legs over Jack who had decided to fall asleep under their table.

'Hello, sexy.' Amy kissed him on the cheek, as she always did, as she did to almost everyone she knew. He blushed, as he always did. 'What's new with you?'

'Me and Libby are dating,' he declared with a huge grin on his face. Libby laughed and Amy nearly spat out her drink.

'Finally! It took you two long enough. You tell me not to date him, but it's OK for you to,' Amy said with a smile, clearly not bothered at all by this new turn of events.

'What?' George asked, taking a big swig of his ale.

Libby's eyes widened as she suddenly remembered.

'I told Libby I was willing to be your rebound sex after you divorced Josie earlier this year, but Libby told me I wasn't allowed. Personally I think she'd be jealous of the amazing sex me and you would have.'

He choked on his ale, but quickly recovered himself. His eyes were almost accusing as he spoke to Libby. 'Why, why would you deny me that? I like sex, especially the amazing kind.'

Libby laughed. 'Ah now, you wouldn't be able to keep up with Amy's sexual prowess, she'd ravage you, leave you broken and beaten. I was saving you from her.'

'I'd at least like to be beaten once,' he muttered.

Amy smiled into her wine. 'What was your reason … oh yes. "I want someone for George who adores him, who treasures him and loves him."'

George's scowl vanished. 'Is that what you said?'

Libby blushed. 'I just want you to be happy. Look, Nick is here.'

George glanced round and Nick waved at him and gestured to the table where they played poker every Sunday night.

'Oh, I better go.'

Amy dug in her handbag and passed him a box of matches. 'Here's your poker money, win big.'

George grinned, took the box and slid out of the booth. He walked a few steps away before he came back and planted a kiss on Libby's forehead. She couldn't help the smile that burst on her face as he walked away. She turned back to face Amy who was watching her keenly.

'I'm happy for you, Lib, George is wonderful and you two belong together. But does this mean you're actually going to stay?'

'No, we're not really dating. George has his eye on the girl who has just moved into the flat above his, Giselle – he's practising on me. It's not real.'

'And that's why you're grinning like the cat that has the cream?'

'He just makes me laugh, that's all.'

'So you would never properly date him?' Amy was pushing it and Libby didn't know why. 'You don't fancy him, not even a tiny bit?'

'No.' Libby knew she was blushing. She knew Amy had seen it too. 'I'm leaving in two weeks. Even if I did have a soft spot for him, I can't pursue anything with him. I'd be in New York, he'd be here, how would that work?'

'Well, maybe you don't go to New York.'

'I have to go for work.'

'You and I both know that's rubbish. There are hundreds of authors out there that never even visit the places they write about, and there are plenty more who just pop over for a few weeks to research.'

'That's one of the things I'm known for: rich settings and detailed locations.'

Amy fixed her with a look.

'George is not remotely interested in me in that way,' Libby said, suddenly feeling like she was protesting too much.

'How do you know?'

'Because I'm just his friend, he just sees me as one of the boys.'

Amy took a sip of her wine, eyeing Libby thoughtfully. 'So, he practises on you and goes out with this Gazelle woman...'

'Giselle, Amy, she's not a deer.'

'And where does that leave you two? The movie nights you two have, the long walks on the beach... You're practically a couple anyway minus the sex and the kissing.'

'I'd be happy for him. Giselle is lovely and I think she would be really good for him.'

'You wouldn't be jealous?'

Libby shook her head.

Amy gave her a doubtful look and Libby glanced over at George, ignoring the feeling of unease this thought suddenly gave her.

—

George watched Libby talking to Amy and smiled. It was beyond stupid to get excited about dating, Libby because it wasn't even real and she was leaving in two weeks, but he couldn't stop the giddiness from bubbling through him.

'Are you shuffling those cards or just giving them a hug?' Matt asked.

George quickly returned his attention back to the table. Every Sunday night was poker night for George. He, Big Dave, Nick and Matt would play for big stakes. Last week he had ended up with the fewest matches at the end of the night and had to buy the others a round of drinks. Tonight he was determined to win back his pride. Nick came back from the bar with two pints and George dutifully shuffled the cards.

Suddenly the door burst open and Big Dave hurried through with his equally big wife. Big Dave rolled his eyes as he quickly left her side and joined George and the rest of the boys.

'Women,' Big Dave muttered, supping the pint that Nick had bought him.

'She's getting so big, Dave,' George said, eyeing Kat as she tried, unsuccessfully, to squeeze herself into the booth with Amy and Libby.

'Oh God, mate, don't let her hear you say that, that's all I get all day: "I'm so fat, I'm like an elephant", and then later on: "I hate you, you did this to me". But yes she is. I swear if she gives birth to a baby cow I wouldn't be surprised.'

'How late is she now?' asked Matt, as he nibbled at his peanuts.

'She's not due till tomorrow, but her two sisters both had their first child really early so she thought she would follow suit. She's so fed up and she's still getting bigger. Nothing fits her any more and I've offered to take her shopping but she flat refuses to buy more maternity clothes when the baby should be here by now. But that's why I was late; she couldn't find anything to wear.'

'Isn't that… what you wore to this year's Halloween party?' George said, eyeing the large black dress, cut in triangles at the bottom.

'Oh please don't say that to her, I said no one would notice.'

'I doubt anyone would dare say anything to her,' Nick said, 'not if they want to live … Oh, look lively.'

George, Matt and Nick all straightened in their chairs, instinctively covering their manhoods as Kat marched over to them.

'You look lovely, Kat,' Nick said.

'Shut up, Nick, I look like a whale. Dave, are you going to buy me a drink or are you going to let your poor wife die of thirst?'

Big Dave stood, getting his wallet out of his pocket. 'Of course, my love, I thought you had your purse.'

'I forgot it. It's not a problem, is it,' she said coldly. 'I mean, you're the reason I'm this big, the least you can do is buy me a sodding drink.'

Big Dave took a wodge of twenties out and thrust them towards her. 'Here, buy whatever you want.'

Kat snatched them from his hand and walked off.

Big Dave sat down heavily and sighed. 'Let's play poker, boys; I think she'll want to go home soon.'

Matt quickly dealt the cards and George glanced over at Libby again. Even the fact that he had a useless three and five couldn't dampen his mood.

—

George was doing badly in poker. They'd been playing for about an hour and he was already borrowing matches from Matt who had won almost every game. George had won once, but he'd just ended up paying back the matches he had borrowed. He was studying his new hand when Libby came to sit with him. God, she smelt amazing.

'How are we all tonight?' she asked, beaming round at the other boys.

'Now, come on, young Libby, we won't have any of your cheating tonight, not when the stakes are so high.' Big Dave indicated the large pile of matches in the middle of the table.

'I'll have you know that Libby is a well-respected member of this community,' George protested, glancing down at her hands in her lap. She quickly gave the sign language symbols for A and Q and drew a heart on her palm. She eyed Nick then dusted her hands off. She had just told him that Nick had the ace and queen of hearts but nothing else worth worrying about. He smiled at her. There was something about her eyes tonight; she looked so happy it almost shone from her.

'Well, if I'm not wanted here, I shall return to my table.'

She got up and walked off, re-joining Kat and Amy without a look back. He was unable to tear his eyes off her.

Nick clicked his fingers in George's face. 'Hey, what's up with you tonight? I mean normally you stink at poker but this is a new level of bad even for you. Why do you keep looking over at Libby for? We all know you love her, that you've been in love with her for months, but why the sudden mooning all over her?'

'I'm not mooning.'

'There was definitely mooning,' Big Dave said, and Matt nodded his agreement.

'It's nothing…' George sighed. 'We're sort of going out on a date tomorrow.'

The boys collectively oooohed so loudly that Libby looked over at them, wondering what all the fuss was about.

'Not a real date, she's just letting me practise my wooing skills on her.'

'You keep calling it wooing, and you're never getting laid again,' Matt said.

'Keep wearing shit jumpers like that and no girl will be seen with you, let alone let you get into her pants,' Nick said.

'Shut up, both of you,' Big Dave said. 'This is a big opportunity for you, George, this is your one chance to make an impression on her, pull out all the stops and make her fall in love with you. Don't screw it up.'

'She's not about to fall in love with me just because I take her out on a few dates. She's had six months to fall in love with me, I don't think she's suddenly going to start now. Besides, she leaves in two weeks. Whatever her feelings for me, they aren't strong enough to get her to stay.'

'Maybe not, but you mooning over her like a love-sick puppy is definitely one way to put her off for good. Play it cool, man, and maybe she'll let you practise your bedroom skills on her as well,' Nick said.

Suddenly the date the next night had a whole new meaning. George knew it would never get as far as the bedroom but maybe Big Dave was right, maybe there was a small chance he could convince Libby he was the right man for her after all. All he had to do was find the balance between pulling out all the stops, making a great impression and playing it cool. He let his head fall into his hands. He was doomed before he could start.

Suddenly the pager in his pocket beeped and vibrated incessantly and as he grabbed it in shock he noticed other people's pagers going off as well, including Big Dave's. Shit.

The pub suddenly went silent as people realised the weight of what was happening.

George had been a volunteer for the lifeboat crew for years, but so were hundreds of other people, which meant that he was only on call twice a month. The lifeboat rarely got called out in their little bay; Port Cardinal, a few miles down the road, got the main call-outs with all the boats coming and going into their harbour, but he knew that the White Cliff Bay lifeboat had been called out to assist them on the odd occasions. George had only been called out himself a handful of times.

Suddenly there were lots of quick hugs and kisses from the husbands and wives of the crew on call. It was always dangerous when they went out – the weather was unpredictable and you never knew what you were going to face. Kat rushed over and kissed Big Dave, her earlier mood obviously forgotten. George had no one to wish him good luck. They all moved to the door, when suddenly he felt a hand on his arm. He turned round to see Libby looking worried. She reached up and kissed him on the cheek, squeezing his hand.

'Be safe, do you hear me?'

He smiled and nodded, and he still had a big smile on his face when he caught up with the rest of the crew a few seconds later.

The RIB was already being prepped ready for launch when he arrived, which suggested it was an inshore rescue not one out at sea.

'George, Dave, Richard, you're going out in the RIB, but we will be ready to assist if you need the other boat,' said Eric, the operations manager.

They quickly got changed into their drysuits, kitting up in record time as they were briefed about what had happened.

'A boy has fallen off the slip near Main Street, a woman has jumped in after him.'

That was going to be a tricky manoeuvre. Even on a calm day, getting in and out of that bay was tricky because of all the rocks; in this weather it would be very difficult, especially with two bodies in the water. A child too. If the boy was panicking and uncooperative, it might require lifeboat crew to go in the water as well.

George started the engine and, as the other two men climbed in, he took off, fighting through the waves easily as he negotiated round the headland towards White Cliff Bay, which gave the town its name.

People were already lining the slipway in the bay and they all started waving and pointing as he approached.

He shifted the boat into second gear, slowing the engine as he got nearer, scanning the water for any bodies.

'There,' shouted Big Dave as he pointed.

The woman and the boy were together. She'd managed to get hold of the boy but they were now bobbing around in the sea as she desperately fought to take them both back towards the slip.

As she turned round to see the boat, George recognised his friend Penny in the water with Sam, one of the Mayor's young boys.

There was a sudden movement on the slip as a man tried to jump in the water. The crowd around him held him back. The man wasn't Sam's dad, which made George think he was more concerned for Penny than Sam. The last thing they needed was another body in the water to rescue. Though George knew if it had been Libby fighting for her life in the waves he would have jumped in the water too, despite knowing the dangers.

He quickly manoeuvred the boat so it was upwind of them.

Big Dave threw the floating swimline to Penny with incredible accuracy and she grabbed it with the one hand she was using to hold on to Sam and they pulled her alongside the boat.

As the boat bobbed closer, she held Sam up out of the water for them to grab, but the action pushed her under the waves.

George reached down and grabbed her, pulling her back to the surface as Big Dave grabbed Sam with ease.

As soon as Sam was in the boat, Richard reached over and grabbed Penny's arm and between the two of them they hauled her into the RIB, where she lay huddled against the cold on the bottom of the boat. Both of them were breathing and conscious. They just had to get them warm and dry now.

Big Dave was tending to the boy and George quickly knelt next to Penny.

'Are you OK?' he said, taking the spare lifejacket from Richard and pulling it over her head.

She nodded.

Seeing Sam's parents lining the slip with the rest of the concerned town, George carefully manoeuvred the boat to the side of the slip. Richard threw a rope to one of the waiting people and they tugged the boat in close. Big Dave leant over and handed Sam back to his dad who whisked him away up the slip, quickly followed by the boy's heavily pregnant mum.

George helped Penny to her feet and Big Dave and a huge man on the slip helped her ashore.

The drama was over.

———

George was lying in bed awake later. After a call-out he was always pumped with too much adrenaline to sleep properly. It had been a simple enough rescue. No one from the crew had had to risk their life by jumping in and he had been back in the Bubble and Froth before his ale had even gone warm. Walking back into the pub to tremendous applause, he had felt like a hero, even though he had barely done anything that could be considered heroic. It was Penny who had saved the little boy, she deserved all the credit. But one proud look and a hug from Libby made him feel like the bravest man in the world.

Suddenly there was the sound of a door slamming and a few seconds later he heard his own front door slamming open. He knew straight away it was Libby.

He quickly got out of bed and went into the lounge. Sure enough she was pacing in front of his sofa.

He watched her for a moment, as she paced barefoot in the Christmas pudding onesie he had bought her a few days before and she'd sworn she would never wear. She was muttering incoherently to herself before he took her gently by the hand and led her back out of his flat.

'It won't work,' she muttered angrily.

'What won't work, honey?' He guided her gently across the hall towards her flat.

'You wouldn't understand.'

'Try me.' He ushered her through her front door and into her bedroom.

'Clint Eastwood.'

'Clint Eastwood, what about him?' He pushed her gently back down on the bed, and covered her with her duvet.

'He's buying my car.'

'Right, I'll look out for him then.'

'Thanks George.' She sighed, sleepily, before closing her eyes and drifting off back into a deeper sleep again. He went back to his flat.

He had become used to her sleepwalking by now. The first time she'd done it, she was standing in the street, in the rain. Just staring into space with a completely vacant expression on her face. He had assumed she had received some bad news and had gone into shock. He had rushed out onto the road and his suspicion was confirmed when all attempts to rouse her had failed. He had taken her back to her flat, wrapped a blanket round her and held her in his arms until she was ready to talk. When she had finally woken a while later, she had screamed hysterically at finding herself wrapped tightly in the arms of a man she couldn't see in the darkness of her lounge.

When she had realised it was him, and that she had been sleepwalking again, she had explained that it was something that happened now and again, particularly if she was worried about something.

Since then it had happened quite a lot, normally once or twice a month. Sometimes she would be pacing, sometimes just staring into the nothingness, sometimes muttering incomprehensibly, and sometimes he could actually have a coherent conversation with her. Well, semi-coherent; 'Clint Eastwood' indeed.

Luckily she didn't walk too far – sometimes to the bottom of the steps just outside the flats, but mostly to his flat. He had found her pacing round his lounge on numerous occasions or just sitting on the sofa staring at the blank TV. One time he had woken up and she had been standing over him. His screams had woken her up that night.

He hadn't minded taking on the role of her protector and returning her back to her bed, in fact he quite liked it. It was just another thing that he found sweet and endearing about her.

The only time it had interfered with his social life was the one occasion he had managed to persuade a woman to come back to his flat. Sinead had been well up for helping him back into the sexual saddle and they had come through the door and fallen onto the sofa in a pile of legs, discarded clothes and kisses. He had looked up to see Libby sitting on the other end of his sofa, staring at her hands like the ill-fated Lady Macbeth.

Sinead had freaked, mostly because of the wild, manic look in Libby's eyes. He had never thought her eyes looked manic before, he always thought they looked lost, scared, and vulnerable.

Sinead was also less than impressed with the tenderness he'd shown Libby, and had suggested he slap her round the face to bring her round, before kicking her out the flat. By the time he had gently manoeuvred her back to her bed, Sinead had gone, leaving a note that said, 'You and the freak deserve each other.' A tad hurtful, he thought.

As he got back into bed he thought about Libby sleepwalking tonight. She had seemed fine today, all cheery and bubbly as normal, but clearly something was worrying her or she wouldn't have been in his flat again. He resolved to ask her about it the next day.

CHAPTER 3

The problem was, Amy decided, as she rubbed the purple dye into her hair, she was nothing like Marie, Seb's late wife – they were polar opposites in fact. Marie was tall and thin, where Amy was a classic hourglass, large breasts, and large bum. Marie was sweet, quiet and kind and Amy was loud, dry and bolshie. Marie dressed in jeans and t-shirts, whereas Amy didn't even own a pair of jeans. For Seb to admit he loved Amy would be a huge slap in the face for Judith, not least because she couldn't stand her, but also because Judith would wonder if Seb had really loved Marie if he now loved someone so completely different.

Amy sighed as she looked in the mirror. The Cadbury's purple hair dye didn't seem to be making much difference to her dark, almost black hair. She lifted a strand of hair and wondered if her other boss, Marcus, had actually heard of wigs, rather than having to go to all this trouble. A purple wig would have made much more of a dramatic statement.

She wandered into the bedroom to wait the twenty minutes developing time and peered out on the view. Up here at the very top of White Cliff Bay, she had an amazing view of the sea in front of her, and the surrounding hills and cliffs.

A movement down below in her back garden caught her eye: evil Philippe, Judith's beloved psycho cat from next door. Philippe was apparently no ordinary moggie, he was an exceptionally rare breed; Judith had proudly told her so. She had explained at length what he was, but Amy had switched off after she had heard the words 'minskin' and 'munchkin', which sounded like characters from *The Wizard of Oz*. Philippe was pure white, with short stumpy legs and huge ears and was actually the devil incarnate. Amy had made the mistake of trying to stroke him once and he had cut her so deep she wondered if he had been bred with razor blades instead of claws.

She watched him now, up the tree in her garden, and realised that he was stuck, his paw wedged or caught somehow. She watched him pulling frantically, starting to panic as he couldn't get himself free. What if he hurt himself, tore a ligament in his plight, or broke his leg? As much as she hated Philippe, she wasn't about to leave the poor animal to suffer. Judith was out – she'd seen her leave earlier – so it was down to Amy to do something about it.

Fastening her robe tighter around her, she ran barefoot down the stairs and out into the garden. Without even thinking about it, she swung herself up into the tree and quickly made her way up the long, twisted branches.

Philippe was howling as she drew close, yanking and pulling desperately at his paw. She reached out for him and he took a swipe at her, slashing her hand so fiercely he drew blood immediately.

'You little bastard, I'm trying to help you.' She went for his paw to try to free it and Philippe sank his teeth into her hand, making her howl louder than him.

Suddenly Philippe managed to free his paw and launched himself at her head, digging his claws into her scalp. She tried to shake him off, but he clung on tight and every time she tried to grab him, he took a swipe at her with his claws.

Somehow she managed to free him from his hold on her head and pulled him into her arms and realised, to her horror, he now had purple patches all over him.

—

As Judith let herself back into her house, her friend Claudia, the local town councillor, followed her into the kitchen.

'Well that's what I told him,' Claudia said, 'he can't just park a caravan outside my house and leave it there…'

Judith moved to the sink to fill up the kettle, looked out the window and froze when she saw Amy halfway up the tree, her purple hair sticking out at all angles. She was struggling with something in her arms, and trying to get down the tree at the same time. To her absolute horror, she saw Amy suddenly whip her robe off, revealing a large tattoo of a shark swimming over her naked bum.

'What are you looking at?' Claudia said as she drew level with her. 'Oh my…'

Judith grimaced as Amy wrapped her robe round something, scratched her bum and then made her way down the tree and ran back into the house, her large breasts bouncing as she ran.

—

Amy ran upstairs with the yowling, struggling bundle and threw it unceremoniously into the shower cubicle and slammed the door.

She looked down at her body. She was bleeding so badly she looked like she had been butchered. She tended to her wounds as quickly as possible then stepped into the shower, closing the door behind her. Her dressing gown howled and thrashed, but Philippe couldn't get out. She had purple dye all over her now, her shoulders and arms covered in purple blotches.

She washed her hair and scrubbed at her body, then turned her attention to the writhing lump.

She grabbed the shower head and untangled her dressing gown. As Philippe launched himself at her she sprayed him with the shower head so he flinched away, backing into the corner, though he continued to hiss. He was almost purple all over now, the dye looking even brighter against his white fur. Grabbing her deluxe shampoo, she squirted it in his direction and, keeping him at bay with the shower head, she managed to rub bits of it into his fur. But as she rinsed him off, much to his disgust, the purple dye didn't shift.

How could she return Philippe to Judith looking like this? Maybe she should just keep him, tell Judith that she hadn't seen him. She could keep him locked up in her house for the rest of his life so Judith would never find out. But as Philippe took another swipe at her ankles, she knew she would probably end up killing the evil monster before the week was out.

Feeling panic rise in her, she grabbed her electric razor and aimed it at the most heavily purple parts. Fur flew off and Philippe yowled, taking a swipe at her, but she kept him pinned in the corner with the shower spray.

Eventually, after she had done as much as she could, she turned the shower off and, leaving Philippe wet and howling in the cubicle, she went to get changed into her uniform.

She surveyed herself in the mirror a few minutes later and rolled her eyes. Dressing as a purple blackberry, complete with purple tights and shiny purple oversized shoes, wasn't an ideal way to spend her Monday, but it paid the bills – paid them very well as it happened.

She called a taxi and then surveyed the damage she had inflicted on the purple monster through the cubicle door. He was still purple – the shampoo had done nothing to change that, the dye having seeped through the fur and marked his skin. Shaving him had achieved nothing either, other than making him look like he had been tortured. The fur had not come off evenly, leaving bald patches all over his body.

She opened the door and threw a towel over him, scooping up the hissing bundle and plodding downstairs, hoping against hope that Judith was still out and that she could leave Philippe on her doorstep.

As soon as she stepped outside and saw Judith's car, her heart plummeted.

Waddling across her garden, she rang the doorbell, hoping that overnight Judith had developed a sense of humour and she would find the whole thing hilarious.

Amy surveyed her neighbour's house. It was lacking in any kind of Christmas decorations at all. Amy never went overboard with the decorations in her own house but to have nothing this close to Christmas was a little sad, though she wondered if that was because the thought of celebrating anything since the death of Marie was not something that Judith could comprehend.

The door opened.

'Judith, hi, I…'

'Amy…' Judith faltered at seeing a large purple blackberry on her doorstep but then carried on. 'I would thank you not to parade around naked in your back garden when I have visitors. In fact, I don't appreciate seeing you naked at any time.'

Amy flushed with embarrassment. 'I'm sorry if my nudity offended you but I was actually trying to help Philippe.' She gestured to the yowling lump in her arms that Judith suddenly noticed for the first time.

'Philippe, that's Philippe! Oh my God, what are you doing to him?' Judith snatched the lump from her hands and he became suddenly still and subdued at the sound of his mistress' voice.

Judith started to unwrap the towel, but Amy reached out to stop her. 'Look, I'm really sorry, he was stuck in the tree and when I went to get him down he jumped on my head and got covered

in purple dye. I tried to wash him, but it wouldn't come off and…
I shaved him. I thought I could shave some of the purple off but
that didn't work either and… well I'm sorry.'

The taxi beeped behind her.

'You shaved him?' Judith stammered and Amy was grateful she
was focussing on the shaving rather than the fact Philippe had
been dyed bright purple.

'I'm sorry.' Amy gestured to the taxi driver that she would be
a minute.

Judith carefully unwrapped the lump and gasped in horror at
the full torture that poor Philippe had endured

'You brute, you horrid girl, how could you…' Judith said,
cradling Philippe in her arms.

'I'm really sorry, I was trying to help him, but he doesn't like
me and—'

'I'm not surprised he doesn't like you, you're a horrible, foul
person. Seb is always moaning about you at work, he doesn't like
you either, no one does, you vile, cruel girl.'

'I really am very sorry.' Amy sighed sadly, as she turned and
shuffled over to the taxi.

'You'll never set foot in his pub again; I'll make sure of that.'

Amy stiffened then turned back to say something. But realising
whatever she said now would just make the situation worse, she
got into the taxi and it drove off.

———

George had been out, helping his mum with an antique wardrobe
she had bought at some fair. He was tired after the night before
and was looking forward to having a small kip on his sofa.

'Hi honey, I'm home,' he called to Candy in the bedroom, the
mannequin he had rescued from a skip a few years before. One day,

he would come home and she would answer him, having changed into the beautiful Kim Cattrall, just like in the film *Mannequin*.

'Hi darling. Dinner is in the oven; I've polished your shoes and starched your shirts for you.'

He smiled, as he moved through to the kitchen, poured two glasses of apple juice and carried them back through to the lounge.

There was Libby lying on his sofa, still in her Christmas pudding onesie, her hair all tousled and unbrushed. She grinned hugely at him when she saw him. She was lying on her front, her legs swinging behind her, busy typing away on her laptop, with several sheets of paper lying around her. Tucked behind her ear was a red biro and tucked between her toes a purple one.

He passed her the glass of juice and threw himself down in his easy chair, flicking up the footrest in one swift movement.

'How's your mum?' Libby asked.

George smiled. 'She's fine. You know what Verity is like. She always has someone she needs to take under her wing, whether they like it or not. She's set her mind on helping poor Judith Axe now. She says Judith has been mourning her daughter for too long and it's time she got over it. Mum wants her married off to Uncle Bob by Christmas because, apparently, "They'd make the perfect couple."'

'I love your mum.'

George smiled. He loved that Libby had so much time for her.

'So, is there a reason you have invaded my territory on this fine Monday morning?'

'Do I need a reason?'

'Not at all, you are always welcome, you know that.'

'I did have a reason actually, Rosie and Alex; I just can't concentrate on writing when they're upstairs going at it like rabbits every second of the day. It seems Alex has a day off today.'

'But you write all that romance stuff. Surely a bit of sex would help to inspire you?'

'You'd think, wouldn't you? It's actually more of a hindrance than a help at the moment.'

He surveyed her. She had always said she didn't want him to read her books and he wanted to respect that, but he was often tempted so he could find out more about the inner workings of her mind. Would there be a clue in there about why she felt the need to always move on?

'So you're having problems writing lately?'

'Yeah, I think it's the lack of romance in my own life, I'm finding it hard to be inspired at the moment.'

'Do you normally have boyfriends and go on dates in the places that you stay to inspire you to write all the romantic stuff?'

'No, I can't say I've ever had a boyfriend. I've had men I've gone out on a few dates with, but there's never been anything serious. When I write, I used to write as Eve Loveheart, my pseudonym, and it was easy to imagine what she would do in the different scenarios I throw at my characters. I also watch other people, draw experiences from real life but make it sound so much better. I write the relationships that women fantasise about. The rugged hero who saves a small boy from drowning at sea, comes back and declares his love for the woman who fills his dreams and every waking breath because he suddenly realises that life is too short and you need to grab it with both hands.'

George smiled. 'Are you writing about me?'

'Maybe.'

He sighed. 'I can see how a dashing lifeboat crewman who perhaps only wears waterproof trousers and no top, with soaking wet abs, who risks his life to save a boy would be miles better than the reality of me coming home from a very quick, easy rescue, sorting out my laundry and never being brave enough to tell the woman of my dreams that I'm completely and utterly in love with her just in case she rejects me.'

'I'm going to help you with that. It's about loving the person you are so other people can love you too. Women love to read about the big, strong alpha males who are mean and broody but in reality they want someone who would take care of them, who is sweet and kind, someone who would make them smile every single day. You have that in spades.'

He looked out the window over the sea. No woman would ever choose sweet and kind over dashing and sexy. He was living proof of that. Josie had left him for the dynamic Chase Kent. George was boring, Josie had told him so on many occasions, along with dull, predictable and pathetic. He quickly changed the subject before he dwelled too long on that.

'And what about you? You write love stories, you're trying to give me advice, but you've never been in love yourself. Don't you think that the thing that's missing, not only from your story but your life, is your own experience of true love in all its spectacular, wonderful glory?'

'I don't need it.'

'Everybody needs to be loved, everyone needs someone.'

Libby shook her head vehemently. 'I don't.'

'How can an author of beautiful love stories be so anti love herself? What happened to you to make you so fearful of letting yourself fall in love?'

'I'm not scared of it, I just don't want it. Falling in love means relying on someone else and I don't want that. Your hopes and dreams for the future tied up in their hands. There can be nothing worse than watching your dreams fade away. To see them slowly crushed and belittled must be destroying. Have you ever seen someone die inside, every bit of joy and happiness just fading to nothing, so all they are left with is this shell. It's heartbreaking. That's what Josie did to you, she put you down, battered your confidence, but at least you were brave enough to get out before you were broken completely.'

'There was nothing left in our marriage any more. I don't think it was brave to walk away from that. She hated me and had no respect for me, something which was proved when I asked her for a divorce and she threw the fact that she had been sleeping with Chase Kent for the last two years in my face. One last-ditch attempt to destroy me once and for all.'

'Christ, who does that to someone they love? Even if you've fallen out of love with them, how could you hurt someone who loves you with everything they have? That's not the kind of love I ever want to be a part of.'

He frowned. 'If you find the right person, then you build your dreams around them, your dreams become theirs and you build new dreams together. Being with Josie destroyed me and, yes, it's made me fearful of dating again in case I'm hurt like that again, but I would never just give up on love. It's one of the most glorious experiences you can ever have – imagine the highs you got from that parachute jump you did in Thailand and double that, no times it by a hundred. I had that with Josie in the beginning and I want that again. You've said before that you want to look back on your life with no regrets. I think the thing you will miss the most, the one thing that you will regret, is never having that heart-stopping, passionate, crazy rollercoaster ride of falling head over heels in love. In fact, while you are helping me back into the dating saddle and teaching me all about first-date etiquette, I'm going to use this time to show you what you've been missing by avoiding relationships all this time.'

Libby stared at him and a smile slowly emerged on her face. 'OK.'

He sensed the tension from the conversation had gone. She'd had a bad experience of love and it broke his heart to see her closed off from love like that, but he'd had a bad experience too and he was determined to show her how great it could be. It wouldn't change things between them, he knew that, but maybe one day in the future she would be open to being in a relationship again. He couldn't bear the thought that she would always be drifting through life alone.

'OK?'

'Yes. OK. I always like to try new things, new foods and experiences. I can try being in a relationship too.'

'So our big date is tonight.' George waggled his eyebrows mischievously, hoping to bring the smile back on her face. 'What can I do to guarantee our date ends in hot, passionate sex?'

Libby laughed.

'I don't want to go overboard and scare you off on the first date but I don't want to be blasé too and not put in enough effort to result in a second date.'

'You're pretty much guaranteed a second date from me and a third. If we're going to do this we have to do this right. For my story, for me to be fully immersed in this new experience, nothing is too much. I want every romantic gesture that you can think of. My fans love the big epic forever-style romances, so anything that you can think of that might be considered romantic is fine with me. I need as much inspiration as I can get. Christmassy too if you can manage it. I've never really had any spectacular Christmases, I've spent most of my Christmases alone. So anything that has that Christmas theme to it will be a great addition to the experience. If you can arrange a reindeer sleigh ride through the snow, I'll be dropping to one knee and asking you to marry me.

But I'll tell you if you do anything that might be deemed over the top for Giselle. The six-foot engagement ring made from ice or a barbershop quartet declaring their love might be a bit much for a first date with Giselle.'

'But for you?'

'Oh God yes, I love all that stuff. Just because I don't want a relationship for myself doesn't mean I can't swoon with that "aww" factor when I see it done for other people.'

'Duly noted.'

Libby smiled. 'Just do whatever feels natural to you – remember I want to help you as well as you helping me, so I need to assess the real George, the one that Giselle will see.'

He nodded, concentrating his attention on a drop of juice on the side of the glass. He honestly didn't think the real George was something anyone would be interested in.

'And we have the upcoming Christmas Eve ball, maybe we treat it like a date. There can't be anything more romantic than a proper ball, being swept around the room in the arms of the man you love.' Libby looked wistful for a moment and quickly tapped out a few lines on her laptop.

'Does that mean I have to dance?'

'Yes, sorry. One of my criteria for my perfect guy is his ability or, more importantly, his willingness to dance with me. All the great heroes do it. Just one night, George, I'm sure you can manage that.'

'I'll try. So an ice carving of a diamond ring, a barbershop quartet, romance, flowers, fireworks, champagne, candles, fudge, dancing, log fires and a sleigh ride through the snow?'

'Yes, I don't want much.'

'And if I do all that we'll be married by New Year's Eve?'

'Yes.' Libby smiled at him. And for a moment, a tiny brief moment, he thought he saw a flash of sincerity in her eyes.

He cleared his throat and looked away and she looked down too, concentrating on typing a few more words on her keyboard.

'Well, I might have a kip for a bit, before we head out for our hot date,' George said. 'Keep up my energy for the night of passionate dirty sex that we're going to have once you are swept off your feet.'

'Shall I go?' she asked.

'No, stay.' He leaned back and closed his eyes. 'I can then tell everyone I slept with Libby this morning.'

———

Libby smiled as she watched George fall asleep, his breathing becoming heavy very quickly. They had become so relaxed in each other's company. He looked so peaceful, so at ease.

She liked that George wanted to teach her about love, it was sweet of him to be concerned for her even though she had convinced herself a long time ago that she didn't need a man to make her happy. If nothing else, all his attempts would be great book fodder.

She glanced round the room. Were there more decorations than there had been the day before?

Above the old Victorian-style fireplace were two huge stockings, one labelled George, one labelled Libby. Her heart leapt when she saw them. He'd said he was going to get her a stocking as everyone should have one at Christmas and he'd said he'd hang it over his fireplace because she was going to spend Christmas with him. It was such a sweet gesture and her heart filled a little bit because of it.

She returned her attention to the computer screen and frowned. She had just started to write the scene where Eliza and Charles got together for the first time but at the moment her characters had no chemistry at all, standing opposite each other seemingly waiting for their cue.

George mumbled something in his sleep and she watched him. She was tired herself. She hadn't slept well the night before and when she woke this morning her feet were dirty, a sure sign she had been sleepwalking again. She never felt completely rested when her body had been up and about while she slept.

She closed her eyes so she could imagine the scene between Charles and Eliza. What would Eve Loveheart do in this scene? But there was nothing there, no inspiration. Everything she had written before seemed fake and clichéd all of a sudden. She wanted to show the reality. Maybe she should think about what *she* wanted, not this fake persona. How would Libby react to being with someone like George? She thought about how they would look at each other, how he would touch her, how it would be making love, not just hot, hard sex.

And as she pictured it, drew the images in her mind, she felt herself drifting off.

——

George woke and immediately looked over to see if Libby was still with him. To his surprise, she was curled up on his sofa fast asleep, her face pressed against her laptop.

He got up and carefully removed the laptop from under her, so she would be more comfortable. As he set it down on the table, the screensaver mode, which had turned the screen off when Libby had been inactive, suddenly sensed movement and switched itself back on. There, in black and white, was her latest story.

He couldn't take his eyes off it. She didn't want him to read her work, which had just made him more and more curious about it.

Eliza knocked on Charles' door, trembling against the cold.

No, he wouldn't read it, that would be a huge invasion of privacy, Libby would be so angry at him.

When Charles answered the door, she nearly wept with relief. There was a log fire burning behind him, filling the room with warmth, and Charles was standing before her, dressed only in his trousers and boots.

Was this…about to turn into a sex scene?

'Eliza, what are you doing out there in this weather? Come in — are you OK?'

'I got lost, and then the storm started…' Eliza shivered.

'Sit yourself down by the fire; get out of those wet clothes.'

Oh my God!

'I'll get something you can change into,' Charles said.

'Charles…stay…with me,' Eliza said, looking away with embarrassment.

He crossed the room quickly, taking her in his arms…

'George,' Libby mumbled, and he nearly threw the laptop across the room in shock. But she was still asleep. Her fist clenched tightly over the blanket on the sofa, stretching out her legs as she sighed his name again.

His eyes bulged. She had gone to sleep writing this sex scene and now she was dreaming about him. Was she dreaming about… having sex with him?

He laughed quietly, shaking his head to clear it of the delusions. Last night she had been dreaming about selling her car to Clint Eastwood, she was probably dreaming about him and Clint in the car together. He closed the laptop down and went to the kitchen to make her a cup of tea.

—

Seb looked at Amy in horror as she came through the door and round his side of the bar. Her arms were covered in purple bruises and large deep scratches. She looked like she had been beaten up. Who would do this to her?

She hung her jacket up in the small cupboard, filled Jack's water bowl and then moved to serve one of the customers, seemingly unfazed by the damage inflicted on her.

A surge of protectiveness rose up in him. He wanted to hug her and hold her and it drove him mad that he had these feelings for her. Swallowing a huge lump in his throat, he took her arm and indicated that he wanted to talk to her out the back.

She followed him into his office and he closed the door.

'Amy... what happened?'

'Don't you dare do this, Seb, don't you dare.' Her voice shook with anger as she spoke.

He looked at her with confusion. 'What? I meant your arms, what happened to you?'

She looked down at her arms and growled. 'Oh, I hate my boss.'

He felt his hands ball into fists in his pockets. 'Your boss did this?'

She nodded. 'Blithering idiot, oh and Philippe, I hate him too.'

'Philippe? Judith's cat?'

'Yes. I take it you spoke to her and that's why you've brought me in here?'

He recalled the phone call from Judith earlier that day; he had completely forgotten it when he saw Amy so badly beaten.

'I had a hysterical phone call from Judith, but she was talking so fast and there was so much yowling and meowing in the background I just held the phone away from my ear and said "yes" and "no" and "I agree" until she ran out of steam and rang off.'

'I swear if you sack me, I'll sue you, I'll hire a big fat lawyer and I'll sue your ass. I've done nothing wrong you know that, I'll—'

'Amy, for God's sake, shut up for a second, I'm about to blow a gasket here. What the hell did Marcus do to you? Did he beat you up?' Seb swallowed at the thought of something worse. 'Did he ... hurt you?'

Seemingly wrong-footed, she stepped back. 'What? Marcus? Are you insane? He's a complete numpty but he's not capable of something like that. What on earth made you think that?'

He stepped towards her, laying his finger gently on one of the bruises. Desire crashed through him as he touched her skin.

She looked down at his finger on her arm. 'Oh Seb, this is hair dye, purple hair dye. Marcus wanted me to dye my hair today as I was dressed like a blackberry to promote one of his new ice cream flavours. Philippe got stuck up a tree in my garden whilst I was dyeing it and I got him out, but I managed to get purple dye all over him and me in the process. Which is why Judith has decided she hates me, well she hated me before... I think now she'd quite like to kill me.'

'All of this over Philippe.'

'Philippe hates me too.'

'He got you good.' Seb stroked one of the cuts, gently, relieved that he had got it so wrong.

'I was only trying to help him, next time I'll just leave him to die up there, or let Judith climb the tree herself and get him down. Now that would be very entertaining.'

He laughed.

'So does this mean you're not going to sack me?' she asked.

He shook his head. 'Not yet.'

She smiled, shaking her head presumably at the 'not yet' comment. Suddenly she stepped closer to him, cupping his face in her hand. 'Thank you.'

He really wasn't comfortable with her hand on his face – it did things in his body that he didn't like, mainly the blood roaring in his ears, his heart thundering against his chest. There was a line between employee/employer relations and she'd just crashed across it. He forced himself to take a step away from her when he really wanted to take her face in his hands too.

'For what?'

'For finally showing that you care for me.'

He did care for; her that was the problem, he cared too much.

'I'm just looking out for the welfare of my staff; I care for all my friends. You're no different.'

But her wistful smile unnerved him. She knew he liked her.

He walked to the door. 'Look, stop slacking off in here and get out there and serve my customers.'

'Yes boss.' She smiled as she scurried past him.

CHAPTER 4

At seven o'clock sharp, George lifted his hand and knocked on Libby's door and then nervously pulled down the sleeves of his suit jacket and waited, his heart doing little rolling thumps.

When she opened the door, he saw her smile at his suit just before he noticed what she was wearing. She looked stunning in a green satin sequinned dress, her dark hair piled on top of her head, with sparkly grips.

'You look lovely, Lib,' he said, softly.

'Thanks, you look very smart too but…' She suddenly stepped forward and undid his tie, sliding it off his neck. He felt her fingers working open the top button of his shirt. He shifted nervously at the intimacy, and couldn't meet her eyes as she surveyed him. He watched her step back to admire her work.

'Much better,' she said. 'The tie just makes it look too formal.'

'Oh, and the satin dress is casual, is it?'

'No,' she said with a laugh, 'but as a girl I can get away with looking formal; men tend to look like they are going for a job interview if they go with a tie and jacket.'

He tutted as he watched her dump his tie unceremoniously over the back of her sofa.

But when she took his arm and he escorted her down the steps to his car, he found he was smiling broadly.

He was feeling nervous on the drive to the restaurant and he couldn't understand it. They had been out to dinner loads of times over the last few months and he had never felt nervous before. But this was a date, albeit a fake one. And though he was only practising his skills, he really wanted to leave her with a good impression.

When they arrived at the restaurant, he realised he needn't have bothered to ring ahead to secure the most romantic table to kick-start his 'date'. They were the only customers; obviously the curry-deprived residents of White Cliff Bay were building up to trying the new place. They were seated in the window overlooking the sea and he was glad she had suggested the place – situated on the peak of a cliff, The Cherry Tree had stunning views over the bay and of the moon sending silvery ribbons over the sea. It was a night designed for romance, for declarations of love and first kisses under the moonlight. In a film, this would be the moment that Tom Hanks and Meg Ryan realised they were perfect for each other. And he was sitting opposite his best friend. He wasn't sure if this was a good or bad thing. What if, caught up in the moment, he suddenly found himself down on one knee, asking her to marry him?

He could see she was impressed. 'You're off to a great start,' she said, 'this table, that view, the Christmas lights and the candles on the table, it's very romantic. With the right setting, even the most unlikely suitor can look appealing. A little bit earlier would have been even better. A sunset is one of the most romantic things in the world, but the moon is a very close second and sitting here looking at it over the sea with you, well, if this was a real first date I'd already be mentally replacing my surname with yours to see if it fits.'

He laughed. 'I thought it might be a bit clichéd, the moon, the sea...'

'There are some things which never go out of date.'

'It's a bit... quiet in here.' He looked around only to find all the waiting staff were watching them keenly.

'I hope that's not a reflection on the food.'

A smartly dressed waiter appeared between them with two menus.

Libby took hers and started scanning through it. 'Ooh, what shall I have?'

He couldn't help smiling. He loved that about her. When he used to go to Indian restaurants with his ex-wife, Josie, she always, always had chicken tikka masala. She wouldn't even bother looking at the menu – she didn't want to risk having something she didn't like. Whereas Libby would choose something different every time, sometimes something a bit obscure. Last time they had gone to their nearest Indian in Port Cardinal, nearly half an hour away from White Cliff Bay, she'd had ostrich curry.

'Oooh, can't choose, it's too hard,' she said finally, her eyes shining with excitement. She put her menu down, closed her eyes and stabbed her finger randomly at it. 'Ha, salmon and plum jalfrezi,' she announced when she opened her eyes, 'might be nice. What are you having, George?'

He quickly looked down at his menu. 'Erm, I'll have the beef handi, do you want to share a rice with me?'

'Yes, and a naan?'

Once the waiter had taken their order they both looked out at the view for a while then Libby turned back to him.

'OK, George, now you have to woo me.'

He stroked the back of her hand with his thumb, hoping that would be enough wooing for now. 'Shouldn't we be wooing each other?'

'Well yes, it should work both ways, but I'm your guinea pig remember.'

'So you won't try to woo me at all?' he scowled.

'OK, OK, I'll do my top three – the things my characters do to make their men fall in love with them.'

'What's your top three?'

'I'm not telling you, the wooing should be a surprise.'

He decided to play for time, it all seemed a bit complicated to him. 'Don't you think woo is a weird word?'

'Mmm, how about entice then?' She fixed him with a sultry smile.

He felt the heat rise in his cheeks as he cast around for a suitable anecdote to put himself at ease.

'Compliments are a good start, women love compliments about themselves,' Libby prompted, fluttering her eyelashes at him.

He laughed, brought her hand up to his mouth and put on his most seductive voice. 'My darling Libby, you have the most beautiful eyes in the world. Twenty shades of green. Olive, jade, moss, shamrock…'

She swallowed as she stared at him. He ran his mouth lightly over her knuckles, not taking his eyes off her.

'…With flecks of emerald, apple and sprout.'

She blinked once then burst out laughing. 'Sprout?'

'It's a colour.'

She laughed again. 'Oh well, when you say such endearing things like that, let's forget the meal and go straight back to your place.'

He smiled.

'How about you ask me some questions instead?' she suggested.

'How can I ask you questions about yourself when I already know everything there is to know about you?'

'Just pretend you don't, that this is the first time we've properly met. Pretend I'm Giselle.' She sipped her Coke.

'OK, er, Giselle, what is it you do?'

'I'm an astronaut.'

He laughed. 'What?'

'What, just because I'm a blonde with big blue eyes, did you think I'd say hairdresser or beautician? Don't judge a book by its cover, I'm actually really intelligent.'

'I'm sure you are. What's the capital of Chile?'

'Yeah, don't do that, don't try to trip your date up – and it's Santiago.'

He gasped. 'How did you know?'

'George, I was at the pub quiz with you last month when that question came up. We're so alike, we both store away useless information for regurgitation later on.'

He smiled. 'OK, so… an astronaut? That's interesting, have you been anywhere cool?'

'This is good, asking lots of questions,' she whispered in an aside, leaning in conspiratorially across the table, 'shows you're interested, and there's nothing women like more than talking about themselves.' She straightened up and more loudly said, 'Yes, just last week I went to Mars for the weekend.'

'Right,' he nodded, seriously.

'Yes, I've got three Martians as friends on Facebook now.'

He laughed. 'Libby Joseph, how can I practise on you when you're not taking this seriously?'

'OK, OK, I'm sorry. So, George, what is it you do?'

He straightened in his chair, finding a smile spreading across his face as it always did when he spoke about his job. 'I write radio adverts, scripts. The companies come to me with a rough guide to what they want their advert to say and I write a script for them. I love it; allows me to be really creative…' He watched her posture change as he spoke; she leaned forward in her chair, staring deep into his eyes and she smiled hugely as he talked. She knew how much he loved his job but she seemed really interested, like she was hanging off his every word. He wanted to carry on talking, wanted to talk forever if it meant that she would continue to look at him like that, but he trailed off, thrown by the intensity of her gaze.

'Lib, you OK?' he swallowed.

'I'm being interested, that's one of my top tips: leaning forward, eye contact, smiling. It's the body language that shows you how keen I am on you.'

'Oh.' He was momentarily disappointed that it was just for show. 'Well, it worked, I felt like I was the most important person in your world right then.'

'That's because you are, plus I genuinely do love listening to you talk about your work, so it wasn't too much of a stretch for me to look like that.'

Just then a man appeared between them; he must have been the head waiter or manager judging by the different coloured shirt he was wearing.

'We are very pleased you've come to us tonight. I am Kamal, the manager. You are a beautiful couple, very much in love, you've even dressed to match,' Kamal gestured.

He and Libby looked down at themselves and then at each other.

She laughed. 'We're both wearing the same shade of green, I didn't even realise.'

'Neither did I,' he said, aware that he had bought the shirt a few months before, because the colour reminded him of her eyes.

'How long have you two been together?' Kamal went on.

'Six months,' Libby said at exactly the same time as George offered, 'It's our first date.'

Kamal looked confused.

'We've been best friends for six months, this is our first date as a couple,' she tried to explain.

'Oh, that's beautiful,' Kamal said, looking a little watery around the eyes. 'A relationship built on such strong friendship, those are the ones that last. I can see how much you mean to each other, how much love is between you. Would you like some music for this special occasion?'

'Ooh yes, that'll be lovely.'

George saw her expectant expression change as Kamal waved theatrically and one of the waiters suddenly appeared at his side with a violin.

'Oh, you meant live music?' she said.

'Yes, Mani is very talented.'

As soon as Mani put his bow to the violin it was evident that Mani either wasn't that talented or the violin badly needed tuning. George winced a bit as Mani squeaked his way through the opening bars of what sounded like 'Jerusalem' and eyed Libby to see what her reaction was. She was looking at Mani as if he was playing a masterpiece, like she was enthralled by the music. Either she was completely tone deaf, or she was a really good actress. He tried to catch her eye but she seemed to be deliberately not looking at him. Then he saw the tiniest twitch of her mouth and he realised she was doing her absolute best not to laugh. He had to keep a really tight rein on himself, knowing that if he smiled he'd soon be laughing. 'Jerusalem' had been one of his favourite hymns at school, but he had never realised how long the song was before, unless Mani, encouraged by Libby's reaction, had repeated it several times. After what seemed like an eternity, by which time tears were forming in Libby's eyes with the suppressed laughter, Mani finished with a final tuneless flourish to his bow.

She clapped enthusiastically, wiping the tears away. 'That was beautiful, Mani. Do you play anything else – maybe something a bit more modern or Christmassy perhaps?'

George stared at her, incredulous. Why was she asking for more? His ears were still ringing from the last piece of music, if in fact you could call it that.

Mani nodded and launched into what could only be 'Angels' by Robbie Williams. Kamal pulled on Libby's chair, gesturing for her to stand up, which she did, looking bemused, until Kamal turfed George out of his seat too and he realised with some dismay, as Kamal pushed them both together, that he wanted them to dance.

'I don't think…' he protested, knowing he was blushing furiously.

'That's a lovely idea, thank you,' Libby said.

George caught her little grin and then she wrapped her arms around his neck, and he found he'd put his around her waist. In an attempt to dance, he started swaying from side to side. He heard her snort into his shoulder.

'You'll pay for this, Miss Joseph,' he muttered into her ear, 'you know how much I hate dancing.'

'Oh, come on,' she said, as Mani attempted to hit the high notes of the chorus, 'admit that there's a tiny part of you that's having fun right now.'

'I can't dance,' he said with some feeling.

'Rubbish. You're not doing as bad as you think. Just relax, just imagine you're dancing with a beautiful woman. Imagine you're dancing with Giselle.'

He smiled. He wouldn't imagine he was with Giselle, he would just enjoy the fact that his lovely Libby was in his arms. He moved his arms round her back, hugging her tightly to him.

'You see,' she said as Mani's strangling a cat impression reached a crescendo, 'a little bit of imagination and you've loosened right up.'

'I don't need imagination, Lib,' he said, 'I've got my best friend in my arms, that's all I need.'

She smiled up at him, looking right into his eyes. 'Well, just to give you a heads-up, if this was really Giselle in your arms right now, this would be the perfect time for your first kiss.'

'Well, Lib, you are my guinea pig.' He bent forward until his lips were moving to enclose hers. Which was when Mani moved seamlessly, or rather unseamlessly, from 'Angels' into 'Agadoo' by Black Lace. Libby's laugh broke the moment and he jerked his head back up.

'I really can't dance to this,' he said.

'Oh, sure you can, the dance moves are in the lyrics: "Jump to the right, jump to the left, jump up in the air and touch your knees,"' she sang.

'I don't think those are the lyrics.'

'Close enough. But you're right, it's definitely not one of the most romantic songs though, shall we sit back down?'

He should have felt relieved that his dancing torment was over, but he was too busy fighting off the disappointment that his beautiful best friend was no longer wrapped in his arms. He gave Mani a scowl as they returned to their seats; after all, it was his fault he'd missed out on his chance to kiss her.

'I really don't dance,' he said, trying to explain away his awkwardness.

'It's not your fault – mating rituals have changed a bit over the years. Time was, men used to have dance lessons. A man was expected to know the waltz or some other romantic dance, and they would swing their women around the dance floor, in order to impress them. Nowadays, in nightclubs up and down the country, the men linger at the bar, and the women dance to impress the men. It's no longer in your genes to be able to dance. Luckily there is only really one time that you'd be expected to dance and that's on your wedding day. But you don't need to worry. You're actually a really lovely dancer. I'm sure Giselle would love to dance with you.'

George was sure that she was only being polite. Besides, if his dancing had been lovely, it was only because he was with his best friend. If he'd had another woman in his arms he'd be a gibbering wreck.

Mani thankfully finished 'Agadoo' just as the food arrived, and Libby attacked it with enthusiasm.

'Oh George, this is wonderful, you should try some.' She held a forkful of food up to his lips and he obediently let her feed him.

'Mmm,' he said, savouring the spices, 'that is really good. Here, have some of mine.' He tried not to stare at her lips as he fed her a forkful of his beef handi.

'Ooh, I really like that,' she said, 'and that was number two of my top tips: sharing food is quite intimate.'

'Oh. I like it.' Suddenly he saw her lean across the table and felt her wipe his lip and chin gently with her thumb. Her touch sent fireworks through his body and he swallowed the lump of beef that had been in his mouth before properly chewing it. He took a long swig of his drink to help the food go down.

'And that was number three,' she said with a wink, 'body contact. Normally my characters might go for the hand, or a nudge of the knees under the table, but as you had sauce on your chin that was the perfect moment.'

He nodded weakly. He was supposed to be falling out of love with her, not falling more deeply in love.

'The food here is amazing.' Libby was oblivious to the emotions now swirling around in him along with his curry and beer. 'Why do you think it's empty?'

'I guess we might find that out later tonight – the food might not be as amazing as it tastes.' He devoured his curry with equal enthusiasm.

'Doesn't that put you off? Doesn't that scare you? This could literally be our last meal, and tomorrow we'll both be dead from food poisoning.'

'It's nice to live life on the edge.'

She nodded.

'Still, I might give them the number of that advertising agency in Port Cardinal, the one that uses me all the time. A little bit of marketing might be just what this place needs.'

She wiped up some of her sauce with the naan bread and for a while they didn't talk. But as he finished off his meal, he realised that a first date was supposed to be about talking, getting to know each other, and if he was with any other woman other than Libby right now, the last few minutes of silence would have been awkward.

'So anyway I'm supposed to be wooing you, aren't I?'

'You're doing fine – the view, the dance. We would have already had our first kiss, and all before we started to eat. It's going well so far.'

'What about the conversation?' He found he was playing with the last few bits of rice on his plate.

'I love talking to you, George, you're funny, intelligent and you're so easy to talk to. I could talk to you about anything for hours, and you listen, properly listen too. That's a great quality. Don't overthink what you should say to Giselle, just be yourself. And if you get stuck, just keep asking her lots of questions about herself, let her do all the talking. She will think you're interested and it doesn't leave room for awkward silences.'

'But why do silences mean something different when we're with different people? With you it's never awkward, is it? It's just silence. But with other people I feel the need to fill it with inane ramblings. What's wrong with silence?'

He was waiting for her to say something when Kamal appeared. 'Dessert?' he asked, beaming proudly at their empty plates.

She shook her head, patting her stomach. 'Sorry, I'm way too full. George?'

He shook his head too.

'Just the bill then please,' she said.

He fished his wallet out of his pocket. 'Now what does the first-date etiquette say about payment?'

She pulled a face. 'It is still kind of expected that the man will pay, or at least offer to pay. It shows generosity, old-fashioned chivalry, and a lot of women like that. It shows you want to care for her. I would just put your card down on the bill and not make a big deal out of it. She really doesn't need to think you are counting the pennies. If I was on a first date, I would offer to pay my half. In this day and age the woman really should offer to pay half, but I wouldn't count on it, and actually you should probably insist on paying unless she throws some kind of feminist tantrum. If she does, by all means let her pay.'

He nodded.

She smiled. 'You don't need to worry, you are incredibly generous. You should just do what feels natural. But you want to watch out for the gold diggers: if you are on your fifth date and she has never shown any sign of reaching for her purse, then I'd start to get a bit worried.'

Her phone suddenly rang in her bag, the *A-Team* theme tune, which always made him smile. But instead of retrieving it, she ignored it.

'Are you not going to get that?'

She shook her head. 'I'm on a date – you need to know there is no one that is more important than you right now. Really I should have left it at home or turned it off, but I forgot.'

'What if it's important?'

'If you're worried then check on it surreptitiously, preferably when you pop to the loo.'

The phone stopped ringing, just as he was wondering whether he should be taking notes.

———

Judith sat in one of the booths in the Bubble, stroking Jack's ears and surreptitiously watching Amy and Seb. Amy was working down one end of the bar, chatting animatedly to Polly and Matt and the other customers. Though Seb was serving behind the bar, she had barely given him a single look all night. To the untrained observer, he held no interest for Amy whatsoever, or if you had some curiosity about the situation you might think the two of them had had a row. But Judith recognised the signs of someone in love, but not wanting to admit it. Deliberately not looking at him was much more obvious than just not looking at him. What upset Judith most though, was that she was pretty sure that Seb was in love with Amy too.

Judith remembered when she first met Seb. When her own husband had died eleven years before, she had moved to White Cliff Bay to be close to her sister, who had then promptly died the year later. Marie had been at university at the time in London and when she finished her course it was natural for her to stay there with her friends, but she visited often and on one of her many visits she'd bumped into Seb.

When Marie was younger and she'd started dating, Judith had in her mind the worst possible person that Marie could bring home. Seb pretty much fitted the bill. His shaved head and tattoos made him look mean and violent. He was a landlord in a pub – hardly the doctor or lawyer that she had hoped for her bright, beautiful daughter – and quite a bit older, twenty-seven to Marie's young, innocent twenty-two.

At first Judith had disapproved but it hadn't taken Seb long to win her round. He adored Marie and anyone could see that they were made for each other. Judith soon loved him like the son she'd never had.

Seb and Marie were married very quickly, just a year after they'd first met, but four years later Marie was dead. A horrible car accident had robbed Judith of her only child and Seb of his loving wife. Marie hadn't died straight away though, and for a few hours, it seemed like she would pull through. Then complications set in and she deteriorated very quickly.

The grief had brought Judith and Seb both closer together. They now saw each other two or three times a week; she would do the odd shift for him in the pub and every Thursday night, his night off, he'd be round her house for dinner. They had become very close over the last five years; she adored him and wanted more than anything for him to find happiness again.

But not with Amy, anyone but Amy. Judith couldn't think of anyone worse than Amy for Seb to fall in love with. She was loud, crude and truly one of the vilest people she knew.

She had to get Amy out of his life and fast.

—

Seb couldn't concentrate on anything tonight. He had messed up several orders already, though thankfully it was mostly the locals and they all took it with good humour. Amy was infuriating. She hadn't so much as looked at or spoken to him all night and it was driving him mad.

The more she ignored him the more he wanted to talk to her, wanted her to notice him. She looked fantastic tonight, sexy in a gorgeous black dress and her favourite red high heels, her dark hair long and gleaming down her back. He wanted to kiss her … he had to kiss her.

She occupied every single waking and sleeping thought and it scared him. He had never felt this way before and although, for the last few months, he had put it down to lust and a need for sex, he knew it was so much more than that. But he couldn't get involved with anyone again. The pain he'd felt when Marie died had been unbearable and he couldn't go through that again, especially not with someone like Amy who he had such strong feelings for. If his heart had broken so painfully when Marie died, what would it feel like to lose Amy when his feelings for her were so much more?

He looked at Judith and realised she had been watching him. He smiled over at her as he moved to serve another customer.

And that was another reason. Guilt. How could he ever explain his feelings for Amy? He'd loved Marie, he knew that, but somehow the intensity of his feelings for Amy was greater and he never wanted to belittle what he'd had with Marie. He couldn't hurt Judith, he owed her so much, and falling in love with another woman would break her heart. Minutes after Marie had died, Judith sobbing, near hysterical in her grief, had made him promise that there would never be anyone else. At the time he had promised without hesitation – he could never have imagined loving anyone as much as he had loved Marie – and he had kept the promise ever since.

But now he had to find the courage to break that promise – and the thought of opening himself up to all that hurt again was one that was utterly terrifying.

CHAPTER 5

'George, I have a question. At what point do you introduce your partner as your girlfriend?'

'I don't know, that is a very good question.'

'OK, say this was really our first date and we bumped into your friends, how would you introduce me?'

'I think I would just say "This is Libby", and then if it was a good friend I might waggle my eyebrows a bit to indicate that I was sleeping with you, or at least hoping to.'

'Oh, the eyebrow waggle, very clever, subtle.'

'And then two or three dates down the road, you might become "my good friend Libby". But I think, to avoid all confusion or awkwardness of introducing you as my girlfriend, if you didn't want to be introduced as such, I'd probably just introduce you as "my lovely Libby".'

'Oh, that's sweet.'

'Yeah, even after we were married I could still use that one.'

'Well, I think once we're married you could safely assume it wouldn't be awkward any more. Once we're married you could introduce me as your wife, I'd be OK with that.'

'Oh, very gracious of you. OK, I have a question for you. When do you tell your partner you love them?'

'When you do love them, never before.'

'But what if she says she loves me?' He thought that was pretty wishful thinking; he couldn't imagine anyone telling him they loved him.

'If you don't feel the same way, you should never say it back, just smile and kiss her.'

He frowned. 'Won't she notice that I haven't said it back?'

'Yes of course she will notice, but you can't say you love her if you don't; it will give her false hope and, if and when you finally do love her, you'll want to tell her. If you've already done that several weeks before, it won't mean as much.'

'What if she asks if I feel the same way?'

'You say that after your divorce you are a bit vulnerable and it will take you a while to completely trust someone. You tell her that you've built all these walls up to protect yourself and that it may take a while to pull them down, to be able to let yourself fall in love again.'

He smiled to himself at how well she actually knew him, inside and out.

'Just promise me you won't ever tell a woman that you love her if you don't, that's the worst thing you could do. And I'm not talking about the kind of love that you feel for Angelina Jolie, I'm talking proper all-consuming, can't-breathe kind of love. Only when you feel that should you declare it.'

He sighed. 'It's hard. It's like, "I love you, here's my heart to do with what you will." I gave my heart to Josie and she stamped all over it, crushed it to a bloody pulp. I'm going to have to find a whole load of courage to do it again.'

Libby smiled. 'When you find that special someone, someone you want to marry, you will. And you will be more selective over who you fall in love with next time.'

'But it's not enough to choose the perfect woman, if she doesn't love you back.'

'Oh George, how could they not love you back?'

The bill arrived, accompanied with two pieces of white chocolate and one piece of dark.

'Oooh, white chocolate.' Her eyes lit up.

He loved white chocolate. It was his all-time favourite thing to eat and he wanted to hug her when he saw her hand hover over the white chocolate before settling on the dark piece. She popped it in her mouth and pushed the two pieces of white chocolate towards him.

He took one piece and pushed the plate with the remaining piece back to her.

She shook her head. 'No, you take it, your need is greater than mine.'

He determined next time he was at the shops to pick up another bag of rum and raisin fudge for her; he knew that was her favourite thing in the world.

She fished out her purse from her tiny handbag, and dug out a twenty, but he waved it away with his card. 'As payment for being my guinea pig.'

'Oh, I enjoyed it.'

Once George had paid, Kamal escorted them to the door.

'Did you enjoy your meal?' Kamal asked.

'Very much,' Libby nodded. 'Especially the music.'

George took his mind off the laugh that was forming in his throat by handing Kamal the business card of the advertising agency and advising him to give them a call.

Once outside the restaurant the cold air blew from the sea and over the hilltops, whistling around them, light snowflakes falling like tiny grains of salt, and Libby shivered.

'Bet my jacket doesn't look so silly now, does it?' he said, whisking it off and wrapping it round her shoulders, hoping the gesture wasn't too cheesy. He put his arm round her too and started to guide her towards the car, but she peeled away, heading towards the cliff top. He saw her stop and just stare at the view. Coming to stand by her side, he saw the inky water below, covered with a dappled silver blanket.

'It's beautiful, isn't it?' she said. 'When I look out on that view, sometimes I want to look out on it for the rest of my life.'

His heart leapt with a sudden sliver of hope. 'Do you think you might ever find somewhere that you would want to stay?'

She didn't answer straight away, which helped turn that sliver into a small bloom.

'What about an extension?' he said, quickly. 'You said you haven't been able to finish your latest story. What if you extended your stay here until it's finished?'

'I can't. I travel because of my job.'

It was such an automatic answer, even she believed it now.

'I want you to stay,' he said, softly.

She turned to him, suddenly giving him her undivided attention. 'I know you would never stay because of me...'

'That's got nothing to do with it, I...'

He stepped closer. Pulling his jacket tighter around her shoulders, he kissed her softly on the forehead, stalling all other words from her. 'It's OK, I get it. You've been running for so long that now you don't know how to stop. But if you stayed, I'd keep the demons from your door.'

She stared up at him and then rested her head on his chest, wrapping her arms around him. He held her tight, wishing more than anything that he had reached her.

'I will miss you so much, George Donaldson.'

His heart sank. He stared out at the sea, wanting to say something to break the tension that was hanging in the air between them.

'Come on.' He stepped back out of her arms, then took her hand and led her back towards the car. 'Our date isn't over yet.'

'Yes, of course, we're going to watch *Psycho* so you can cuddle me when you get scared.'

He laughed. 'I cuddle you because you get scared, not the other way round. Anyway, that's not what I meant. There's something I thought you might like to see.'

—

'Where are you taking me?' Libby asked as George drove through the steep windy roads of White Cliff Bay. They drove past the huge Christmas tree in the village square and Libby smiled at the carollers who were singing a version of 'Silent Night' as people wrapped up in hats and scarves stood by and watched. She glanced over at George as he drove. They were clearly going to ignore that little moment up on the cliff tops. There were lots of things they were going to ignore lately and Libby couldn't help the feeling that they were just papering over the cracks.

'All that talk of that engagement ring ice carving today, I remembered there's some ice carving competition tonight in the town hall. Now that sounds pretty Christmassy to me. I'm sure there's room for a couple of ice carvings in your book,' George said.

He drove past the ice rink at the top of the slipway. The whole town looked magical, as if ready for Christmas. Decorations and garlands of lights were strewn from every building and across the streets, creating golden puddles on the wet cobbled streets below. The beauty of the place, all dressed in its Christmas best, had never failed to make Libby smile over the last few weeks.

'It's very late – are you sure the town hall will still be open?' She had been ready to snuggle up with George for another movie but he had taken a different way home, driving through the town instead. It was bitter cold out and she didn't really want to drive across the town and find the place was closed. Everything seemed to close really early in White Cliff Bay. Most of the restaurants even stopped serving food after nine.

'Apparently it's open till ten thirty for people to go and have a look at the carvings so I think we should be OK.'

George pulled up outside the town hall which was decorated with garlands of lights and two sensibly dressed Christmas trees stood sentinel either side of the door.

Inside, the town hall was completely empty of people and almost in darkness apart from the spotlights underneath the six ice carvings, causing the sculptures to glow with an enchanting ethereal beauty. She was suddenly very glad George had suggested this.

'See, there's an angel and a snowflake, that's very Christmassy.' George pointed across the room and Libby went to investigate the two carvings. The angel was beautiful, with every line of hair, every feather, carved intricately. She looked round to see if anyone was watching but she and George were completely alone. She reached forward and touched the angel's face, feeling the cold almost burn through her skin, but she was surprised how dry the ice felt. Surely it should be melting. She looked down at the rosette to see it had come first place in the competition. She could see why.

'This is Penny's. She lives in the town,' George said as he admired the angel too.

Libby moved on to the snowflake, which, although small, was carved with incredible talent. She moved to a vase of flowers, admiring the roses, tulips and orchids that had been carved with delicate petals and leaves. She felt incredibly humbled to see this huge amount of talent all together in one room and a little bit sad that by the time the morning came there would be nothing left of any of them other than a puddle of water. It felt special somehow that only she and George were there to witness this brief moment of beauty. The other people from the town, the competitors and the judges had all been and gone, leaving the ice carvings all alone. But whether George realised it or not, standing there just the two of them and these incredible carvings was actually really romantic.

She slipped her hand into his and he looked surprised at the gesture. 'Thank you for bringing me here tonight.'

He smiled. 'My pleasure.'

'I feel bad that they'll all be gone by tomorrow.'

'Some beauty is fleeting, some lasts a lifetime.'

She stared at him, stunned at this rare moment of sincerity and soulfulness from him.

He turned to look at her. 'I guess it's like friendships. Some people come and go from your life like ships passing in the night, some people stay forever. It's funny though, when you meet those forever friends, you just know that they are going to be your friend for the rest of your life – there's that connection there that you don't get from those fleeting friendships. I thought we had that connection.'

'We do.' She had felt it too, there was no denying that. 'Friendships are not just about proximity. We can still be friends even if we are far apart. We can keep in touch.'

'And you keep in touch with a lot of the people you meet on your travels, do you?'

There was no one, no friends. She very rarely allowed herself to get close to people; some places she stayed, she came and went without anyone even knowing her name. Even the people that she did become friendly with, she left them with a hug and a promise to keep in touch, even though she never had any intention of keeping that promise.

'It's different with you.'

He smiled sadly, before he looked away.

'Wow, look at this.' George pointed to what was obviously supposed to be Hogwarts Castle. It was quite simply stunning. Every tiny brick, every spire and turret was carved beautifully; even the tiny dragon on the roof was portrayed with minute detail.

She swallowed down the emotion that had bubbled to the surface with their conversation. 'This is just… amazing.'

She looked at the rosette next to the carving and saw it had come second place in the competition. She looked back at the angel.

'How did the castle come second place? The angel is beautiful but the castle is something out of this world.'

George looked across the room at the angel and back at the castle. 'I agree. Penny was the woman who I saved from the sea last night; she had jumped in to save one of the Mayor's boys. I'm guessing that had something to do with her winning. Though if I know Penny she will hate that she won that way. Maybe we should award the rosette to the rightful winner.'

He quickly grabbed the second place rosette and ran across the room and swapped it for the first place rosette on the angel. He came back and silently awarded the castle with first place.

'George! You can't do that.'

'No one else is going to come here. It'll be closed in the next few minutes and a pool of water tomorrow, but at least the rightful winner has now been awarded as such.'

They walked past and admired a wonderful lighthouse, the exact copy of the one out in the bay, and a spectacular mermaid.

'Well, after all that ice, I think we should go home and watch *Titanic*.'

Libby smiled. It was a film she had watched with George probably twenty or thirty times and he still cried every single time.

George looked through his imaginary telescope. 'Iceberg dead ahead.' He ran to the front of his imaginary boat and stood with his arms stretched out to the side. 'Jack, I'm flying.'

Libby moved to stand behind him, extending her arms out too so she was flying with him. As George launched into 'My Heart Will Go On' by Celine Dion there was suddenly a polite cough from behind them. They whirled round to see a security guard at the door.

'We're locking up in two minutes.'

George nodded, looking like a naughty school boy who had been caught smoking behind the bike sheds, and the security guard left them alone.

'I suppose we should go,' Libby said.

'Hang on,' George said, running to the vase of flowers. He looked over his shoulder and then, with a great deal of difficulty, he snapped off a tiny ice rose.

'George!'

'What? No one will know.' He gave it to her and she was touched by the sweet gesture. She cradled it in her hand, afraid it might break or suddenly melt. 'You can put it in your freezer when you get home.' He started singing, '*Nine days before Christmas my true love gave to me, an ice rose that was all slippery.*'

'Your poetry is terrible.'

He shrugged as she stared down at the tiny memory from their wonderful date. He took her by the hand and she quickly slipped it into her pocket as they walked past the security guard trying not to look guilty.

'Come on, we have a date with Leo and Rose.'

'I thought we were going to watch *Psycho.*'

'Your choice, Lib, do you want to watch something scary so you can cuddle up to me, or watch *Titanic* so I can cuddle up to you?'

'*Psycho* definitely. There's no better way to end a date than cuddling with your boyfriend on the sofa. But we'll watch *Titanic* tomorrow, I know you need your weekly fix.'

He smiled and she followed him out.

—

The pub was slowly emptying, the locals shouting their goodbyes to each other across the pub, and Amy was just getting her jacket on ready to leave herself when Seb walked past her with a tray of empties.

'I need to speak to you. Stay back after everyone else has gone, will you?' he said, as he moved behind the bar.

She surveyed him. 'My shift finished fifteen minutes ago. Whatever you want to say to me you can say when I'm next on shift.'

He banged his tray down, stirring Jack from his slumber, and started forcefully throwing glasses into the dishwasher.

'What's wrong with you tonight? You've been snappy, getting orders wrong. You're like a bear with a sore head.'

'Oh, you noticed, did you? I didn't think you would have. Matt and Polly seemed to hold your attention avidly all night.'

She looked away so he wouldn't see the smile of satisfaction on her face. So it had worked. 'I have to be up early for work tomorrow, so I'd appreciate you discussing the finer points of my shifts or how to clean the dishwasher either right now or leaving it till tomorrow.'

'Damn it, Amy, you make me so angry. Nobody gets under my skin like you do. For God's sake, can you not spare me a few minutes?'

She slung her bag over her shoulder. 'We both know why I make you so angry, it's because you want me and you continue to deny it. And no, I can't spare you a few minutes. I don't want to be alone with you any more, it's driving me insane to be with you and not touch you or kiss you.'

'That's what I want to talk to you about,' he muttered, as she moved to leave, freezing her in her tracks.

Judith suddenly approached. 'I'm off now, my love, unless there's anything you want help with?'

'No, that's fine, I'm nearly done here and then I'm going straight to bed,' he said, shooting Amy a quick look of desire and her mouth nearly fell open. Did he mean he wanted to go to bed with *her*? He walked round the bar towards Judith. 'I'll see you Thursday.'

She hugged him, giving him a fond kiss on the cheek then looked at Amy.

'Amy, would you like a lift home?'

Amy was sure that if her mouth hadn't fallen open before at Seb's surreptitious offer of sex, it certainly had now at Judith's sudden generosity.

'I... actually need to talk to Amy about something to do with work, so...' said Seb.

'I don't mind waiting,' Judith smiled cheerfully and Amy suddenly wondered if she planned to kill her, to get her in the car and then do away with her, burying her body in a shallow grave in the hills between here and their road.

'It will take a while actually, Judith, so there's no point in waiting.'

Judith stood in the silence that followed, her eyes narrowed, her nostrils flaring, before she admitted defeat.

'OK, I'll cook your favourite Thursday, spaghetti bolognese.'

Seb smiled and Amy watched him as Judith let herself out.

The pub was empty now and she found her mouth was dry as he turned towards her.

There was a silence, punctuated only by the ticking of the clock and his breathing, nervous, accelerated. She didn't seem to be able to breathe at all.

'I want you, you know that,' he said, stepping towards her.

She couldn't speak either, so she simply nodded.

'I need you.'

She found her hands were trembling as she reached up and touched his face. She watched as his eyes filled with desire and suddenly his mouth was on hers.

—

Seb's heart hammered against his chest. There was so much heat in that kiss, so much pent-up need, passion and desire. Amy was already reaching for his jeans, undoing his button. He had planned to take her upstairs, to do it properly, but he wouldn't make it, he would have her here, on the floor of his pub.

He moved his mouth to her neck, tasting her, devouring her.

'Shit, Seb, stop,' she muttered, trying to push him away.

He didn't think he could.

'What?' he growled, but then he saw the look of guilt and horror on her face and he whirled round to see what she was looking at, but he already knew.

Judith was standing horror-stricken in the doorway.

'Judith…' But there were no words he could find which to explain.

'How could you?' Judith said, her voice choked with grief. 'With her of all people, did Marie mean nothing to you?'

'Judith. I'm sorry,' Amy started.

'Don't talk to me, you disgusting… you whore.'

'Judith!' Seb said. 'Don't talk to her like that.'

'I should go,' Amy said quietly, and he watched her leave, his heart aching for her.

He turned back to Judith, not sure what he could do or say to make this better. If he had taken Amy into the office or upstairs Judith would never have known. Greed was a horrible thing; he hadn't given Judith a single thought as he had kissed Amy, his only thought had been of Amy, of touching her, kissing her, being with her. Shamefully, Marie hadn't entered his thoughts either.

'I left my handbag here.' Judith stalked back to where she had been sitting and snatched it up.

'I'm sorry, I really am.'

'For kissing her or that I found out?'

That she found out obviously; he never wanted to hurt her. But he could never regret that kiss.

'And in case you've forgotten, tomorrow is the fifth anniversary of Marie's death. I didn't want to mention it, thought you'd honour her in your own way. I had no idea you planned to do it by jumping into bed with the town slut.'

Seb opened his mouth to protest but she was already gone.

He sat down in a chair with his head in his hands and Jack nuzzled against him, sensing he was upset. He pulled the dog's ears absently – he hadn't remembered. The date of Marie's death had meant nothing to him. When she first died, he had no idea what date it was. For the six or seven weeks immediately after her death, he had been a mess, life had moved as if in a thick fog, and he had very little recollection of those weeks, even the funeral was a blurry haze. His friends had rallied round and kept the pub running in his absence, while Judith had arranged the funeral, sorted out all the paperwork, cooked and cleaned for him, made him get dressed in the mornings, until slowly he could cope on his own, until the grief became manageable. But if he thought his grief was bad, it was nothing compared to what Judith went through a few weeks after Marie's death. It shocked him to his core to see this woman, who had always been so in control, now a complete wreck. The grief did not subside for months and there was now a role reversal where he did everything for her instead. Judith eventually stopped crying, but he knew she'd never really got over it.

About two years after Marie's death, he had been asked out on a date and had said yes. When he had told Judith about it, she was livid. They'd had a big row and she'd stormed off. That night she'd had a heart attack. Seb, still recorded as her next of kin, had been called out in the early hours of the morning, and to see her looking so vulnerable, so small, made him writhe with guilt. He also felt an enormous amount of responsibility too; he was all she had now and Marie would have wanted him to look after her. He felt so ashamed, as if *he'd* nearly killed her. Judith had insisted it wasn't anything to do with him, that she had been feeling a bit poorly for a few days, but it was a bit too much of a coincidence for him. He swore to himself he would never put her through that again. The girl hadn't been anyone important, she was lovely, but not someone he could see himself spending the rest of his life with. So why fight with Judith over her? Why hurt her over someone who was just a nice girl, no one special?

But if that had been Judith's reaction when he was tentatively going out on a first date, what would her reaction be to him falling in love again? Would it be different now that so much time had passed?

Five years. He shook his head. He deliberately did not want to mark the day of Marie's death. He preferred to honour her, to remember her on happy occasions, the date of their marriage and her birthday. But five years was too long to grieve. Marie was a firm believer that life was for the living, that you only have one life and you should grab it with both hands. If she had been here now, she would have slapped him round the back of the head – as she used to do when he did something to infuriate her – to see that he hadn't moved on in the last five years, that he was honouring a promise he had made to her mum across her death bed. It was high time he moved on, found someone else to love, someone he could take to Judith and say, this is the person I'm going to marry. So why had fate decreed that the one person he wanted would be the one person who Judith hated? He smiled, wryly to himself as he stood up. If Marie was here now, she would have found the whole thing hilarious.

———

'Popcorn,' Libby said, coming in from the kitchen with a large bowl. George lifted the duvet so she could crawl under and, taking her usual place on the opposite side of the sofa to him, she plonked the bowl of popcorn between them. The log fire was roaring nicely, sending golden shadows across the room, *Psycho* was ready to watch on the TV, everything was perfect. He hoped the film would scare her enough that she would need his arms around her for protection. One night they had been watching *The Blair Witch Project* and after about twenty minutes Libby had left her side of the sofa, lifted his arm and curled up into his chest. He'd barely registered what the rest of the film was about, just that there had been a lot of running around the woods and screaming, which had made her press herself tighter against him.

He had tried many different horror films since then, and occasionally he got lucky and found one which scared the crap out of her. Usually the psychologically disturbing ones rather than the gory had the desired effect, which meant she needed his arms around her, but mostly she stayed resolutely and annoyingly on her side of the sofa.

'So, as first dates go, how did ours rate, marks out of ten?' he asked.

'Ten definitely. There was romance, a great meal, the view, great conversation, and even funny moments with Mani's violin playing, plus the incredible ice carvings afterwards. If that was a real first date, you'd definitely get a second.'

He smiled. He wanted a second date with her, and a third and fourth.

'So tell me, is this the sort of thing you'd do with Giselle on your first date – that after your meal you'd come back to your sofa to watch a scary film?'

'I guess this is the sort of thing couples who have known each other for a while would do. Me and Josie used to do this occasionally, but she didn't share the same taste in films as I did. Nor did she like popcorn.'

'How can she not like popcorn?' she asked, incredulous.

'Exactly.'

'So what would your ideal first date be?'

'Well, a drink down the Bubble and Froth, maybe a meal. You can tell a lot about a woman by what she eats – is she only going to be on the rabbit food, or does she like her food as much as I do? Then afterwards a walk along Silver Cove beach. It'd be cold so we'd have to cuddle together, and the wind would be whipping around us but we wouldn't care because we would be with each other.'

'Aw, George, you really are rather romantic, aren't you?'

'Yes, of course. Then it might start to rain and we'd have to run back to the flat, we'd be all rosy-cheeked from the wind and giggling about getting caught in the rain, and we might share a kiss for the first time, a sweet, tender kiss.'

'Aww.'

'Then I'd rip her clothes off and have really dirty sex.'

She laughed loudly. 'How romantic, what a perfect end to the evening.'

'Sounds pretty perfect to me.'

'So a few years down the line, and you and Giselle are still together, would you get married again?'

'Yes, of course. Just because my first marriage didn't work out doesn't mean it won't work out the second time. I've grown as a person now.'

'OK, so you're married. Kids?'

'Yes, definitely, two girls and a boy.'

'Sounds wonderful.' Her smile was wistful.

'Do you not want that – marriage, babies, the happy ever after?'

'Maybe. No. I don't know.'

'You don't want children?'

'Yes I do, lately more than ever, but…'

'That requires trusting the man you're with.'

She nodded.

'What happened to you, Lib, what happened that made you so scared of that?'

She glanced over at the TV and he knew she wasn't going to tell him; she never revealed anything from her past.

She sat up and he thought he had pushed her too far and she was going to leave. He didn't know why he'd felt the need to rock their happy little equilibrium. They had two weeks until she left, he wanted everything to stay wonderful between them until then. There was nothing he could do to make her stay, so why spend their last few weeks together pushing her and knocking the way she lived her life? It was none of his business.

She moved the popcorn from in between them onto the coffee table and, to his great surprise, shifted closer to him, lifting his arm and cuddling into his chest. He didn't do anything, unsure if she just wanted him to stop talking and watch the film.

'My dad died earlier this year and you have no idea how relieved I was. He was a vile man,' Libby said, quietly. He swallowed, tightening his arm around her. She was going to talk and he wasn't sure if he wanted to hear it.

'He was never physically abusive and I suppose I should be grateful for that but he abused my mum in so many other ways. I remember when I was little she was so full of life and joy and over the years I watched it just fade away until it was gone. She wanted to travel and see the world – when he was at work or out at the golf club we would watch all these travel programmes and documentaries together and she would tell me about all the places she wanted to see. We never went anywhere. So many times I heard her trying to persuade Dad to go on holiday to these places but he always refused, he didn't want to fly, didn't want to eat strange food and go to countries where they didn't speak the language, there were many reasons. But I often wondered if the only reason was he didn't want to do anything that would make her happy. He had a horrible temper. He would pick holes in everything she did, she never ironed his shirts well enough, the dinners she cooked were disgusting. He would scream at her until she cried. There was nothing loving about their marriage and that's what scares me. She married him because she loved him. I saw their wedding photos and they were happy and very much in love. How does that love turn to so much hate and disrespect?'

'I guess people just grow apart. Me and Josie got together so young, I guess as we grew up we both wanted different things. Maybe it was the same for your mum and dad.'

'Growing apart I can understand, but I could never hate the person I had loved so much. My dad constantly put her down, insulted her and then those comments passed to me. He told me I was worthless and that no one would ever love me. There's only so many times you can hear that before you start to believe it.'

'What? You think you're worthless?'

'No, I don't think that, not any more. I've proven I have worth. The stories I write bring happiness to thousands of people, the money isn't bad either. But I don't think I'll ever find someone who loves me.'

'You don't stay still long enough for that, and I bet you'd be surprised at how many hearts you've broken when you pack up and walk away.'

She laughed. 'I don't think there are any broken hearts left littering the road I've walked.'

'Trust me on this, you're incredibly loveable.'

She smiled up at him and he wanted to tell her how much he loved her but the fear of rejection was too much. If he told her how he felt and she still walked away at the end of the year it would break his heart just months after it had barely healed.

'So you keep moving on because you're scared of letting yourself fall in love only to have that love be betrayed?'

'No. Well, maybe that's part of it. My mom got sick. Cancer. They caught it too late and by the time they realised she was given months left to live.'

'Christ, Lib, I'm so sorry.'

She looked up at him with tears in her eyes. 'She was my best friend and there isn't a day that doesn't go by that I don't miss her. But I was so angry at her when she died. Still am, I suppose. A few weeks before she died she told me she had some money put aside for me in a locker in the train station near where she worked. She said it was for me to escape so I would never have to live the life she led. She told me she wanted me to see the world, to seize every opportunity that came my way. After she died, Dad immediately passed all her duties to me, shouting at me to clean and cook for him. It was happening all over again. I wasn't allowed out, I wasn't allowed to see my friends. I took the locker key my mum had left me and retrieved a bag full of cash. I took it home and counted it and there was over fifty thousand pounds. She said it was all her tip money. I guess over the years it all added up. The next day I took the bag and walked away. There was no way I was going to stay and live that life. I changed my name, flew abroad and haven't stopped running ever since. I was so scared that he would track me down and find me, so I kept moving on, but he never did. Though I don't know whether that's because he just didn't bother to look or he was unable to find me. The money meant I didn't have to worry about food or rent for the next two years and by that time I had already written three books and got them published. I was so angry at my mum, though. She should have left him, lived the life she wanted to live. Life is precious and so short and she should have seized it and visited all those places that she wanted to see. She had the money to do it and instead she wasted her life with a man who hated her. All her hopes and dreams, and she never did anything to fulfil them.'

'It's hard to walk away, Lib. You shouldn't judge her too harshly.'

'You walked away from Josie.'

'It took me four years to find that courage. Probably more. Four years where I pathetically hoped things would get better, where I tried to pretend it was just a bad patch and we would get through it. We had so many good memories and it was hard to believe that we'd never get that back. Things got worse and I still didn't leave. I loved her and it took a long time for me to fall out of love with her. Maybe it took a long time for your mum to realise there was no love left in the marriage. Sometimes you can convince yourself that one person's love for the other is enough for both of you. It sounds to me that she was planning to leave – she saved fifty thousand pounds in cash. That sounds like an escape fund to me, not just for you, but for her too. Maybe cancer caught up with her before she could escape so she gave the money to you instead.'

She stared at him. 'Is that what you think?'

He nodded. 'For her to create an escape fund for you shows that she knew there was a serious problem. But she couldn't just leave, she had to have somewhere to go, money to spend. So she saved up. If that was tip money, that's quite a few years she spent plotting her escape. It's heartbreaking that she never got the chance to live her life and see the world. I think it's wonderful that you've taken on her dreams of travelling – she would have been so proud to see what you have achieved and the places you've seen – but I don't think for one minute that she ever meant for you to spend your whole life running, seeing the world at the expense of making real friendships and falling in love. Your dad is dead, there's no one going to come banging on your door. But by constantly running and moving on, you're letting him win and you don't want to give him that. Maybe it's time you stayed in one place for a while.'

Libby was silent for a long while and he wondered whether she was even thinking about what he'd said, or just thinking of another excuse.

'But what about my work? My publishers are expecting a story set in New York next.'

'Then you go there on holiday. I'll come with you.'

'You would?'

'In a heartbeat. Seeing the world must be an incredible experience but surely seeing it with someone, having someone to share those memories with, would be infinitely better.'

She looked back at the TV. 'I don't know, George. I've never stayed anywhere longer than six months. What if I get bored?'

'What if you don't? You love it here. I think that's why you are struggling to finish your story because you know finishing it will mean you have to leave. What if you don't finish it? What if you stay here and create your own story? One that involves movie nights with your best friend and quiz nights down the pub. A story that includes a stupid scarecrow festival in the spring, the summer fete with one of the few places left in the world that still does maypole dancing and scuba diving in one of the most beautiful places in the world to dive. People love you here. Amy and Kat would be very sad to see you leave.'

She looked back up at him. 'And what about you?'

'I'd be heartbroken.'

She stared at him for a second and then burst out laughing. 'Put the movie on, George.'

'Is that a yes?'

'It's a maybe.'

He felt the smile spread across his face. He'd take a maybe.

'So.' He broke the tension, and then put on his most sinister voice. 'You ready to be scared?'

She nodded and picked up the bowl of popcorn and plonked it on his lap. She didn't move from his arms as she took a big handful of popcorn. He pressed play on the movie and the room was lit by the flickering of the old black and white film. As the haunting music drifted out from the speakers, she cuddled closer against him.

He would just have to do everything in his power to turn that maybe into a yes.

CHAPTER 6

Libby woke the next day to snow falling in light flurries outside her window and smiled hugely. She had never really appreciated the snow before, but George's love of all things Christmassy was obviously having an effect on her. So many Christmases had been spent moving on from one place to the next or sitting alone in the only restaurant or pub that insisted on staying open. This year she would spend it with her best friend. For the first time in a long time she was really looking forward to Christmas.

Could she really stay in one place? Put down roots, get married, have a baby? OK, she was getting ahead of herself. She just had to work out if she could stay first, the other stuff could come later.

It was still early, and she guessed that Rosie and Alex hadn't started yet. Though Tuesdays, she gathered, Alex worked from home, so it tended to kick off a bit later than other days. She smiled to herself. It came to something when you set your clock by the sexual antics of the couple upstairs.

She got up, got undressed and then pulled on her robe to walk from the bedroom to the bathroom, just in case George was in her flat. He wasn't. She pulled back the shower curtain. But standing in the shower was a large old woman with a knife. The woman lunged forward to stab her.

She screamed hysterically. Staggering backwards away from this maniac, she tripped over the bath mat and went flying into the wall, cracking her head painfully on the bathroom cabinet. Everything went black.

—

Judith was busy sweeping her drive when Verity Donaldson, the newest member of their book club, came round. Verity and her husband Bill had moved opposite her a few months before, after living their entire life on the beach of Silver Cove, and although Judith didn't really have many friends it seemed that Verity wasn't to be put off.

'I bought some new books round for you,' Verity said, indicating the shopping bag.

'For the book club?'

'No, for you.' She rooted round in her bag. 'I'm not quite sure what you like, though I know it's not the rubbish that we read at the book club, so I bought you a selection. Michael McIntyre's autobiography is very funny, *The Girl with the Dragon Tattoo* is brilliant, the latest book from Jill Mansell, one from my new favourite author Aven Ellis, she's fantastic. Ooh, have you read these? I know they're meant to be for teenage girls but I just love them.' Verity pulled out the first two books in the *Twilight* series and Judith smiled; she suddenly liked Verity a whole lot more.

'I'm reading *Eclipse* at the moment. I've just got to the bit where the vampires and the wolves are training for the big fight.'

Verity smiled. 'I knew I'd spotted a kindred spirit. Why don't you put the kettle on and we can talk about it?' She took her arm and started guiding her towards the house. 'Are you Team Edward or Team Jacob?'

'Oh, Edward, obviously.'

'Yeah, I thought that until I saw the films, but that Taylor Lautner who plays Jacob is a very fine specimen…'

Suddenly Judith stiffened as a blue car pulled up outside next door. How embarrassing that Verity would be here to see this.

Jackson Cartwright got out, flashed them both a smile and knocked on Amy's door. Every week, without fail, he would turn up at the same time like clockwork. Amy would greet him at the door, wearing nothing but a dressing gown and a saucy smile. He'd go in and shortly after she would be seen closing her bedroom curtains. An hour later, he'd re-emerge, with a huge grin on his face. She had seen money exchange hands on numerous occasions. Slut. The worst thing was Jackson Cartwright was a respected member of the community, a teacher at the local senior school, and here he was on his one day off, clearly paying for sex.

Amy opened the door and Jackson slipped past her into the house.

'Hello, my lovely,' Verity called, waving at Amy as if she were her new best friend.

'Hello, Verity, thanks again for dinner the other night, it was lovely to see you.'

'You're welcome, any time.'

Judith watched the exchange with some annoyance. Verity obviously didn't know how vile Amy was, otherwise she wouldn't be inviting her round for dinner.

'I better go, Jackson's waiting, and as he's paying by the hour, I better get upstairs and earn my money.'

Judith flushed with embarrassment as Amy closed the door.

'Lovely girl, that Amy. Shall we go inside and get that kettle on?' Verity said, moving back towards Judith's house.

Judith shook her head at Verity as she walked past; she was very naïve if she hadn't realised that Amy was a prostitute.

—

'Shit, Libby, open your eyes, please open your eyes,' George begged, kneeling by her side and shaking her gently.

There was blood, quite a lot of it, and no amount of begging or shaking her was bringing her round. He eyed the blood-stained knife discarded on the floor.

He stroked her face, softly. 'I love you Lib, you have to wake up, you just have to, please.'

But there was no response.

—

'How is your George?' Judith asked, putting the kettle on.

'Oh fine, still madly in love with his best friend...'

'Amy?' she asked. Surely not.

'No, Libby, but he seems happy enough.' Verity opened the biscuit tin and helped herself to a Bourbon. Judith liked that she felt comfortable enough with her to do that. 'I don't know, Judith, you want the best for your children, don't you? And George hasn't been with anyone since his divorce from Josie. He's a lovely man, he deserves someone to love him, but Josie hurt him so badly I just don't think he will risk his heart again.'

Judith handed Verity a mug of tea.

'But you must worry about Seb in the same way? I know he loved Marie, but it's high time he found someone else, isn't it? It must be nearly five years now – that's way too long to grieve over someone, don't you think?'

Verity's eyes were kind, but they were watching her carefully.

'Five years exactly,' Judith said, quietly. 'Five years today.'

'Oh I'm sorry, dear, you must think I'm so callous, don't pay any attention to me and my ramblings.'

Judith turned away to put the milk back in the fridge. 'You're right though, I do want him to be happy again. Marie would have wanted him to find someone, she would have hated that he stayed on his own for all this time. And I feel obligated to him, to look out for him until someone else comes and takes the reins, when actually all I really want to do is go around the world, see the sights before it gets too late for me.'

'Life is too short and too precious to live it for someone else; you have to live it for yourself.'

Judith turned back, clasping her mug protectively to her chest. 'I know…but I…I guess I want someone for Seb that Marie would have approved of.'

'We can't live our children's lives for them. I know Seb isn't your son, but he's as good as. If I could live George's life for him, I would march straight round to Libby's flat and shake her by the shoulders until she saw what was right under her nose: that she and George were made for each other, that if she were to give him a chance, he would make her the happiest girl alive. But I can't do that. If he's too scared to tell her his feelings, I have to let him live his own life, make his own decisions, and trust that those decisions will ultimately bring him happiness. It's the same with Seb. Who you think will bring him happiness and who he thinks will make him happy will probably be two very different people and in the end you have to let him choose for himself.' Verity dipped a biscuit into her tea and chewed it, obviously thinking how to phrase what she wanted to say next. 'Love comes in many different shapes and sizes, and more often than not it comes in the shape we least expected. Libby, I think, would be perfect for George, but if he came to me tomorrow with a six-foot punk rocker called Bert who had a pierced face and green shaved hair and said this was the man he wanted to spend the rest of his life with, I would be delighted that he was finally happy again.'

Judith smirked at the thought of George hand in hand with a shaved, leather-clad punk rocker and knew Verity was right. She couldn't choose for Seb. She had tried to choose for Marie and, against Judith's better judgement, Marie had chosen Seb who had made her deliriously happy.

'I don't know if he will ever love again though, Verity. Like you say, it's been five years; he should have found love by now.'

Verity helped herself to another biscuit. 'I think…that he hasn't found love because he's too worried that it will upset you.'

Judith felt her mouth fall open. Had she really been holding Seb back all this time? She wanted him to be happy and had he been protecting her? But he couldn't possibly find happiness with Amy, any fool could see that that was a recipe for disaster. He didn't love Amy. She meant nothing to him surely. The night before had just been a kiss, nothing more than that. For all of Verity's liberal attitude to George marrying some bloke called Bert, Judith couldn't be that relaxed. In fact, Judith would prefer it if Seb did turn round and say he was marrying Bert; anyone would be better than Amy.

—

Libby was aware of pain before she could open her eyes, aware of her face lying against the cool bathroom tiles. She forced her eyes open, the bathroom was a blur but there was no one there. She tried to get up, forcing her hands under her and pushing herself off the floor, but her arms were shaky and she couldn't get enough leverage. She groaned as she fell back to the floor.

Suddenly she heard footsteps running from the lounge towards the bathroom, and the blurred figure of the old lady in a purple dress came towards her. Panic rose up in her again and she desperately and unsuccessfully tried to scrabble up. She reached out blindly to find something to defend herself with and grabbed the first thing that came to hand, the toilet brush, swinging it round in the direction of the old lady. It made contact with her face, and to her surprise, as she hit her, the old lady's hair suddenly fell off.

'Ewww, Libby, that's disgusting, that's been around your loo and now you're smacking me round the face with it...' said George's voice and she stopped trying to defend herself in confusion.

'George?' she groaned.

The old lady crouched down and Libby put a hand out to stop her getting closer, but as she stared at her, trying to clear her head of the grogginess, George's face came into focus, his eyes filled with concern.

'Are you OK, Lib?'

Libby's eyes closed again against her will. The pain was immense. She forced them back open again and nodded, trying to raise herself into a sitting position. George helped her sit up straight.

'What happened?' she muttered.

She saw a flush seep over his features. 'I'm sorry, honey, it was meant to be a joke, I thought it would make you laugh. I'm so sorry.'

She looked at him in confusion and then, taking in the dress he was wearing, the grey curly wig on the floor lying next to what was clearly a rubber blood-stained knife, she realised what he'd done. The shower scene in *Psycho* had never before been so real.

'Oh, you idiot,' she laughed but doing so made her brain bounce inside her head. She groaned.

'I'm so sorry,' he repeated. 'Stay there, I'll get you some ice.'

He raced out the bathroom and she could hear him rooting around in her freezer and then he was back, gently pressing a bag of peas to her head.

'You scared the crap out of me,' she muttered, watching him care for her.

'You know what, Lib, whatever fear you felt, times that by a hundred and you might get somewhere in the region of what I felt when you knocked yourself unconscious. I honestly thought I might have killed you. I was just about to call an ambulance.'

'You don't want to do that, you want to dump my body in the sea, before anyone found out that you killed me.'

'Good point, though I'd have to cut off your fingers and take out your teeth so you couldn't be identified by fingerprints or dental records.'

'And probably pour honey or something over me so the fish eat all my flesh.'

'Nice.'

'I need to get up.'

He put the peas down and, with his hands round her waist, pulled her gently to her feet. Her head spun, the blood rushing to her brain making her feel suddenly very drunk, and she leaned heavily against the wall as the bathroom swam around her.

—

George watched the colour drain out of her; as he helped Libby to her feet, she went a very sickly shade of grey.

'I think I need to lie down.'

'I don't think that's a good idea.'

'I do.' She took a step forward and staggered, losing her balance, but he caught her. She leaned against him and he wrapped his arms protectively around her.

'I think you might need stitches, Lib, the cut is pretty deep.'

'Urgh, I'm sure it's fine.'

'We really should get you to a hospital, you might have loosened some brain cells when you fell, they can push them back in, if need be.'

'George, the nearest hospital is nearly an hour away. I'm sure I'll be OK after I've slept.'

'You're not supposed to go to sleep after a bang to the head.'

'It's OK,' she mumbled.

'OK, how about I call a doctor, and ask their advice?'

'Hmmm.'

'I'll take that as a yes.'

He guided her out the bathroom and into the lounge, where she flopped uselessly onto the sofa. He found the phone book and quickly dialled the number for the local surgery.

'Yes hello, my friend banged her head and knocked herself out and I'm wondering if I should take her to the hospital? Yes… Right… Just a few minutes… she's a bit dizzy… I'm not sure, it probably isn't that deep… Right… OK… Thanks.' He put the phone down. 'Yeah, they said I should bring you in just in case.'

She giggled, holding her hands out like she had been hand-cuffed. 'Bring me in.'

He pulled her to her feet. 'Come on, Miss Joseph, get some shoes on.'

She giggled again. 'I can't go like this; I'm naked under this robe.'

He had noticed. As soon as she'd knocked herself out, she had slumped unconscious on the floor, and the robe had fallen open in the most indiscreet manner.

'Well, go and put some clothes on.'

She nodded thoughtfully and started to walk towards her bedroom. She wobbled a bit, her legs not performing as she wanted them to. He caught her arm.

'You might need to help me.'

He nodded.

'But no peeking.'

'Right, so I have to help you get dressed with my eyes closed?'

'Exactly,' she giggled.

Honestly, with her giggling like this, it was like she was drunk. Maybe she really had dislodged some of her brain cells.

They went into the bedroom and she sat down on the bed.

'Underwear first,' she said, dispensing with her robe.

His eyes bulged as he tried to look everywhere but at the beautiful, naked woman before him.

'Right, where shall I look?'

'Top drawer.'

He went to the top drawer. It was filled with all manner of tiny, delicate things. He grabbed the first one that came to hand, a lacy black pair of knickers with tiny red roses and took them over to her.

She giggled when she saw them. 'Not those, George, they're my sex knickers.'

He laughed. 'You have sex knickers?'

She nodded.

'I thought the whole idea of sex was that you didn't wear knickers.'

'Those are the knickers I wear when I'm going to have sex; the unwrapping is part of the process, as well you know. I have a matching bra in there too.'

There was so much he didn't know about relationships. In his limited experience of sex, it normally involved getting the underwear off as quick as possible.

'If I wear those, the doctors will think I'm a prostitute.'

'Why is the doctor looking at your underwear when you've banged your head?'

She clearly thought about this for a moment. 'Good point.' She took the knickers and stood up. But it was like watching Bambi on ice, as she wobbled on her legs. He took her arm to steady her, as she precariously lifted one leg into the hole and then the other. She pulled them up and then sat down on the bed again.

He went back to the drawers and pulled out a white bra and passed it to her.

'Oh George,' she sighed in disappointment. 'Do I not even get to go to the hospital in matching underwear? The shame of it.' She put it on anyway, sighing theatrically.

'Right, jeans and a hoodie and then we can be off.' He went to the wardrobe, dug them out and turned back. She was lying across the bed, clearly asleep.

He sighed. 'Libby.' He shook her gently. 'Libby, you really shouldn't go to sleep after banging your head. Libby. Libby.'

She jerked awake. 'What?'

He pulled her back into a sitting position, pulled the hoodie on over her head, struggled to get her arms through the sleeves, as she was now not helping at all. He pulled her jeans on up to her thighs, helped her to her feet and pulled them up the rest of the way. Doing up the flies was quite embarrassing as his hand was so close to her crotch.

He bent and put her feet into a pair of trainers and then, with his arm round her shoulders, he guided her out the flat.

'George,' she whispered theatrically, 'you've seen me naked.'

'Yes Lib, that's twice now.'

She leaned heavily against him as he shut her flat door behind him. They turned around and came face to face with Giselle.

CHAPTER 7

Giselle clearly didn't know where to look first — at the drunken Libby staggering in George's arms or the fact that he was dressed as an old lady.

Deciding ignoring his freakish behaviour was probably the safest tactic, she focussed on Libby instead.

'Oh God, is she drunk?' Giselle said with disgust. 'It's nine o'clock in the morning.'

'No, she banged her head, knocked herself out, I'm taking her to the hospital,' George explained. No need to mention that it was his stupid joke that knocked her out in the first place. Though maybe he should explain that, considering he was standing there dressed as a woman.

'Oh no, is she OK?' Giselle's face changed to one of sympathy.

'I think so, just a bit dizzy. Actually, would you mind holding her for a second, while I grab my car keys?'

'Of course.' She stepped forward and put her hands round Libby's waist. Libby didn't even seem to notice.

He quickly ran into the flat, grabbed his keys, put some shoes on and ran back out. There wasn't really time to change. Besides, if he left Libby with Giselle for long, Libby might say something embarrassing to Giselle about his feelings for her. Or just something embarrassing.

'You're very pretty,' Libby was saying to an embarrassed Giselle, as he came back out 'Very, very beautiful.'

Too late.

'Thanks,' Giselle said awkwardly.

'And George is lovely, isn't he?'

Oh God. He was frozen to the spot, like watching a car crash and being unable to do anything about it.

'Yes,' Giselle said.

'Very, very lovely. And lovely looking too. Lovely eyes, don't you think?'

'Um... yes,' Giselle said, blushing as she caught his eye.

'Lovely bum too,' Libby surmised. 'I'm just saying you're beautiful,' she held out her left hand, 'and he's lovely,' she held out her right hand. 'That's all I'm saying.' She brought both hands together, meshing the fingers and making kissing noises, as if the two hands were kissing each other. 'That's *all* I'm saying.' Libby waggled her eyebrows at Giselle.

George ran forward before it could get any worse. 'Erm, thanks Giselle, I better get her to the hospital. I think she banged her head harder than I thought,' he laughed nervously.

'Yes, that's probably a good idea,' Giselle blushed.

George took Libby in his arms and guided her out the flat.

'And another thing, Giselle,' Libby called. 'George has seen me naked...'

Oh God.

'Twice.'

He quickly ushered her out the flat and round the back to where his car was parked. He managed to get her into the front seat, strapped her in and then took off up the road. Libby was silent, and judging by the soft snoring sounds coming from her side of the car, she had fallen asleep again. He wasn't happy about that, but he couldn't keep her awake and drive at the same time. And as long as he could hear her snoring, that meant that she was OK. He hoped.

How had it gone so spectacularly wrong? He'd wanted to make her laugh after her revelation the night before and he had nearly killed her.

The nearest hospital was a good forty-five minutes from White Cliff Bay, on the other side of Apple Hill. And this time of the morning in the run-up to Christmas, it would be packed with shoppers. The traffic would be horrendous. At least the road between here and Apple Hill would be relatively quiet; he could really put his foot down.

Unfortunately the road towards Apple Hill was a bumpy, twisty one and every bump and lump in the road caused Libby to bang her floppy head against the window. As they careened round a corner, he heard a loud thud as she smacked her face against the glass. This was no good; she would be in an even worse state by the time he got her to the hospital.

He quickly stopped the car, ran round to the boot and pulled out the tow rope, then tied it round her head, and round the back of the headrest of her seat. At least it would stop her head from banging against the window.

He got back in the car and put his foot down on the accelerator again. They were making good time now, the countryside whizzing past in a blur of green. But as he tore up the road, he was suddenly joined by a police car, its blue lights flashing furiously behind him.

'Shit,' he muttered, as he pulled over onto the side of the road.

The policeman got out the car and leaned into his window.

'George,' he nodded, seriously.

'Uncle Bob,' he nodded back, equally as serious. People might think that he would get preferential treatment having his uncle in the police. But no, Uncle Bob took his job very seriously.

Uncle Bob looked him up and down in his purple dress and pearl necklace and, like the elephant in the room, decided not to address his nephew's transgender tendencies.

'Do you have any idea what speed you were travelling at?'

'Erm, probably about sixty miles an hour?' George ventured, though he knew it had been probably more like seventy.

'Do you know what the speed limit is round here?'

'Yes, Uncle Bob, it's forty. But it's an emergency.'

'What kind of emergency would require you to break the law so flagrantly?'

'Uncle Bob, you remember Libby, my friend.' He indicated the tied-up, slumped, pale and bleeding figure next to him. Christ, this looked like something out of one of those action films, a kidnapped girl, a speeding car. Bob's eyes bulged as he noticed her for the first time.

'She banged her head, knocked herself out, so I'm taking her to the hospital.' He decided it was time for some of that drama he was so famous for when he was at school. 'Please Uncle Bob, I'm scared she might die, she's unresponsive and I didn't know what to do,' he cried. This surely had to work, appealing to Uncle Bob's softer side. Uncle Bob always reminded him of the heroic gentlemen in the older movies he loved so much. A cross between Cary Grant and Rock Hudson in looks and his chivalrous attitude. If anyone was going to swoop in and save Libby it would be Uncle Bob.

'Well yes, son, I see, but you should really have called an ambulance.'

Maybe not.

'I know,' George sobbed, 'but I thought that it would take ages to get here and then it would be too late.'

'Well, son, we can't have that now, can we?' Bob straightened his shoulders as if this was the most daring thing he'd done in his life. 'I will give you a police escort to the hospital – we'll save the little lady, don't you worry about that.'

Bob hurried off to the police car and a few seconds later it whizzed past him, with the sirens blaring and blue lights flashing furiously. George quickly followed him. Bob was driving a lot slower than he would have done, but he was certainly grateful for it once they reached Apple Hill. The roads were packed as predicted, but as Uncle Bob forced his way through the traffic the cars parted and George followed closely behind.

When they finally got to the hospital, Bob ran in shouting about a medical emergency and seconds later a couple of nurses came running out with a trolley, obviously expecting some kind of massacre. George blushed with embarrassment at the fuss he had caused as he ran round to the other side of the car, untied Libby and pulled her out of the car.

The nurses helped him to get her on the trolley, though from the loud snores that she was now emitting, it was quite clear that she was asleep rather than unconscious.

Bob looked at her in confusion.

'Erm thanks, Uncle Bob,' George said, awkwardly, shaking his hand and then running after the trolley before Bob could say anything.

—

Amy lay back on the bed, naked apart from a thin sheet draped over her. Her hair was thick and tangled as it hung over her shoulder. The sun drifted through a chink in the curtains, lacing her shoulder with a ribbon of gold. She smiled across at Jackson as he watched her from the other side of the room.

Initially when he had first suggested this, she had been horrified at the thought. But the amount of money he had offered her had been more than she got in a month from her other jobs. She would have been silly to turn it down. It was a one-off, she'd told herself the year before. But Jackson had been coming to her house every Tuesday ever since. They had come to an arrangement now, a weekly fee rather than a lump sum, but the weekly fee was still huge and actually if she only continued with this job, forsaking all others, she could still afford to pay her mortgage and have some left over for her bills.

She had been embarrassed about it at first, but when Jackson had finished, he actually made her feel really beautiful and desirable. No man had ever made her feel what Jackson had achieved. She loved what Jackson did; it actually took her breath away. The first few times she had actually cried tears of joy when he'd finished. No man had ever made her cry before, and she was glad that Jackson had been the first.

But still no one knew. Jackson was very discreet and, though he now relied on her to get him through his week, he swore to her that no one would ever know. Until now.

Jackson was becoming quite famous in his own circles and he wanted to go public before people found out and, though she was a bit nervous about it, she agreed that the time was right.

'I need to go, my darling,' Jackson said, pulling on his jacket.

'So… Saturday, that's when everyone will know?' she said, quietly. Once word got out it would spread like wildfire.

'Yes, four o'clock. You'll be there, won't you, when I reveal it? You can stand at my side and I'll hold your hand.'

She nodded. 'I'll be there.'

———

Libby woke later to find herself in a hospital bed. Her head hurt but she was no longer dizzy and her vision had returned to normal. She had been woken rudely on her arrival at the hospital, but after a CT scan, and a few other observations, which were all a bit hazy, she had been allowed to sleep. She looked round and smiled when she saw George asleep in the chair next to her, holding her hand, and still wearing that awful purple dress.

She carefully sat up and was glad to see the room didn't spin. Her movements woke George up though.

'Hey Lib.' He smiled. 'You OK?'

'Who are you? Why are you holding my hand? Where am I? Who am I?' she stammered.

His face fell. 'Oh God, Lib, do you not remember? I'm George.'

She so wanted to drag this out a bit more, but she couldn't keep a straight face any longer. She snorted with laughter. 'Sorry George, couldn't help myself.'

His face set angrily. 'Oh, I suppose you think that's funny.'

'Yeah, about as funny as you leaping out the shower in a dress with a knife in your hand, it scared the bloody life out of me.'

'Touché.'

She stretched. 'Can I go home now?'

'I think so, the doctors say there's no swelling on the brain, no permanent damage, just a bit of concussion, you didn't even need any stitches. I've got to keep an eye on you tonight though.'

'You're an idiot, you know that, don't you?'

'A loveable idiot though?'

'Yes, I suppose so.'

She swung her legs off the bed and carefully stood up. George held her arm just in case, but the effects seemed to have passed.

'*Eight days before Christmas my true love gave to me, a bump on the head and a fright that was very scary,*' George sang.

Libby laughed. 'Worst present ever.'

She followed him into the main reception, and he signed some papers, the nurses and doctors all bravely ignoring the fact that George was in a dress.

They got in the car and he started driving back towards White Cliff Bay, explaining to her how he nearly got arrested by his own uncle. She laughed. 'I imagine your mum wouldn't be too impressed.'

'She'd kill me… and er… Giselle saw me, in this.' He gestured to the dress.

'Oh.' Wearing a wetsuit, a snorkel and flippers was one thing, but dressing up in women's clothes was a whole different kettle of fish.

'Do you remember talking to her as well?'

She bit her lip, trying to remember.

'"You're very pretty",' he mimicked. '"And George is very lovely, lovely eyes, and a lovely bum, don't you think?"'

She flushed with embarrassment. 'Is that what I said?'

They had reached some traffic lights at this point and George stopped in front of the red lights that he had apparently torn through a few hours before with his police escort.

'Yes, which was nice,' he grinned. 'But then you did this.' He pressed his hands together and moved them against each other, making kissing noises.

'What was that?'

'Me and Giselle, apparently.'

'Oh God, I'm so sorry.'

'It's OK; I think I'd already done enough damage by that point by carrying a half-drunken girl out of your flat whilst wearing a dress. Bet she thinks she's moved into a right mad house.'

'And White Cliff Bay used to be such a respectable place.'

'Yeah, but it's the quiet places like White Cliff Bay that you have to watch out for, who knows what happens behind closed doors. Mrs Kempston from number fifty-six might be a secret drug lord, selling Ecstasy and Speed to the kids.'

Libby laughed. 'She's ninety-three.'

'So? It doesn't mean she's not capable, she's quite a wily little minx.'

'And I suppose Mr and Mrs Gillespie might secretly be making porn films in their back bedroom?'

'Exactly, and that Mr Alexander, he's definitely a KGB agent.'

'And I guess Mrs Baldwin is making weapons of mass destruction in her cellar.'

George laughed as he manoeuvred down the windy lanes back towards the seedy underbelly that was White Cliff Bay.

She leaned back in her seat for a moment, closing her eyes against the glare of the early afternoon sun. On the radio, WCB FM, Nick was introducing the next song and reminding people about the forthcoming cake sale that was happening in aid of the Lifeboat appeal. A front for tobacco smuggling or money laundering if ever she heard one.

'Oh,' she laughed, letting her head fall into her hands as she remembered. 'You saw me naked again, didn't you?'

He grinned, proudly. 'Yes I did.'

'You're such a pervert.'

'You're such an exhibitionist. "Oh George, can you help me get dressed, oh is that my robe that's just fallen to the floor."'

'That's not how it was at all.'

He laughed. 'It so was.'

She grinned, shaking her head.

He parked his car next to Libby's round the back of the flats and they walked back round to the front together.

'I'll get changed and then I'll make us some lunch. I bet you're starving?' he said.

She nodded. 'I am. I do really need a shower too, since I didn't get one this morning.'

'OK, I need to pop down to see Seb at the pub for a second, he wants me to do a radio advert for their new menu so I'll just have a chat with him about what he wants. But just come round whenever you're ready?'

She nodded.

She had a quick shower and got dressed just as George was leaving for the pub. She watched him go and smiled. He really was the loveliest man she had ever met. But as he disappeared up the road, the smile on her face changed and she knew exactly what she was going to do for him.

———

When George got back to his flat, he froze. The curtains had been drawn and lit candles were everywhere. The room was in darkness apart from the flickering glow from the hundred or so tea lights that had been placed over every surface of the room.

As he moved into the lounge, something crunched under his feet. He looked down and saw dried rose petals in a path leading through to the bedroom. His bedroom door was open a crack and more candlelight flickered from the room within.

His mouth went dry. 'Lib?' he called. Maybe she really had dislodged a few brain cells.

There was no answer.

CHAPTER 8

Fluttering on the floor just outside his bedroom was a note. He picked it up and his eyes nearly fell out of his head when he read it.

> I can't deny the attraction between us, I want you
> Big Boy, so come in here and ravish me,
> Giselle x

Surely not. He had seen this sort of thing in the movies – candles, flower petals, the girl waiting in her sexy lingerie to seduce the gorgeous man – but never in his wildest dreams had he ever expected it to happen to him. And with Giselle of all people. Especially when he had made such a startling impression on her.

A part of him was disappointed that it wasn't Libby waiting for him in his bed but he had to remind himself that she was leaving. And even if by some remote chance she stayed, she wouldn't be staying because of him. If she had any feelings for him at all, she wouldn't be encouraging him to go out with Giselle. He liked Giselle too, she was sweet and beautiful. She was perfect for helping him to get over Libby once and for all.

George pushed open the door, wondering what he was going to see. The room was in complete darkness apart from one tiny tea light on the side. But it was enough to see the silhouette of a woman waiting for him in his bed. The blonde hair glistened in the candlelight.

He swallowed. 'Giselle?'

There was no answer. He wasn't prepared for this. A part of him, a huge part of him wanted to run away. What if he wasn't any good? What if… In fact there were a million 'what ifs' running through his head right now that told him this wasn't a good idea.

Well, he thought, she's made the first move; she's made all this effort. I can certainly make the next move. He quickly got undressed, hoping she wouldn't look up from the pillow whilst he was standing there naked, hoping he could get into bed before she saw him. She didn't move. She was just lying there, waiting for him. The beautiful Giselle, waiting for him.

He got into bed by her side. 'Giselle?'

There was still no answer.

His heart was pounding as he reached out for her and stroked her hair. It was a lot coarser than he thought it would be, but these women put so many products into their hair and with all the straightening and crimping many had completely damaged their wonderful locks. Libby's hair was soft, though. He quickly put the thoughts of his best friend out of his head and brought his hand out to touch Giselle's shoulder. To his surprise it was cold. He moved his hand down her arm and realised her arm was hard to the touch, almost like… plastic.

A flash went off in the room and Libby's cackle of laughter came from the wardrobe.

He quickly sat up and flicked on the bedside lamp. Turning back to the woman in his bed, he realised he had been stroking Candy.

Libby fell out the wardrobe, laughing, holding her digital camera. 'Oh God, that worked so much better than I thought it would,' she cried, literally holding her sides from the pain of the suppressed laughter.

'You bitch,' he said, flushing with embarrassment.

'Come on, it's funny, it really is,' she said, wiping the tears from her eyes. 'Look, look at the picture.' She dragged Candy out unceremoniously and dumped her on the floor and leapt onto the bed by his side. 'Look.' She showed him and even he had to laugh at himself lovingly caressing the shoulder of what was clearly a mannequin.

'Oh, this is what the stuff of great blackmail is made of; this photo would be worth millions.'

He shoved her, playfully. 'Bitch.'

She was unperturbed as she continued to laugh. 'I never really expected you to believe the note, but I figured you would suss it as soon as you saw Candy in the bed. But you completely fell for it. Oh, that was brilliant.'

He shook his head.

She suddenly sat up. 'And I got to see you naked. That's revenge for the two times you've seen me.'

'I feel so violated.' He pulled the duvet up to his chest protectively.

She nudged him. 'Hey, you certainly have nothing to be shy about.'

He blushed. How was he sitting in his bed, naked, listening to Libby talk about his penis? Life certainly wasn't dull with her around.

'Go on, get out, leave me to get dressed in peace, or there'll be no lunch for you.'

Libby, still giggling, rolled off the bed and left the room. He could still hear her laughing as he got dressed.

———

Seb watched the last customer disappear through the pub door and glanced across at Amy, sitting in one of the booths and studiously making her glass of wine last an extraordinarily long time. Judith hadn't been in the pub that night. They were alone. There was nothing to stop them now. Oddly the thought terrified him. He had been awash with guilt all day, about Judith and for Marie. But fear had been the predominant feeling. If he let anything more happen between him and Amy, he would fall deeper in love with her and it would hurt even more when he lost her. And he would lose her, he knew that. Fate would take her just like it had taken Marie.

He poured himself a glass of whisky and went and sat opposite her in the booth.

He sipped the warm, amber liquid, letting the burn hit the back of his throat, and felt the glow spread in his stomach. He swirled it around in his glass, staring at it, hoping somehow it would give him the answers. It was a young whisky in comparison to some of the bottles he kept. Only five years old. There was an irony in there, he was sure. Five years ago his life fell apart when his wife died, while up in Scotland they were carrying on with their lives as normal, distilling whisky, ageing them in their wooden casks. Life went on. It carried on regardless even if for some people it just stood still.

Amy reached across the table and took his hand and his eyes snapped up to hers.

'I'm sorry,' he said.

She frowned at him in confusion. 'What for?'

'For kissing you, for not being brave enough to tell Judith I wanted you more than anything. I never meant to hurt you, that's the last thing I want. I can't let anything happen between us, Amy, I'm sorry. It wasn't my intention to lead you on or to tease you. I thought I was ready to move on but I don't think I ever will be.'

'Is this about Judith, about not wanting to hurt her? She doesn't have to know.'

He shook his head. 'For so long I've been telling myself that I never wanted to hurt her, that I couldn't get involved with someone again because of her, but I've just been using her for an excuse. It's the anniversary of Marie's death today. Five years ago today I was standing in hospital holding her hand as she passed away. I went down to her grave today. I haven't been for a while because it just hurts too much. I… I told her all about you, how I think she'd really like you, that you make me smile… and then it all came back, those heartbreaking feelings I felt when she died. I can't go through that again.'

Her face fell. 'Damn it, Seb, so that's it then, one kiss and it's over – we're just going to carry on pretending there isn't this thing between us? It's torture.'

'I'm sorry.' He stood up, leaving the whisky on the table; it was leaving a bad taste in his mouth. He bent to kiss her on the cheek, breathing her in. 'I can't give you what you want.'

He turned away from her and, whistling for Jack, he headed upstairs to bed, wanting more than anything to take her hand and bring her with him.

———

As the end credits of *Titanic* started to roll, George turned off the TV and wiped his eyes.

'George?' Libby said, her voice slightly muffled by the duvet. 'Are you crying?'

'No, I just have something in my eye.'

She sat up to look at him. 'In both eyes?'

'Yes, probably hay fever or something.'

She rolled forward so she was kneeling next to him and, taking his face in her hands, she wiped his tears away.

He laughed. 'It's pathetic, isn't it?'

'No, I think it's sweet that you cry over sad films.'

'But I've seen *Titanic* about twenty times, how can I still cry over it?'

'Because you're an emotional person, it's a good thing.'

They heard the main front door close and footsteps running up the stairs; there was a giggle that was undeniably Giselle, and she said something before she went into her own flat above them. The talking continued, but as it appeared to only be one-sided, George guessed she was on the phone.

'We need to do something to bring Operation Giselle into fruition,' Libby said. 'You haven't made the greatest first impression but I know she'll fall in love with you if she had the time to get to know you properly. Are you going to ask her out?'

He absently fiddled with one of her toes. 'No, I'm not sure if she's the right one for me.' He glanced over at Libby, the woman who was perfect for him in every single way.

'Oh George, you can't let the fear of being rejected and hurt rule your life. I know it's scary but you have to find that courage to start again.'

He sighed quietly. If only she knew.

'I just want to get it all sorted in my head, to know everything that I'm going to do and say before I do it. I want to get this right. So I know what I'm going to wear, what I'm going to say and where I'm taking her on our first date and, assuming that went well, we'd now be on to our second.'

'The first date that ended with you having really dirty sex?'

'Yes, now of course that *will* go well, she'll be impressed with my prowess between the sheets so of course she'd want to see me again.'

'Of course,' she said, smiling.

'In all seriousness, the second date is where I have to impress her. If she thinks I'm quite nice on the first date, she might be prepared to give us a second chance. If I'm only quite nice by the end of the second date, there won't be a third.'

'You're right; I've had many dates like that. Things went well on the first, there was a lot of laughter and we'd talked constantly. But that meant that by the second date there was nothing left to say. I had one torturous second date with a very, very sweet guy talking about the weather.'

'Exactly.'

'OK, so what do you have in mind?'

He opened his mouth to speak but then changed his mind, then opened it again. 'To be honest, Lib, I have no idea. I don't really do dating, you know that. Sinead was the last woman I dated, if you could call it that – three dates over seven weeks. The second date was so disastrously boring that I was very surprised that she called for a third. In fact, I didn't even want to go to the third date because I knew I'd be bored out of my mind, and I was, it was like wading through treacle. Which was why I was very surprised at the end of the night, when she stuck her tongue down my ear and dragged me back to my flat to have sex.'

'Yeah, sorry I spoilt that for you.'

'Ah that's OK, Lib, it was never going to last anyway. So I have no idea what constitutes a great second date.'

She thought for a moment. 'Well, it depends. If the first date went really well, then a repeat performance isn't always a bad thing – a meal out or just a drink down the Bubble. I think if I found someone special, I could do the same sort of thing with them every day, long walks on Silver Cove beach, drinks down the pub, sitting by the fire in the winter, righting the world's wrongs over a glass or two of wine.'

George swallowed down the lump in his throat as she had just described their relationship perfectly without even realising it. The fire crackled in the fireplace, punctuating her point.

'Dating doesn't need to be a big song and dance; it's just about spending time with the one you love,' Libby went on.

'Libby, you are so sweet, but even in my limited experience of women, I know that to be bollocks. Women like to be wooed, spoiled, lavished with jewels and pearls and only then will they possibly consider you for a serious relationship. All that stuff that you described comes much later.'

'OK, OK, you're probably right. Then your second date needs to be something different, something a little exciting. A man once took me paintballing. All that running round the woods, rolling round the ground, hunting down the enemy, running from the enemy, it was exhilarating. I was so pumped with adrenaline by the time we got home; we had the most amazing sex.'

'Right, so paintballing it is then, problem solved.'

She laughed. 'Most girls don't go for that sort of thing – you get covered in mud and it's bloody painful, and the welts on your body last for weeks. But you need to do something like that, something fun and different.'

He nodded thoughtfully. 'OK, let me practise on you again.' A second date with Libby would kill two birds with one stone. He would get in practice for if and when he did finally pluck up the courage to ask Giselle out, but most importantly he would get to spend romantic moments with Libby and that couldn't be a bad thing. Pretend dates meant they could both dabble in having a relationship to see what it would be like without spoiling their beautiful friendship. Anything that might blur the line between friendship and love was definitely a good thing in his eyes. But it was safe; there was a way back: if things got too close it could just be laughed off, put down to research.

'OK,' she said.

'We've already been out on a first date and it went well.'

'Yes it did. Now, just so I can get into role, did our date end with or without the dirty sex?'

'Erm… for the sake of realism, I suppose without,' he mumbled, regretfully.

'OK.'

'Let me take you out on a second date, tomorrow. I'll pick you up and take you somewhere fun and then at the end of the date you can tell me how it went. Mark me out of ten, so to speak.'

'Sounds good … ooh, what shall I wear?'

'I can't tell you that, it'd ruin the surprise.'

'Love, surprises are good, but the girl needs to be slightly prepared. She doesn't need to turn up wearing her favourite summer dress and high heels to find out she's hiking twenty-five miles over the Pennines.'

'Right, OK, well, just something really warm and bring a waterproof coat.'

'You have a plan, don't you?'

'Yes I do.'

'Right, I'm going to bed. Night George.'

'Hang on, you have to sleep with me tonight,' he said, wiggling his eyebrows in what he hoped was a saucy way.

'What?' she looked confused.

'Doctor's orders.'

'The doctor ordered that I have sex with you? I didn't know that was a prerequisite for a bang on the head, to be banged elsewhere as well.'

'The doctor's actual words were that I should keep an eye on you tonight, just in case you fell into a coma or something careless like that. I can't keep an eye on you if you're over there and I'm over here. Besides, you might go wandering again, you might stagger vacantly onto the beach in a confused concussed state. You'd trip, smash your head on the rocks and then the tide would come in and take your body out to sea. You'd wash up in Skegness in a few days' time, dead and mutilated by the fishes, and they'd only be able to identify you through your dental records.'

'Oh no.'

'Exactly.'

'Skegness? Really?' she said, disdainfully.

'Yes.'

'You paint quite a picture. So what you're saying is that if I don't sleep with you tonight, I'll be dead by the morning, and fish food by the afternoon?'

'Yes, case in point I think.'

'OK, if it's doctor's orders, I guess I have to,' she shrugged. 'Though I'm still not sure that having sex with you will help, but if it's doctor's orders…'

She started walking towards the bedroom, pulling off her hoodie and throwing it over the chair, so she was only in her pyjamas. She flashed him a sexy look before she disappeared into the bedroom.

He stared after her in shock for a second. He had expected her to laugh at his proposal and go back to her own flat. And he hadn't actually meant that they should have sex, he'd just meant to insinuate it by suggesting that she sleep in his bed. Was Libby now lying in his bed, naked? He quickly stood up and followed her in. She was lying with the duvet pulled up to her chin. He had no idea if she was still wearing her pyjamas. Luckily he didn't have to undress in front of her as he was already wearing his Christmas tree pyjama bottoms and a t-shirt with a huge snowman on it. He switched off the light and slipped into the bed by her side. In the light of the moon he could see her watching him and, as soon as he got himself settled and comfortable, she slid across to his side of the bed, cuddling up to him with her head on his chest. He wrapped his arms around her, swallowing nervously.

'I've never had this with a man, not really. I never had a man who I wanted to spend all my time with. Dating is nice but it seems like a big front and, once you're used to the person or slept with them, then no one makes any effort any more, so I don't really miss that. But this. I like this. Did you and Josie used to cuddle?'

'We never cuddled, ever.'

'Oh, do you not like cuddling?' She started to pull away but George held his arms tight around her.

'She didn't, I do. You ever want to cuddle in bed, you can come over here any time.'

She snuggled into his side again. 'And if Giselle is here?'

'Well, there's probably room in the bed for the three of us.'

Libby laughed. 'We could make a George sandwich.'

'Yes, I like the sound of that, a rose between two thorns.'

Libby laughed even louder and then she leaned up and kissed him on the cheek. 'Good night, George.'

He watched her close her eyes and within minutes she was fast asleep. Though it took significantly longer for him to go to sleep. It had been a long time since he'd had a woman in his bed. And it wasn't just any woman, his best friend, the most beautiful woman in the world. Every time he dozed off, he kept waking himself back up to check he wasn't imagining it. She lay there all night, with her head on his chest, arms wrapped round him, their legs entwined, her breath warm on his neck. It didn't matter that they weren't making love, this was infinitely better. It was quite simply the most beautiful moment of his life and he never wanted to let her go.

CHAPTER 9

Libby woke the next morning and smiled to find that she had spent the whole night wrapped in the arms of her best friend. She also found she had a burning desire to write. She carefully extracted herself from George's arms without waking him and left a note on the pillow that said Last night was amazing, thank you Big Boy *x* before heading back over to her flat.

Unfortunately as she opened the door to George's flat and walked out she came face to face with Giselle who was heading out the main front door. She faltered for a moment as she saw Libby, clocking her pyjamas and her hair everywhere, and pennies quite clearly dropped into the wrong place. Giselle quickly regained her smile and hurried out the flat, leaving Libby with her mouth flapping as she desperately tried to think of a reason why she could be leaving George's flat in her pyjamas so early in the morning. The door closed behind Giselle and Libby sighed. George's chance with her was getting slimmer by the day.

She couldn't let it distract her though, she was inspired to write for the first time in months and she had to get it down before she forgot it completely.

———

Libby was writing furiously, the words coming easier than they had for a long time, when she was disturbed by the buzzer being pressed insistently. She glanced at the bottom of her screen and realised she had written over two thousand words since she had left George earlier that morning. As the buzzer didn't seem to show any sign of stopping any time soon, she rushed to the intercom, pressed the entry button without checking and flung open the door.

A big bunch of flowers were suddenly shoved into her face. Yellow roses. They smelt amazing.

'Delivery for Miss Joseph,' came a muffled voice.

She took them in confusion. 'Thanks.'

The delivery man, who clearly didn't get a lot of satisfaction from his job, mumbled something to himself, and left.

She took the flowers to the dining room table and admired them. They were beautiful. But who was sending her flowers? She took the envelope from the depths of the bouquet, and opened it.

To My Lovely Libby, I'm very much looking forward to our second date tonight, yours George x. PTO

She flipped it over and read the message on the back.

Seven days before Christmas my true love gave to me...

She smiled, grabbed one of the roses and ran across the hall, letting herself into his flat. George was in the shower; she hovered for a second, then clamped a hand over her eyes, and pushed open the bathroom door.

'Jesus, Libby,' came George's angry voice as what sounded like a bottle of shower gel clattered to the floor.

'I can't see anything.'

The shower was suddenly turned off and the cubicle door was opened. There was something very tantalising about having him naked and wet and so close. She stifled a giggle, as she heard him get out in front of her and wrap a towel round himself.

'I just wanted to say thank you for the flowers, they're beautiful.' She risked a peep through her fingers, and thankfully he was now decent. She took her hand away and tried to gauge whether he was really angry. She brandished the flower as a peace offering and he took it begrudgingly.

'The normal response is to text your thanks,' he said, grumpily.

'I'll text you when I get back.' She checked her watch. 'I better get back actually. I did say I would pop up and see Kat later, what with Dave being out on the farm all day.'

'Good luck. She's one mad, scary pregnant lady.'

'George! She's not mad, she's just fed up. I hope you'll be more understanding when you have your own kids.'

'Sorry, you know I love Kat, but you've got to admit, she has gone a bit... unhinged.'

Libby didn't say anything, knowing it would be disloyal to Kat to do so, but she did think that poor Dave was having a bit of a rough time.

'Polly and Linda are holding a cake sale at lunchtime, all the money they make this afternoon is going straight to the Lifeboat appeal. If I get back in time I said I'd go,' Libby said.

'Mmmm, I do like Polly's cakes; I'll probably pop along myself.'

'You like Polly, you mean,' she said, feeling a sudden unexpected surge of jealousy.

'What's not to like? A beautiful woman who can bake, she's like my dream wife.'

George must have seen the frown on her face, because he caught her hand. 'But I bet her bacon sandwiches aren't anywhere near as amazing as yours. I hear rumours that there are white chocolate and raspberry muffins.'

'I hear...' Libby looked around to make sure no one could hear them, 'that there's rum and raisin fudge.'

'Well, that's definitely my treat then.'

'I'm a very cheap date, George, one bag of rum and raisin fudge and I'm anybody's.'

'And what if I buy you every scrap of fudge in the shop?'

'Mmmm, I wouldn't let you out of the bedroom for a week.'

'Jesus Lib, what are we still doing here, there's fudge to be bought.'

She laughed. 'Well, I'll see you this afternoon for our date – if I don't see you drooling all over Polly at the cake sale later?'

She left, suddenly vowing that she would learn to cook.

———

Wednesdays were Amy's day off, in the sense it was the only day she didn't work; well, not for money. She volunteered for the local charity Cancer Awareness. Her boss, Mia, was one of the most colourful people she knew and she loved her dearly. Mia had lost her own husband to cancer years before, and had since set up the charity to bring more awareness to people. Every Wednesday Amy would be doing something different, sometimes face painting in White Cliff Bay or selling cakes to raise money for cancer research, sometimes it would be liaising with the local surgery and taking a tour bus to nearby towns and villages offering free health checks and sometimes… her day was… a little bit odd.

She surveyed herself in the mirror, laughing at the costume that Mia had brought round the day before. If she thought dressing up as a blackberry was bad, this was a million times worse.

Today she was a penis. A seven-foot-tall penis complete with two large round hairy testicles that her feet had slotted into. Mia wanted her to promote awareness of testicular cancer. Amy's job was to go up and hug as many men as she could and once they had calmed down from being attacked by a seven-foot penis, she was then to hand out a leaflet about testicular cancer and the importance of regular checks.

Mia certainly had a good imagination.

Amy had a short while before the taxi came, so she walked backwards and forwards across the lounge trying to get used to moving with the costume. The head of the penis kept dragging on the ceiling, rather painfully she imagined.

As she neared the back window, her heart dropped. The wind was up today and her little rotary line had been blown over. Her knickers that she had washed and hung out earlier were nowhere to be seen.

Opening the French windows, she stepped outside, wondering where they were. Then she saw a spotted pair, fluttering like a flag on one of the bushes that divided her garden and Judith's. Shuffling closer, she saw to her horror that every single pair of her knickers – stripy ones, lacy ones, flowery ones – were now dotted over Judith's garden like rare tropical butterflies.

What was the protocol in a case like this? Could she go round, knock on her door and politely ask for her knickers back like a kid asking for her ball? But what if Judith refused and spitefully kept all her knickers? Those were some of her best ones out there in the garden. Would it be best to forget them and buy a whole new drawer full? But that would still mean Judith finding them, and knowing her, she would probably think that Amy had done it deliberately. Realising that the only course of action was to retrieve them before Judith noticed, she shuffled closer to the small dividing wall at the top of her garden. The penis costume had taken ages to get into and she didn't have time to get out of it and back into it before the taxi came.

She eyed the low wall and, praying that Judith wasn't near her window, she took a deep breath and rolled herself over the top.

—

Judith was sitting in her lounge, bored. The book club she had started many years before had seemed a good idea at the time. But the ladies who frequented it were as dull as ditch water. They talked about their plants, their grandchildren, the latest cake recipes, none of which interested her. And the books they read, she hated every single one of them. Over the last four years, they had read and deliberated over *Pride and Prejudice*, *Jane Eyre*, *Wuthering Heights*, *Great Expectations*, *Oliver Twist*, *Moby Dick*, *Middlemarch*, *War and Peace* and even some of the works of Shakespeare. She had rented *Much Ado About Nothing* on DVD, rather than reading it, just so she could have something to talk about. She'd actually really enjoyed it, though that might have something to do with the rather lovely Denzel Washington, rather than the quality of the book. Upstairs, by her bed, waiting to be read, was *Eclipse*, the third instalment in the *Twilight Saga*, the latest story by Eve Loveheart and a romance thriller by her favourite author Nora Roberts. None of which she would admit to in front of these well-to-do ladies.

What Judith wanted more than anything was to go on a world cruise, where she could curl up on a sun lounger with all manner of trashy books en-route to locations she had only dreamed of. If only Marie hadn't made her promise to look after Seb after she had gone, she would have left White Cliff Bay years ago. Her lifestyle bored her, White Cliff Bay and its elderly residents bored her. Nothing exciting happened; it was the same day in and day out.

She looked out on her garden as Brenda, the chairwoman of the Woman's Institute, waxed lyrical about *The Christmas Carol* that they were reading. Brenda was talking about the character of Scrooge and how he hadn't changed his ways because this was the right path but because he was scared of what the future held.

Suddenly a penis rolled over the wall of the garden and started shuffling around her hedges.

Had she gone mad? She had just been reading Eve Loveheart's book that morning, the sex scene was quite detailed; with Chad's very large manhood, was Judith now manifesting her very own large penis?

But as the book club grew deathly quiet, and they all turned round to look at the seven-foot penis as it strode purposefully round her rockery, she knew she wasn't hallucinating after all.

Verity Donaldson, next to her, burst out laughing. 'Well now, that's not something you see every day.'

'Disgusting,' Brenda said, huffily.

'I don't think so, there's nothing wrong with the male sex organ, especially not one that big, eh, Judith?' Verity nudged her in the side.

Judith looked at Verity, and felt a smile spread across her lips. The first smile she had felt in five years. She liked Verity, she decided. She liked her a lot.

———

Libby sped up the drive of Two Hill Farm as quick as the windy road would allow. She beeped her horn at Big Dave as she drove past him in his tractor and he waved hugely. Pulling up outside the large farmhouse, she let herself into the cosy warmth of the kitchen.

'Kat?' she called, moving into the empty hallway.

'Up here,' sobbed Kat and Libby's blood turned to ice in her veins. Taking the stairs three at a time she ran quickly into their bedroom. Kat was sitting on the bed, sobbing.

Libby quickly enveloped her into a big hug, not an easy feat considering how huge she was.

'What's wrong, what's happened?' she said, into the side of her hair.

'I can't put my shoes on, I've been trying for the last hour and I just can't do it.' Kat wiped her nose, noisily.

Libby sighed with relief, and pulled back. 'Well, I can help with that.'

She kneeled at Kat's feet, tugged her boots on and did up the shoelaces, then she heaved her to her feet, noticing she was wearing one of Dave's shirts and his tracksuit bottoms today.

'So, where are you going now you've got your shoes on?'

'I was going to go down to the field and shout at Dave,' Kat said, like a petulant child.

'Well sure, that sounds like something worth doing … but how about I take you out for an ice cream instead, and then if you really want to shout at Dave when you come back, we'll both go down there and throw our shoes at him?'

Kat wiped her nose again. 'I do like ice cream.'

'Well, you can have a sundae if you want, with marshmallows, and sauce and chocolate brownie pieces. Amy's not working there today but she's working nearby. If we're lucky we may see a big penis molesting some poor unsuspecting men as we eat.'

'A penis?' Kat sniffed, her eyes lighting up.

Libby grinned. 'I'll explain on the way.'

—

Kat sat opposite Libby with love in her eyes. The sundae she had chosen, the triple chocolate, strawberry and coconut dream, was almost as big as her head.

Libby's two scoops of mince pie ice cream looked tiny in comparison.

Sucking the chopped nuts off her spoon, Libby glanced out the window as the seven-foot penis chased a man down the road. The man looked genuinely terrified but Amy was unrelenting.

For a big girl, dressed in what Libby presumed was a heavy costume, Amy was very fit – the penis was moving very quickly.

She smiled. It was when Amy had been working for Mia that they had first met. Libby had been living in White Cliff Bay for about three weeks and had been driving back from Apple Hill along the windy lanes when Amy's little red Mini had swerved across a sharp bend, cutting Libby up and ending up in a field of sheep that barely moved as the Mini came to rest amongst them.

Libby had leapt out to see if the occupant of the car was OK, but when the six foot tall, oversized breast struggled to remove itself from the innards of the Mini, its nipple getting caught in the steering wheel, Libby had burst out laughing. It had taken a full five minutes for the breast to get out of the car, and Libby had been almost powerless to help, she had been so crippled with laughter.

Eventually, Amy had emerged, the nipple looking decidedly deflated, apologised profusely, and they had been best friends ever since.

It was, she supposed, her fault that Amy had now developed this inappropriate infatuation with Seb. The Bubble and Froth hadn't even registered on Amy's radar until she made friends with Libby as it was on the far reaches of the town. Amy had moved to White Cliff Bay with a previous boyfriend two years before Libby had moved there, and once they had become friends Libby had persuaded her to come to the Bubble and Froth. Since then Amy had been coming two or three times a week. She had started doing the odd shift there and that was when the crush had properly started, though perhaps the reason for her working in the pub was because of the crush.

They had laughed about it, when it first started. Amy would talk, out of Seb's earshot, quite lewdly, of what she would like to do to him. But they both knew that it wasn't going to lead anywhere, like having a crush on Chris Hemsworth. But as the months went by, the feelings Amy had for him had gone from being a silly little crush to being full-blown head over heels in love. Libby felt for Amy, because Seb just didn't see her like that, not at all. He was, as far as Libby could tell, still in love with his dead wife, and always would be.

Suddenly, outside, Amy stumbled and, as the penis came crashing to the ground, she managed to knock the poor man she was chasing over as well.

Kat nearly choked on her ice cream as she spluttered with laughter and Libby would have found it funny as well, if she had been watching a comedy sketch on TV and not her best friend hitting the ground so hard.

Leaving Kat to chuckle into her ice cream, Libby ran outside.

'Get off me,' said the man, struggling to extricate himself from under the penis.

'Ow, my hair,' came Amy's muffled voice, somewhere near his groin.

The head of the penis was smacking the man in the face.

'Stop moving, please,' Amy whined.

Libby barged through the crowd that was already starting to form and fell to her knees as the penis and the man struggled.

'Stop, both of you,' she ordered and to her surprise they both froze.

'Are either of you hurt?'

'No,' mumbled Amy and the man shook his head.

'My hair is caught in his belt,' Amy mumbled again.

Crouching closer to the man's hips, Libby bent her head to have a look. Amy's face was resting on the man's crotch, a large chunk of her fringe trapped in the belt buckle.

'You alright kid?' Libby asked softly.

Amy nodded, then winced when it was clearly painful to do so.

Sliding her hands under the large penis, Libby very slowly, very carefully undid the belt. It was awkward, and her hand was almost certainly brushing against the man's groin as well. Eventually, after a few minutes, she managed to free Amy from her constraints.

Amy sat up, smacking the man in the face one last time with the head of the penis.

The crowd around them now was huge – clearly this was the most entertaining thing that had happened in White Cliff Bay for some time now.

Deeply humiliated, the man scrabbled to his feet, and shooting Amy a scathing look, he barged his way through the cheering throng and disappeared.

Libby looked back at her, biting down a smirk.

'Libby Joseph…'

'Come on, Amy, you've got to see the funny side.'

She scowled at her.

'Would you like an ice cream to cheer you up?'

'That would drive Marcus mad, me going into his ice cream shop dressed like this.'

'Then all the more reason to do it.'

Amy smiled wickedly and Libby stood and hauled her to her feet.

Amy followed her into the shop and sure enough Marcus came running round the counter, waving his hands at Amy to stop her.

'No, no, no, you can't come in here,' Marcus said trying to push the penis out of the shop.

Kat's laughing in the corner went up an octave.

Marcus was a small, very round man with a moustache like a walrus, but he had some strength in him. With Amy planting her feet and refusing to leave and Marcus trying to shove the penis out through the door, the head of the penis kept banging the bell above the door, so even if the customers hadn't noticed the arrival of the seven-foot penis, they certainly had now.

'Please leave,' Marcus murmured, wrestling with one of the testicles as he tried to prise it back through the doorway.

Kat was now crying into her ice cream, finding it hard to draw breath she was laughing so hard.

'Marcus, stop pushing, stop it,' muttered Amy, 'get your hands off me or I'll sue you for sexual harassment.'

Marcus froze mid push, his face going pale.

Libby looked away so Marcus wouldn't see her smirk. Amy had threatened Marcus with a lawsuit almost every week since she started work there. Every time they had a disagreement she threatened to sue him. Over the last six months she had accused him of sexism, ageism, racism on account of Amy being Welsh, heightism and weightism. She just had to mention the words solicitor or lawsuit and Marcus backed down.

'I'm just going to sit over here with my friends, have an ice cream and a cup of coffee and then I'll go, I promise,' Amy said.

Suddenly an elderly lady bustled over. 'It's disgusting, you should be ashamed of yourself.'

'Hey!' Kat said, defensively, suddenly finding her voice and standing up with a great deal of effort. 'She's giving up her free time to raise awareness of cancer, she doesn't get paid to dress up like that and be humiliated, she does it out of the kindness of her heart. So before you get on your moral soap box, consider what good she's doing.'

The elderly lady gaped like a fish.

'Does anybody else have a problem with Amy dressed like this?' Kat said, defiantly. If anybody did, they certainly weren't brave enough to voice it in front of the highly deranged pregnant lady.

Marcus sighed heavily. 'Just be quick.'

Amy nodded and shuffled into the booth opposite Kat, knocking over three chairs and a menu stand en-route.

Libby stopped to tidy up the trail of devastation behind her friend, then noticing there was no room left in the booth now it had been taken over by the heavily pregnant lady and the penis, she pulled up a chair to sit at the table.

'Thanks Kat,' Amy said, picking up a menu.

Kat leaned over the table. 'Amy Chadwick, I've laughed so hard today I nearly wet myself, so really I should be thanking you.'

—

It was as Kat went to the toilet for the third time since their arrival in the ice cream shop that Amy, finishing the last mouthful of her ice cream, leaned across the table and fixed Libby with a stare.

'How's the dating going, fallen in love with George yet?'

Libby smirked. 'No, of course not…'

Amy watched her for a moment. 'You bloody have, haven't you?'

'No, I promise, I haven't. I just enjoy spending time with him, he makes me smile, a lot.'

'There's a reason you haven't dated anyone since you moved here and I think George is a huge part of that.'

'No one has taken my fancy.'

'Because you have everything you need with George.'

Libby sighed. 'He is my favourite person in the whole world, I can't deny that, but you can't force something that isn't there. He doesn't want me in that way. He's in love with Giselle.'

'And if he did love you, would you stay?'

'I don't know, Amy. I've been thinking I might stay a bit longer, not for George, just because I like it here. I haven't decided yet but maybe, if I stayed and George wasn't with the beautiful woman upstairs, maybe we could date.'

Amy smiled hugely. 'I would love it if you stayed, I love you, Libby Joseph. Even if George doesn't love you, I do. So if you're not going to stay for him, stay for me, because you seriously don't want to see me cry, that's a whole lot of tears and snot that no one wants to deal with.'

Libby stared at her across the table. 'You love me?'

'Yeah I do. Not in a gay, I want to marry you kind of way, just you're my best friend and I love you … and stop staring at me like I've got three noses. Tell anyone I said that and I'll shave your head.'

'OK,' Libby said, the smile erupting on her face.

'Stop smiling too.' Amy pretended to scowl at her.

Libby forced the smile off her face but a few seconds later it was back again. She was still smiling when Kat came back.

'Do you know how hard it is to wipe your arse when you have a belly the size of small car?' Kat said. 'Even getting into the cubicle was a problem.'

'We should sue Marcus for being anti-pregnant women,' Amy said.

Marcus, who was passing with a tray of empties, nearly dropped them in horror.

—

That afternoon Libby was waiting in the lounge for her date to arrive. She was surprised to feel that her heart was beating nervously in her chest, which was silly. This was George, her best friend; they'd been out hundreds of times before.

There was a knock on the door and she went to answer it. George, she was pleased to note, was dressed as she was, in jeans, a hoodie and walking boots, his waterproof coat slung over his arm. But in his hand was the single yellow rose she had given him earlier. 'It missed its friends.'

'Thank you, that's so sweet.' She took the rose from him, put it in the vase with the others and kissed him on the cheek. 'It's lovely to see you again, George, I was so pleased you called after our date the other night.'

'Well, I'm glad you agreed to see me again. I had such a great time the other night. And can I just say you're looking very pretty today.'

'Oh thank you.'

He took her hand as they walked to the door. 'How am I doing so far?' he asked in a whisper.

'Very well,' she whispered back.

'What about the flowers? Too cheesy?'

'No perfect, as was the compliment.'

'Holding hands?'

'A bit soon for a second date, but it's OK, it's very sweet, women like sweet.'

He led her down the steps and held the car door open for her. He eyed her hopefully, but she shook her head. 'Too clichéd,' she whispered.

He closed the door again. 'Get your own bloody door then,' he huffed as he went round to the other side. She giggled as she got in.

'Do you want to do my seatbelt as well? You know as a little lady I might not be able to manage it.'

She saw him shake his head with a smile as he drove off.

They drove down the road that ran parallel to Silver Cove beach away from White Cliff Bay. It wasn't long though before George parked up by the side of the road. Libby looked around, intrigued as to what they would be doing tonight. They were in the middle of nowhere, the sea was still on one side and large hills grew up like mushrooms on the other. So it was either hiking or maybe… she looked at the sea … fishing from that jetty over there. Fishing would be fun. George could help her to cast out, though her mum had already taught her that when she was little, but she wouldn't tell him that. She could play the role of the helpless female today. He got out the car and removed a cool box from the back of the car. The cool box didn't tell her anything; it could be for a picnic up on the hill, though it was a bit grey for that today. Or the cool box could be filled with wiggly maggots.

He came to her side, took her hand and headed out towards the jetty. Excellent, it was fishing. They could have a competition to see who caught the biggest one and later, if it stayed dry, they could light a fire on the beach and cook the fish and eat it. Very romantic.

But as they thudded onto the wooden jetty, she looked around and realised they didn't have any fishing rods. Confused, she followed him until she noticed something at the end of the jetty that made her go cold. Oh no, not good, not good at all.

He led her to the end of the jetty and carefully lowered the cool box into the orange boat, then hopped down into it and turned back for her.

She looked out on the waves. It would be fine ... it was slightly choppy but it'd be fine. Besides, she couldn't spoil his carefully constructed plan now, he'd be crushed. She would just take deep breaths and keep her eyes on the horizon and pray really hard that the boat journey would be a very, very short one. It'd be fine, really.

It so wasn't fine. Five minutes into the journey and she was already feeling violently sick. She always prided herself on trying anything once, on being brave and having a sense of adventure. She loved to do boys' stuff like clay pigeon shooting, quad bike racing, potholing and abseiling. She didn't get scared of the dark, heights, confined places, spiders or snakes. But her only weakness was seasickness. She had tried many things over the years to try to stop it, from elastic bands round her wrist, special drops of some ointment on her clothes and a multitude of anti-seasick tablets. Nothing had worked.

But today would be different. She was so not going to be sick. George was at the wheel, skilfully manoeuvring the speed boat through the waves. But the sea was choppy and the boat was bouncing hard over the water. In normal circumstances she might have found this ride exhilarating, which was obviously what he was hoping for as he gunned the boat to go faster, but with every wave came a surge of sickness in her belly. She drifted to the back of the boat, she'd heard that the back was the best place for sufferers of seasickness, but she had never found the back, middle or front of the boat to be any different. She wasn't going to be sick. Definitely not. It was a case of mind over matter. She was not going to be sick. She was not going to be sick.

Oh God, she was being sick, her head was over the side, and everything she had ever eaten in her whole life was coming out of her mouth. In actual fact she was pretty sure she had just puked up a kidney, or maybe her appendix.

And George hadn't noticed, he was too busy driving. She had to do something; at this rate she'd be too ill to do anything, especially eat. She took a handful of seawater, washed her face and sat up. She forced herself to her feet and her stomach lurched. Carefully she made her way back to his side, swallowing down the sickness.

He looked up at her, grinning hugely, though the smile faltered when he saw her face and how pale she probably looked. He quickly stopped the boat as it lurched to a halt and caught her arm to stop her from falling over.

'You OK?'

'Yes … can I drive?'

His face fell; clearly he was enjoying being in control. The boat bobbed on the waves and she swallowed another wave of sickness, feeling sure that she was just about to vomit again. Before she could explain or he could ask questions, she quickly sat down on his lap and took the wheel.

'How does it work?' she called over the dull thud of the engine.

'Erm…' His hands were at her waist, her thighs, then on her shoulders, clearly not knowing where was appropriate to put them. He settled for one hand on the wheel, reaching round her to help her control it and the other hand on the throttle. 'It's just like a car in many ways, first, second, third.' He indicated the increments next to the throttle. 'Just push it into first and it will move and then you just need to steer it.'

She pushed the throttle into first and the boat started moving slowly forwards.

He pulled the wheel slightly to the right. 'We're heading for the islands, over there.'

She nodded and steered in that direction, pushing the boat quickly into second and then third, the force of which pushed her back further into his lap. But the quicker they got there the better. And now, sitting down, concentrating on driving the boat, it had pushed the seasickness to the back of her mind. Her stomach still lurched, but she was pretty sure now she wasn't going to be sick any more, although that was possibly due to there being nothing left in her stomach.

She just had to concentrate on driving and nothing else. Well, almost nothing else. She couldn't ignore the fact that George's hands had returned to her waist and felt very nice there.

As they drew close, his hands went back to the wheel again, reducing the speed down to its slowest as he slowly guided the boat in. He skilfully avoided the rocks and parked the boat next to a small metal pole, then picked up a rope which he threw round it and then cut the engine.

'Well, that was… fun,' he said, clearly bemused how his best friend had ended up sitting on his lap.

She turned round to face him, praying she didn't have sickie breath. 'Actually it was.'

She climbed over the side of the boat, onto the rocks at the edge of the island, relishing the feel of the solid non-moving ground beneath her feet.

He grabbed the cool box and joined her.

She took a few deep breaths as she walked up. She was OK now, the seasickness almost completely gone, though her belly did feel tender, and she felt a bit wobbly. She looked around. They were on a tiny patch of land probably about thirty metres long and the same across, large boulders jutted out from the middle. Sea stretched out for miles in every direction, though there were more tiny islands not far away. A thin black line in the distance and the tiny green hills indicated where they had come from. Though she couldn't make out George's car, they were too far away for that.

He put the box down and turned to look at her. 'You OK, you look a bit pale?'

'Just a bit seasick.'

'So this wasn't such a good idea, was it?'

'No, George, this was a brilliant idea: the exhilarating boat ride, the picnic on a deserted island, it's romantic, it's exciting, it's perfect.'

He brightened visibly. 'Really?'

'Really George, if this was a real second date, I'd be glad I was wearing matching underwear right about now.'

His mouth fell open. 'Sex outdoors?'

'No! Well, maybe if it was warmer, but I meant for later tonight.'

He grinned. 'I know it's not really Christmassy but I have that sorted too.' He reached into his bag and pulled out one Santa hat and one pointy green elf hat with a bell on the end. She quickly grabbed the Santa hat, but only because the comedy value of seeing George in an elf hat was too good to miss. He put his hat on and nodded his head obligingly which jingled the tiny bell. Libby laughed, suddenly feeling a surge of love for him.

'If this is really what you are going to do with Giselle I would just check she doesn't get seasick first. Sickie breath is not conducive to a romantic snog.'

He laughed.

'So this is nice.' She looked round. It was barren and wild and remote. She loved it.

'Oh, this isn't half of it yet. Just you wait.'

She looked confused, as he dug into the cool box. He pulled out two large packs of cocktail sausages and walked down to the shore. She followed and he passed her one box, opened his and started flinging handfuls of sausages out into the sea.

Libby, bemused, copied him.

'Don't throw them all, just a couple of handfuls – we'll save the rest,' he said, softly.

She nodded, sensing that they had to be quiet.

'What do we do now?' she whispered.

'Just wait.'

They waited, silently. She was almost holding her breath in anticipation. Then suddenly she saw it. A small grey head in the water, a grey head with big black eyes.

She gasped and she saw George grin by her side at her reaction.

The grey head disappeared and reappeared again a bit closer; this time he had another grey-headed friend with him.

'Seals,' she whispered.

He nodded. 'There's a whole colony out here, they live on the islands over there.'

Five heads, with black wet eyes, were staring at them now, as curious about the humans as they were about them.

The seals swam closer and she could see they were eating the sausages, floating in the water.

'They like sausages?'

'They love them.' He grabbed another handful and flung them out to sea.

The water was clear and she could see the silvery bodies gliding and twisting playfully through the waves.

'George … they're beautiful.'

He grinned and slung an arm round her shoulders. She leaned into him as she watched the seals play in the water. Periodically, they would throw another handful of sausages into the water, until eventually neither of them had any left. The seals hung around for a bit, hoping for some more, but when none was forthcoming they slowly drifted away.

'You ready for dinner now?'

She nodded, still in awe.

He took her hand and walked back to the cool box. He pulled out a blanket, then spread his bounty on it just in front of the rocks which created a welcome barrier from the cold sea wind. An array of meat, salad, crackers and cheese was laid out on the blanket, along with strawberries, chocolate and champagne.

'Wow George, you've gone to so much trouble.'

He shrugged, shyly.

They sat for ages chatting, eating and drinking champagne. When the food was all finished, he packed all the rubbish away. He picked the blanket up and wrapped it round them, sitting with his arm round her as they watched the sun set. The sky was a tangerine and plum colour tonight, the sun looking very orange as it sank beneath the waves.

'So how have I done?' he said, when the sun had vanished completely and the moon was making sporadic appearances between the clouds. 'Marks out of ten?'

'Twenty, no fifty,' she said, cuddling into his arms. 'George, this was the perfect second date; in fact this would be the perfect place to propose one day, when you find that special person.'

'Really, that good, eh?'

'You really are the perfect boyfriend. You're sweet and incredibly romantic.'

He laughed. 'Sounds like I've made a good impression.'

Libby swallowed. He *was* the perfect boyfriend. Maybe it was the champagne, but she was suddenly looking at George differently. Maybe Amy was right, maybe he would make the perfect boyfriend for her. She liked him so much and lately whenever she looked at him she felt this ache in her heart for him. She knew he would never do anything to hurt her. She hadn't trusted anyone ever since she had left her dad fourteen years before, but she trusted George, she had done from the very first day they met. She slugged down the last of the champagne. She was feeling all warm and fuzzy now; she had polished off most of the bottle on her own.

The moon peeped out from the heavy clouds, sending a momentary white glow across the waves.

'I've had the best date, George, thank you.' She kissed him on his cheek and he looked down at her. He was going to kiss her, she was sure of it. Maybe he felt the same way.

Suddenly a loud roaring rumbled angrily across the sky

'Shit,' he said, scrabbling to his feet. Over where the hills used to be, the sky suddenly lit up in a fantastic fork of lightning.

'Shit,' he repeated.

She got to her feet. 'That's not good, is it?'

'No, we need to get back before the storm hits us. We do not need to be on the water when the storm breaks or on this island with no shelter.'

He grabbed the cool box and ran down towards the boat, threw it in and then came back to make sure she got over the slippery rocks without falling.

'I'm alright,' she called, 'get the boat started.'

He ran back to the boat and started the engine, just as another rumble groaned across the sky.

'I checked the weather report, it said it was going to be clear skies all night. I didn't see this coming.'

'It's OK, we'll be back before it hits.' She tried to offer some hope where she felt none.

He leant over and unhooked the rope, then turned the boat and headed back for the mainland.

The boat was soon speeding along but the wind had got up and the waves were much bigger. As they bounced over the water, the waves crashed over them. She could see him handling the boat with a sense of urgency and panic. They had to get back before the storm hit.

But then she suddenly didn't care about the storm any more as she threw up violently over the side. The champagne, the strawberries, the chocolates, the chicken, the salad, the cheese, everything came out, but not just through her mouth, it streamed out her nose as well. Projectile vomit through her nose. Great! The waves crashed over her, as she sat at the back of the boat, soaking her to the skin, even dripping down into her shoes. She couldn't even find it in her to care as she threw up again.

The sky lit up with distant lightning at periodic intervals, punctuated with more rumblings and more throwing up.

This was so much worse than the journey out. She didn't think she had ever been this sick in her entire life. It came out with such force that she honestly thought she might have torn something in her stomach. In between her heaving over the side, she was able to note that she was soaked, numb with cold, and that the thunder was getting closer. They were heading straight for the storm now.

Suddenly the boat hit a big wave and rolled onto its side, depositing them both roughly into the sea. The waves closed in over her head, the icy cold stabbing her skin like a thousand knives. She fought back to the surface, but the weight of her clothes dragged her down. Her head broke the waves above her and she gulped in deep breaths of much needed air. The salt water stung her eyes as she looked around for George, but he was nowhere to be seen.

CHAPTER 10

'George!' she screamed, thrashing around in the water trying to see him.

Suddenly an arm burst through the water near the boat but was gone again a second later. She swam as quick as she could to where she'd seen him, and realised his leg was caught in the boat at such an odd angle that he must be almost completely upside down under the waves.

Taking a deep breath, she plunged under the icy water, and saw him flailing around trying to pull himself to the surface. She grabbed a fistful of his coat and with immense effort yanked him back to the surface, treading water and supporting his head as he gasped for breath.

Her arms and legs screamed in protest as she struggled to keep him afloat long enough for his breath to return back to normal.

'Hold your breath,' she stammered with the cold. He nodded as she let him go and as he disappeared underneath the water again, she quickly turned her attention back to his foot. His boot was caught in the rope around the side of the boat. With trembling fingers, she managed to yank the boot off and throw it in the boat, freeing him from his constraints.

He burst from the waves like a sea monster, his curly hair matted to his face. She climbed quickly back into the boat, with his hand on her bum, shoving her unnecessarily hard. She turned round to help him in, but he was already throwing his leg over the side as he joined her on the floor of the boat.

She reached for him, wanting to touch him all over to make sure he was OK, wanting his arms around her to calm her down, to sooth the adrenaline pounding through her veins. But he was already on his feet, shoving the emergency cut-off cord back into its slot and somehow miraculously starting the engine again.

Within seconds the boat was bouncing along the waves and if she thought the adrenaline, the panic of nearly losing her best friend, would be enough to stop the sickness, she was wrong. She was thrown around in the back of the boat and the sickness started again.

A lot sooner than expected, the engine cut out and the boat was left bobbing in the water, like a toy tossed round in the wind and rain.

George's hand was round her arm, round her waist as he pulled her up and half-dragged her to the jetty. She hauled herself up and, as he grabbed her hand, she ran on shaky legs back to his car. The thunder roared above them, and the rain lashed down on their heads. He flung open the door for her before running round the other side and jumping in as another rumble of thunder boomed around them.

He started the engine and turned the heating on full blast, but it barely made a difference in the painful numbness that was searing through her body. He turned the car round and floored the accelerator.

'I hope we don't meet Uncle Bob again.' His voice was shaking with the cold.

At least, she thought as she shivered violently, she wasn't being sick any more.

They got back to the flat very quickly and staggered, shivering, through the door. She made to go towards her flat but he pulled her towards his. They fell through the door and he put on both the electric fires in the lounge, then dragged her on trembling legs to his bedroom.

George started fighting out of his clothes, his fingers shaking with the cold. She kicked her shoes off and pulled her jeans down. She struggled with the buttons on her coat, her fingers unwilling to do the job required of them. He moved to stand before her and tried the buttons himself, but his fingers wouldn't work either. She pulled his t-shirt off as he struggled with her coat. He resorted to ripping the coat off, the buttons pinging off round the room. She pulled off her hoodie and then her t-shirt as he struggled with his shoes.

She quickly went to the wardrobe and found a jumper which she pulled on and a pair of his jeans, which were way too big but she pulled them on as well. George, completely naked by the side of her, was also pulling on a jumper and jeans, then he grabbed the duvet and pulled her back to the lounge. He positioned the electric heaters next to the sofa, then lay down on it, pulling the duvet over the top of him. She crawled under the duvet, cuddling into him. He pulled her tightly to him as they shivered and trembled against each other.

'You see, I said, you'd be getting to see my underwear by the end of the night,' she said.

'Yeah, if there was a checklist for a perfect second date, tearing each other's clothes off would certainly be on there.'

—

George woke up, stiff from lying on the sofa all night. Libby was nowhere to be seen. He rolled onto his back, and thought back to the previous day. Even with the storm, the near-death experience and Libby throwing up as if it was an Olympic event, the second date had been pretty spectacular. And in fact if that had been a real second date, he was quite sure there'd be a third. They would talk and laugh about the seasickness and the storm just added drama to it.

The seals, the picnic, the sunset had been very romantic too. At one stage, just before the storm broke, he had nearly got carried away with the romance of it all and kissed her.

He wondered how she would have reacted to that. But he could have just laughed it off and said it was all part of the date. They were pretending after all. He frowned. He had to keep reminding himself of that. None of this was real. Everything he and Libby did was supposed to be preparing him for his date with Giselle not making him fall deeper in love with Libby.

Yes, he would definitely take Giselle to the islands if he got a second date with her, she would love it.

But then a niggling doubt settled into his mind. Had it been so perfect only because it was Libby? They had chatted for hours, but that was because they were already so comfortable with each other. The silences were easy, not tense and awkward. And she had just laughed off her seasickness. Would Giselle really be that gracious? After throwing up she'd probably have refused to eat anything, if they'd gotten that far; she might well have insisted he take her home.

The whole point of the second date was doing something fun together. But if there was all that time for talking, and they didn't have anything to say to each other, then it'd still be the last date they'd have. Giselle would perhaps appreciate the romance, but not the fact that it was so awkward and stilted between them.

No, ideally the second date would involve something fun, exhilarating and romantic but leave very little time for talking. Then on the third date they could talk and laugh about the second date. The islands would make a great fourth or fifth date.

Suddenly a loud squealing sound snapped him out of his reverie. He scrambled up, wondering what on earth the horrid piercing noise was. Realising, from the plume of smoke coming from the door, that it was the fire alarm, he ran towards the kitchen. Libby, half naked, came running out of his bedroom at the same time. They collided with such force that she somehow managed to punch him in the groin and his teeth smacked into her forehead. They both staggered apart, injured. She was the first to recover, as he was bent double with pain.

He watched as she yanked the tray from underneath the grill, which was smouldering nicely, and put it on the unit, seemingly burning her fingers in the process.

'Ow, fuck, shit,' she muttered, blowing on them.

She opened a window to let the smoke out, then grabbed a towel and jumped up and down, flapping it over the smoke alarm to try to stop the incessant squealing.

He couldn't help smiling, despite the pain, because every time she jumped up, he got a glimpse of her underwear underneath his jumper. Somewhere between last night and this morning, she had lost his jeans.

The smoke alarm finally stopped and their ears rang in the silence. She turned back to the bacon, which was decidedly black, and sucked her sore fingers. 'Crispy bacon OK?'

'Perfect.' He winced as he stood up, trying to ignore the searing pain in his nether regions. He took her hand. 'Did you burn your fingers?'

She shrugged. 'Ah, it's OK.'

He put her fingers to his mouth and kissed each one in turn. Libby watched him, speculatively, and he realised that what he was doing was hugely intimate and quickly dropped her hand.

She laughed. 'I would offer to do the same for your injury,' she eyed his groin, 'but maybe I'll save that for our fourth or fifth date.'

'Excellent, something to look forward to.'

She picked up a rasher of bacon, and nibbled sweetly round the burnt bits. She looked adorable dressed just in his jumper.

'I can't help noticing, Miss Joseph, that you seem to have misplaced your jeans.'

'They were too big for me; I had to hold them up whilst I was cooking. That's what I was doing in your bedroom, looking for some shorts. I didn't realise the bacon would cook so quickly.'

Over mugs of tea, and the remains of the bacon, he discussed his concerns about the second date: that going to the island still gave too much time for talking and awkward silences.

Libby nodded. 'Yeah, I can see that, stuck out on that island, it could get awkward. If we were in the pub, then we could always play pool if the conversation got desperate. If we were at your flat, and you were cooking me a nice romantic meal, if the conversation halted we could always put the TV on, or watch a film. But being on that island, there's no escape, there's just each other. And the toilet facilities lacked the *je ne sais quoi* that some women prefer.'

'So what then, any ideas?'

Libby bit her lip, as she thought. He loved that she did that.

'OK, you should let her choose. You can suggest that you do something fun, something different for your second date. You could suggest a competition for who can come up with the best date, she can choose the second one and you'll choose the third one. There can be certain rules like a maximum budget of fifty pounds. That way, if she plans the second date you can get a sense of what she likes and can plan your third date round that. Also, you are almost guaranteeing there will be a third date, even if the second date was rubbish, because she will be intrigued to see what you come up with after her date.'

He grinned broadly. 'I like it, I really like it. It kind of brings an element of fun to our relationship right from the word go. It's brilliant. But you know what this means, don't you?'

She finished off the rest of her tea. 'What's that?'

'Our next date, our next second date, you have to plan it.'

'OK, you're on,' she grinned.

He let out a small sigh of relief that she had accepted his proposal so readily. Another date with Libby. How many more of these could he realistically go on for research purposes? But the dating competition was a brilliant idea, mostly because they were now back to their second date, instead of their third. A perfect reason to go ahead with it.

'Tonight?' he asked.

She pulled a face and he quickly backtracked. 'Of course you've probably got other things planned, we can do it some other time.'

'No, tonight's fine. I was just wondering what I could pull out of the hat at such short notice.'

'It doesn't matter what you choose, nothing will outdo the island, with the seals, the picnic and the sunset.'

'No, that doesn't count any more. If the date I'm planning is actually our second date, then the island date never happened. We had our first date at the restaurant...'

'With the dirty sex at the end?' he asked hopefully.

'No.'

'Damn it.'

'So we had our first date and that's when you've suggested this dating competition. So we are starting off from an equal footing, we're both on nil–nil.'

'OK, OK,' he sighed, 'nil–nil.'

'Right then, our second date…' She trailed off thoughtfully. 'Wait, am I Giselle or Libby?'

'What do you mean?'

'Am I doing a date that I'd enjoy or that I think Giselle would enjoy?'

'That you'd enjoy, definitely.'

'But how is that going to help you practise for Operation Giselle? I have what you might call an eclectic taste when it comes to things fun.'

Damn it. He should have said a date that Giselle would enjoy. Otherwise it was too obvious that he wanted another date with Libby.

'It will just give me a sense of how the female brain works.'

'OK, something I'd enjoy…'

She smiled as she stared off into the distance and he was relieved that her competitive streak had her focussing on the details of the date rather than the actual reason behind it.

'You have a plan, don't you?'

She grinned mischievously. 'Oh yes, there's definitely a plan.'

'What should I wear? I don't want to turn up in my high heels and find we're abseiling down a cliff.'

'Something old, something that you won't mind getting a bit dirty.' She smiled, somewhat evilly he thought.

'Oh, that reminds me, let me give you your daily present before you go. It's just something small.' George walked off into the bedroom and opened his wardrobe and hauled out the huge snowman he had bought the day before. It was bigger than him and had somewhat of an evil facial expression, though he didn't think that was intentional. With great difficulty he dragged it into the lounge and Libby burst out laughing.

'*Six days before Christmas my true love gave to me, a promise for no more bad poetry.*'

Libby laughed again. 'George, how on earth will I take that with me to New York?'

'Well if you stay, you won't have that problem.'

She smiled. 'Maybe I will.'

—

Amy was late, she was never late. It was Seb's only day off and she was in charge. He would be waiting for her and she hated to let him down.

She had done her shopping and was just carrying the bags out to her car when she saw Carol, Mia's sister, in the car park, struggling with several heavy bags as she made her way over to the bus stop as light flakes of snow swirled around her. Amy had stopped her and insisted she drove her home. When she'd got there, Amy felt obliged to help Carol unpack all her bags as the old woman talked non-stop about some man called Sean who she'd had some passionate affair with. As much as Amy had wanted to stay and hear all the gory details, helping her had made her late and Carol, living the furthest point away from Silver Cove, would make her even later.

There was a short cut: Cow Bell Lane, which she was now racing along. She hated this road, it was narrow, windy and steep, and she would much rather add the fifteen minutes' drive to her journey to avoid it but today she had no choice – even taking this road would mean she'd still be a bit late.

The only good thing about this route was that no one ever used it: it was dangerous and the locals knew better than to drive on it. Passing an old wooden hut, she put her foot down.

Suddenly flying over a blind summit, a silver sports car tore towards her. The road was only wide enough for one car so she swerved just in time to miss it. Everything seemed to happen so slowly as her car flew through the air. It hung there for ages, almost suspended from the grey clouds, and she vainly found herself trying to steer the car to safety, pumping the brakes to stop what happened next. The car tilted downwards and a flash of green came tearing towards her. With the sickening sound of metal buckling around her, she knew nothing more.

—

Seb had only just opened the pub doors, but Big Dave was already waiting outside for his lunch.

'Where's the lovely Amy today? Didn't expect to see you, I thought Thursdays were your day off?' Big Dave followed him back to the bar and took up his regular stool.

'She's late,' Seb muttered.

Big Dave frowned. 'Not like her.'

'I think she's trying to prove a point.'

'Well, point proven: the specials board hasn't been changed since yesterday, there's no peanuts on the bar and I have to put up with your ugly mug glowering at me rather than her lovely face. Whatever she wants, give it to her. I know better than anyone that you've got to keep your women happy.'

'She's not my woman,' Seb said defensively.

Big Dave smiled knowingly. 'Your *women*, Seb, not your woman, but lord knows you need one of them in your life. But I'm talking about all the women in your life: Amy, Judith, Sally, your mum, your sister. Keep them all happy; agree to anything for a quiet life.'

Seb checked his watch for the tenth time as more customers drifted in. How exactly was he supposed to keep both Amy and Judith happy?

He was going to have stern words with Amy after this stunt, though that just seemed to turn her on even more. He looked at his watch again. She was half an hour late and his friends would just be arriving at the Winston Churchill in Apple Hill now, wondering where he was. Damn her. One day a week off and she was cocking that up for him.

'Can we bring our dog in?' asked a man who had the look of someone already stressed out by the thought of Christmas approaching. Two kids, a boy and a girl, were playing tag behind him. Seb had heard the day before that White Cliff Bay primary school had closed early for the holidays and clearly this man had had enough of looking after them already. A small red setter sat patiently at the man's feet.

Seb indicated Jack, lying snoring in a shaft of daylight, his large belly rising and falling with each breath. 'As long as she gets on with other dogs.'

The man nodded. 'Oh, she's very friendly.'

Seb nodded and the family moved into one of the booths. The children, having had their game of tag temporarily thwarted, fell on Jack with excitement. He opened a bleary eye and sat up so he could be stroked more thoroughly. The red setter sniffed him, Jack's eyes lighting up at the female attention. Seb smiled, though his smile fell off as a steady stream of young couples, families and locals suddenly came through the doorway. Where the bloody hell was Amy?

———

On his way out to the tiny shop to pick up some milk, George bumped into Giselle in the foyer. Literally bumped. Not looking where he was going as he shut the door, his thoughts on his wonderful date with Libby that night, he turned and slammed into her so hard she nearly toppled over. He quickly reached out to stop her from falling.

'Shit, sorry. God, are you OK?' he said, feeling his cheeks glowing crimson.

'Yes, I'm fine.' She smiled at him politely.

'Erm…' he said, trying to find something to say. Anything would be good right now. Anything that wasn't 'erm'. She really was so beautiful, cute in a pixie type way and he was painfully aware that he was just staring at her.

'I, er…' This was good, he had nearly knocked her over and now couldn't even string a sentence together. She was bound to be bowled over.

OK, he was funny, Libby always said that he made her laugh, he just had to say something funny. Oh God, Giselle was shuffling away now, he had to say something. A knock, knock joke, he knew loads of those, or a limerick maybe, he'd written quite a few himself for his radio adverts. No, he couldn't just launch into a limerick; he would look like a madman.

'Well, see you, George, I've still got a bit of unpacking to do, so I better get on and do it.' She turned away quickly.

'How are you settling in?' he blurted, pleased that he'd finally found something to say, something that wasn't a sodding limerick.

'Fine thanks, I was thinking of having a house warming party actually. Maybe in a week or two once all the boxes have been unpacked, a sort of a "get to know my new neighbours" type thing.'

'Ooh, you want to be careful about doing things like that – I hear Bridget Whittaker, your landlord, is a bit of a tyrant when it comes to the "rules".' George used his fingers to show quotation marks in the air around the word rules, then cringed. Who actually did that – who used quotation marks?

'Oh really?'

'Yes, she doesn't like her tenants to have parties or smoke or have pets or have guests to stay or put pictures up or cook tomato soup on a Thursday.'

Giselle smirked and, emboldened by this, he pressed on.

'I've never met the woman, but I imagine with a name like Bridget Whittaker she's a horsey type.'

'What's a horsey type?'

'Oh, you know, walks around in jodhpurs and riding boots, with a tweed jacket that's too small for her big boobs. She'll have very short hair, cut for convenience rather than style, or she'll have it long but always tied up in a bun. She'll carry a riding whip around with her everywhere, probably tucked under her arm, and she'll march, not walk.' He was getting into his stride now and as he started trotting round the foyer on his pretend horse, he put on a high-pitched posh female voice. 'Tristan, you must work on your rising trot. Harmonica, we simply must get together at the meet next week and Magnus, why don't you meet me in the stables for a quick romp in the hay.'

He pulled his horse to a stop in front of her. There, that was funny, energetic and witty.

'Bridget's my mum.'

Shit.

'Oh … well, I, erm…'

Yes, he really knew how to make a good impression.

—

The phone rang and, after finishing serving Big Dave, Seb rushed to answer it.

'Seb,' Amy croaked.

'Amy, where the bloody hell are you? You were supposed to be here over an hour ago. I'm late for my friends and the place is packed.'

'I… don't think I can make it in.'

'If you can't be bothered to come in then don't bother turning up for any of your other shifts. If you're ill you should have phoned me hours ago so I could have arranged cover. This isn't good enough.'

'I…' A strangled sob caught in her throat, which caught him off guard. 'Christ, there's blood everywhere.'

His heart stuttered. 'What?'

'I don't feel well… I think I need an ambulance.'

'Amy, what's wrong?'

'There was a car, on my side of the road, I swerved and then my car flew over the edge and… my God everything hurts. I'm not sure where I'm bleeding, but there's blood everywhere.'

He swallowed uneasily, the noise of the pub vanishing, his brain only tuning in to Amy. 'Where are you?'

There was silence from her, and her breathing sounded strange.

'Amy, where are you?'

Another sob. 'I can't get out the car… I'm on Cow Bell Lane, somewhere near the old wooden house.'

'I'm on my way.'

'No, I'm OK; well I'm not but just call an ambulance for me.'

'Shut up, woman, I'm coming.' He quickly hung up. 'Big Dave, get your arse round here and start serving. That goes for you too, Nick.'

Big Dave and Nick immediately moved round to the other side of the bar, sensing the urgency.

'Dave, call an ambulance and the fire brigade, tell them to go to Cow Bell Lane, near the old wooden house.'

Big Dave nodded and Seb ran out the pub, not caring if it fell into complete ruin whilst he was gone.

—

Amy sat in the car wiping the tears from her face. The car had come to rest at an odd angle, her door was smashed in and the seatbelt was jammed. Everything hurt. How was it possible to feel so much pain? Blood was splattered against the windscreen, over her clothes, the dashboard; as if something inside her had been ripped open. If she was that badly injured, it was likely that she wouldn't live through this.

There had been so much she had wanted to do with her life – she'd wanted to travel, to see the world. But more than that she wanted to get married, have children, spend her life with the man she loved. How could she have missed out on all of that? It seemed so unfair that her life was over before it had really begun. But then life wasn't fair. Marie had died at twenty-seven, much younger than Amy was now, leaving behind a loving husband and mother.

Amy looked up at where the road was, though it hurt her neck to do so. What had happened to the silver car; why hadn't they stopped when they realised they had forced her off the road? What kind of person doesn't stop?

She would be difficult to spot from the road from down here. Seb could be driving up and down Cow Bell Lane for ages trying to find her. What if something happened to him too?

She had to get out, try to get to the road so she could be spotted. With trembling fingers she fumbled with her seatbelt but it wouldn't budge.

She heard a car approaching; it was moving fast, taking the corners too quickly. Shit, it had to be Seb, either that or the bastard driver of the silver sports car coming back.

The engine sound stopped – or had it just driven past and she could no longer hear it? She waited but she could hear nothing now and there was no sign of any help coming at all.

—

Seb stood on top of the hill, unable to move. Amy's little red Mini was sitting battered at the bottom and she was inside, hurt and alone. The sheer amount of blood all over the windows was horrifying. It looked like someone had been slaughtered. If she was not dead now she soon would be; no one could survive after losing that much blood. He couldn't face it, he couldn't face going down there and seeing her dead body, or watching her die. He couldn't bear the thought of seeing her so badly injured, it was heartbreaking.

But what if he could save her? The ambulance was on its way but maybe there was something he could do in the meantime.

Scrabbling down the hillside, he reached the car on shaky legs and tried to wrench open her door. Inside she was moving, peering through the blood-stained glass to look at him. Her eyes filled with tears when she saw him and he wanted to hold her so badly. Her face was covered in blood too. He felt sick.

He ran round the other side and pulled the door which came away loosely in his hand.

'Seb,' she sobbed as he knelt on the passenger seat too afraid to touch her.

'Amy, shit, where are you bleeding?' He was already pulling off his shirt ready to stem the blood when the smell of strawberries hit him.

'I don't know, I hurt everywhere.'

He looked around the car suspiciously. Something wasn't right, blood was everywhere but, apart from her face and a tiny bit on her clothes, it was hardly on *her* at all. In fact she didn't seem to be injured in any way. Well, obviously she was injured, she was hurting but there certainly weren't any cuts, any great gashes that had severed several major arteries. He wiped his finger down the windscreen and sniffed it. It was strawberry juice.

'Amy, this is fruit juice.'

'Is it?' she asked in confusion.

He nodded, suddenly spying the smashed carton of mixed berry juice lying in the foot well of the passenger side along with a broken packet of eggs. A squashed loaf of bread and two mutilated oranges were on the dashboard and there was a damaged packet of condoms lying next to the gear stick, ironically next to a sausage that had escaped its packet.

He reached down to grab the carton of juice and showed it to her and she let out a weak laugh.

'Oh thank God, I thought I was a goner for sure, losing that much blood.'

'You and me both,' he laughed. He tossed the carton back into the foot well and shuffled closer, almost wanting to cry with relief. 'Anything broken?'

'I don't think so, it's hard to tell.'

He shuffled closer still. He picked up the packet of condoms. 'Did you have plans for these?'

She blushed. 'I was hoping you might have a change of heart.'

He eyed the pack of thirty condoms. That was some change of heart she was hoping he would have.

'Is there anything I can do?'

She touched his face. 'You can kiss me.'

He looked up. 'The fire brigade are here.'

'Then kiss me quick.'

He smiled and leaned forward to do just that.

CHAPTER 11

Having just finished writing three scripts for radio adverts, George had decided to go for a walk on the beach. However, as he reached the main front door of the flats he saw Giselle running down the stairs towards him. He froze. Twice in one day. He tried to decide whether he was lucky or really unlucky.

But instead of the look of annoyance he was expecting when she saw him, she flashed him a huge smile and stopped to speak to him.

'Hey George.'

'Hi.'

He should just ask her out. He could ask her out, it was easy, it was just eight little words: 'Would you like to go out with me'. He could do this. He could.

'Giselle, would—'

Libby suddenly threw open her door with such force it shook as it banged against her wall.

He looked at her and saw that her face was pale and shaken.

'It's Amy, she's been in a car accident,' she said as she ran past him and he bolted after her, Giselle suddenly forgotten.

—

Libby looked at Amy and burst into tears. She looked pale, tired and so tiny and vulnerable lying in Seb's king-sized bed. There was the beginning of a big bruise under her eye.

'Come on now, Libby, I'm fine, just a few cuts and bruises, nothing to worry about.'

'Can I hug you?' She knelt next to Amy on the bed.

Amy nodded. 'Gently.'

Libby wrapped her arms round her and felt George hug Amy too, though one arm was round her own shoulders.

Pulling away, she wiped the tears from her eyes. She looked at Seb, standing on the other side of the room. 'What did the doctors say?'

When Seb had phoned her he had explained what had happened, how the fire brigade had had to cut Amy out, by which time the ambulance crew had arrived and taken her to the hospital in Apple Hill. After a few hours of tests, scans and close observation, it was clear she was suffering from nothing more than a bit of mild concussion, and a few bruises.

'Only what I told you on the phone, that she just needs rest. He said I'm to keep an eye on her and that she may be a bit stiff and sore over the next few days.'

'Well, you need to come home with us, Amy,' George said, wiping his eyes. 'It's great that you were there, Seb, and that you went with her to the hospital, but I think it's best her friends take care of her now.'

Libby watched Amy and a look passed between them. It was so subtle, you would barely have noticed it, but Libby received it as loudly as if her friend had shouted it.

Seb coughed awkwardly. 'I don't think she should be moved. Besides, you two don't have spare rooms like I do, I can sleep in the room down the corridor.'

'Seb's right, Amy can't stay with us,' Libby said hurriedly. 'If she sleeps in my bed I'd have to sleep on the sofa and that's not a good sofa for sleeping on, it's hard and lumpy, I'd get no sleep at all.' She eyed Amy to see if she was doing the right thing. The slight smirk on Amy's lips told her she was.

George stared at her incredulously, but finally he seemed to find his voice. 'Well, she can stay with me. I don't mind sleeping on my sofa.'

'George, you snore,' Libby lied. 'You'd keep her awake.'

'Well, you can sleep on my sofa then and I'll sleep in your bed.' He really wasn't going to let this go.

'Chenille affects my asthma,' said Libby. 'It's OK for sitting on but I couldn't lie on it.'

'You don't have asthma.'

'It's very mild.'

Libby saw Seb roll his eyes. 'I'll get you some painkillers, Amy,' he muttered.

Libby watched him leave with a smile. He knew exactly what she was trying to do; it was a pity that George couldn't pick up on the subtleties.

'I can put sheets on the sofa,' George was saying.

'I'll still be able to smell the chenille.'

Amy stifled a giggle.

'Then what? She can't stay here,' George said, plumping Amy's pillows up so aggressively, Libby was surprised they didn't burst. 'I'm sure Seb's just being polite by letting her stay. She needs to be looked after by those who love her.'

Libby tutted at him. 'Why don't you go and see if Seb needs help?'

'With a packet of tablets? I'm sure he can cope.'

'George, for goodness' sake, I want to talk to Amy.'

'Oh... well I'll be back in a minute.' He scowled at her as he left.

She turned back to Amy. 'You know you would be very welcome to stay with me. I would wait on you hand and foot and treat you like a queen.'

'That's OK, I'm fine here,' Amy smiled and Libby returned her grin.

'And you're OK, really, truly?'

'He loves me, Lib.'

'I meant the cuts and bruises.'

'Oh that, yes, very sore, but yes, I'm fine.'

Libby took her hand. 'He loves you?'

'He hasn't said it, but he kissed me. It was sweet and tender, not lust filled like the last time. He loves me I know it.'

Libby's heart leapt with joy. 'Wait. There was a last time?'

'The other night. It just sort of happened. Although truth be told, it's been a long time coming.'

'Then you need to drag out this convalescence as long as possible.'

'I may need help bathing and getting dressed.'

Libby laughed just as Seb and George came back into the room.

'Well, Amy's very tired so we should leave her to rest.' Libby smiled as Amy yawned loudly behind her. 'Do you need any clothes or anything brought from your house?'

'No, Seb stopped off on the way back from the hospital and helped me collect a few things.'

'He looks like he's got everything covered.' Libby ushered a scowling George out of the room. 'We'll check in on you tomorrow.'

—

Out on the street George turned on Libby. 'What the hell was that about? I've never known you to be so selfish before.'

'Oh George, you couldn't see the truth if it came out and bit you. Do you think I'd really leave Amy to stay with her boss for no good reason?'

'Well apparently you had a good reason: "my sofa's too lumpy, I have asthma".'

'Let me know when the penny's dropped, won't you, and in the meantime you carry on thinking I'm a cruel heartless bitch.'

George walked in silence next to her. Poor Amy, having to stay with her boss. Seb was a great guy, he would help anyone out, but he clearly hadn't reckoned on having a house guest when he woke this morning. He probably offered to be polite and hadn't thought Amy would accept. Why did Amy accept? Unless she knew Libby better than George did and had expected her to be selfish. What if she needed help getting dressed, Seb couldn't do that. Amy would be so embarrassed having Seb put on her bra and knickers for her. But it would be weird for Seb too. The last woman who had lived in his pub was Marie. George supposed it would be nice for Seb to have some company, someone to talk to who wasn't Jack. He could cook for Amy and they would eat together and it would be nice for Amy to have someone to look after her for a change, she was so used to doing everything for herself. But why would Libby not want Amy to stay with her? If Libby had been involved in a car accident, he would insist that she stayed with him, or he stayed with her so he could look after her. That's what friends did. Though there would be an ulterior motive to having Libby living with him. Having her there, with him twenty-four hours a day would be heaven and…

'Oh,' George said, suddenly.

'There it is,' Libby said next to him. 'Took you long enough.'

'Amy likes Seb?'

'I'm pretty sure the feeling's mutual.'

'Seb likes Amy?' George was incredulous. 'But there hasn't been anyone else since Marie died.'

'Then it's high time there was. She loves him, George, has done for months but I was always sure that he didn't return the feeling.

176

Amy swore that he did. Now it seems he loves her too; the car accident probably jolted him out of his stubborn reverie.'

George smiled. He liked the idea of Amy and Seb together.

'But don't say anything to anyone, I'm sure Judith wouldn't be happy if she found out. Don't mention it to them either. Not until they feel ready to talk about it. We've got to let them sort this out themselves and any interference on our part could shake the foundations before it's even started.'

'And making up a lumpy sofa and asthma isn't interfering?'

'That's giving a helping hand.'

George grinned in relief. He couldn't bear the thought of Libby being selfish.

'So, still want to go out with me on a date tonight, or have you changed your mind since I'm so self-centred?'

'I'll go with you anyway. We can't all be perfect like me. Being with me will give you something to aspire to.'

George was surprised and confused to see Libby blush as she looked away.

'In more ways than one,' Libby muttered.

'What?'

'I'll see you at half six then.' Libby smiled brightly and closed the door to the flat behind her.

—

Seb had called in Sally and Mandie to work the bar whilst he tended to Amy. Normally he would call on Judith if he was short-staffed, but he could hardly call her and say that he wanted her to come round so he could look after Amy in his bed upstairs. He had called to cancel their long-standing arrangement of dinner, but he'd just said something had come up and hoped his vagueness hadn't piqued her curiosity.

Apart from George, Libby and his chef, Gavril, who had seen Seb bring Amy through the back, no one knew he had Amy upstairs – and he'd like to keep it that way. It was none of their business and quite frankly he needed to figure it all out in his head first before he announced it to the town.

She was asleep now, lying in his bed, facing away from him with her hair over her bare shoulder like a satin black scarf. She was beautiful. Today he had nearly lost her without telling her how he felt.

It wasn't just lust and a desire to sleep with her, he was kidding himself if he thought it was. With the fear of her dying, before the blood turned out to be fruit juice, the feelings he had for her crashed over him like a tidal wave. Afterwards those feelings had turned to relief and complete euphoria that she was alive. He had been given a second chance with her, something he never had with Marie. Every single part of him was now screaming at him to grab her and make the most of life with her while he had the chance. Life was so short and ultimately very unfair so he needed to live it now and not spend it worrying about the future. He hadn't looked to the future since Marie had died, spending the last five years looking over his shoulder for the grim reaper. Now he wanted that future with Amy … but it scared the hell out of him. She had escaped death today but would she be so lucky again? It was stupid living his life with this utter fear of losing those around him but the pain of losing Marie had been immeasurable and he was scared to open himself up to that level of pain again. But he knew he couldn't walk away from Amy again either.

She stirred and slowly sat up.

'Ow, ow, ow, ow, ow,' she whimpered quietly as she moved.

'What are you doing?' he growled, and she jumped at the sound of his voice.

'I didn't know you were there.'

'Evidently. Why are you getting out of bed?'

She stood gingerly but he came round quickly to her side of the bed.

'I don't want to have to tie you to the bed, you're supposed to rest.' He swallowed as he realised she was wearing a long black satin nightie that clung beautifully to her hips and breasts. Damn it, even in bed she was glamorous.

'I need the loo, Seb, and then I need something to eat.' She shuffled to the door.

'Well, I'll help you go to the toilet and—'

'You will not, I'm not quite ready for you to wipe my butt for me just yet. Not when we haven't even slept together.'

'I actually meant I'd help you down the corridor.' He put his arm round her waist and relished that he had an excuse to touch her. 'And then I'll make you some soup.'

She slid her arm round his waist too, leaning on him. 'Do you not have a pub to run? You can't sit up here and watch me sleep for the next few days, least of all because it's a little bit creepy.'

'I wasn't going for the stalker approach, just came to see if you were OK and you happened to wake up while I was standing there,' he lied. He actually had been watching her for fifteen minutes or more.

They passed a small room, with a single bed that he had hastily made up.

'Is that where you're sleeping tonight?'

He nodded.

'That's silly; you'll never fit in there. I'll sleep there instead.'

'No, it's really uncomfortable, trust me. Here, the bathroom's just through there.'

'Then sleep in the bed with me.'

He opened his mouth to protest but she pressed on.

'I promise not to molest you in the middle of the night; besides, your bed is huge, we can both spread out and still not touch each other.'

'You might be able to control yourself, Amy Chadwick, but there's no way I can lie in bed with you and not touch you.'

She leaned up, sliding her arms round his neck, and instinctively his hands went to her waist. Her body was pressed against his, her lips just centimetres from his own. 'Then touch me.'

He swallowed. 'You're enjoying this, aren't you?'

'Every second and if I wasn't in a whole lot of pain right now, I'd be enjoying it a whole lot more.'

He kissed her forehead, the only part he could safely kiss without getting carried away.

'Now if that's all you're going to offer me, I'm going to the loo and you can go and see Gavril about doing me some soup.'

Still holding her, Seb pressed his face to her hair. 'I'm quite capable of opening a can of soup.'

'I'm sure you are, but I want some of that leek and potato I saw him cooking when we came in, and I'm very demanding – something you may learn one day.'

He released her and watched as she smiled sexily at him, closing the bathroom door. She was going to be trouble, having her here was going to be trouble. And he was enjoying every second of it too.

—

Judith was sitting at her computer. She had been annoyed that Seb had cancelled their dinner plans that night without explaining why. She'd wanted to talk to him, about Marie, about moving on and that he shouldn't feel obligated to her. She wanted to tell him of her plans to travel the world. And she wanted to talk to him about Amy, dissuade him from going down that path if he was inclined to take it any further than that kiss. She didn't know what she could do to persuade Seb from being with Amy, but maybe he should be told that she was a prostitute; he had a right to know that at least.

Being free tonight had given her the excuse to look at world cruises. Turquoise waters, golden sands, lofty skyscrapers, beautiful cathedrals, quaint cottages, great French villas, jagged mountains, emerald green rainforests and towering waterfalls had drifted out from the web pages, dazzling her senses. She had found one cruise that took in all the sights and sounds of the world in a hundred days. It was pricey, but affordable. It was discounted too as it was leaving in four weeks and they wanted to fill the last remaining cabins. For the last half hour, her fingers had hovered over the keys to book it. If she left, Seb would be free from any obligations to her or Marie. She would get the chance to see things that she had never experienced before in her lifetime, to do the things Marie had wanted to do but never got the chance. Judith could release herself from the tedium of life in White Cliff Bay, to read the books she wanted without judgement, to meet people, to make friends.

There was a knock at her door just as she pressed the 'book it now' button and a form had appeared asking her for all her details.

To her surprise it was Dave Wilson and his heavily pregnant wife Kat.

'Hello?' Judith said in confusion.

'Hi,' Kat said, looking flustered, 'do you know where Amy is?'

Judith found herself bristling at the very mention of Amy's name. 'Well, I presume she's in the pub. She works when it's Seb's day off.'

'No, she had a car accident today, Dave's just retrieved her car with his tractor.' Kat indicated the tiny red Mini, battered and broken on the road behind her. 'We brought it round and came to see if she's OK, but she's not answering and I'm worried about her. Do you have a spare key?'

Judith found herself going cold. As much as she despised Amy, she wouldn't wish what Marie went through on anyone.

'Is she OK?'

'Well, Seb said she was,' Dave said, looking concerned.

'Why… why would Seb… Was he with her, is he OK?'

'Seb was in the pub when she called from the car. I've never seen anyone look so scared before in my life, the colour literally drained from his face and then he was gone, shouting at me to man the bar and call an ambulance. He came back several hours later, said she was OK, just cuts, bruises and mild concussion, but…' Dave gestured vainly at Amy's door.

'Oh no you're mistaken,' came Mary's thin voice from next door; her neighbour was quite possibly one of the nosiest people Judith had ever met. 'Seb and Amy came back from the hospital late this afternoon, about four o'clock. She looked very shaken and sore, the way she carried herself I imagine she was badly bruised all over. They went into the house for about ten minutes and then they both came back out, he was carrying a bag for her and they got in his car and drove off. She hasn't been back since.'

Judith found her heart was beating, furiously. Not Seb and Amy. He would be worried about his staff, about any one of his friends who had been involved in a car accident, but to just leave his pub without a second thought was unheard of. And to go to the hospital with Amy and then where? Where was she now? In his bed, in the bed he had shared with Marie? Judith felt sick.

'I bet he took her to stay with Libby or George,' Kat said.

Yes, that was it, Amy would be staying with Libby, her best friend.

'No I don't think so.' Mary grinned hugely. 'My Peter saw Libby and George race into the pub and go up the stairs at about four thirty and then come downstairs again about ten minutes later. George looked very worried apparently, though Libby was beaming. My bet is Amy's staying with your young Seb.' Mary looked positively ecstatic to be imparting this news to Judith.

'Makes sense I suppose,' Kat said, turning to Dave. 'You said Seb has had a thing for Amy for months now.'

Dave eyed Judith, his eyes bulging. 'No I didn't, I never said that.'

'Yes you did,' Kat said, angrily.

'I bloody didn't, pregnancy must have addled your brain, woman. Seb doesn't like Amy.'

'Oh yes he does.' Mary was grinning from ear to ear. 'Any idiot can see that, the two of them are besotted with each other. Rumour has it he's been sleeping with her since she started work at the pub. About bloody time too, I say.'

Judith turned and slammed the door.

She stalked to her computer and turned it off. There was no way she was going on this world cruise now, she couldn't possibly leave Seb in that slut's clutches.

—

'Come on, George, we're going to be late,' Libby said, racing down the hill past The Pilchard towards the village square. George ran by her side, his blue coat flapping in the wind behind him, making it look like a superhero's cloak.

Suddenly Suzanna from the chemist called across the street to Libby, stopping her in her tracks.

Suzanna ran across the road towards her, which made Libby smile. She must be in her nineties but that didn't seem to slow her down. Libby had seen her running round town after her grandchildren on many occasions. Suzanna eyed George with some embarrassment.

'Might I have a word in private?' she said.

'I'll wait for you,' George said, strolling off to the bottom of the hill.

Suzanna slipped out a copy of Libby's latest book from her bag as if it was some illegal contraband. Although everyone in the town knew the real Libby, most people in the town knew she wrote under a pseudonym.

'I was hoping to run into you, I've been carrying this around in my bag for the last few days just in case. I wonder if you would sign it for me,' Suzanna whispered, looking around to see if anyone was watching. It made Libby laugh that some of the older generation were so coy about Libby's books. They weren't erotica, they were certainly a far cry from the whips and handcuffs of the *Fifty Shades* series. Her sex scenes did get a bit steamy sometimes but the books were definitely more romance based than sex based.

'Of course,' Libby said, taking the book and the pen and signing her name inside. She passed it back.

'Thank you so much, dear.' Suzanna slipped the book back in her bag. 'I hear you and young George are dating now?'

How on earth did she hear that? But nothing stayed secret in White Cliff Bay. 'Oh no, not really. He… We… He's helping me with my next book, it's research more than anything.'

'Oh, of course, dear, but really, if you want to research dating, you need to go the full hog. Maybe you should see what he is like in bed too, I'm sure that will help you get inspiration.'

Suzanna smiled and walked off leaving Libby wondering how she would even begin to suggest to George the idea of platonic sex.

She ran down the hill towards George and as a man stepped out from one of the shops in front of her, she swerved to try to avoid him, slipped on the icy wet ground and ended up sitting at his feet.

'Shit, are you OK?' the man said, offering her his large hand to help her up. She took his hand and he pulled her to her feet. He was huge – easily the biggest man she had ever seen in her life – and good-looking too, with those gorgeous soft grey eyes and long lashes.

Libby suddenly realised her bum was soaking and probably bruised and her pride was in tatters; this really wasn't the romantic start to her date with George that she had envisaged.

The man was joined by a blonde teenager who looked at her with amusement and George arrived on the scene a second later.

'Are you OK?' the man asked again.

Libby nodded. 'Yes, thank you, sorry I nearly knocked you over.'

'Come on, Lib, we'll be late,' George said, wrapping his arm round her shoulders possessively and flashing a glare at the man who had helped her.

They walked down the hill and Libby heard the girl laugh. 'Jeez Dad, women are literally throwing themselves at your feet.'

'Are you OK?' George asked, softly.

'Yes, I'm fine.'

'I didn't take you for the "swooning at a man" type.'

Libby laughed. 'I didn't take you for the "being jealous over me talking to another man" type either.'

George looked back at the man. 'Looks like he fell out of a bloody Gap commercial.'

'I don't go for big men,' Libby said. 'I go for men with curly hair and a wicked sense of humour.'

'Really?'

'Oh yes,' she teased and George smiled as they walked into the bakery.

Linda Forbes, who ran the bakery with her daughter Polly, had already started her talk and they snuck onto a table at the back hoping she wouldn't notice their lateness.

'What are we doing here?' George hissed as Linda went over the ingredients on the table in front of them and told them all they would get the recipe on a sheet before they went home.

'We're making mince pies.'

'I can make mince pies, jars of mincemeat, ready-made roll-out pastry, job done, or buy a box of six Mr Kiplings. Nobody can beat Mr Kipling.'

'We're making the mince pies from scratch,' Libby whispered back just as they got shushed from a couple right in front of them.

George opened his mouth to speak and she clamped her hand over his mouth.

'So you can use as much or as little of the ingredients in front of you as you like to make the mincemeat,' Linda said. 'There are suggestions on the laminated sheets on your tables but really these are your mince pies so just throw whatever you like into the saucepan and then heat it for about ten minutes or until the ingredients start to bind and become sticky.'

There were some murmurs about the various methods and ingredients the different tables were going to use and Libby released George's mouth.

'So off you go … and for our latecomers,' Linda flashed her and George a smile, 'perhaps you should go and wash your hands first.'

Libby blushed as everyone turned round to look at them, some of the people of the town shaking their heads with disapproval. They quickly moved off to the bathrooms to wash their hands and when they got back people were already throwing ingredients into their saucepans with gay abandon.

'What shall we put in then, George?' Libby asked, rolling up her sleeves.

George looked seriously at all the ingredients in little glass bowls that filled their table. 'Well, currants, sultanas, they're a must surely.' He grabbed the two bowls and tipped them into the saucepan.

'Brandy?' Libby offered the small jug.

George took it from her and poured no more than a teaspoon into the saucepan. She laughed and, taking the jug back off him, poured the rest into the pan.

George laughed. 'Should we just pour everything in then, see how it turns out?'

Libby nodded and they grabbed the chopped apples, the orange zest, the sugar, the apple juice, the cinnamon and the cloves and poured every last ingredient into the saucepan, giggling like school kids. They put the saucepan onto the little camping hob that sat in the middle of their table, turned the temperature up high and leaned over to stare at the ingredients – like the witches in *Macbeth* standing around their cauldron, Libby thought.

Linda, moving between the tables, arrived at theirs. 'Oh, you're on to the cooking part already. Which ingredients did you choose – did you go more apple based or more orange based?'

Libby looked at George guiltily; were they supposed to choose one or the other? Linda followed their eyes to the empty bowls on the table. 'You used everything?'

George nodded reluctantly.

'Even all the cloves? You're only supposed to use half a teaspoonful,' Linda said, in shock.

'We like it strong,' Libby said, trying not to laugh. Their pies were going to taste disgusting. Already the potent smell of cloves was drifting from their saucepan.

Linda laughed. 'Well, remind me not to taste your mincemeat when it's finished. Keep stirring it so it doesn't stick to the pan and you could make a start on making the pastry. The recipe is on the tray with the ingredients.'

Linda walked away as the smell of cloves got stronger, making them cough.

'Shall we try to be a bit more exact with the pastry?' George suggested.

Libby shrugged. 'I suppose so.'

They measured the dry ingredients carefully and then added the butter.

'So we just shove our fingers in and rub the butter into the flour and sugar?' George asked, looking at the butter with some distaste.

'Yep, come on, it's fun.'

Libby started massaging the butter between her fingers and George followed suit, the look of disgust very evident on his face.

She laughed at him. 'It's only your hands, you can wash them afterwards, it's not like it's your face.'

Libby quickly dragged her fingers down his face, leaving buttery smears across his cheeks. He stared at her in horror. With his fingers in the bowl, he flicked his hands up at her, coating her in a snowstorm of flour.

Other couples nearby looked at them with disapproval as Libby shrieked and laughed.

'You're such a child, George Donaldson. Wait till I tell your mum.'

George laughed, not ashamed of his behaviour for one second.

Libby put her hands back in the bowl with George, eyeing him warily just in case he tried anything else for revenge, her fingers brushing up against his for a second, causing his eyes to snap up to hers.

'You know our pie is going to taste like shit,' George said.

'I know but at least it'll be added to the many memories that we'll never forget.'

George looked at her. 'We make a good team, don't we?'

She smiled, feeling her heart fill for him. 'Yeah, we do.'

She watched him as he rubbed the pastry together, a huge lump forming in her throat. She didn't recognise the pain in her chest but she was pretty sure she was falling for him.

The noise of the pub below Amy had gone silent an hour or so before and after a while Seb had been up to see her, to make sure she didn't need anything before he went to bed. She refrained from saying she needed him. But she was still awake now, looking out the skylight at the clear sky peppered with thousands of stars. Judging by the size of the single bed she saw earlier, she bet he was awake too. It was weird being in such close proximity to him and yet still being so far away. How could he kiss her and then still not do anything? She understood about Judith – she had picked up the pieces for him after Marie had died and then he had done the same for her when she fell apart. They were close, Amy got that, and she didn't want to hurt Judith either. She understood the pain of his grief too. Her own dad had died ten years before and it had been utterly heartbreaking, but that's why they should enjoy the time they had with each other while they could. To deny each other when they loved each other so much didn't make sense. Real love didn't come round very often, and when it did, and when you were lucky enough to have it reciprocated, you should grab it with both hands, not run in the other direction.

She stood slowly, stepped over Jack, who was snoring loudly at the foot of the bed, and carefully walked over to the window. She stared out on the view for a moment and opened the window so she could hear the sound of the sea. Sitting on the windowsill, she stuck her head out, feeling the damp, salty air on her cheeks.

'You better not be smoking, Amy Chadwick, my pub is a non-smoking establishment,' said a rough voice in the darkness.

She leaned back in, smiling, and looked around, waiting for her eyes to become accustomed to the gloom again. 'Did you not knock? I could have been naked.'

'I did knock, you must not have heard me.' His tall frame appeared from the shadows. 'And a part of me was kind of hoping you were naked.'

She swung her legs off the windowsill and stood, wincing when it hurt to do so. His arm was suddenly around her waist, supporting her, and she leant into him. 'And what would you have done if I was naked?'

He sighed. 'I don't know, I'd hope I'd have the strength not to do anything.'

She leaned her head against his chest. 'How long do you think we can do this for? This thing between us isn't going to go away.'

'I know, but...'

'What did you come in here for?'

'I couldn't sleep, I'm not sure if it was the hardness of the bed or the fact that you're sleeping just ten metres away from me, or...' he sighed. 'Amy, nearly losing you today scared the crap out of me. And I don't think my heart has stopped pounding since. I'd quite like to hold you for a while.'

'You just want to sleep in your own bed, holding me is just an excuse.'

He pulled away and got into bed, lying exactly where she had been lying moments before. 'I get the best of both worlds – my nice comfy bed and a beautiful woman in my arms.'

She bit her lip, while she watched him. Was he deliberately trying to torture her? She could lie in bed with him, hug him but not make love to him.

'Will you get over here, woman?'

She sighed then slid into the tiny gap he'd left by his side. With a bit of careful rearranging, she lay down with her head on his chest, and he wrapped one arm round her back, the other in her hair, stroking her. And although she thought she would never get to sleep, finally being wrapped in the arms of the man she loved, a few minutes later she was snoring softly.

CHAPTER 12

Amy was standing in the bathroom, trying to remove her nightie. But she had woken that morning feeling so much more stiff and sore than she had been the day before, and she couldn't now lift her arms to get the nightie over her head.

It was early and she'd left Seb asleep in bed. She needed a bath – hopefully that would ease some of the aches and pains.

It had been weird waking up in his arms this morning, lying on top of him as if they had shared a night of passion. It had been almost painful, being so close, but not being allowed to do anything. That had been another reason for her getting up so early; he certainly had more strength of mind than she did. She couldn't lie in bed with him and not touch him.

She whimpered as she tried again, her arms were so stiff, so painful.

Suddenly the bathroom door opened, and Seb was standing there, looking at her in confusion.

'What are you doing?'

'Trying to get my nightie off, but my arms are so sore I can't do it.'

He swallowed then moved into the bathroom. 'Let me help you.'

'I…' she started but he had already pulled the material at her hips and was very gently and carefully sliding the nightie over her head. The nightie slithered out of his fingers to the floor and she was standing there naked before him. He was so close to her, she could feel his heat, his breathing was strangled, his lips so close to hers they were practically touching. She closed the gap and kissed him. For a second, maybe two, his lips responded, he kissed her back. But just as soon as it started, he pulled away and walked out of the bathroom, closing the door firmly behind him.

———

Libby's fingers were moving so quickly across the keyboard, she was surprised steam wasn't coming from them.

After her lovely date with George the night before, the silliness at the bakery and the wonderful moonlit walk along Silver Cove beach afterwards, she'd had trouble sleeping, her thoughts awash with him. So she had got up, switched on her laptop and started writing, eventually crawling into bed at three in the morning.

Now she had been up and writing for hours, even waking up before Alex and Rosie's bed squeaking started, and her back was starting to ache.

She stood up and stretched, just as George walked in.

'Morning.' She smiled at him.

'Hey. I have a proposition for you – a contract if you will,' he said seriously, though his eyes twinkled with mischief as he waved a formal-looking document at her.

'Do I need my agent to look at this? Normally she has to go through any contracts with a fine-tooth comb.'

'I don't think we need to involve outside parties, not yet anyway.'

'Well, let me make some tea and we can discuss it formally over the boardroom table.'

George nodded to accept these conditions and when she returned from the kitchen with two steaming mugs of tea, he was already sitting at the dining table with the contract.

She passed him his mug and sat opposite him.

'In the interest of our dating competition, I've taken the time to draw up a checklist of rules for the perfect second date. You get a point for each one of the rules that's included.'

'Hang on, these are your criteria for a perfect second date, what about mine?' she asked.

'OK, you can look at my list. If there's anything you want to add or change we can discuss terms.'

She looked at the list:

1. *Gift* – *Normally in the form of flowers given at the beginning of the date but can also be in the form of Mars Bars or other such confectionery items.*
2. *Food* – *This could be in the form of something cooked or prepared by one of the participants or the purchasing of food from an establishment such as a restaurant or pub.*
3. *Chat* – *There should be time in the date for at least thirty minutes of talking time. This is not the time to find out about your partner's first pet, or their deepest darkest secret, this is merely enough time for the participants to feel comfortable with idle chat. Maximum one hour of talking.*
4. *The special element* – *Under no circumstances should the date involve going to the cinema, bowling or the pub unless pub falls under category two, see above. If pub is chosen for food it should form a small part of the date and not be the whole date. The special element must be something different that the participants in the date have not done before.*
5. *Fun* – *Both participants in the date must have fun for this category to be ticked. Fun is described as something that is enjoyable and amusing. For this reason both participants must be seen to be smiling for a minimum of ten percent of the date. If the date lasts for four hours then smiling time must be at*

least twenty-four minutes. Both participants do not need to be smiling at the same time.

6. ***Romantic gestures** – This can be in the form of hand-holding, a hug, kiss, or arm round the shoulders. Can also include holding the door open for the date. Minimum of two such gestures.*

7. ***Romantic moments** – This can be in the form of a sunset or an amazing view. Generally considered to be a moment that takes your breath away. Minimum one moment.*

8. ***Additional features** – The moments that are not planned but happen as a circumstance of the day. These moments are measured by those times the participants' hearts raced. For example, a smile that sends the heart aflutter, an accidental touch that sends goosebumps up the participant's arm. The moment when you look into your partner's eyes and realise this is the person you want to spend the rest of your life with. Minimum one feature.*

9. ***Nudity** – Full or partial nudity is acceptable here.*

10. ***Dirty sex** – This can take the form of sex on a table, in a shower, on the sofa, on the floor, in the car or outdoors. Ripping clothes off is a prerequisite so you may wish to wear old clothes that you don't mind getting torn.*

She laughed, loudly. 'This is quite a comprehensive list.'

He nodded, a smile twitching on his lips. 'Well, I wanted to make clear the expectations.'

'You've certainly done that.' She studied the list again. 'I like the chat part, that there should only be a maximum of one hour. We don't want any awkward silences.' She read on. 'How can sex be dirty in a shower?'

'I don't know, it just sounded like somewhere dirty sex would take place.'

'So I can only get ten out of ten for my date last night if I slept with you?'

'Yep.'

'Well then you're only going to get a maximum of nine for your date as well.'

'You don't know that. You haven't experienced the date yet; you might be so bowled over by my date tonight that you jump straight into bed with me at the end. You never know, Lib, it might just be one of those moments, those go-with-the-flow moments.'

'OK, I won't rule it out.'

'Good, that's all that I'm saying, keep an open mind.'

'So how much would my date last night get? I did buy you that Mars Bar when we stopped at the newsagents on the way.'

'I know, that's why it's on the list.' George took the list back and quickly did a mental calculation. 'No nudity and no sex, but you got everything else.'

Libby smiled as she thought about the 'Additional features' rule. Had she done something that caused his heart to flutter? The hug on the beach – had that meant as much to him as it had to her?

'And how much would the island date get?'

'Well, despite me throwing up all of my intestines, and us nearly being killed in the storm, it was still one of the best dates I've ever had. And we had the nudity at the end so nine, although we did agree your island date didn't count as our second date. So I'll have to mark you tonight for your official second date.'

'How long are we going to keep these practice dates going?' George asked and Libby's heart dropped.

'Are you not enjoying them? We can stop if you want.'

George looked alarmed. 'No, of course I'm enjoying them. It's been brilliant so far. I just wondered how far we would take it, whether we would be practising marriage and babies next year.'

Libby laughed. 'How about Christmas Eve, that could be our finale. We have the Christmas Eve ball and there can't be anything more romantic than that. After that, the day after Christmas, you march straight round to Giselle and ask her out. You're very good at this dating thing, I don't know why you're so scared of asking Giselle out, she'd be very lucky to have you.'

'You're very sweet, Lib, but it's different with you. If I was with Giselle, I'd be second guessing my every move. Shall I hold her hand now, what if my hand is sweaty, shall I put my arm round her, shall we have fish and chips for lunch or would she prefer to go somewhere more classy, would she prefer to go somewhere that serves salad, why is she looking at her watch, is she bored, what is she thinking, what shall I say, do I smell OK, does my breath stink, shall I kiss her, what if the kiss isn't very good, if I kiss her where do I put my hands, do I use tongue or not, how long should I kiss for. With you it just sort of works, I don't second guess anything. I wouldn't be this relaxed with Giselle; I'd be a sweaty mess. That's what I'm afraid of.'

'You really think all that stuff?'

He nodded.

Her heart went out to him. 'You're overthinking it, George, you just do what you want to do. If she doesn't like it then she'll let you know one way or another, but at least she will be going out with the real you, not the man you are pretending to be. If you don't hold her hand or kiss her because you're scared of the reaction, then she might go home thinking that you're not very affectionate, that you obviously didn't like her. Just be yourself.'

'OK, but what about all that kiss stuff? The first kiss matters, people have broken up over the first kiss.'

'True, but when Kat first met Big Dave she said it was like kissing a lizard but they've been together for five years now. If

Giselle really likes you and the kiss is crap then she'll just gently teach you how she likes it.'

'Tongue or no tongue?'

'It depends. If it's a sweet tender first kiss then no, if it's a passionate kiss then for me yes, but some women don't really like tongues. Let her lead by example, or if you really want to then maybe just a little bit of tongue and see if she reciprocates.'

'OK, where do I put my hands?'

'Just where it feels right to do so. Round the waist is nice, round the face can be good as well. One hand round the back of the neck is very nice too; the back of the neck is a very sensitive spot.'

'Bum?'

'Sure, some women might like a little stroke, but don't squeeze it. Not on the first date, it's a bit too soon for that. Stuff like that can come later, when you're comfortable with each other.'

'OK, good to know and, erm... what about dirty sex, what would that entail?'

'What?' she asked, sipping her tea.

'I need help with that too, Lib.'

She stared at him. Were they really going to practise having sex? But as shocked as she was that he might be suggesting that, the idea was suddenly very appealing.

—

Seb was downstairs in the pub, bouncing the white cue ball off the far side of the pool table, catching it and bouncing it again.

The pub wouldn't be open for hours yet.

He heard a noise behind him and he turned to see Amy in her robe, her hair wet from the shower. He turned away from her, leaning his hands on the pool table.

'I'm going to stay with Libby for a few days. I can't do this – I thought it would be fun, but it's hell.' He heard her walk closer and then she was by his side, leaning her back against the pool table.

He swallowed. 'I don't want you to go.'

'We both know this isn't working. I can't be here and not touch you, not be touched by you, it's driving me mad.'

'I agree. I can't have you here and not touch you.'

'You think I should go then.'

He turned to face her. He put a hand on her waist and slid her along the edge of the pool table so she was standing in front of him, her eyes were wary.

'I was actually thinking of touching you.' He slid a hand underneath her robe, rubbing his thumb over her nipple.

To his surprise, though, she slapped his hand away. 'Don't do that, don't tease me. You can have me, you know that, but don't tease me with what could be, it's not fair. You can either have all of me or none of me.'

With blood burning through his veins, he undid her robe. 'Then I'll take all of you.'

———

'Sex?' Libby asked. 'You want me to help you with that?'

George nodded and she choked on her tea. 'How do you suppose I help you with that, we go into the bedroom now, roll around for the next few hours and then I'll mark you out of ten for that too?'

'No, of course not.'

Libby couldn't help the feeling of disappointment that suddenly crashed through her.

'I just need a few pointers,' George explained. 'What do women go for these days?'

'I can't help you with that, sex is very personal. I have no idea what Giselle would like in bed. Women go for lots of different things. Some like it hard and fast, some like it soft and gentle. Some women like it on top, some like the man to go on top, some like oral sex a lot, some can't stand it, some like anal sex, sex in the shower, against a wall, on the kitchen table, on the stairs, outdoors, indoors, places where you're likely to get caught...'

He visibly paled, looking suddenly panic-stricken.

'...and if you believe some of these magazines, some people go for all sorts of positions, the cobra, the elephant, the palm tree, the crab, the scales, the—'

'Hang on, hang on, are we still talking about sex here?'

She smiled at his naivety, and nodded. 'Your Giselle might be into whips, handcuffs and gimp masks for all I know.'

He sighed. 'What's wrong with the good old-fashioned missionary position? OK, OK, you look relatively normal, how do you like it?'

She smirked at the 'relatively normal' comment. 'I guess I'm old-fashioned really, sex for me is really intimate. Lots of people close their eyes when they have sex, and I don't know why they do that. Are they imagining they are with someone else? I always keep my eyes open; I want to look into the eyes of the one I'm with. I'm not really bothered which position, I just want to be held really, I want to be stroked and kissed all over, sex for me should be beautiful and tender and soft,' she said, wistfully, staring off into space.

'Sounds perfect,' he said.

'I bet sex with you would be good, you can get a feel for how someone would make love by the type of person they are.'

There was a stunned silence from him then he laughed, and she sensed he did so to break the tension.

'What do you like in bed?' Libby asked.

He took a deep breath, clearly to prepare himself to answer that question. 'Well, you know I've only ever been with one woman?'

She smiled; she found that so endearing.

'Yeah, don't laugh. It's just the way things turned out. Josie was my childhood sweetheart, we were together since we were sixteen, married when we were twenty and divorced when we were twenty-eight. There hasn't been anyone since.'

'So what was sex like with Josie, before she cheated on you? I bet it was beautiful, sex with the woman you loved.'

'I think sex was ultimately the reason we broke up,' he sighed. 'I guess neither of us really knew what we were doing when we started having sex. At first we were just fumbling around, but then later it was beautiful. I used to hold her in my arms, and kiss her and to just feel her under me, her hot skin against mine, was the most amazing feeling. To watch her come, to see her getting pleasure out of something that I was doing was the best feeling ever.'

Libby smiled.

'But slowly she seemed to lose her appetite for it. She was never really a sexual person, it would always be me that instigated sex, but over the years she just didn't want to do it any more. I was OK about it, at first – I just wanted her to be happy. We were so good together, in many other ways, maybe sex wasn't the be all and the end all. It turns out she was getting sex elsewhere, with Chase Kent, the sexiest-looking bloke I've ever seen. I'm not gay, as you know, but even I could appreciate how bloody good-looking he was. When we finally broke up she said that sex was amazing with Chase, that he was so adventurous. All the things you spoke about before, sex in the shower, in the garden, on the beach, they'd done all of that. But she never said anything to me that she thought our sex was boring. In fact, we'd watched this porn film together once; this couple were having sex everywhere. I suggested that we could try some of those positions. She laughed and said sex wasn't like that, that most of the positions looked really uncomfortable and she was more than happy doing it in bed like a normal person. If she'd said something I would have done something different, I would have gladly done all those things, we could have experienced them for the first time together. I just thought she wasn't interested in sex, and I didn't push it. I just wanted her to be happy. I was gutted, when I found out. Not just because she had cheated on me, but that it was sex with me that was so bad that I had driven her away.'

'Oh George, you can't think like that, you can only grow sexually if the person you are with wants to grow with you. With you just wanting to make her happy and her not saying anything to you, you would never have changed, why would you?'

'Lib, it's nice of you to say but if you cook me carrot soup and I tell you I love it, you're not going to cook me carrot soup every time I come round, are you? You might try tomato soup one day, onion soup the next. Josie got carrot soup almost every day for the first few years. No wonder she went elsewhere for sex. She was bored stupid by it.'

'She should have said something, men aren't mind readers. In fact, my experience of men shows they don't pick up on subtleties at all.'

'Well,' he sighed, 'I've kind of been put off sex a bit since then. What if the next woman I'm with finds me boring as well? What if I really am crap in bed?'

'You won't be. You're lovely and sweet and kind, I bet you make love like that as well. Any woman would appreciate that. The fun stuff can come later.'

'But what if Giselle is into all that weird stuff? What if, during the throes of passion, she shouts, "Hey, big boy, do the cobra on me." What do I do then?'

Libby smiled to herself at the 'big boy' reference. 'Well then you just have to be honest and say something like "Sounds lovely, but you're going to have to point me in the right direction, I'm not sure I know that one."'

'Won't she mind, that I'm completely clueless?'

'Nah, she'll like to educate you, to teach you in the ways of Giselle.'

George looked doubtful.

'Look.' She stood up. 'If you're worried, why don't you have a look through these?' Libby went to the bottom shelf of her bookcase and picked up a pile of magazines. 'This one does position of the week, it gives you step-by-step instructions on how to achieve it. This one has tips for how to please your woman in bed and this one has tips on how to please your man in bed – she should be doing stuff for you too, it shouldn't just be about making her happy. This one has tips for giving good oral sex, a lot of women like oral sex, receiving it, especially. Ooh, this one references the Kama Sutra. There are some mad ones in there; one involves some pulley-type system where the maids lower the woman onto the man's penis.'

He looked stunned as she handed him the pile.

'And if that's not enough, read a few of these erotic fiction books. There's *Belinda and the Bulge*, *Sex on the Beach* – that one's particularly good, there's a cracking sex scene in there involving a hammock.' Her hand hovered over her own books. She hadn't wanted him to see them before because George knew the real her and she didn't want him to read who she had pretended to be for the last fourteen years. But while her books weren't erotica they did have sex scenes in them and George might find them more of a gentle introduction to sex in fiction. 'Try these: *The Night of the Storm*, *Après Ski* and *Cocktails on Ice*.'

George handled the books carefully, like they were bombs about to explode. 'You read this stuff?'

She smiled. 'I write it.'

His eyes bulged. 'You write porn?'

'No, mine aren't erotic fiction, they're just romance with sex, there's a big difference. The top three are mine. I am Libby Joseph by day, Eve Loveheart by night.'

'You write porn?' he managed again. 'You've just been telling me that you like to be held, kissed softly, gently and all the while you're writing this kind of stuff.'

She shrugged. 'It's not real though, that's not what sex is really like, it's fake.'

'But women read this stuff and then expect it from us poor men. This is just false advertising.'

'Women know this stuff isn't real. Besides, most women don't actually want stuff like that.'

He was quiet for a moment as he stared at the books she had given him, then he stood up. 'Well I should go, let you get on with your work. Thanks for… this.' He gestured with his collection of porn. 'I'll see you later.'

She nodded and watched him go, wistfully. Sex with him would be amazing.

—

Amy clung to Seb, her screams still echoing around the pool room, her body shaking as he held her to him. The man was certainly good with his hands. He had kissed her first, done nothing but kiss her, but then his hands had explored, caressed, finding the exact areas that made her weak. He had sat her on the edge of the pool table and as he kissed her deeply he had stroked the one spot that had sent desire and need crashing through her. She had wanted their first time together to be a mutual gratification, both simultaneously taking what was needed, but he was still fully clothed when she clung to him, screams of pleasure ripping from her throat.

'Lie down,' he ordered her, somewhere in the distance.

'I don't think I can move,' she muttered, into the side of his neck.

He carefully disentangled himself from her arms and started to undress in front of her.

Suddenly feeling nervous, she looked away, but then she looked back. She had waited too long to deny herself this pleasure now. His body was beautiful, toned, muscular and long.

He moved closer, gently pushing her legs open so he was standing between them.

'I think you'll be more comfortable lying down, but I'll take you here if need be,' he said, his eyes watching hers as he moved his hands to her hips.

She smiled and lay down and he climbed up onto the pool table too, lying down on top of her, kissing her deeply. His mouth moved to her throat, then her breasts, his tongue hot against her flesh. His mouth was back on hers as he thrust into her, fast and hard. She flung her arm out, knocking a glass off the side of the table, where it smashed on the floor. He moved against her again, lifting his mouth from hers for just a second.

'I'm taking that from your pay,' he growled.

'I don't care,' she laughed, and he smirked as he kissed her again.

—

Amy watched Judith knocking on the door of the pub from behind the upstairs curtain. Despite Seb's best efforts, word that she was staying there had obviously spread fast and Judith clearly didn't like it and had come to tell him just that. Really, Amy thought, she should just go down completely naked and open the door. Any misconceptions that Judith was harbouring or hoping for would be dispelled there and then. Anyone looking at her now would know she'd just had sex, amazing, fantastic sex, on his pool table of all places. She had that glow about her.

She smiled now as she thought of him. Yes, not even Judith banging angrily on the door below could snap her out of this good mood.

—

Judith was walking back through White Cliff Bay when she spotted Seb carrying a bag of shopping and a bouquet of flowers. It wasn't hard to guess who the flowers were for, especially when he looked so guilty when he saw her.

'Seb, I just came to see you, do you have time for a cup of tea and some cake?'

'Of course, is everything OK?' He ushered her into Linda's bakery. Straight away the smell of mince pies and gingerbread assaulted her senses. Everyone was celebrating Christmas, but Judith still didn't feel the season held anything to celebrate. He ordered them both a mug of tea and they sat down at a table.

'It's about Amy ... I...'

Seb sighed. 'Why do you hate her so much?'

'I...' The directness of his question threw her, not least because his tone was protective. There was so much she wanted to say to him. He had to know that her reasons for not wanting him to be with Amy had nothing to do with Marie or dishonouring her memory, but because she wanted the best for him, and Amy wouldn't give him that.

'Do you love her?'

Judith had his full attention now, his eyes were ablaze, but she couldn't identify the emotions playing across his face.

'No, I don't.'

'Are you sleeping with her?'

'No.'

She strongly suspected he was lying to her and that hurt her too.

'I don't think you should see her.'

He reached out for her hand. 'I know it must have been difficult for you to see me kissing her the other night, I understand that the prospect of me moving on must be hard. I never want to do anything to hurt you, but who I go out with is my business.'

'Amy's not good for you, you must see that.'

'Why is she not good for me?'

'Well amongst many, many reasons, one of the worst is that she's a prostitute.'

He stared at her in shock for a second then burst out laughing. 'Judith, that's ridiculous. I know you hate her but you can't start spreading rumours about her, and to be honest I expected more of you than—'

'I'm not lying,' she said, affronted. 'I don't like the girl, I admit that. After what she let her nephew do to my gnomes last year, and then the way she embarrassed me in front of my friends by running round her garden naked and dressed as a penis, and after what she did to Philippe, I think the girl is vile, but I would never make something like that up.'

Seb stopped laughing, suddenly taking her seriously. 'What makes you think she's a prostitute?'

'Every Tuesday morning Jackson Cartwright turns up at her house. She opens the door, only in her dressing gown, they go upstairs, she closes the bedroom curtains, and then he leaves after an hour, and pays her on the doorstep. Sometimes she doesn't bother to close her curtains, and I've seen her wandering around naked in her room and he's been in there as well. I mean, I've not actually seen them having sex, but I think it's pretty obvious what they're getting up to.'

Seb's face was very readable now, he was hurt and angry. Judith hadn't wanted that but he had a right to know.

'I'm sorry,' she said quietly.

'I've got to get back. The pub opens in an hour and there's lots to do.'

She watched him go, his whole body tense, and she couldn't help the relief that flooded through her.

—

Seb drove back to the pub, his mind elsewhere. Amy had a past, he knew that, knew there'd been other men before him, but for her to prostitute herself... She had a lot of jobs though to pay the bills – had she resorted to prostitution as well? He'd always assumed she wasn't short of money, that she could have more shifts in any of her jobs. Hell, he'd have given her more shifts if she was short of cash.

He pulled up in the small pub car park and got out, scowling at his bedroom window. Maybe Judith had got the wrong end of the stick. But what else would Amy be doing naked in her bedroom with a man who then paid her afterwards? It made him feel sick to think of this Jackson, he thought contemptuously, shagging her, paying her for sex, taking advantage of her and her desperation for money. He knew Jackson – not very well, but well enough to think he was a decent bloke. Obviously Seb had been wrong about him.

He walked in and realised Sally had already opened up; she had keys so she could do just that if she arrived when he wasn't there. Jack was sitting watching her astutely and Seb guessed she was eating a packet of crisps and smuggling some to him.

'Are you OK down here for a bit?' he asked, moving to the bottom of the stairs. 'I need to send some emails, make some phone calls regarding stock.'

'Yeah sure, you go ahead,' Sally said, writing the specials board in her beautiful sloping handwriting.

'And stop feeding him crisps.' He gestured to Jack.

Sally turned and laughed at him. 'You caught me.'

As she turned back, he watched her. She was very pretty, young, tanned, blonde hair. She reminded him a little of Marie, when he'd first met her, in looks anyway. It would be so much easier if he'd fallen in love with Sally instead of Amy. Why was love so inconvenient, not giving any thought to the problems it caused as it weaved its spell over the heart?

He walked up the stairs and found Amy asleep in his bed. Yesterday had probably done more damage than he'd thought and her body needed time to heal. He smiled; either that or he'd worn her out that morning.

He gently shook her awake. She blinked a few times, then seeing him she smiled.

'I need to talk to you,' he said, sitting down in the chair on the other side of the room, so he wouldn't be tempted to touch her.

Her face fell, and she sat up, holding the sheet to her chest. 'Please don't tell me this morning was a once only thing, that it can never happen again, I couldn't take it.'

'I hope not. Listen… you know you're the first since Marie, that there has never been anyone else?'

She nodded in confusion.

He sighed. 'I'm falling for you.'

'I love you too, you know that,' she said, a frown creasing her forehead.

'Yes, well I thought so... I know there have been other men for you but...'

'There's been no one since I fell in love with you, no one for six months.'

He swallowed. She had been in love with him for six months, he had denied her for all that time but she'd never given up, never found someone else.

'I guess what I'm saying is that I would hope that whilst we're together there won't be anyone else for you.'

A look of hurt crossed her face. 'I would never... I may have been with a few men in my time, but I never screwed around. I don't cheat on my boyfriends and I never will.'

'I know, I didn't think you were the sort to sleep around. I'm sorry, I...' This was so difficult. He could hardly come out and ask her if she was a prostitute. He didn't think she was the sort to do that either, it was a ridiculous accusation, but what else would she be doing in her bedroom, naked with a man who paid her?

'Are you... OK for money?'

She pulled her knees up to her chest protectively, and he knew he'd struck a chord.

'What's happened? This morning, you were all over me, couldn't keep your hands off me. Now you sit over there, afraid to touch me, accusing me of sleeping around and asking me if I'm OK for money. Who have you been talking to?' Then her face cleared. 'Judith, she told you about Jackson, didn't she, told you that I'm a prostitute?'

'Yes.'

'And you want to know if it's true?'

He didn't answer but his silence spoke volumes.

The look of hurt that crossed her face pierced straight through his heart, but it was quickly replaced by anger. She got out of bed, completely naked, and started throwing her things back in her bag, stuffing them in so angrily that the bag ripped around the zip.

'Amy, what are you doing?'

'What does it look like I'm doing? I'm leaving. I'm not sharing a bed with someone who has so much contempt and so little regard for me.'

He quickly got up and moved round to the other side of the bed to stop her, but she pushed him away when he came close.

'Amy, stop, please, this is ridiculous, talk to me.' He caught her wrist, but she slapped his hand away. Grabbing her shoulders instead, he swung her round to face him, and was surprised to see tears in her eyes. Apart from in the car after the accident yesterday, he had never seen her cry before. 'Tell me then, tell me how wrong I've got it?'

'No, I won't tell you anything, you can make your own mind up about me, which clearly, with a little help from Judith, you already have. I've seen the looks that Judith gives me when Jackson leaves, I know what she thinks. I'm a slut, you've slept with a slut, and now you're wondering how much I'll charge you for this morning's antics. Well, I tell you what, darling – that one was on the house.'

She shoved him hard and threw on a knee-length blue wrap dress, which she quickly tied around her waist.

'God damn it, Amy, what am I supposed to think? A man turns up every week and you go up to the bedroom for an hour, closing the curtains. Judith has seen you walking around naked in the bedroom whilst he's in there and he pays you for it after.'

She sat on the bed and pulled on a pair of black leather knee-high boots. He was so turned on right now, her anger, her being completely naked under the dress, now these boots, did she have any idea what she did to him?

'You're supposed to trust me. If you loved me, you'd trust me.'

'You've not given me anything to trust, you've not told me anything. If you tell me you're not a prostitute I'll believe you – even better than that, tell me exactly why Jackson Cartwright is in your bedroom whilst you're naked and then I can truly trust you.'

She stood up. 'I told you there hasn't been anyone else in the last six months, longer than that in fact. No one has kissed me or touched me since I fell in love with you. That includes anyone that might pay for the privilege. But that isn't enough for you…'

'It's enough.' He was actually starting to panic now, he couldn't lose her.

She stared at him with contempt then walked past him to grab the last few things. 'I'm not going to have a relationship with anyone who thinks so little of me.'

He caught her hand as she walked back past him again. 'I'm sorry, I really am. I trust you. I guess I got scared that this didn't mean as much to you as it did to me.'

She stared at him for a moment, then took his hand still holding hers and pressed it to her heart. It was thundering against her chest. 'That's how much you mean to me.'

He bent his head and softly kissed her chest, between his fingers, then lifted his head to kiss her on the mouth, but she put a finger on his lips to stop him.

'I'm sorry,' he said and was relieved to see the fire in her eyes lessen slightly. He put his arms round her waist. 'Look, if you walked into my bedroom and found me walking round naked in front of another girl, would you just smile and walk back out again? If you saw me then paying the girl would you still be smiling?'

'I'd trust you.' Her voice was calmer now, quieter.

'You'd never ask me about it, you'd just carry on as normal? Because that's all I was doing – I was asking, not accusing.'

'No, I wouldn't ask.'

He smirked. 'Bullshit.'

She looked away so he wouldn't spot the smile, but he'd already seen it.

'OK, I'd kill her, then I'd kill you, then I'd ask questions later.'

He laughed.

She looked back at him and sighed. 'I don't want to tell you now what it is I do with Jackson. I don't want to see that same look of disgust that I see when Judith looks at me in your eyes. Telling you doesn't do it justice, but I will show you. Four o'clock, Saturday afternoon at White Cliff Bay town hall.'

He frowned slightly.

'Trust me.'

'Does this mean that you're going to stay?'

She looped her arms round his neck. 'What will you offer me if I do?'

He moved his hands up her back and deftly undid the bow holding the dress together, then pushed the dress off her shoulders, letting it fall to the floor. 'Anything you want.'

She kissed him, and he pushed her gently against the wall, his hands wandering down her thighs.

'Anything?' she asked, already undoing the buttons on his shirt.

'Anything, on one condition.'

She closed her eyes as his hands explored her body. 'Mmmm, what's that?'

'You keep those boots on.'

She laughed loudly but then the laugh was gone as he found the one place that had made her scream so loudly earlier that morning.

—

George was waiting in his lounge, nervously. This was his fourth date with Libby, even though it was technically their second date – or was it their third as his beautiful island date didn't officially count? Either way, he was damned sure he was going to get a kiss out of it. He had been thinking about it all day. They had held hands, he had held the door open for her, hugged her, danced with her and did all the things normally associated with a date apart from a kiss. So tonight he was going to get one.

He had thought about asking her to kiss him, as part of his research. She could rate him out of ten maybe, but then he thought she might say no and that would be awkward.

So he had thought about creating a romantic moment where, if it had been a real date, he could kiss her. And then after, it could easily be put down to research, going through the motions of a date; it could easily be laughed off. But there might not be any romantic moments tonight.

So he had decided he would do it now, when she came to call for him. He would greet her as he would do any other date and then kiss her. But now he had decided it, he was a bag of nerves; his palms were sweaty, his heart thundering in his chest. What if he was a crap kisser? But if he was bad, she would be sweet enough to teach him how to do it, how she liked it, which could only mean more kissing.

So he would just grab her and kiss her and…

There was Libby's door. She was coming.

He quickly wiped his palms on his jeans and opened the door. She was standing right in front of him, gesturing to her flat, her mouth open about to speak and he bent his head down and kissed her.

CHAPTER 13

Libby stood frozen in shock for a moment, her words still trapped in her throat, so as he kissed her, a noise came out of her mouth that sounded like 'amerghhst'. She wondered if this was what it was like to pass out, to faint. Her mind had shut down, all thoughts went out of her head, she wasn't aware of anything, there was nothing else but his hot lips moving against hers, his hands on her face. Her hands moved almost instinctively to his waist, her heart pounding in her ears, and just as her brain kicked into life, just as she moved her lips against his, just as she started to move her tongue into his mouth, he released her.

'Hi,' he said, sheepishly, still holding her face.

'Hi,' she said, her voice coarse. She felt a stupid grin cross her face and could do nothing to stop it. She cleared her throat and tried to find something else to say, but her head was blank. 'Hi,' she said again, when nothing else was forthcoming.

'Was that OK?' He stepped back, his eyes suddenly anxious.

'What?' There had been something she had been going to say, but all that was gone now.

'As the start of our date, was it too soon, too intimate?'

Her mind started to clear, the fog suddenly lifting. 'Our date, yes of course, I… I… no, a second date would probably be the right time for a first kiss. Though maybe not at the beginning, normally at the end. If you kiss like that you'd probably not actually get on the date, I'd be pushing you back into your flat and grappling you onto the sofa.'

She touched her lips nonchalantly. God, she had to step back away from him just to stop herself from doing just that.

'Really?' He grinned. 'And… my technique?'

What had his technique been like? It had taken her so long to catch up with what he was doing and then it was over. She wanted more, she knew that. She wanted to kiss him back properly this time, not just stand there with her mouth half open.

'I… don't think it went on long enough for me to judge that,' she said, awkwardly, suddenly hoping he would give her a second chance.

To her absolute delight he stepped forward, bending his head to kiss her again just as a flash of blonde hair caught her eye at the bottom of the steps leading up to the flats. Giselle.

Libby quickly pushed George back before Giselle saw them. He looked disappointed and hurt but realisation crossed his face as the front door swung open. Giselle smiled at them both as she went up the stairs. The last thing Libby wanted was for these practice dates to ruin George's chances with Giselle, although the far more selfish side of her wanted to carry them on forever. Christmas Eve was in four days and then they would stop and she would hand over her best friend to the woman upstairs. She suddenly couldn't help the feeling that she would also be handing over the other half of her heart.

They heard Giselle's door close upstairs.

'Should we…?' George looked like he didn't know whether to kiss her or not. The moment had gone.

'How about if the moment grabs you tonight – one of those "go with the flow" moments you were talking about – you take it. And I'll mark you out of ten on it if you do.'

'And maybe, if the moment doesn't present itself whilst we are at the ski centre, we could come back and… practise kissing later.'

Libby smiled at this new confidence that was starting to bloom. George would never have kissed her a week ago or tried to plan a session of kissing either.

'Maybe,' she said, noncommittally.

She honestly didn't know how much further she could take these practice dates. She had never fallen in love before, but she knew she had never been with a man who evoked such feelings in her. It didn't feel like he was her friend any more, it was more than that. Her heart was filled with him. She wanted to touch him, to be touched by him and not just in the sense of sleeping with him, although she did want that too, but she wanted to hug him, be held by him. She wanted to spend every spare second with him. All her worries about trusting someone enough to be with them for the rest of her life hadn't even reared their head when she was with George. Every romantic moment she was spending with George was another step closer to falling in love with him. If she was going to stay, would they still be able to be best friends at the end of this? Did he have any interest in her at all? And if he didn't, would it break her heart to watch him walk away with Giselle?

George's voice interrupted her thoughts. 'We really should go or we'll be late again.'

—

Libby laughed as she watched George climb up the slope towards her, shaking the snow out of his hair. Despite falling off the sledge every time he hit the bottom of the slope, he still had the biggest grin on his face. She had an overwhelming urge to hug him, so in the spirit of the date she flung both arms round his back as she leaned her head on his chest. He didn't even bat an eye as he hugged her back.

George had pulled out every stop, making sure that every item on the list was ticked off. A gift of a teddy dressed in a full ski suit and goggles was stuffed inside her locker which he had presented to her with his 'five days before Christmas' song. They had shared a portion of chips before their sledging session had started. And as for the part of the checklist that mentioned looking at the person she was with and realising she wanted to spend the rest of her life with them, she knew she was already there.

'Thank you for tonight, I've had the best time,' Libby said.

George kissed her forehead. 'Me too. Last go. Shall we go down together?'

'Won't we be too heavy?'

He shrugged. 'It'll be fun though.'

She nodded and he sat on the back of the sledge and she sat in between his legs. He wrapped his arms around her and they used their legs to push themselves off. They zoomed off down the slope and, where Libby thought the extra weight would slow them down, it had the complete opposite effect and made them go much faster than she had ever gone before on her own.

She laughed and screamed before the scream died in her throat as they began to head for a bank of snow with no sign of stopping or slowing down. The sledge hit the bank, slid to the top and deposited them both over the edge. Libby hit the soft snow on the other side hard and a second later George landed on top of her.

They were hidden there between the snow bank and a poster advertising skiing lessons and she stared up at her best friend with a smile.

'Are you OK?' he asked, gently brushing the hair from her face but making no move to get off her.

She nodded and before she could say anything else he kissed her. This time she was prepared for it, she had seen the softness and the intention in his eyes as he looked at her. The taste of him was exquisite, his lips were soft and his wonderful warm scent was a heady mix. She ran her hands round the back of his neck, fingering his curls, but before she had a chance to relax into it, there was a polite cough from nearby and they quickly pulled apart.

One of the instructors was peering over the bank, smirking at them with amusement.

'Sorry to interrupt but we're closing up now and although I'm sure you'd like to be locked in here all night, it can get quite cold after a while.'

George quickly scrabbled up and held out a hand to pull her up too.

'Shall we go home?'

Libby nodded as they walked towards the door, still feeling the taste of him on her lips. There really was no way back from this now.

—

On the way back from the ski centre George drove through the town of White Cliff Bay. It was late, snow was falling and the streets were almost deserted.

Libby was silent next to him; she hadn't said a word since the kiss, leaving him wondering if he should have done it. She had kissed him back though, there was no doubt about that and she had seemed to be enjoying it as much as he was. It was too much though – the lines of their friendship were blurring so much it was hard to see what was for practice and what was real any more.

'Look!' Libby shouted, snapping him out of his reverie.

On the side of the road a man was loading two live reindeer into the back of a horse trailer. There was a large sleigh on wheels nearby.

'Oh yes, I heard there was someone in town doing reindeer sleigh rides,' George said, relieved that they were speaking again but annoyed slightly that she had spotted it – it had ruined the surprise slightly for what he had planned for the next few days.

Libby turned to him accusingly. 'And you didn't think to mention it?'

He laughed. 'I think it's for children. But if you want that could be one of our dates.'

'I'd love that.'

They drove down the hill towards their home, lapsing into an uneasy silence again. They parked up and walked back into the block of flats.

'Want to come and watch a movie?' George asked, hoping to get things back onto normal ground again.

Libby yawned and it was very obvious it wasn't genuine. 'I'm actually really tired, so I'll catch you tomorrow.'

She waved at him and disappeared into her flat, leaving George feeling hurt and confused. He had kissed her and now she was pushing him away.

—

Seb slowly disentangled himself from Amy's arms and got dressed. He had persuaded her to call in sick again today, so where she would normally be up and out by now, she was still sleeping in his bed and he liked it a lot. Holding her whilst she slept, waking up to her, the thought of coming back from his walk with Jack and making love to her again, he could get used to this.

He sat down and watched her.

Fear still circled at the edges of his heart but when he was with her it all just went away. At the moment only a handful of people knew about their relationship and by keeping it secret it was almost like he was keeping it safe. By not admitting how much he loved and cared about her, it meant that she couldn't be taken from him. He rubbed his face, sighing with defeat. Losing Marie had messed him up spectacularly.

Could he ever truly embrace a future with her or would he always be looking over his shoulder for the grim reaper?

Suddenly his mobile phone rang on the drawers next to the bed. He moved to grab it before it woke Amy up but it was too late, her eyes snapped open at the shock.

He looked at the caller ID and saw it was his sister. Panic raced through him – why would she be ringing so early? Amy wasn't the only one who had to live with his fears, his family bore the brunt of it too.

He answered it and heard a soft giggle on the other end which was instantly recognisable and immediately melted his fears as he remembered what day it was.

'Uncle Seb, it's me,' came the sweet voice of his niece, Angel.

He sat down on the bed, next to Amy, leaning against the headboard. 'Hey Angel, Happy Birthday.'

Amy stretched, grabbed her own phone and sat next to him as she quickly read an email.

'Thank you for my present,' Angel said. 'I love it.'

'Oh, I'm so glad you like it.'

Amy was smiling at something in the email; it was obviously good news.

'It blows snowflakes from my wrist just like Elsa. And with the crown I feel like a real princess.'

'You are, Princess Angel, I shall bow and curtsey to you when I see you.'

Angel let out a squeal of giggles. 'I might turn you into a snowman if you don't.'

'You will? Now that's no way to treat your favourite uncle.'

'Are you coming to my party today? We have jelly and ice cream and chocolate cake with bits on the top.'

'I do love jelly and ice cream, I wouldn't miss it for the world.'

'Will you play Pass the Parcel with us?'

He smiled. 'Of course.'

He was aware that Amy was now looking at him with a big grin on her face.

'I love you, Uncle Seb, I'll see you later.'

'Love you too, Angel.'

He hung up and looked at Amy who was smiling hugely.

'What?'

'Was that your niece?'

'Yes. Angel.'

'Angel is such a pretty name, is it because she was born at Christmas?'

'I think it was more that she came along when they had all but given up hope of having children. My sister, Rebecca, had five miscarriages before she fell pregnant with Angel. I don't know where she found the courage from to keep trying when every time would end in heartbreak.'

'Because if you want something more than you want to breathe, you keep trying regardless of your fears or the consequences.'

He stared at her, knowing that she was right. Some things were worth fighting for.

'What was in your email that made you smile so much?'

'You know I do this Cancer Awareness work? Well, on Wednesday I was dressed as a penis to bring awareness of testicular cancer and the importance of having regular checks. I had to hug all these men and hand out leaflets.'

He smirked at the thought of it.

'When I was chasing this one man, I tripped up and ended up flooring him, then my hair got caught in his belt and he couldn't get away. He was so embarrassed by being molested by this giant penis. Anyway he went home and told his wife and she said if that wasn't a sign that he should get checked out, she didn't know what was. She's a doctor at St Mary's, the private hospital on the far side of Port Cardinal, and she got him checked out that afternoon. He was mortified, being checked out by the girl who had been bridesmaid at his wedding. His wife made him go through all these tests and even her friend thought it was a bit extreme, but they actually found micro traces of cancer, very small, just a few cells. He was gutted, but because they've caught it so early, a simple operation will probably eradicate it. He's going to talk through his options with the doctor, but they're confident that it's treatable. He emailed Mia to say thanks which she passed on to me. If it hadn't been for me it might have gone unnoticed and untreated for years. I actually made a difference; it's such an amazing feeling.'

Seb looked at her, her eyes bright with excitement, and his heart swelled with love for her. He leaned forward, cupping her face in his hand and kissed her softly. 'You do make a difference, not just in your cancer work, but to your friends and to me. You're healing me, making me stronger.'

She smiled, her eyes soft with love for him.

'I know you have this thing down the town hall this afternoon, but do you fancy going to a kids' birthday party at lunchtime? It will be loud and noisy but my sister makes the best jelly and ice cream and I'd really like you to meet them.'

'I'd love to. You're so good with her. Your conversation made me smile so much.'

He smiled, sadly. 'I always wanted children. That was one of the things me and Marie would disagree on, I wanted them, she didn't – she thought she was too young. And now… it's too late.'

'It isn't too late … Well, it's too late for you and Marie but not too late for you – you could still have that. We could still have that… one day.'

'I'm not sure I can give you that. The thought of losing you terrifies me, the thought of losing our baby is not something I can even bear to think about.'

Amy shifted so she was straddling him, facing him eye to eye.

'No one knows what tomorrow will bring, but that's why we need to enjoy what we have now. Life is for living, it's for jelly and ice cream and spending time with loved ones, it's for long walks on the beach with a fat retriever, it's for dancing in the rain, it's for amazing sex and making a difference, it's for making every second count. This is all new for us and I understand you are scared but you're going to have to grow some balls and man up. If we are going to be together then we are going to have children so you're going to have to deal with that. And if you can't then you need to tell me. You can't live your life in shadow, afraid to step into the sun. And I won't live like that either.'

Seb swallowed down the lump of emotion that was sticking in his throat. He couldn't let her walk away when he had only just found her. He tried to change the subject away from the sudden fear of losing her, but this time not through death but his own stupid stubbornness.

'Any more clichés you wish to share?'

'Life is a cliché, Seb. You're born, you die and you try to have as much fun as you can in between.'

'Tell me more about this amazing sex we could have.'

She smiled. 'I'm happy to enjoy the next few days with you. Christmas is in four days and I'd like to spend it with you. After that you need to make a decision about our future and how much you want it.'

She kissed him and, as with every time they were together, the fear just faded away. He needed her in his life. He just had to find the courage to take what was on offer.

—

Libby woke to the smell of bacon and she smiled with love for George. It was weird knowing that she was falling in love with her best friend, after all this time. She had never fallen in love before, she had never allowed herself to, but somehow her feelings for George had sneaked up on her without her knowing. She still didn't know what she was going to do about it or whether her feelings would be reciprocated, even if she did do something about it. Could she stay if he turned her down and watch him go out with Giselle instead? George was a large part of her wanting to stay, but he wasn't the only reason. Beyond George, Amy and Kat were the first friends she had ever had, her relationships with the people of the town were also something she hadn't had before. She wanted to stay but the whole George thing was so complicated and really it shouldn't be at all.

She got up, wrapped herself in her robe and padded out to the kitchen where George was dishing up bacon onto doorstep-sized pieces of bread.

'This is nice,' Libby said, following him into the lounge.

'Well, I just thought…' He trailed off and she knew he was still thinking about that incredible kiss the night before. It was all she had been thinking about as well.

She sat down opposite him and he watched her carefully.

'We're OK, aren't we?' George asked.

'Of course we are.'

He rubbed his hand round the back of his neck. 'You feel weird about the kiss?'

She didn't, not really. The kiss had been perfect and beautiful. What was awkward was she was slowly falling in love with her best friend and he was blissfully unaware about her feelings for him.

She reached across the table and took his hand. 'I don't feel weird about it. I'm worried that it means something different to you than it does to me.'

He stared at her in shock but he didn't say anything else. She relinquished her hold on his hand and turned her attention back to her sandwich.

'We'll always be friends though, right, George? Whatever happens between me and you and Giselle or whoever, whether I stay or go, that won't change, will it?'

He shook his head. 'I don't want to lose you.'

She nodded, satisfied by his answer. She just had to pluck up the courage to tell him her feelings at some point.

He focussed on eating his sandwich and she switched her attention to the light flakes of snow swirling past the window. Outside there was a black motorbike, a beautiful old classic Honda Shadow.

'Whose is the bike?' Libby asked.

'I think it's Giselle's.'

Of course it was.

'I do love a woman on a motorbike, there's something incredibly sexy about that,' George said.

'I used to ride a bike,' Libby said, wondering why she felt like she now had to compete with Giselle for his affection. 'A red Ducati.'

George looked surprised. 'You had a Ducati?'

'Yes, it was my pride and joy, a big shiny red beast of a machine. Until I had an accident and completely wrote it off.' She slid her robe over her shoulder and pointed out the faint silvery scar there, then pointed out a similar larger scar on her elbow and her knee.

'There was a sheep in the road and I skidded to avoid it. The worst thing was, I was lying in the middle of this dark road, in agony. I had a broken collar bone and two ribs, I couldn't move, couldn't get up, my bike had slid off the road somewhere and I could see this car coming. Its headlights were careening round the corners so fast and I knew he wouldn't see me till it was too late, knew he was just going to run straight over me and there was nothing I could do about it. It was terrifying, that moment when you know that death is coming. Luckily he did see me at the last second and swerved off the road to avoid hitting me. The guy in the car ended up almost as bad as I was and I felt so guilty about that. The only one not to get hurt was the bloody sheep. Anyway, after that, I decided to give up on the bike and get a car instead. Though I do miss it. I keep thinking about getting another bike, one day.'

'You know, Lib, if you fall off the horse, you just have to get straight back on again.'

'Yes I know you're right, but it's a bit scary…'

'But that's why you have to do it, you can't go through life scared of the "what ifs".'

She nodded as she stared at him. He was right in more ways than one.

His phone beeped and he fished it out of his pocket.

'My mum,' he indicated the phone, 'texting to remind me that I offered to help her clean out the loft this morning. Well, offered would probably be pushing it, coerced is probably more accurate. I better go, I'll meet you outside the town hall at four?'

She nodded and watched him go, deciding that straight after they left the hall she would tell him exactly what was going on in her heart.

—

Judith had just finished throwing the dirty plates into the dishwasher when there was a knock at the door. Rumour had it that Amy was still staying at the pub, so she and Seb were obviously still together, despite Judith telling him she was a prostitute. Slamming the dishwasher door closed, she stormed over to answer the front door and was surprised to see Verity Donaldson on her doorstep.

'Judith, how are you doing? Are you busy?'

'I'm fine, come in, do you want a cup of tea?' Judith opened the door for her. In the kitchen she set about making tea, as Verity selected a chocolate chip cookie from the biscuit barrel.

'So how are you doing, really?' Verity asked, taking the mug of tea from Judith.

'I take it you've heard about Seb and Amy? I'm sure the whole town knows by now.'

'I have, yes.' Verity dipped her biscuit into her tea. 'Why is this such a problem for you? I thought you wanted him to be happy again, after all this time?'

'Yes, of course, it's just that...' Judith swallowed. 'Seb and Marie would have been married nine years now, they would have had children and it seems weird, wrong somehow that he might have that with someone else. I don't think I'll ever get over Marie's death, and it doesn't seem right that he will. When Alan died, Marie's father, I knew there would never be anyone else for me, and there never has been. I... just don't want him to forget her, and for him to have the life with Amy that he can never have with Marie doesn't seem fair.'

She looked at Verity as she sipped her tea. What was it with her that made Judith bare her innermost feelings? And she didn't pussyfoot around either, she just told it as it was.

'Fair on whom? Is it fair that Seb's life stops just because Marie's has? He might as well have died too if that's the case. Do you think that Marie would have wanted that for him? Do you think Alan would have wanted that for you? Do you honestly think that Seb will ever stop loving Marie, or that it's not possible to love two people at the same time?'

OK, maybe that was a bit too honest.

'He doesn't love Amy, how could he? She's nothing like Marie.'

'Do you think we have one type that we are attracted to, that we have any control over who we fall in love with?'

'But she's vile.'

'Is she? From what I remember of Marie she doesn't seem that different.'

Judith felt her hands clench into fists in her lap.

'Marie spent a lot of summers down here with your sister, Alice. She was accident-prone, clumsy, always getting into scrapes. She nearly killed Alice's dog when she was cleaning out Alice's car and accidentally released the handbrake. She had a very kind heart. I remember she used to mow the lawn for my dear old mum before she passed away and walk the dogs for some of the other elderly neighbours. Not that far away from what Amy does now for the some of the old ladies at the far side of White Cliff Bay. Marie spent most Saturdays when she was down here collecting money for the PDSA, selling cakes and rattling a tin. Did you know that Amy volunteers for the local Cancer Awareness charity every Wednesday, raising money, handing out leaflets or, as was the case the other day, dressing up as a penis to raise awareness of testicular cancer?'

'I didn't know that, no.' Judith swallowed. That's what Alan had died of when the cancer had spread to his prostate. If they had caught it earlier…

'And Marie had a wicked sense of humour. When she came to stay in winter one year, and it snowed on the beach, she made a whole row of snowmen that were very well endowed. She put clingfilm over the toilets in the public library; she put salt in the sugar pots in Alice's cafe. And I remember her using condoms as water balloons in a water fight with some local kids. I think she would have found what Amy's nephew did to your gnomes last year absolutely hilarious.'

Judith shifted awkwardly. Verity was right; Marie did have a brilliant sense of humour. She always made Judith laugh a lot. Had she completely lost her sense of humour the day Marie had died?

'Maybe we are drawn to a certain type, but not in looks, in personality. And even if Amy is different to Marie, isn't it better that Seb doesn't go for a Marie clone? If he did he would always be reminded of Marie every time he kissed her, looked at her. How could he ever realistically move on if the person he moved on with was her exact replica?'

'She's a prostitute.' Judith tried her last attempt to win Verity round to her way of thinking.

'Yes, I heard that's what you thought. I doubt you will approve of this any more than her being a prostitute. If you really want to know what Jackson Cartwright has been doing with Amy for the last year then you should go down to White Cliff Bay town hall this afternoon around four o'clock. I'm going, you could meet me there.'

'I'm not a prude, Verity, I'm as open minded as the next person. I just don't think...'

'...Amy's good enough for Seb. Yes, I got that. But I think you have to let Seb decide that for himself. It's rare that we get to fall in love twice in our lifetime, I don't think it's fair to stand in the way of that.'

'I wouldn't... I...'

'Look, I better go, I can see I'm upsetting you and I don't want that. I brought round these brochures.' She pulled out a stack of brightly coloured brochures from her bag. 'There's a group of us going on a cruise in January, thought you might like to come with us. Don't answer now, just have a look through these. I've marked the pages of the ones we are considering. I may see you later then at the town hall. Thanks for the tea, I'll see myself out.'

Judith watched her go, unsettled. Verity was certainly honest; she had to give her that. She certainly hadn't got the tea and sympathy she'd been hoping for when she came to her door. Verity had made her out to be quite the bad guy and Judith didn't like it.

She glanced at the holiday brochures. But maybe it was time to leave White Cliff Bay, if only for a little while, let Seb lead his own life.

She looked at her watch. Maybe she'd pop along to the town hall to see what all the fuss was about.

—

Later, after George had cleared out several boxes of what appeared to be bank statements that were older than him from his mum's loft, he was driving back towards the town centre. He had to pop in and see Matt before he met Libby. Over poker on Sunday, Matt had asked him to do an advert for his jewellery shop. He was going to take him the first draft of it for his approval.

As he rounded a corner, he saw a car with its hazard lights on at the side of the road. It was quite an old car, a classic MG roadster convertible, in racing green. It wasn't a car he recognised so he guessed it belonged to one of the tourists.

But as he pulled over to see if he could help, he spotted the most beautiful woman on the side of the road, desperately trying to get a signal on her mobile.

Part of him wanted to carry on driving. He didn't do well with beautiful women; his startling impression on Giselle had made that obvious. He really didn't want to make a fool out of himself by getting out of his car and staring at her, no words forming in his mouth. She would think he was a right idiot, either that or an axe murderer.

But the chivalrous part of him wasn't about to leave a woman, no matter how beautiful, stranded on the side of the road.

He could do this. Libby was always telling him how lovely and sweet and funny he was. How any woman would be lucky to go out with him. Surely he could offer his help without coming across like a weirdo.

He would just ask if she needed some help. Yes, that was very simple, very easy … So why was his heart thundering against his chest?

He took a deep breath and got out the car.

CHAPTER 14

Amy was pacing inside the town hall, feeling nervous. Jackson had deliberately chosen this time of day because the Giant Gingerbread House Race was happening in the marquee. He didn't want a big audience and Amy had to agree, but what if no one came, or – even worse – what if everybody came? Would they all look at her with the same disgust that Judith looked at her? Would they chase her from their quiet unassuming town before she even got a chance to pack? Most importantly, what would Seb think?

Conrad approached her, a tall dark, beautiful man who had the gorgeous lilt to his voice of his South African heritage.

'Stop pacing, Amy, you will wear a hole in the floor.'

'Is it OK, Conrad, really?'

'It's beautiful, but then you know I'm so very proud of Jackson. I don't think he could do anything that I didn't like.'

She smiled and took his hand and squeezed it. 'He's very lucky to have you.'

Conrad looked down at her. 'No, I am the lucky one. We drift through life finding people to amuse us along the way. But to actually find my soul mate, the one person I want to spend the rest of my life with, I feel very blessed indeed. If you find it, Amy, if you find true love, then hold on to it with both hands and don't let go.'

She looked over to the other side of the room, where Jackson was pacing too. She just had to hope that Seb had the same attitude.

—

Libby stood outside the town hall, waiting for George. It was snowing lightly, tiny flakes swirling through the late afternoon sky. Quite a few people had filtered past her now. The three old ladies from Flower Cottages that Amy did the gardens for; Verity and Bill, George's parents; Bob, George's uncle; Polly from the cake shop; Kat and Dave; as well as a handful of other people she didn't know. Lots of people were at the annual Giant Gingerbread House Race, which was probably why Jackson had chosen this time slot, so he wasn't swamped with people, but Libby was a little bit sad that she wouldn't get to see the race, it sounded like a lot of fun. Would she even be here next year to see it?

She watched as George waved at her excitedly from the other side of the street, and disappeared into Matt's jewellery shop.

Matt's jewellery was beautiful, all handmade, individual pieces, some of it simple and elegant, some of it contemporary, obscure twists of gold woven with jewels. But every piece was ridiculously expensive. The tourists seemed to like it though, and Matt did very well out of it.

She checked her watch; she would have to go in on her own in a minute. Amy would kill her if she missed it.

Just then George appeared from the shop and literally bounced across the road towards her. He kissed her on the cheek, which surprised her, as they didn't normally greet each other that way.

'I have a date, Lib, the most beautiful red-head you have ever seen, she's like Venus. She's stunning and funny and lovely and she wanted to go out on a date with me. Here, I bought you something, we better get in,' he gabbled as he passed her a small paper bag and grabbed her hand and ran up the steps.

'Wait, George, you have a date? Who with? Where did you meet her?' Libby couldn't help the sudden wave of disappointment that crashed over her with his words. She tucked the paper bag, which she assumed was a bar of fudge by the feel of it, into her bag as she ran in his wake.

'Shush, it's about to start,' George said.

—

Libby looked at the beautiful painting of Amy hanging in front of her and wanted to cry for her. She looked stunning. Of the twelve nude or semi-nude paintings of Amy adorning the walls of the town hall, this one was her favourite.

Jackson had given a speech about the paintings, about his muse, how she had inspired him, but how everyone always asked the same question: who was the girl in the painting? Eleven of the pictures showed Amy from different angles, but not one of them showed her face. When she was looking forward, her face was partly obscured by a sheet of black silk hair. Amy had said she was worried that when Jackson had wanted to obscure her identity with her hair the paintings would make her look like the creepy girl from *The Ring*, but every single one of them made her look beautiful.

One, titled 'Waiting', was Amy from the back, naked, looking out the window. Another, titled 'Sunday Mornings', had her curled up in bed with a book. The other side of the bed from her had clearly been slept in, and there were two champagne glasses on the bedside table. Libby liked that one; although the title of the book wasn't clear, the cover was quite obviously one of her own books.

Another had Amy wrapped in a towel, sitting on her bed drying her hair while behind her in bed the lump of a man slept on. Another was of her getting dressed, from the point of view of the man in the bed as he watched her – you could see his hand on the bed in front of him, fingering a strap of her satin nightie.

Two others were hung side by side. One showed Amy, completely naked as she admired her heavily pregnant belly in the mirror, and the other was of her breastfeeding an adorable chubby baby, the baby clutching at Amy's finger, kicking his legs as she held him.

But Libby's favourite, the one she was standing in front of now, was Jackson's latest. In number twelve he had revealed Amy's identity, showing her face in full as she lay in bed, a thin sheet covering what was clearly a naked body. Her hair was ruffled, and she was propped up on one elbow as she looked out, laughing freely. In her eyes, the silhouette of a man could clearly be seen. She looked amazing.

'Well, what do you think?' asked Amy from behind her.

Libby tore her eyes from the masterpiece before her and turned around. 'Amy, you are so beautiful, these paintings, every single one of them, are... incredible. I can't believe you did this and never told me.'

'Ah, some people are not that understanding about posing nude.' She shrugged and looked around the room.

Libby looked too, but from where she was standing everyone seemed to be enjoying the pictures as much as she was. Verity, Bill, Bob, the old ladies from Flower Cottages, they were all looking at the different paintings in awe. George, she could see, was standing in front of the one where Amy lay asleep in bed, her hair over her face, her mouth parted slightly as she slept deeply. He was clearly looking at it in admiration.

Libby looked round the other side and her heart leapt when she saw Judith, studying the 'Sunday Morning' picture.

'Oh,' she said.

'Yes exactly. I'm not quite sure what she's doing here. It's certainly not to support me, but I guess curiosity got the better of her. I better go; I've got some more people to thank before they leave.'

Libby watched Amy move over towards Verity and then glanced back to George. Curiosity getting the better of *her*, she wandered over to speak to him.

'Come on then, George Donaldson, spill.'

He turned to look at her, breaking into a huge smile. 'I don't know what you mean,' he said, innocently.

'You know full well what I mean. Your date?'

'Libby, she's beautiful, her name's Cerys Andrews, she works in Apple Hill, owns her own flower shop…'

'Wait, back up, where did you meet her? Last I heard you were going to clean out your mum's loft. Was she lurking up there amongst the dust and cobwebs?'

'She'd got a flat tyre on the road between Mum's and Apple Hill. I pulled over to offer to help.'

'Very gentlemanly of you.'

'Well, I could hardly leave her stranded. Anyway, whilst I changed her tyre we were chatting, and we were getting on so well. When I'd finished, she just asked me out. Can you imagine that, Lib, she actually asked me out?'

'I can imagine it actually. As I said, you really are lovely.'

Libby cursed herself, she was an idiot. Why hadn't she told him she was falling for him when she realised it. Why had she waited? Was it her fear of rejection or commitment? Maybe her fear of staying. Whatever it was, now she was too late. She had been pushing him into dating again and although the date wasn't with Giselle, she couldn't be angry that he had a date with someone else, that's what they had been practising for all this time.

'At first I was going to say no, that I wasn't ready. But I kept thinking about our dates, and how well you said they went, and...' he looked suddenly awkward as he rubbed a hand round the back of his neck, 'and how lovely you said I was, and I thought "I can do this".'

He was so excited she had to try to be happy for him. 'That's great, George, I'm really pleased for you. So when's the big date?'

'Tomorrow, I'm taking her to The Cherry Tree, just as we practised.'

'It's poker night tomorrow.' She felt affronted on behalf of the other boys.

'Ah, the boys will understand.'

'Well, you'll have to practise this dating competition on her then.' She looked away, rummaging in her bag for the much needed fudge.

'I could,' he said, doubtfully.

'What?'

'Well, it seems a bit silly.'

She looked back at the painting, for want of something to do, though she wasn't really looking at it. She felt stung by his comment.

He somehow knew he had upset her. 'Lib, it's different with you, I can completely be myself, we can be silly and do fun things together, and you make me laugh so much. I like being silly with you, but Cerys seems more...'

'Sophisticated, mature,' she suggested, rummaging in her bag again.

'Libby Joseph, OK, if you want to get down to the nitty gritty, yes, she isn't as silly as you, she seems a bit more... mature. But you know what, I like the silly and fun in our relationship. I'd want that in any relationship. If I was to get married again, it would have to be to someone fun like you. But I should give her a chance, right? The fun stuff can come later, once we know each other a bit better. I want to impress her, and handing her a sheet of paper on our first date that talks about dirty sex and partial or full nudity I think would send her running for the hills.'

She conceded this. 'I see your point, but you have to be yourself as well. If she's going to fall in love with you, she has to fall in love with the real you, the funny, silly you, not the person you think she would like.'

'You're right, Lib, but let me just get through this first date. If I can string a coherent conversation together and she wants to see me for a second date, then maybe the fun element can come in then.'

She nodded. Finally finding the bar of fudge that he had given her earlier, she freed it from the jumbled contents of her bag.

'Have you not opened that yet?' He sounded slightly affronted.

'No, the whole Amy nude painting thing kind of took over for a while. Want a piece?'

'What?'

She opened the paper bag, but inside was a black velvet box. She looked back at him in confusion. 'What's this?'

'Oh, just something I saw and thought of you,' he said, casually, looking away back to the painting again.

She pulled out the box, still confused, half expecting to see some fudge in there when she opened it. But when she did, her heart leapt.

Inside, nestled against the black velvet, was a beautiful jewel-encrusted starfish, on a thin gold chain. Its legs were bent slightly, as if it was caught in a strong tide, but each leg had a multitude of different coloured jewels running along the ridge. It was stunning.

Oh no, this was not good, not good at all. She was falling for him and this was making it worse. He clearly didn't return the feelings when he had flitted so quickly from kissing her the night before to agreeing to go on a date with Cerys. But this gesture was so sweet.

'Do you like it?'

She looked up at him in shock. 'I… it's beautiful. Did you get this from Matt's?'

'Yeah, I was in there giving him the script for his new advert, and I saw it and thought of you. You remember last week, we were on the beach and we found that starfish and you said how you loved them, that they were a little bit of magic washed up on the sand?'

She swallowed. How on earth did he remember that? She barely remembered it. This was making the situation worse.

She looked back at the starfish, running her finger lightly across one of the legs. 'But… his stuff is really expensive.'

'Ah, it's OK. It's your "four days before Christmas" present. Besides, I owe you, for all the dating advice. I couldn't have agreed to go on a date with Cerys if it wasn't for you. You've made me realise that what I have to offer is quite good – so I wanted to say thank you.'

Libby looked back up at him again, and reached out to touch his face. 'What you have to offer is more than quite good, George Donaldson. You are one of the most beautiful people I know.'

He blushed. 'Well, put it on.'

Taking it carefully from the box, he gestured for her to turn around, which she did. He put it round her neck and she swept her hair up so he could fasten it at the back. His fingers fumbled on the clasp for a second, but his touch sent goosebumps straight down her spine. This definitely wasn't good.

The necklace sat perfectly in the hollow at the base of her neck, and she admired how it looked against her throat in the reflection of a nearby glass door. She couldn't help looking at George standing behind her, his hands on her shoulders as he too looked at her reflection.

'Thank you,' she said, quietly.

—

The last few people were drifting out of the town hall now, and as Amy stood awkwardly in the middle, Kat and Big Dave made their way over to say goodbye.

'Amy, you should be very proud, these paintings look beautiful,' Kat said, hugging her.

'Yes, we especially like the pregnancy one, you look lovely. Almost as beautiful as my wife,' Big Dave said, fondly stroking Kat's pregnant belly.

Kat beamed at him, and with an arm round her shoulders, Big Dave escorted her out.

Amy turned back to see who was left. Seb still hadn't turned up yet. She'd left him at the party and he promised to be there but there had been no sign since the exhibition had opened an hour before. She noticed Judith was still amongst the stragglers, standing now in front of the 'waiting' picture.

Taking a deep breath, Amy walked over to her.

'Of course, you'd be one of the few people in this room who'd see what's missing from this picture,' she said, coming to stand at her side.

Judith looked at her and then looked back at the painting, not willing to talk to her.

Amy stepped forward and pointed to her bum in the painting, and she saw a tiny trace of a smirk appear on Judith's lips, which surprised her.

'I asked Jackson not to include my shark tattoo, and he agreed that it wasn't the look he was going for.'

Judith looked down at her handbag, fiddling with a stray thread. 'I'm sorry for saying you were a prostitute.'

'That's OK.' Amy eyed her carefully. 'And I'm sorry if I've ever done anything to upset you. I never wanted to hurt you. I'm clumsy and accident-prone and bad things just happen around me, like your shed setting on fire. I'm sorry about what my nephew did to your gnomes and that I managed to dye Philippe purple when I was helping him out of the tree. I'm loud and crass too, and I'm sorry if I embarrassed you when I was naked in my garden and when I was a penis in yours. I'm sorry for upsetting you, truly I am. It was never my intention. I was thinking of moving house actually.'

'You're moving because of me?' Judith said quietly.

'I've realised that I've become a neighbour from hell and I never wanted that.'

Judith shifted awkwardly, which Amy hadn't expected. She'd thought Judith would do cartwheels of joy across the hall.

'What about Seb? Are you two not… do you not love him?'

Even the mention of his name made Amy's heart thunder.

'I love him, I've never loved anyone like I love him.'

'Does Seb love you?'

'I… can't speak for him. I won't.' There was no way she could tell Judith what had happened between them; she wouldn't betray Seb in that way.

Judith's eyes flittered over her shoulder and her jaw set angrily. 'Well, him being here certainly speaks for something.'

Amy whirled around and saw Seb standing in the doorway. He looked over and saw Amy and he took a step towards her, before he no doubt spotted Judith behind her and stopped.

More than anything Amy wanted to run over and jump into his arms. But she couldn't do that with Judith here.

Seb looked awkward, and she knew that he hadn't expected to see Judith and, judging by Judith's stony face, she hadn't expected to see him here either. Nobody moved and the tension could have been sliced with a knife.

Until George swooped in. Wading through the tension, George suddenly ran up to Seb and greeted him like a long lost brother, then took his arm and guided him to one of the paintings, at the furthest point in the room away from her and Judith. She could have kissed George. That was until she realised they were looking at the painting of her getting dressed after what was clearly supposed to be a night of passion. That was too close to the truth for both of them. But then looking around the room, none of the paintings were particularly safe to look at.

And what would Seb's reaction be to her posing nude? Would he be disgusted?

Obviously feeling Judith's eyes burning into the back of his head as he looked at the painting of Amy getting dressed, he quickly moved on to the painting of her in bed on a Sunday morning, which Amy supposed was a safer picture.

George, who was clearly embarrassed looking at nude paintings with a man who was obviously more familiar with the subject matter than he was, was loudly talking about the beautiful brush strokes and the lighting and even postmodernism.

Seb was standing at the side of the room now, so they could both see his face from the side as he looked at the paintings. If he was trying to keep his face neutral, he wasn't doing a very good job. He looked in awe.

Amy quickly glanced back to Judith again, but she was watching him intently, her eyes narrowed.

But as he moved to stand in front of the pregnancy and breastfeeding pictures, something happened. He reached out to touch the painting of Amy breastfeeding, which Jackson would have had a fit about if he hadn't been distracted by Conrad. Seb gently touched the baby's head, his face filled with emotion. He looked like he was about to cry.

Amy took an involuntarily step towards him, but just managed to stop herself as she remembered Judith. She looked at Judith, who was pale now, her eyes hurt, wet with tears herself. But if she thought the tears were for Seb, she was mistaken, as Judith suddenly turned and walked out of the hall.

Amy stared after Judith for a moment, unsure whether she was going to come back, but when she didn't she quickly crossed the room to Seb's side.

On seeing her, he quickly pulled her into his arms, holding her tight.

She held his face in her hands. 'What's wrong?'

He gestured to the painting, to the baby. 'I want that, Amy. I want a family with you.'

'I want that too.'

Seb glanced over her shoulder. 'I want that as well, more than anything.'

She turned round to see the picture of her laughing openly.

'I want to have fun with you. Watching you today with Angel at the party, dancing with her, I loved seeing the smile on your face. I want the jelly and ice cream, and the walks on Silver Cove beach and the amazing sex. I want...'

He took her hand and pulled her towards the fire exit, then pushed the door open and dragged her outside into the tiny courtyard where the snow was now coming down thick and fast. In the middle, a stone fountain that had faded over time stood with frozen icicles sparkling in the light of the moon. He took her in his arms and started moving around with her.

Amy laughed. 'What are we doing?'

'We're dancing in the rain.'

'It's snowing.'

'It's close enough.'

She leaned her head against his chest and let him sweep her around the courtyard.

'I love you and I want to share my life with you,' Seb said.

She felt her smile spread across her face. 'Well, that's good, because I love you too.'

He bent his head and kissed her under the light of the moon. Everything faded away. It was the two of them, and that's all that mattered.

When he finally pulled away, she had to fight for her breath, and she leaned her head against his chest to steady herself for a moment.

'I won't lose you, Amy, I won't,' he said into her head and she pulled back to look at him.

'I don't want to hurt Judith…'

'I'll talk to her, but I'm not about to lose the woman I love for the second time in my life. I love you, Amy, I want to get married to you and have a child with you, and nothing is going to stand in the way of that.'

She smiled as he kissed her again.

—

George was quiet as he drove Libby home. What had he been thinking – he wasn't ready to go out on a date with a complete stranger. He doubted whether he'd ever be ready. And what was worse was the only woman he wanted to go out with was sitting next to him.

'Are you nervous about your date, George?' Libby asked.

'Yeah, I am now it's sunk in a bit. I don't exactly have high hopes for it. Anyone who asks out someone they've only just met is either desperate or has a whole heap of issues. I don't think it's going to end well.'

'*You* agreed to go on a date with her. By your standards what does that say about you?'

'I know I have issues, Lib, I have only ever been with one woman. I haven't had sex in a very long time, and the sex was so bad my ex felt the need to go elsewhere for it.'

He sighed. And his biggest issue was that he had been in love with his best friend for the last six months, desperately holding out for her to fall in love with him.

'Exactly, we all have issues.' Libby fiddled with a stray thread on a hole in her jeans. 'You shouldn't be so judgemental about others when you have your own.'

'That's the problem, two of us with issues, insecurities and baggage.' He put on a high-pitched whiny voice. 'Does my hair look OK, did I wear the right shoes, does my breath smell, does my bum look big?'

'Not all girls have those issues.'

'I wasn't talking about her, I was talking about me. God, it's hardly a good start to a relationship if we're both like that, is it?'

'But it doesn't have to be a relationship, George. It could just be a bit of fun, a few dates, someone nice to talk to. What's the worst that could happen?'

'She takes one look at me and runs a mile.'

'She's already seen you and fallen for your dark rugged looks. If she runs away then it would be her loss and she would have missed out on knowing one of the most beautiful people I know.'

George nearly swerved off the road as Libby picked up her phone to reply to a text from Amy.

'What time is the date?' she asked, absently, drinking from her bottle of water.

'Seven thirty.'

'I'll do your make-up for you if you like.'

'What?'

'It's what we used to do when we were teenagers. If one of us had a date, the others would rally round lending handbags, shoes, doing hair and make-up.'

He tossed his hair. 'Will you give me a blow job?'

She spat her water out with such force it splattered over the inside of the windscreen. 'What?!'

He looked at her in confusion. 'You know… make it more curly…' He trailed off as he suddenly realised what he'd said. 'Oh God, I meant… I…' But she was already laughing.

'It might be a bit beyond the call of duty but if it will help…'

'It will help, it would really help,' he insisted.

She laughed as he pulled up round the back of their flats.

'You coming for dinner? I was going to cook a curry.'

She hesitated again and it worried him that these practice dates had driven a wedge between them.

'I really need to crack on with some work actually. My publishers are hassling me for the first draft. Quite why they need it a year in advance I have never worked out but I need to get it finished, preferably before Christmas.'

'OK, I'll see you tomorrow?'

She nodded vaguely and disappeared into her flat. Maybe this date with Cerys would be a good thing. If Libby stayed, they needed some normalcy back in their relationship and with George finally dating other women it meant they could go back to exactly how they were before. He would just have to ignore the heartbreaking feeling that giving up these dates would cause him.

—

Libby sighed as she stared out the window at the moonlit sea the next night. She had successfully managed to avoid George all day. She had signed up for an ice carving lesson in town and gone last-minute Christmas shopping and somehow had managed to make this task last until it got dark. It felt so weird to her that, only two days before, George had been lying on top of her at the ski centre kissing her as if he was in love with her and now he was going out on a date with someone else. She couldn't be angry at him though. This was what the whole practising had been for. Admittedly it had been with the idea of asking Giselle out and they had agreed that they would continue their practice until Christmas Eve but it was going to come to an end eventually. George had no idea that she had these feelings for him. Just because she had started having feelings for him didn't mean he should feel the same way. It wasn't his fault that she had suddenly started wanting more from the friendship. He was still plodding along in the role of best friend, none the wiser that she had moved the goalposts.

She looked at her watch. He would be freaking out about his date right now and, in her role as best friend, she needed to be supportive. If George was happy then she would be happy for him. She would just ignore the voice that was screaming in her head that said she wanted him to be happy with her more.

—

George was pacing his flat nervously. He eyed the pile of discarded shirts on his bed, wondering if the red one he had tried on first would be better than the blue one he was currently wearing.

'Hello?' called Libby, letting herself into the flat. 'I've come to give you a blow job.'

The colour of his shirt suddenly forgotten, he stood there in shock for a moment, then stumbled out quickly into the lounge. He laughed when he saw the hair dryer in her hand.

'Aw, George, you look fantastic. I'd lose the tie though, it's a bit too formal, especially with the jeans. You're only going for a curry after all.'

He quickly loosened the tie and slid it off his neck.

'Shirt tucked in or left out?' he asked, pulling at the ends of it self-consciously.

'What do you prefer?' Libby asked, spraying a small lump of mousse into her hand and running it through his hair.

He swallowed at the intimacy of it. 'Erm … out.'

'I think out too. You're so hot, are you OK?'

'I feel sick, Lib. My stomach is churning, I'm a sweaty mess. She's going to take one look at me and run a mile.'

'OK, OK, sit down, take a few deep breaths. Let me have a look at you.' Libby held his face, looking deep into his eyes. 'You have beautiful eyes, George. Deep pools of melted chocolate filled with kindness. Your hair has that gorgeous Poldark look to it, all dark and curly.'

George had often likened his hair to Alan Davies in *Jonathan Creek* rather than the sexy Poldark, but he smiled slightly at the thought.

'And you have the loveliest smile, very sexy.'

'Thanks.'

'Do you feel better now?' she asked hopefully.

He shook his head; his stomach felt like it was in a tumble dryer. 'It's just… I've been thinking about the worst-case scenario, you know – she thinks I'm hideous and makes some excuse that she left the gas on and leaves, or we're on the date and she turns out to be more unhinged than Kathy Bates in *Misery* – but then it occurred to me, what if everything goes really well? What if it goes so well we end up back at her place or back here and…?'

'And?' she prompted.

'I haven't had sex in years, Libby, and by all accounts I wasn't very good at it in the first place. What if I'm crap?'

'Practice makes perfect, George; just tell her it's been a while. I'm sure, unless she's a complete cow, she'll be very understanding about it, and if she is a complete cow then you probably won't end up back at her house anyway.'

He sighed heavily.

'Just try to relax, be yourself. If she sees the George I know, you'll be fine.' Libby moved to the door. 'I should go. Look, text me, if you can, let me know how it's going.'

George smiled weakly as he watched her go, wishing more than anything that he could spend the night with her instead.

CHAPTER 15

Libby sat at the table that George normally sat at to play poker, with four pints sitting in the middle. George had asked her to buy the boys a pint and explain that something pressing had come up. But she knew the boys would be upset that he had cancelled. One time when Matt was sick, they had decided not to play as it wasn't right playing as a threesome. So she hoped, somehow, she could make it up to them by playing in George's place.

Nick and Matt were the first to arrive and they stopped dead when they saw her at their table.

'Nick, I heard you on the radio the other day, you sounded brilliant.'

Nick blushed. 'Thanks.'

'And Matt, did you make this?' She gestured to the starfish around her neck, and he nodded. 'It's beautiful, you really are so talented.'

Matt sat down and sipped from his pint, eyeing her suspiciously.

'George couldn't make it tonight, something's come up, and I know you like to play as a four, so I thought I would take his place.'

Nick gave a sharp intake of breath as he too sat down. 'No wives, girlfriends or significant others, them's the rules. Poker night is a strictly boys' affair.'

'Well that's OK. I'm not a wife or girlfriend.'

'You're a significant other though,' Matt said.

Libby thought about this for a moment, not sure if she liked being an 'other'.

'Big Dave won't like this,' Nick said, shaking his head.

She rolled her eyes and stood up. 'I'll leave you boys to it then, I'd hate to get in the way of any male bonding.' She turned and walked straight into Big Dave. Literally butting her head into his ample chest.

'What's going on here?' Big Dave said.

'Oh nothing, George can't make it and I thought I'd play the fourth man, help you out a bit, but apparently it's boys only,' she said, catching Kat's eye over Dave's shoulder. Her friend rolled her eyes in sympathy with Libby's predicament.

Big Dave narrowed his eyes. 'Did you buy the drinks for us?'

'Yes, but it doesn't matter, I—'

Big Dave looked suddenly furious. 'Boys, where are your manners? A girl buys you a drink, offers to help you out of a hole and you're ready to cast her out in the cold.'

'Dave, really, it's not a problem.' Libby really didn't want to play poker that badly, she just wanted to not land George in hot water with them. In truth the fact that they didn't want her to play had been something of a relief.

'Lib, we were only joking, of course you can play with us,' Nick said, patting her recently departed chair enthusiastically.

Matt nodded. 'Sorry Lib, we were honestly joking, and I can't turn away anyone wearing one of my ridiculously expensive necklaces.'

'Your stuff is stupidly overpriced,' Nick said to Matt, catching Libby's hand and pulling her into the chair.

'I caught your show too, thought you sounded like Mickey Mouse,' Matt said, shuffling the cards, as Big Dave kissed Kat on the cheek and sat down too.

'I thought he sounded brilliant,' Big Dave said. 'You really made me laugh and, Matt, your jewellery is beautiful and I think you should charge more for it.'

Nick and Matt looked at Big Dave suspiciously.

'Why are you so happy tonight?' asked Nick, then looked over at Kat who was smiling inanely at the bar.

'Nothing, just, you know… happy,' shrugged Big Dave, and Libby could see the truth of his words straight away.

'You dirty dog,' Matt muttered. 'You've had sex, haven't you? She's nine months pregnant!'

Big Dave blushed and shrugged again. 'Yeah. And you know what, it was bloody amazing.'

As Matt stole a crisp from her bag, Libby smiled at her acceptance of her into their little gang. Her mum would have loved this. It was she who had taught Libby how to play poker, dragging her along to her weekly poker nights with her friends, the only time in the week her mum had been allowed out and the only time Libby had ever seen her really happy. Libby's mum had wanted to travel the world and see the sights but the one thing that had brought her happiness was her relationship with her friends and that was the one thing that Libby had been missing out on all these years. She looked around the pub at the people who had become her friends. No one looked at her as an outsider, they had all welcomed her into the fold so naturally and easily. She had real friendships here: George, Amy and Kat, and so many others who loved her exactly as she was. Regardless of what might happen with George, Libby wanted to stay here now. It was time to stop running and she couldn't think of a better place in the world than White Cliff Bay to call her home.

—

George paced the lounge nervously. Libby had been gone quite a while now, Cerys was late and the nerves that Libby had helped to calm were creeping back in. He would have preferred Libby to stay holding his hand until Cerys arrived – hell, if it had been appropriate he would have taken Libby on the date with him. She could have sat next to him and prompted him with things to say or do.

Just then, as he was debating whether he needed more after-shave, Cerys arrived, looking stunning in a red dress that showed a lot of cleavage.

'Hey.' He smiled shyly as he opened the door. 'You look fantastic.'

'Thanks,' she said, looking him up and down.

He waited for some reciprocal comment about how he looked – a comment about his shirt perhaps, but none was forthcoming.

'Where are we going tonight?' Cerys asked, when the silence became palpable as she moved past him into his flat.

'Oh, The Cherry Tree, on the far side of White Cliff Bay. It's a new Indian place, just opened a few weeks ago.'

Cerys nodded but he couldn't help but notice the small pout of disappointment that crossed her face. She moved into the lounge and looked around with disgust at all his decorations and inflatables. For the first time in his life George was utterly embarrassed about his love for all things Christmas.

'Well, shall we go?' he said, suddenly feeling the nerves that Libby had calmed earlier erupting from his chest. He picked up his keys and wallet and moved to the door.

'Yes but… are you not going to wear a jacket and tie?'

He looked down at himself self-consciously. Libby had said it looked too formal for an Indian restaurant, like he was going to a job interview, but he supposed, in a way, he was. This was where he had to make a good first impression.

'Yes of course, I'll just get them.'

He moved quickly to his bedroom and pulled out a jacket that went with his trousers. But now he would have to tuck his shirt in and the shirt Libby had chosen, one of her favourites, wasn't really the sort that could be tucked in – and which tie could he wear? He wanted to ring her up and ask her, but he knew he couldn't.

George started to unbutton his blue shirt and grabbed a red one instead, but suddenly Cerys was standing in the room with him. He quickly wrapped his shirt round himself, to protect his body from view.

She looked at the red shirt on the bed and then moved to the wardrobe. She fingered his brightly coloured shirts and pulled out a black one.

'Why don't you wear this instead? It will go better with the jacket. Where are your ties?'

He gestured to Candy, suddenly feeling embarrassed about the mannequin standing in his bedroom.

Cerys didn't seem too impressed either, but taking it in her stride, she walked over and flicked through his tie collection, and pulled out a black satin one.

'Here, this will finish it off nicely.'

She stood watching him, clearly waiting for him to get undressed, but he wasn't ready for her to see his body yet. When he didn't make any move to get changed, she seemed to get the message and walked back into the lounge, closing the bedroom door softly behind her.

He quickly got changed, then surveyed himself in the full-length mirror.

Libby was right. He looked like he was going to a funeral. He looked drab and boring. He sighed.

Then he remembered what else Libby had said, how Cerys had to fall in love with the real him. Feeling suddenly mischievous, he slid the black tie off his neck and grabbed the Wily Coyote and Road Runner tie that Libby had bought him. He quickly put it on and then looked back in the mirror. At least there was a small part of the real him that would go on this date.

He went back into the lounge and watched for Cerys' reaction. There was a slight scowl as she took in the cartoon tie, but she picked up her handbag and waited for him near the door.

He grabbed his wallet and keys and followed her out. He felt sure she'd be scowling even more if she knew the tie went 'beep-beep' when you pressed the bottom of it. Smiling to himself, he followed her down the stairs to the street. He had a feeling it was going to be a long night.

———

As Amy pulled a pint for one of the customers, she watched Libby win another round of poker – the fifth that night if the groans of despair were anything to go by.

Tonight had been lovely. Whereas, before, Seb had been studiously ignoring her whenever they had been together in the pub, tonight he had been friendly, chatting to her as much as he was chatting to Sally. Amy loved it; she wanted to work alongside him like this every night. If only she could kiss him, hug him when she wanted to, her life would be complete. He still wanted to keep it quiet at the moment, just until he had told Judith. Though any stragglers left at the town hall the day before would have seen them kissing and dancing in the courtyard and it wouldn't take long for word to get around, if it hadn't already.

Amy so wanted to believe that they had this bright and happy future together, but she refused to believe in it yet. Not until it was cast in stone.

Somehow, something was going to take away her bliss. After another night of passion, Seb would change his mind, or Judith would throw a tantrum or at the very least make a voodoo doll of her and stick it in a bowl of acid. Marriage and children were a very long way off indeed.

———

George had been determined to win back some of that magic from the day before; while he had changed Cerys' tyre they had chatted a lot. Surely that didn't mean they now had nothing left to talk about. But unfortunately, during the short drive to the restaurant, it did seem that was the case. Everything he tried resulted in blank stares or one-word answers. Cerys seemed to lack any kind of sense of humour at all. How could she be so different just twenty-four hours later?

Still, at least things might perk up a bit at The Cherry Tree. With Mani playing his violin, who couldn't fail to be amused?

They walked into the restaurant and Kamal greeted him like an old friend. 'You have come back, you enjoyed the food?'

'Yes, very much.'

Kamal looked behind George and his face fell when he saw Cerys. 'Where is your beautiful girlfriend?'

George flushed with embarrassment; he hadn't thought about this problem.

Cerys glared at him. 'So you bring all your dates here then?'

'No, it's not like that. Me and Libby came here, the girl from the flat opposite mine, we wanted to try it out. Kamal obviously thought that we were a couple,' he explained. Because they had told him they were. What was it Libby had said? That they had been friends for six months and that it was their first date as a couple? Kamal had been delighted, that their relationship was built on such love. George swallowed.

Cerys smiled tightly. 'It's fine, George, you don't need to explain. I know you've been out with other women before me.'

But Kamal was not to be put off; if he had any customer relation skills or sense of social etiquette, they seemed to have completely deserted him. 'I thought you loved her, it's rare you see such love between two people. I said to my wife that night that you two were going to grow old and grey together. Your girlfriend loved you too, so much. I could see that. Why are you not with her? Did you two fall out?'

Cerys arched an eyebrow at George as they sat down in the window.

'No, Kamal, she's just a friend.' Just a friend, how could he describe Libby like that? She was so much more than that, she was the single most important person in his life. But thinking about Libby like that was certainly not going to help his already flagging date.

He just had to ask Cerys questions about herself. Libby had said women like to talk about themselves.

'So Cerys,' George started after they had placed their order, 'have you always lived round here?' He knew she hadn't – she had a slight northern accent, and this he hoped would start a conversation about her life prior to White Cliff Bay.

It did. She quite simply did not stop for breath. He listened, he ate and he listened. At least, he thought wryly, it didn't leave time for awkward silences.

—

Unfortunately for George, Mani wasn't working that night, and he desperately needed something to lighten the tedium of the date. Mani's violin playing would have been right up his street. But instead he had to wade through numerous awkward silences. He had run fresh out of questions and all funny anecdotes had fallen on deaf ears. Whenever the silences dragged on, Cerys would think of another story to tell him about herself. He now knew that her colleague at work could never get her tea the way she liked it, that her favourite flower was a poppy, and that her dog when she was a child was called Tripod and only had three legs. He could actually feel brain cells dying; it was almost as if his brain had decided he wouldn't need the cells responsible for intellectual or humorous conversation any more and as such was removing them to make way for the layers of inane babble she was torturing him with.

Occasionally, probably more out of politeness than interest, Cerys had asked him questions. George had talked about his job, which she actually seemed vaguely interested in. He told her briefly about his ex-wife, and a bit about how insecure it had left him. Weirdly though, Cerys had decided that the moment when he was vulnerably baring his soul was the moment to suggest he needed a haircut. When his phone rang at that point, it was something of a relief.

Suddenly remembering Libby's advice about not answering the phone on a date he quickly fished his phone out of his pocket to turn it off. He was about to divert the call to the answer machine when he noticed the caller was Libby.

Frowning, he hesitated. She knew he was on the date with Cerys; she wouldn't call unless something was wrong.

'Erm…sorry, I won't be a moment,' he said, getting up and walking out the restaurant. He quickly answered the phone.

'Lib, are you OK?'

There was a very manly laugh. 'You arse,' said a very familiar voice that definitely wasn't Libby.

Confused, he looked at the phone, but the ID clearly said Libby. He put the phone back to his ear again.

'Hello?'

'It's Nick, I knew you wouldn't pick up if you saw my name ringing, so I'm using Libby's phone whilst she's popped to the loo. What the hell are you playing at, lad, you send a woman to do your dirty work for you?'

George looked through the window at Cerys drumming her fingers impatiently. 'What?'

'You afraid you would lose again tonight so you sent Libby to win for you? That's cowardly. And we all thought, "Aw sweet lovely Libby, sure we'll let her play, what's the worst that can happen?" Bloody woman has only gone and cleared us out. Every single match between the four of us is sitting in front of her place right now. She's bloody lethal. Next time you can't make it, you just send your apologies, don't send the bloody poker genius to play on your behalf. You keep her at home where the woman belongs. Ooh, look lively, lads, here she comes.'

George shook his head in confusion. 'Libby's playing poker with you?'

'Yeah, don't pretend you don't know, George. Next you'll be telling me that you didn't know she played poker...oof.'

He heard Libby's voice in the background. 'Is that George? Why are you phoning him, give me the phone...' There was a scuffling noise and then she came on the phone. 'George, I'm so sorry, I had no idea the idiot would call you...'

'Libby, why are you playing poker?'

'Oh...I didn't want you to get into trouble with the boys...'
He smiled fondly.

'...How's it going?' she asked.

'Good...' He looked at Cerys through the restaurant window. 'Well, OK, I guess.'

'Look, I'm going to go home to bed now, the boys are bad losers and I'm tired. Come by when the date's over, we can dissect it together if I'm still awake.'

'I better go too.' George looked back at Cerys again, wishing he could just stay on the phone to his best friend rather than go back into the restaurant.

'Yes you should, enjoy the date, George. Even if she isn't the person you're going to spend the rest of your life with, just put it down to practice for your big date with Giselle.'

Libby was right; regardless of the outcome, tonight would be a good thing.

'I'll see you later then, Lib.'

He hung up and went back in and Kamal looked at him as he walked past, shaking his head regretfully.

'Sorry about that… bit of a family thing,' he said, sitting down, disappointed to see that his plate had been whisked away whilst he had been gone.

'It's OK.' She smiled tightly. 'Shall we get dessert?'

He nodded, wearily. This really was going to be the longest night of his life.

—

Libby put her phone back in her bag and glared at Nick. 'Why did you phone him for? He's on a date and it doesn't look good that he answered his phone in the middle of it.'

'He's on a date, bloody hell,' Nick spluttered into his beer. 'Well, the silly arse shouldn't have picked up the call then.'

'Good for him,' Big Dave said, still grinning stupidly, as he had been all night.

'Can't believe he would cancel our poker game for a date with some girl,' Matt said, surreptitiously trying to steal some matches back from Libby's pile. She slapped his hand away. 'It… is with a girl, isn't it? Not that I'm judging, I wouldn't care if George was gay, just… it's been a long time since he's been with a woman, I was beginning to wonder if maybe…'

'It's a girl, a beautiful red-head who looks like Venus apparently. Cerys somebody,' Libby said, sipping the last of her drink and standing up.

'Cerys Andrews?' Nick said, his eyes bulging.

'I think so.'

'Oh God, poor chap, we've all been there, haven't we, boys?'

Matt and Big Dave nodded solemnly.

'She's like a mermaid, beautiful, like a gift from the gods, but that's how she lures men in, and then she strikes.'

Libby sat down again. 'What do you mean?'

'Halfway through my first date with Cerys, I had actually planned my untimely demise in several different ways. The most appealing being cutting my ears off so I wouldn't have to hear her and then letting myself bleed to death. She is quite possibly the most boring person I've ever met. When she suggested a second date, I made up some ghastly disease and she soon lost interest after that,' Matt said.

'You got out easy, I suffered three dates with her before I got out,' Big Dave said, shuddering as he remembered. 'Don't forget her Mr Perfect complex. After my first lunch date with her, I went straight to the barber's for a haircut and a shave. I'd booked an appointment with some beauty salon to have my back and chest waxed and spent five hundred pounds on new clothes. I mean, I work on a farm, what use to me is the latest Ralph Lauren shirt, but I was under her spell. Oh, poor George doesn't stand a chance.'

'Five dates,' Nick said, grimly. 'I slept with her, the most unpleasant experience of my life. "Put your hands here, don't do that, do this, harder Nick, not that hard, go gently, kiss me, touch me here, stop that, harder Nick, for fuck's sake harder, HARDER, that's pathetic, what are you doing, for goodness' sake, stop fucking around…" I was a gibbering wreck by the end.'

'Oh God no,' Libby said, suddenly scared for George, that just as he was venturing out of his shell he would be sent scuttling back into it. 'I should probably warn him.'

Big Dave smiled kindly. 'Libby, we have to let him make his own mistakes. This way, when someone perfect for him comes along, he'll appreciate it all the more. I think it's best he's left to sort this one out for himself.'

Libby sighed. She knew he was right. George was a grown man; he would have to stand on his own two feet eventually.

'Look, it's been a pleasure playing with you gents,' she said, standing up and eyeing the big pile of matches smugly, 'but for now I'm off to bed.'

Nick grumbled and Matt shook his head in a mixture of admiration and annoyance.

She turned for the door and watched as Judith marched through it and straight to the bar. She clearly meant business. Seb and Amy paled guiltily. This wasn't good at all.

—

Finally the bill came and, remembering the advice that Libby had given him, George put his card on the bill to cover it.

Cerys noted this gesture but just smiled.

When Kamal came back with the receipt he also gave a small tray with the traditional two white chocolates and one dark chocolate.

'White chocolate is my favourite thing in the world,' he said.

'I quite like white chocolate too,' she said, popping one of the pieces in her mouth and offering him the other white piece. He took it, begrudgingly. She quite liked white chocolate? *Quite* liked it? He had just said it was his favourite thing in the world and she had taken a piece because she quite liked it. But it was just a bit of chocolate. He wasn't going to spoil his date because of a piece of chocolate.

When they stood up though, she smiled almost as if she was amused by something, which was an encouraging sign.

She giggled. 'I never realised how short you are before.'

He frowned as he looked down. 'Cerys, you're wearing six-inch heels.'

'But I always wear heels, George; it looks silly that you're shorter than me.'

'Looks silly to who?'

'Other people.'

'I'm sure "other people" have better things to worry about than whether I look shorter than you. Besides, I'm not actually shorter than you, am I, I'm five foot nine. How tall are you?'

'The same, but in my heels I obviously look taller. You could wear heels too.'

'What, stilettos?' he laughed.

'No, boots or shoes with a heel. There are many actors who wear heeled boots. It looks good on a man.'

'You could wear flats,' he suggested.

'George, I'm not wearing flats. I look good in heels, don't I?'

He looked down at her legs. Her legs did look fantastic in heels. Libby never wore heels, well not stilettos like these. He had to admit Cerys did look very sexy wearing them.

'Yes, you do.'

'Well then,' she said, as if the case was closed.

'Cerys, I'm not wearing heels.'

She sighed. 'How about if I bought some for you, some nice fashionable ones, would you wear them?'

'No.'

'George, will you at least think about it? I think we look silly, that's all, I don't want people to laugh at us, do you?'

He couldn't imagine people standing and laughing at them just because he was now a few inches shorter than she was, and if they did he didn't really care. 'No, but...'

'Just think about it.' She suddenly kissed him, running her hands round the back of his neck, and all thoughts of wearing heels or arguing with her about it went from his head. He was standing in a restaurant being kissed by a beautiful woman. This date was suddenly looking up.

She pulled away. 'You really do kiss well. So you'll think about it?'

He opened his mouth to protest but changed his mind. 'I'll think about it.'

She smiled, smugly.

'Let's go back to yours,' she whispered in his ear in such a way that left no room for misunderstanding. Though if there was any doubt in his mind about what she meant, that was quickly dispelled when she grabbed him through his trousers, and stuck her tongue down his throat.

This was not good, he hadn't had time to read the stuff that Libby had given him. He didn't want this at all. But the longer he kept putting it off, the worse it would get. If he didn't sleep with Cerys now, if he went and hid under his bed like he wanted to, the next time he was with a woman, he would be even more scared.

He nodded reluctantly, his heart hammering with fear as they stepped outside and the wind whipped over the cliff tops.

———

Seb closed the office door behind him and faced Judith. And for a while, no one spoke. But here was the opportunity he wanted, to tell her he had fallen in love again. He just hadn't figured out which words to use yet. Words jumbled through his mind as he tried different variations.

In the end Judith helped him out.

'Do you love her?'

He stepped forward away from the door, and reached out to take her hand. 'Yes, I do. This isn't just some little fling, I love her.'

Judith snatched her hand from his. 'You lied to me. I asked you if you loved her and you said no.'

'I know. I didn't want to hurt you. I promised you there would never be anyone else after Marie and…'

She frowned. 'When did you promise me that?'

'About ten minutes after Marie had died. You made me promise that I would never love anyone else.'

'Oh, for goodness' sake, Seb, is that what's been holding you back, some silly promise I made you make minutes after my daughter had died?'

'Well, there have been many reasons why I've been holding back: being scared of falling in love again, of losing Amy, fear of hurting you. I kept thinking about the heart attack. I couldn't bear the thought of that happening again…' He trailed off. What if Judith had another heart attack now? Not only was he in love with someone else, but it was Amy of all people. Judith looked OK – angry certainly, and hurt, but she didn't look like she was about to keel over.

'That had nothing to do with you, I told you that – that I'd been feeling ill for a few days, that the doctors said it was high blood pressure, that I needed to sort out my diet, take more exercise. It wasn't anything to do with you going out on a date.'

'But you were so angry about it.'

'Of course I was. I was still grieving. I guess I always will grieve over Marie, miss her. I can't expect that from you.'

Seb's heart leapt angrily, and he had to swallow down the anger from his voice. He was not going to get into another row with her. 'That's not fair. I will always love Marie, that will never go away for me. But do you not think it's possible to love two people at the same time? I'm not going to suddenly forget her just because I've found someone else.'

Judith sighed wearily and she leaned against the edge of his desk. He quickly moved to her side; she looked so old all of a sudden. He took her hand again, and this time she let him.

'I know you loved Marie,' she said. 'I know you still do, but... I guess I find it hard to watch you carry on with your life when she can't.'

Seb looked away. It wasn't fair, none of this was. He moved to his cupboard and grabbed a bottle of whisky and poured himself a glass.

'You can pour one for me too,' she said behind him. He felt his eyebrows shoot up in surprise, but he did as he was told and turned back to hand her the glass. She took a big gulp.

'Marie would have wanted you to be happy again, and so do I.'

He found himself taking a big swig of the whisky now. 'You're saying you're OK with it, but... you hate Amy.'

'I hated you when Marie first brought you home. I didn't want her to go out with you, but I changed my mind. I love you now like a son. I don't think I'll ever love Amy, but... I don't hate her. Not any more.'

He hardly believed this was happening. 'What about marriage and children, what happens if... when it gets that far?'

'Then I'll buy a big hat.' Judith smiled, sadly. 'I want a happy future for you, Seb. Our lives shouldn't stand still just because of what happened. Marie wanted to travel, to see the world. After her father died, we spoke about doing that together, but we never got round to it. Life is short and precious and I want to do what we spoke about before it gets too late for me. I want to see every little tiny pocket of the world, so I may not be around to see the wedding anyway. It'll probably be a good thing if I'm not around for a while, if I'm not lurking over your shoulder.'

'You don't have to go away; this doesn't change anything between us.'

She smiled and reached up to touch his cheek. 'I know that. We'll always be a part of each other's lives, but I think you need some space now, some time to enjoy your new relationship. She loves you, you know.'

'I know.'

'Then why are you still in here talking to me and not out there taking her in your arms and kissing her?'

Seb smiled but still didn't move. He'd just declared his love for Amy to Judith, something which he never thought he could do. He wasn't sure if he could declare it to the whole pub yet.

'Come on.' Judith put her glass down and moved to the door. He followed her, his heart pounding.

She stood back and let him open it, which he did, and his eyes sought out Amy straight away. She was clearing tables of glasses and as the door opened she looked up at him, her eyes filled with worry. Judith gave him a little nudge from behind. He smiled at Amy, and the rest of the pub faded. The woman he loved was standing just a few metres away from him, and there was no reason to hide from it any more, he could finally shout it from the rooftops. He loved her and he didn't care who knew it.

He took two large steps forward and took her face in his hands and kissed her. The tray she was carrying clattered to the floor as her hands moved round his neck. The pub went silent and someone somewhere gasped, but he didn't care.

—

Amy's head was spinning as she kissed Seb, wanting to touch him all over, to hold him tight and never let him go. Was this it, were they really going to spend the rest of their lives together? Could they? Her heart pounding in her ears, she pulled away. He smiled at her, his eyes filled with love.

Someone cheered, probably Nick. Someone else clapped and then suddenly everyone was clapping and cheering. Seb kissed her fondly on the head and she gently pulled out of his arms, trying to find Judith in the sea of clapping faces. But Amy couldn't see her – had she gone? Had he told her he was going to be with Amy and he didn't care what she thought? Had she walked off in disgust? Amy suddenly felt panic-filled, she didn't want to hurt her.

But then she saw her and Judith was smiling.

'Thank you,' Amy said.

'Take care of him,' Judith said and Amy smiled as she kissed Seb again.

—

George pulled up outside his flat later. The drive back had been silent, the tension between them hanging heavy in the air like a thick smoke. His mind was racing wildly, his heart pounding, his stomach churning so violently he thought he was going to throw up. But as soon as they got back into his flat, Cerys pounced, sticking her tongue down the back of his throat and rubbing herself up against him like a dog on heat. She started pulling him towards the bedroom. So this was it, no backing out now.

But as they approached the bedroom door, his heart leapt at what he saw over Cerys' shoulder. Libby was lying on his bed, curled up like a black cat in her pyjamas, fast asleep.

CHAPTER 16

'Argh!' was all he could manage as he pulled back from Cerys in shock.

'What's wrong?'

'I… I'm a bit nervous. It's been a while since I've been with a woman – do you mind if we…watch a film for a bit, maybe… calm myself down.'

'George, I'll be very gentle,' she whispered, nipping at his ear, as she started to inch back into the bedroom. Something told George that the way Cerys would have sex would be a million miles away from gentle.

He let out a hollow laugh, and resisted as she tried to pull him into the bedroom with her. His heart was beating so loudly now, he was sure it would actually wake Libby up.

'Come on, I've got some great films. What's your favourite, I bet I have it.' His strength won out and he dragged her, unwillingly, back into the lounge.

'Do you have any porn?' she pouted as she threw herself down on the sofa.

He turned to look at her incredulously. He didn't really go in for porn. He and Josie used to watch it together sometimes, but he always ended up feeling very inadequate afterwards, in comparison to the great godly male specimens that starred in them. That's just what he didn't need right now, another reason to feel bad about himself.

'How about a comedy, *His Girl Friday*, now that's a classic.'
He quickly grabbed the DVD, loaded it, then pressed play. 'Here, you watch it, I'll grab us some wine.'

He hurried over to the kitchen, stopping en-route to the bedroom. He watched Libby sleeping peacefully in the middle of his bed. Cerys would not take kindly to finding another woman in his bedroom. He looked back into the lounge. Cerys was already looking decidedly bored, but she hadn't noticed anything was amiss.

Not really knowing what to do about the Libby situation, he quickly closed the bedroom door. Like an ostrich with its head in the sand, he thought if he ignored the problem it might just go away. Maybe once the film got underway, Cerys might actually enjoy it, or she might be so bored she might fall asleep. Either way might buy him a few more hours to think of something he could do about the Libby situation.

'George? You OK?' asked Cerys, eyeing him leaning against the bedroom door.

'Yeah… yes I'm fine, so… red wine or white?'

'White.' She turned her gaze back to the TV.

He opened up a bottle of wine and slugged back a glass. He didn't normally drink wine. Wine always got him stupidly drunk and really quickly too. He looked at the wine bottle, thought about Libby on his bed and refilled his glass, then took both the bottle and two glasses through to the lounge.

He finished his glass, refilled it and sat down. Cerys immediately cuddled into his arms, which reminded him of how Libby cuddled him when they watched a scary film. Thinking of her, he took another big mouthful of wine.

Cerys cuddled him tighter, running her hand round his waist.

'George, do you go to a gym?'

He looked down at his belly distractedly and shook his head.

'You should, it's good fun. I always feel so much better, so energised after I've been to the gym, and you'll notice the difference after just a few short weeks. You should go. I bet you'd love it.'

He nodded as he looked over to the door of his bedroom. He'd heard something, he was sure of it, but the door stayed closed.

The film continued, but he couldn't concentrate. Every minute that ticked by was another minute closer to the time when Libby would wake up and come out into the lounge. There was no way he was going to get through the whole film without her waking up. He just wasn't that lucky. And even if he was, what was he going to do afterwards? He finished his third glass of wine and poured himself a fourth.

Sure enough, about halfway through the film, he heard a loud yawn come from the other room. This was it. He finished his wine, waiting for the big confrontation. Cerys had not heard the yawn, but it was now only a matter of seconds before Libby appeared looking dishevelled and sleepy and gorgeous. He started tapping his fingers on the arm of the chair, as the long seconds stretched on.

The bedroom door opened, and George closed his eyes. He heard Libby gasp and then the bedroom door slammed again.

'What was that?' Cerys asked.

He shrugged, pretending he hadn't heard it.

'Your bedroom door opened and closed again.'

'Did it? Oh, the window's open, it probably got caught in a draught or something.' He shrugged again, trying to pull off an air of nonchalance.

Cerys sat up and looked towards the bedroom door and then back at him.

'George, is there someone in there?'

'No, of course not,' he said, his voice high with anxiety.

Detecting the note of anxiety, she got up and walked towards the bedroom and he quickly followed. What was he going to say, how could he explain it? Maybe he could say he had a flatmate, or… a live-in maid or a… There really was nothing he could say that would justify a woman in his bedroom, in her pyjamas.

Cerys opened the door and his empty bedroom stared back at them, the window pushed open, the curtains blowing in the wind.

'You see, no women lurking in my room. Did you want to check my wardrobes as well?'

'No, sorry, George, I just… I was sure I heard someone gasp.'

He laughed. 'I might just shut the window, it's started to rain.'

He went to the window and saw Libby outside in her pyjamas, already soaked to the skin. He laughed nervously and she put her hand over her mouth to stifle her laughter as well. She motioned with her hand that she was going round to the front. He nodded as he closed the window and turned back to Cerys, grinning, he thought, in a very inane way.

He sat back down on the sofa with Cerys and she took her place in his arms again. He bit his lip as he heard the faint sound of the buzzer in Giselle's flat above him. Libby was trying to gain access to the building. But he knew that Giselle was out; her lights had been off when they'd got home. George knew Libby would be trying Rosie and Alex next, but he also knew that they had gone away for the weekend. He laughed to himself as he poured himself another glass of wine. He would have to let Libby in, but how could he explain to Cerys why he was suddenly going to the front door, or why he was buzzing someone in who hadn't actually rang his buzzer?

Cerys looked at George in confusion, wondering why he was laughing. This made him laugh even more.

He needed an excuse, a reason to go outside. He patted his pockets.

'I think I might have left my wallet in my car, I'll just go and get it.'

'Get it later.'

He drummed his fingers nervously.

'George, are you OK? You seem really... highly strung all of a sudden.'

'I'm fine, I'm fine, but I might just get my wallet, there's been a spate of car break-ins round here lately,' he lied.

'Really?' She sat up in alarm. 'I might come out with you then, put the steering wheel lock on my car, just in case.'

'No, I'll do it for you, it's raining, there's no point in both of us getting wet.'

She conceded this and passed him her keys.

As soon as he had closed the flat door behind him, he yanked open the main front door, grabbed Libby's hand and pulled her towards her flat.

She laughed as she followed in his wake, despite the fact that she was already soaked to the skin.

Inside the flat, he turned to face her. She was shivering violently, but laughing hard. He laughed as well.

'Libby Joseph, you will get me into so much trouble one day.'

She couldn't stop laughing, as she trembled. 'I must have sleepwalked again. I'm sorry, George.'

'Yeah, I'm sure you are.'

'George, are you drunk?'

'Yes. Completely.' He laughed. 'I can't actually remember the last time I was this drunk, but I imagine I was very young.'

She giggled. 'Have you been drinking wine?'

He nodded, sheepishly.

'You know you shouldn't drink wine, how many have you had?'

'Five, six, I'm not sure. I was very stressed.'

Libby laughed, shivering against the cold.

George pulled her to her bedroom and without thinking he pulled her t-shirt off. As soon as he had done it, he realised how inappropriate it was, but as he was on his fifth glass of wine, he found it really funny and started laughing again.

He grabbed another t-shirt and pulled it over her head, but it was very low cut.

'Did you want to do my pyjama bottoms as well?'

He blushed and grabbed a blanket from the bed and wrapped it round her, holding her in his arms.

She giggled. 'God, it feels like we're having a sordid affair, creeping around behind your wife's back.'

'Well in that case, I better give you a quickie before I go back.' And not really knowing why, he took her face in his hands and kissed her. Just a brief kiss, feeling her hot mouth against his, made his heart explode.

He stepped back, and laughed at what he had just done. God, he was stupidly drunk, and the adrenaline coursing through his body was just making the situation worse.

Libby looked stunned, but then laughed as well. 'I'm not taking the blame for that. I take full responsibility for turning up in your bedroom in the middle of your date, but I'm not taking the blame for that kiss.'

'You should, Libby Joseph, you drive me wild.' With that he stepped forward and kissed her again, grabbing her shoulders and pulling her tightly against him.

But to his great surprise, after a few seconds of her standing in shock, she started to kiss him back. Her mouth was moving softly against his lips, her tongue tentatively sliding against his, her hands in his hair.

George pulled back in shock. 'Good God, woman, what are you doing to me?' He laughed. 'I better go. Get changed for goodness' sake, you'll catch your death, sitting around in wet pyjamas. I've got to go back now and have sex with a beautiful woman, wish me luck.'

He was confused slightly by the look of disappointment that suddenly crossed Libby's face. 'Check under your bed for your next present. *Three days before Christmas…*' he sang as he raced back to his flat, burst through the door and vaulted over the sofa. 'Hey!' he said to Cerys, with a big grin on his face.

She frowned. 'You OK? You're practically glowing, like you've just won the lottery or something.'

'No, I'm fine, I just… I just ran back here so I wouldn't get too wet in the rain.'

She surveyed him. 'You don't look very wet.'

Oh what a tangled web we weave. 'Like I said, I ran.' George turned away so she wouldn't see him smirk. He grabbed his glass of wine and drank it down. His heart was beating so fast. But now amongst the fear of sex, the panic of Cerys discovering Libby, was another feeling: lust and desire for Libby, for what had just happened with Libby.

—

Libby stood in her bedroom in shock. What had just happened between them? She knew she shouldn't read too much into George kissing her, he had been very drunk, but she had really enjoyed it. It hadn't been part of a date or for practice, it had been purely because George had wanted to kiss her.

But why had he kissed her? Was it at all possible that he had feelings for her? But then why was he with Cerys if he liked her? Libby wanted to talk to him about it, but he was with Cerys. At this very moment they might be having sex, she could hardly walk in and say, 'Excuse me, George, but about our kiss…'

Libby wondered what he would do if she walked over there now and said that she wanted him to finish that kiss, that she wanted him to choose her. Would he? Would he politely show Cerys the door and then take her into his bedroom and make love to her as beautifully as he had kissed her? Would he laugh and say something like, 'Libby, that's really sweet but I'm with Cerys now, I don't need you any more.' She didn't think she could bear that. But she couldn't bear the thought that he and Cerys would be having sex either.

There was a tiny part of her that wanted it to go well tonight, for George to get what he wanted out of it. But the wholly selfish part wanted it to go badly, wanted him to be thinking of her, comparing her favourably with Cerys.

She knelt down and dug under the bed to find a large paper bag. Inside were two oversized green elf shoe slippers with curly toes and bells on the end. She smiled with love for him.

She got changed out of her wet pyjamas, switched on her laptop; she needed some distraction now, and paced the lounge whilst it loaded up.

She wanted to finish that kiss, she knew that much, she wanted George's hands on her just like he had held her when he had kissed her. It was so…commanding.

The laptop flickered to life, distracting her with its usual ping, with her emotions whirling out of control. She sat down in front of it.

She opened up her latest story, ideas suddenly whirring through her head. She closed her eyes, remembering how lovely it felt to be in George's arms, remembering his kiss. She opened her eyes, and started writing.

—

George and Cerys watched the rest of the film in silence. Well, 'watched' was probably an overstatement, especially on his part. He stared at the screen, experiencing a rollercoaster of emotions. Part of him wanted to come up with another excuse to leave the flat just so he could run over to Libby's flat and kiss her again. But another part of him was wracked with guilt. Had he just cheated on Cerys? Could it be classed as cheating when they were only on their first date? Either way he felt absolutely crap about it.

Now, the pressing problem of sex was also creeping back into his mind. With Libby out the picture there was nothing else to stop the forthcoming coitus. He finished the bottle of wine that Cerys had hardly touched and opened a second.

The film finished, way too prematurely for his liking, and he turned it off. Playing for time, he ejected the DVD and put it back into its box. 'Well, what did you think?'

She shrugged. 'Yeah, it was OK, I suppose.'

He felt incensed by this. How could she not enjoy it? *His Girl Friday* was one of his all-time favourite films. She should at least have a bit more of an opinion than just 'it was OK'.

There was a silence as he stood in the middle of the lounge, a long silence punctuated only with his heart thundering in his ears. Cerys stared at him, clearly waiting for him to make the first move. She'd have a long bloody wait. In fact, he seemed to be paralysed with fear, his feet glued to the carpet where he stood.

'Erm, Cerys, you should know, I'm not that… experienced in this department.'

'You don't need to worry, George, where you lack in experience, I more than make up for it. I've been with many men.'

She patted the chair next to her but he couldn't move at all. What she had just said hung in the air. Was that supposed to make him feel better, that she'd been with many men? If anything, that made him feel worse. What if Josie had been right? What if he was crap in bed? What if Cerys laughed at how bad he was? What if she told everyone and anyone how awful it was? He could imagine her laughing loudly about it in her local, telling everyone who would listen.

Cerys stood up and launched herself at him like a rabid dog.

So this was it, there was nothing that was going to interrupt him now, no other reason to stop her. He told himself that sex with Cerys would be a good thing, an end to his long sexual abstinence.

Cerys kissed him hard, forcing her tongue into his mouth. She seemed to be quite enjoying herself. He was not. He couldn't decide where to put his hands, her bum seemed too familiar and her waist seemed too polite for what she had in mind. Her tongue was so far down the back of his throat, he was pretty sure it could be classed as a choking hazard. He didn't know whether to close his eyes or keep them open, or whether he should just keep one eye open and one closed, though he realised that might be a bit weird. She was pulling his hair so hard, licking all over his face like some kind of dog. It was gross. What was wrong with him? He should be enjoying this. She was pulling him back towards the sofa, kissing and licking all over his face.

She put his hands on her breasts and he tried to decide whether he should squeeze them, stroke them or rub them. He tried squeezing the left and stroking the right, but neither seemed to provoke any reaction in her, she was too busy licking his chin.

She leaned into his ear, licking it, nipping at it with her teeth. She whispered, 'I'm not wearing any underwear.'

Strangely that was a huge turn-off.

Her hands were under his shirt, stroking his chest, his stomach, his belly. She looked down at his stomach, patting it with some amusement. 'George, you really must go down to the gym, you're a bit wobbly.' She leaned in to kiss him again.

He turned away, hurt, but Cerys wasn't to be put off. She kissed his neck and then forced his head round so she could kiss him on the mouth once more.

This was so not what kissing should be like. Kissing should be beautiful; it should be romantic and tender. It should be like it was when he was kissing Libby, the perfect kiss. But kissing could only be like that when you were in love with the person you were kissing. And he certainly wasn't in love with Cerys. How could he kiss her when he felt nothing for her? How could he have sex with her? There was a reason it was called making love – it was because you should do it with someone you loved.

Clarity tugged at the periphery of his brain. He tried to focus on it, on the nagging doubt that was filling his mind. This wasn't right.

'Take your shirt off,' she ordered.

He smiled wryly. 'Cerys, you just told me I was fat, so excuse me if I don't feel ready to take all my clothes off in front of you just yet.'

'I didn't say fat, just… not toned. But that's why you should go down the gym – it will help you feel more confident in the bedroom department. If you feel that self-conscious you could keep your shirt on, then I won't see it.'

He thought that what he really needed to feel more confident in the bedroom was not to be told he was fat in the first place, or to be told that he should cover it up with his shirt so she wouldn't be repulsed by him.

Libby had said that he was beautiful, that Cerys had to love him for who he was, or not at all.

And suddenly the lucidity he had been grasping for slammed into his brain. He didn't want to sleep with Cerys. He wanted Libby and sleeping with Cerys wouldn't be fair to him or to her. Libby probably didn't want him in that way but there was no way he should settle for a poor substitute, someone who didn't like him for who he was.

'This isn't going to work,' he said, quietly.

Cerys' face fell and he felt horribly guilty. 'I'm drunk and…' He gestured vainly to his groin.

'Is it me, George?' she said, quietly. 'Do you not find me attractive?'

'Cerys, it's not you at all, it's me, stage fright, being with a beautiful woman, well … it's kind of intimidating.'

She pouted as she bent to put her shoes back on in what she clearly hoped was a suggestive way. She obviously wasn't used to getting this reaction.

He sat down on the sofa.

'Can I see you tomorrow?' she asked.

Was she kidding? There was no chemistry at all between them and she still wanted to try again?

'Erm…' George tried to find the right words to turn her down, but couldn't. Though she obviously took his silence as an assent.

'I'll… bring something to help with your little problem,' Cerys grinned. 'You can cook for me, and I don't want you to drink so much tomorrow; that probably hasn't helped tonight.'

Then she kissed him on the head and left.

He sighed as he stood up. He would call her tomorrow and make some excuse.

His thoughts strayed back to Libby. He had made a complete fool of himself kissing his best friend too. And he knew he had cheated on the first woman he had dated in years in the process.

He well and truly felt like an arse. He had no right to be with Cerys if his mind was on Libby the whole time, it wasn't fair. And he certainly shouldn't be kissing Libby behind her back. He really wasn't cut out for the 'having his cake and eating it' kind of lifestyle. He leaned his head against the coolness of the door. But annoyingly his brain didn't agree. Because knowing that he shouldn't be kissing Libby made him want it even more. He wanted nothing more now than to go over to her flat and kiss her again. To spend the rest of the night, holding her in her bed and kissing her. Oh, this was dangerous. He turned round and, spotting the second bottle of wine that had been opened, he decided pouring himself another glass might help him to make his mind up. Failing that, it might at least render him unconscious and unable to kiss her again, which was probably the safer option.

——

After Libby had written several pages of beautiful, detailed love scenes between Eliza and Charles, she scrolled through, reading what she had written. With George uppermost in her mind, she had written possibly her best sex scenes ever. And now there was nothing she wanted more than to make those words a reality, but that wasn't going to happen any time soon. He was with Cerys right now, making love to Cerys, a beautiful woman – 'a gift from the gods,' Nick had said. How could Libby have let this happen? He belonged with her. She had spent so long dithering about whether this was something she wanted or not over the last few days and now it was too late. She stood up and wandered sadly over to the window. The moon was no more than a sliver in the cloud-filled sky.

Just at that moment, she heard George's flat door close. A moment later, the most beautiful woman she had ever seen in her life came running down the steps, her long red hair flying in the wind like scarlet ribbons.

So this was Cerys, and Libby could see what all the fuss was about: she was stunning. Though as she moved round the car to get something out the back, Libby did think that the shortness of her dress and the lethal-looking stilettos did mar the effect of her beauty somewhat. As did the rather plunging neckline, her breasts practically falling out. Less Venus, more page three girl. Though Libby supposed George hadn't minded it.

As Cerys closed the back door, she dropped the keys on the ground, and when she bent to pick them up, Libby was treated to something she would have preferred not to see. Was the lack of underwear designed for easy access? Libby shuddered at the thought. Cerys did look a bit… ruffled. Had they had sex?

Libby shook her head and, turning from the window, she headed for bed.

But dreams were very far away as she lay in bed. The memory of George kissing her was fresh, vivid, and she knew she had to talk to him. But she was hardly going to get anything coherent out of him tonight. But maybe she didn't need anything coherent – maybe just going over there and kissing him again would be enough to give her the answer. No, that would be dangerous. Kissing him when he was drunk and probably horny would not be good. Who knew what it might lead to? She rolled over in bed and closed her eyes, determined to go to sleep.

——

George was lying in bed, the room literally spinning around him. He couldn't quite believe how drunk he was.

Libby. The woman of his dreams. She was the only one he wanted, the only thing in his mind. She had definitely kissed him back. And the only thing he could think of now was to go over to her flat and finish that kiss.

He sat up decisively. He would go over. Maybe he couldn't finish that kiss, but he would at least give her the option. Or maybe it was better to kiss first and ask questions later. He walked across the foyer with a bit of difficulty and let himself into her flat.

Heading straight for her bedroom, he opened the door and saw she was lying in bed, clearly awake.

'George? Are you OK?' Libby sat up, pulling back the duvet for him, which he took to be a very good sign. If he could only make it into the bed; unfortunately his legs seemed to want to take him straight to the wall.

'Are you actually more drunk than the last time I saw you?' Libby giggled.

'Completely drunk, more drunk than anyone has ever been in their lives.' George finally made it to the bed and sat down. In a most ungraceful way he pulled his jeans off and then lay down, propping himself up on one side to look at her. Both of her. She seemed to be very close, but then that was probably his fault; there was a whole half of bed behind him. He hadn't left her much room to lie in at all.

'You only have yourself to blame.'

'No, I'm blaming you entirely. Had you not turned up on my bed in the middle of my date, I wouldn't have got stressed out and wouldn't have drunk myself into a coma.'

'So you're not going to take any of the responsibility yourself, it's all my fault?'

'Completely,' George agreed, catching her hand and kissing the back of it. 'I got very stressed at seeing you in my flat when I came home with Cerys. I thought she might shout at me and I didn't want that, then I thought she might shout at you and I definitely didn't want that – like Sinead when she saw you, she wanted to slap you and I didn't want Cerys to do that.' George was aware he was talking shit, but his mouth seemed to have completely disengaged from his brain now. 'Then when we kissed I felt guilty that I had cheated on Cerys and that would make me no better than Josie and so I drank some more and then I was nervous about sex with Cerys, and then I kept thinking about you and kissing you. Then me and Cerys tried to have sex but that didn't work and after she left all I kept thinking about was you, about coming here and kissing you and making love to you and I didn't want that, so I drank a bit more because really I did, I always have and—'

'Shhhhh,' Libby soothed, bending his head down and kissing his forehead.

Oh God. He had to close his eyes quick because, naively or deliberately, she had put his face almost to her breasts. She was wearing a low-cut t-shirt and his mouth was now almost touching her cleavage. He had to keep his eyes closed so he wouldn't be tempted to slide his hands up her ribs and touch them. Or kiss them. He opened one eye. She had a tiny freckle just above her left nipple, and he wanted nothing more right now than to kiss it.

He let out a frustrated sigh, which to his surprise sounded like an angry snarl. Libby jolted slightly in shock.

'I should go, I shouldn't have come,' George said, his voice thick with anger and desire.

'Why did you come?'

'Because I wanted you so badly.'

Shit. That was subtle, wasn't it?

He moved his head up to look at her, waiting for the look of revulsion, or the 'I only want to be friends' speech, but she was still holding his face, her eyes kind.

'Can I kiss you again?' On the inside he could feel himself dying with embarrassment – had he no shame?

'That depends.'

George moved his mouth to her jawbone and kissed it softly. He knew he wasn't going to be able to look her in the face the next day, but right then he didn't care. 'What does it depend on?'

'Well, if you are kissing me just because you are completely drunk and will regret it in the morning then I'd say you probably shouldn't kiss me again. But if you are kissing me because you want to, because you really want to and not just for practice, then… yes.'

His head swam with the conditions. He didn't really understand any of it, except he really wanted to kiss her right now and he was pretty sure she had just said it was OK. Only one way to find out.

And the next thing he knew he was kissing her. He waited for the slap round his face, or for her to push him off, but to his delight, she was kissing him back, wrapping her arms round him.

Quickly, before she changed her mind, he pulled away and kissed that freckle just above her nipple, which made her moan softly, then catching sight of another freckle on her neck, he kissed that too, which made her push her hips against his.

His mouth was back on hers again, her soft hot mouth against his. Fireworks exploded in his head, his heart, his veins. This was what kissing was supposed to be like, beautiful and amazing.

He could feel his lips on fire, his heart pounding against his chest. His senses were exploding, suddenly acutely aware of everything that was Libby. She tasted so sweet, like Starbursts, and she smelt of coconut. Her skin, as he stroked her face, was so smooth, so soft and warm. Oh God, now his tongue was in her mouth, exploring her, tasting her. What would she think of him? A tiny little moan escaped involuntarily from her throat, which made his heart leap into his mouth. Instinctively he wrapped his arm round her waist and pulled her tightly against him. Her hand tightened round the back of his neck, caressing his hair.

The kiss became more heated, more passionate, and he found himself rolling on top of her as the kiss continued. She looped her arms round his neck, kissing him hungrily.

He found his hands wandering down to her hips, and he moved his hands under her top, feeling her hot, silky skin around her waist, her back, her stomach. Then his hands moved back to her hips and slowly started to pull down her pyjama bottoms.

CHAPTER 17

Her hand stopped him, pulling her bottoms back up.

He stopped kissing her. 'Sorry.'

'It's OK, it's just… if you wake up tomorrow and regret kissing me, then you're going to regret sleeping with me even more. I don't want to be a drunken mistake.'

'I would never regret being with you, Lib, I… I adore you.'

She kissed him fondly, on the head. 'Kiss me like that when you're sober and I promise you I won't be stopping you.'

He grinned. 'I better get sober quick then.'

'Black coffee helps.'

He laughed, as he rolled off her onto his back and she found her place with her head on his chest.

—

Libby heard George's breath become heavy, and fingered his hair, absently. Instinctively, in sleep, he pulled her tighter against him.

Oh God, that kiss. She had never been kissed like that before. Her heart had almost exploded with joy. When he had stroked her, it felt like her skin was on fire. And it was so tender, so soft, so…

So there was no going back now. She was falling for him; no doubt about it and she had to tell him. Well maybe not now, he was drunk. She would wait till morning and tell him that she thought she was in love with him, that that kiss had been amazing and the reason that their dates had been so successful was because they were so good together and they should give it a go.

First thing tomorrow, before he left, before he talked his way out of the kiss, she would tell him. Regardless of the outcome or his opinion of it, he had to know what she was feeling. He was her best friend, after all, and she told him everything.

—

George woke the next day, his head feeling like it had been ripped open. He was surprised to find Libby in his arms and was more surprised to find he was in her bed. He really had no recollection of getting into her bed. He thought back to the night before, which was a hazy, jumbled mess of images. He remembered coming home with Cerys and that Libby had been in his bed, and after that it all got a bit grey. He remembered kissing Libby in her flat, both of them giggling like naughty school kids. He remembered kissing her in her bed, and he remembered making love to her, beautiful, amazing sex. But as he still had his shorts on, it was quite unlikely that had actually happened. So had the kissing in the bed not happened either, had that been part of a dream as well?

He forced himself to remember. But the sex seemed so real, so vivid, he wondered if they had.

He quickly checked under the covers to see if Libby was wearing any clothes. She was wearing pyjama bottoms and a low t-shirt. So definitely no sex but, as he spotted a tiny freckle on her chest, a memory jolted in his brain about kissing her there.

George quickly put the duvet back over her.

He had to remember last night. He had a feeling it was important.

Something. Something he was going to do when he was sober, something she wanted him to do when he wasn't drunk.

He sighed. No more memories were forthcoming.

Suddenly his phone exploded into life next to him, echoing round his brain. Libby gave a little jolt as the noise dragged her from her sleep. He didn't move. He just continued to hold her, closing his eyes against the pain of the ringing.

'George,' she mumbled sleepily. 'Your phone.'

'I can't, Lib, it hurts too much,' he muttered.

'Answering it will stop the ringing.'

He ignored it and eventually it stopped. She cuddled back into his arms again.

A few minutes later it started ringing again.

'Make it stop, Lib, make it stop,' he murmured.

She rolled over on top of him, fished his phone out of his discarded jeans and was about to answer it when she spotted the caller ID.

'It's Cerys,' she said, quietly, holding out the ringing phone for him.

He took the phone and she moved to leave, but he caught her arm and pulled her back, enveloping her in his arms. He cancelled the call, diverting it straight to the answer machine, then turned the phone off.

Silence descended on them and he closed his eyes, wanting sleep to take him, thinking that maybe when he was less hungover things would be clearer.

'George, what are you doing?'

'I'm sleeping, Lib.'

'I meant cancelling a call with your girlfriend, and holding me in your arms. Isn't it sort of supposed to be the other way round?'

He kept his eyes closed. 'She's not my girlfriend, she's someone I'm dating, there's a big difference.'

'And what does that make me?'

'The most important person in my life.'

There was a long silence.

'George?'

'Shush, woman, let me sleep.'

He closed his eyes again, pulled her tighter against him, and drifted back off to sleep.

—

George woke later to Libby shifting round on the bed. He opened one eye and looked at her. She was sitting up, stretching her arms widely above her head. She turned round to look at him, and grinned when she saw him awake.

'Hey you.'

'Hey.' He smiled, reaching out and resting his hand on her knee.

'How's the head?'

'A bit better.'

'And do you remember anything from last night?'

He shook his head, and winced because it hurt to do so. 'Not really, just flashes, I'm not sure how much of it actually happened and how much was me dreaming. I remember us having sex, but that didn't happen, did it?'

Her eyes widened. 'You dreamt we had sex?'

'Apparently, if it didn't happen, I must have dreamt it.'

Libby laughed. 'You had a sex dream about me?'

He nodded.

'Oh my God, that's so funny, was I any good?'

'It was amazing.'

'That's brilliant,' she laughed, then to his surprise she blushed. 'Would you like some breakfast?'

He nodded.

'Full English?'

He beamed. 'Yes please.'

She rolled off the bed and padded out into the kitchen. She came back a minute later with a glass of water and some painkillers. He kissed her hand and she left again.

He put his hands behind his head and closed his eyes, smiling to himself. The night before had been weird. He remembered the attempt at sex with Cerys, which had been awful, and kissing Libby, which had been fantastic. She had kissed him back, he definitely remembered that. What was going on? The first time he had been on a date with a woman in years and he was in the flat opposite kissing his best friend.

Libby came back in a few minutes later, carrying two plates of breakfast. He sat up to take his plate and she settled down next to him.

He kissed her cheek. 'Thank you.'

She smiled as she tucked into her breakfast.

After they had finished, he put his plate down and lay down with his arm round her.

'No, you're not going back to sleep, you're going to have a shower, and you should probably get on with some work, God knows I need to. Come by later and we'll go for a walk, that will blow the cobwebs out.'

'OK, OK, I'm up. I'll have a shower, I promise,' George said, forcing himself into a sitting position. He pulled his jeans on and, kissing her on the forehead, he left.

But as soon as he got back into his flat, he collapsed back onto his bed.

His head was still woolly, his memory nothing more than a blur. There was a reason he didn't drink, hangovers knocked him out for the rest of the day.

He closed his eyes and went back to sleep.

—

Finally, later, much later, he felt able to get up. He showered and dressed and walked over into Libby's flat, but as he walked into her lounge he leapt back in shock. Walking towards him, arms outstretched, was a headless body, wearing his favourite sweatshirt.

'George? Is that you?' came the mumbled disembodied voice from within the folds of his sweatshirt.

He stared at Libby, in amused confusion.

'Well, if it's not George, if it's a burglar, would you mind helping me before you steal all my precious jewels?'

He quickly ran to stop her from bumping into the wall. He caught her in his arms and instinctively she put her hands on his waist to steady herself.

'Do you have many precious jewels then, Lib?'

'Tonnes, all in the vault out the back. George, can you help me?'

'What's up?' he asked the headless figure before him.

'My hair is caught in the zip, and it won't move up or down and I can't get the bloody thing past my head now. I've been stumbling around like this for the last five minutes.'

'Why didn't you come and get me?' George carefully took the zip and tried to ease it down.

'Well partly because I thought you would laugh and partly because I couldn't find the front door.'

'Honey, of course I'd laugh, but mostly after I'd helped you.'

Libby laughed but then the laugh turned to a squeal as he tried to force the zip past the clump of hair.

'Sorry Lib, let me try something else… by the way this sweat-shirt looks very familiar.'

She was quiet for a moment. 'Does it?' She giggled. 'I wonder why that is, you've probably seen me in it quite a bit, it is one of my favourites.'

He smirked as he carefully pulled strands of hair from the teeth of the zip. 'And where did you get it from?'

'Um…'

He saw her twisting round inside to get a look at the label at the bottom.

'It's from Prague,' he whispered in an aside.

'Prague,' she said triumphantly.

'Really? Prague? And when did you go to Prague?'

She giggled. 'I haven't but I have a friend who went and he bought it for me.'

'Really? Are you sure he bought it for you, it seems a bit on the large side?'

'I like them big.'

He rolled his eyes at the innuendo.

'Besides, this one has the best smell in the world, that's why it's my favourite.'

He stepped closer to smell it. 'What does it smell of?'

'You,' Libby said, her grip instinctively tightening round his waist. He looked down at her hands and smiled.

'Lib, I can't do this, I need to cut your hair from the zip. It's caught up pretty bad.'

'NOOOOO!' she wailed. 'Not my precious locks, I'm like Samson, my strength is in my hair.'

He sat her down on the sofa and grabbed a pair of scissors. 'Well I guess that makes me Delilah.'

'NOOOOOO!' she sobbed theatrically.

'Shush, woman, I'm trying to concentrate.'

George carefully cut away the hair that was attached to the zip. When Libby was finally free of the zip, he gave the zip a big yank and it came loose, freeing her from her prison.

She pulled the sweatshirt down and looked at him. She looked all dishevelled and gorgeous. 'How bad is the damage?'

He pulled a face. 'You'd hardly notice it, Lib.'

She shrugged. 'Fancy a walk?'

He nodded and he watched her put her trainers on.

'So…' she said, almost shyly, 'last night?'

George groaned. 'It was a disaster, Lib, a horrible mistake. You know those moments you wish you could rewind and do over? If I could do it over, I would never do it at all.' He shuddered for effect, but stopped when he saw the look of hurt cross her face. 'What?'

'Nothing.' Her jaw set determinedly as she walked towards him. 'Just thinking I'm pretty glad we didn't have sex last night.'

He felt hurt by this.

'Oh don't look at me like that, like I've wounded you in some way,' she snapped. 'You can deliver a death blow yourself. So that's all last night was, a drunken fumble, a horrible drunken mistake, never to be repeated?'

He looked at her in confusion. 'What are you talking about, what happened last night?'

'Oh, I'm glad it was so memorable for you.'

Libby stormed past him, slammed the flat door and ran onto the beach. George stared after her in shock, watching through the window as she kicked a large stone in her path.

He ran after her, running onto the beach in her wake.

'Libby, stop.'

She turned round, her hair flying theatrically behind her.

'Look… I'm not sure what I did last night. I was more drunk than I've ever been, but I'm sorry if I did something to upset you. That's the last thing I want.'

'What you did last night didn't upset me, it's your attitude to it today that has.' She turned and walked away from him.

—

Libby went down to the sea. She stood staring at the water for a moment, then took off her trainers and stepped into the icy waves. She rolled her jeans up to her thighs and waded out until the water covered her knees.

She watched the icy water surging past her legs, the white-tipped waves rising towards her then crashing behind her onto the shore. The sea, even when it was grey and rough like today, was still beautiful.

For George to kiss her like that in bed the night before and then dismiss it as a horrible drunken mistake, that hurt. Mostly because for her, the kiss had been beautiful and amazing. It had made her fall further in love with him, whilst for him it had been nothing more than a drunken fumble. Or maybe he had just tried to laugh it off because he was embarrassed by trying it on with her. Still, she felt weird about it. Waking up in his arms this morning, she had thought about waking up in his arms every morning, and how much she actually wanted that. But tonight he would probably go back to Cerys; maybe tomorrow even wake up with her in his arms instead.

Libby sighed, scrunching her toes into the sand.

But what was he doing kissing her? And not just the last kiss, the beautiful, amazing kiss, but the two other kisses in her flat, when his date was sitting just yards away across the hall. The other kisses on their dates could be put down to just kissing for practice but none of the kisses the night before had been about that. If George liked her why was he going out with Cerys? Why didn't he just tell her he liked her?

'Shit, fuck, that's freezing,' George said, behind her, and she turned to see him hobbling out through the waves to her side. He hated the cold, hated it with a passion, so she couldn't help smiling slightly as he made his way through the icy water.

'I'm quite glad we didn't sleep with each other last night too,' he said, visibly shivering. 'Because if we had, I'd be like this right now.' He suddenly knelt in the water, the waves sloshing over his thighs and threw his arms round her legs, leaning his head against her hips. 'Please sleep with me again, please, please, just one more time, please. I'll pay you, PLEASE!!!'

Libby couldn't help but laugh as he rubbed his head against her side, much like a cat would do.

'PLEASE, LIBBY, PLEASE.'

'There's nothing quite like quiet desperation, and there's nothing quiet about that.'

He looked up at her. 'I know, it's quite pathetic, isn't it.'

'Very.'

He stood up. 'You're my best friend, Lib, and I like our friendship, that we would drop anything and everything to be by the other's side. I like that when you sleepwalk you come to me, as if subconsciously you feel you're safest with me. I like that our friendship has deepened to the extent that we can now cuddle in bed, and OK, maybe the kissing is… was pushing the boundaries a bit, but I sort of liked that too… didn't you?'

'But…you just said it was a horrible drunken mistake.'

George looked horrified. 'Not kissing you, I could never regret being with you. I was talking about Cerys. She tried to sleep with me last night, it was an absolute disaster.'

'Oh.' Libby's heart leapt at his answer, at her mistake. 'What happened?'

'She started kissing me, started taking it in that direction and… I didn't want her. I actually realised that I didn't want to be with her before we even went on the date and I probably should have stopped it then.'

Her heart went out to him, knowing how much he had been looking forward to it. 'Oh George, I'm sorry. What happened?'

'Well amongst other things, she called me fat and that filled me with no end of confidence, let me tell you.'

'You're not fat, George, not at all,' she protested.

'I'm hardly a Peter Andre with a perfect six-pack though, Lib.'

'You're not fat,' she muttered defensively. What an absolute cow. She had to say something to turn this around. 'Besides, six-packs are overrated. Most women don't go in for that sort of thing any more, it just screams that you're trying too hard, that you're self-obsessed. I like your shape, that's who you are. You are very attractive, don't ever think otherwise. And you give the best hugs, I love hugging you, it's sturdy.'

He smiled. 'Anyway, I just kept thinking about you, what you said about her loving me for who I am and I realised that she wasn't the person I wanted to be with.'

'Oh George, what did she say?'

'Well, she was a bit upset, but she wants to try again tonight. I can't think of anything worse. She actually said she'd bring some Viagra. I'm going to call her later and cancel.'

Libby was silent for a moment, watching the waves as they swept past them. 'And… what about what happened with us?'

'We kissed?'

She bit her lip. 'You kissed me, admittedly I did kiss you back, but you certainly instigated it.'

George looked down. 'In your flat?'

'And in my bed.'

His face went bright red.

'You do remember.'

'I… also remember making love to you in your bed. As that definitely didn't happen, I wasn't so sure about the kissing.'

'It was a bit more than just a kiss, George.'

He looked down, colour flooding his cheeks.

'So… was it just a silly drunken kiss, or was it something more?' Libby asked.

George stared at her, but no words seemed forthcoming.

'Was it because you like me… as something more than just friends?'

He opened his mouth to speak but then looked away.

He didn't feel the same, he just didn't know how to tell her. She swallowed the pain of the rejection. 'Are you going to see her again?'

'No. I can't say last night was a huge success, there were plenty of awkward silences, she seemed to lack any sort of sense of humour and there was quite a lot about me she didn't like. And the chemistry was awful. Then there's you, my favourite person in the whole world. There's no comparison between spending time with you and spending time with her. The few minutes I spent with you last night were much more enjoyable than my whole date with Cerys.'

Libby swallowed, her mouth suddenly dry. Hope bloomed in her heart. 'What does that tell you?'

'I… don't know, I… the thing about olives is when you first try them they're disgusting, but when you keep eating them, you start to develop a taste for them. With chocolate. I could eat chocolate all day, every single day for the rest of my life and never get tired of it.'

George looked confused by his own analogy and Libby wasn't any closer to understanding him either.

'You should be with someone who makes you laugh, who loves every little thing about you, who wants to make you happy.' *Someone like me.*

'You're right.'

She reached up to touch his face. 'I want you to be happy, George; more than anything I want that for you. And when you find the person who makes you happy, who you love, grab hold of her with both hands and don't let her go. Don't settle either. She has to be perfect for you in every way. It has to be her mission in life to make you as happy as you make her, and don't accept anything less.'

George nodded as he looked down at her and for one glorious moment she was sure he was going to kiss her.

CHAPTER 18

But whether George would have kissed her or not, Libby would never find out. At that second with her hand still on his face, his mouth just centimetres from her own, Jack chose that moment to gallop between them, obviously curious as to what they were both doing standing in the sea. With his nose in her crotch, and then slamming his wet bum into George, the dog bounced out of the waves onto the beach and then back to them, bringing his ball for them to throw.

Libby stepped back from George, their moment – if indeed there was one – completely broken. She took the ball and threw it down the beach, and Jack tore after it.

She looked up the beach in the direction of the pub to see Amy and Seb walking towards them, holding hands. It filled her heart to see it.

George was already making his way back onto the beach. He stopped to see if Libby was coming and held out his hand for her, a peace offering. She took it and he pulled her gently in his wake as he struggled through the waves, though once safely back on the beach, he let her go.

They walked towards Amy and Seb.

'Sorry about him,' Seb said, gesturing towards Jack who was lumbering back up the beach towards them. 'He has no discretion.'

'Yes, I hope he didn't interrupt anything,' Amy said, looking meaningfully at Libby.

Libby shook her head, staring at Amy with equal weight. 'No, not at all, we were just discussing George's date with Cerys.'

The look of disappointment that crossed Libby's face was obvious and Amy looked at her, seemingly trying to convey her thoughts without a single word. Libby knew what she was thinking. *Why the bloody hell is he going out with Cerys and not you?*

'Cerys Andrews, George? She has very high standards,' Seb said.

'So?' Libby said, suddenly angry. 'Are you saying that George can't meet those standards, any woman would be lucky to go out with him and—'

'Easy, Lib, I wasn't saying that at all. I was diplomatically trying to say she's a complete cow. And in my opinion, George, you can do a hell of a lot better than Cerys.' Seb's eyes flittered to Libby for a moment, but when George failed to notice the meaningful stare in her direction, Seb walked away shaking his head.

Amy hurried to catch up with Seb, taking his hand again, but looked back sadly at her friend as she walked.

Libby watched them go, walking towards the far end of the beach, where it sloped gently up into a small cliff that jutted out into the sea. She looked back to George.

'I'm going to call her, finish it with her,' he said.

Libby's heart leapt with joy.

George was already taking his phone out of his pocket. 'She's not the woman for me; I can do better, a lot better.'

He dialled Cerys' number. Libby took his hand and squeezed it encouragingly as it rang.

He put the phone on loudspeaker.

Cerys answered. 'Hello?'

'Hi it's me, it's George.'

'Hello.'

Libby couldn't help thinking how cold Cerys' voice was.

'Look… about tonight, I… don't think it's a good idea…'

'Are you dumping me?' Her voice was incredulous, angry.

'I just… don't think we're good together,' George said, pushing his hair nervously off his face.

'Well, we would have been if you could have got it up,' Cerys said, sulkily.

Libby opened her mouth to protest, but George clamped his hand over her mouth.

'It's not just the sex though, Cerys, it's the whole package. I want to be with someone who can make me laugh, someone I can be myself with, someone who actually likes me.' He eyed Libby and smiled.

He was talking about her, about being with her. To distract George from her heart beating so loudly, Libby poked her tongue through the gap in his fingers and he looked at her in disgust. She snorted with suppressed laughter and he clearly had to bite back the laughter as well.

'I like you,' Cerys said, quietly, and Libby saw George swallow. She just hoped he wasn't going to change his mind.

'Cerys, it's taken me a long time to realise that I actually have something worthwhile to offer a woman. That the package I come in is actually a good one. You're too hung up on the little things: my hair, my clothes, my shoes, my weight. If you like me, you should like all of me, you should be able to see past those things, and see the person on the inside.'

'I do, George, I like you.'

'Well, what if I don't want to change those things – what if I keep my hair long, don't lose any weight, wear what I want to wear. Would you still like me then?'

Cerys hesitated, long enough for Libby, at least, to see the truth behind her words. 'Yes of course.'

'Cerys, I hope you find him, your Mr Perfect. But I don't think he's me.'

And with that George hung up.

Libby smiled with admiration; as dumping went, that was one of the nicest. He had managed to do it without insulting Cerys once.

He shoved his phone in his pocket and finally released her mouth, wiping his hand on his jeans.

'You're my Mr Perfect,' Libby said, without even thinking about it first. And then it was out there, and there was nothing she could do to get it back.

But he hadn't even noticed, his eyes were on a truck that had just pulled up outside their flats.

Suddenly a huge grin spread on his face and he grabbed her hand and ran towards it singing, '*Two days before Christmas, my true love gave to me...*'

As they drew level, she gasped. Being wheeled down the ramp at the back was a shiny, gleaming red Ducati.

'It's a rental,' he said, quickly. 'We have it for a week. I thought as you've helped me to get back in the saddle I could do the same for you.'

'Oh my God, George. That's fantastic... terrifying but fantastic,' she said in awe, as she lovingly caressed the bike. 'She's beautiful, isn't she?'

'Yes, she is.'

Libby stared at it in wonder for a few moments. A huge lump formed in her throat and she looked back at George. In that moment, she knew without doubt that she was in love with him, completely, unequivocally head over heels in love. Whereas before she thought she might be falling in love with him, she had now fallen, and there was no climbing back out the other side. He was the most beautiful, kindest, sweetest man she ever had the fortune to know. Why had she never seen this before, why had it taken six months, why had it taken these dates over the last few days, that kiss, this unbelievably kind gesture for her to realise it? She loved him. And this huge realisation literally took her breath away.

'Well come on, I didn't rent it so you can stand there staring at me. Are you going to ride it or what?' George passed her the helmet.

'Yes, of course, but…' Libby leaned forward to hug him, and closed her eyes as he hugged her back. 'Thank you, this is so kind of you. Now listen, I want to tell you something…'

'My pleasure.' He pulled back from the hug. 'You've given me so much confidence over the last few days, and you're right, I shouldn't settle – aim high, eh? I'm going to do it, Lib, I'm finally going to ask out the woman of my dreams.'

Libby's heart soared. The woman he had kissed so passionately in bed the night before? The girl who made him laugh, the one he had dumped Cerys for?

He stared at her and a look of fear crossed his face.

George's eyes slid past her to the entrance of the flat. 'Excuse me.' He left Libby and ran up the steps to greet Giselle.

Libby stared in horror. What had just happened? The very moment she had realised she loved him, completely, the moment she was just about to tell him how she felt, and he was running up the stairs to ask out the woman of his dreams, the woman who wasn't her. She tried to find her voice to call him back, but he had already reached Giselle, running his hand through his hair nervously.

Selfishly Libby prayed Giselle would say no. Though there was a small part of her that couldn't bear to see George rejected and hurt, it was overpowered by the part of her brain that was screaming at Libby to march up the steps and snatch him back from Giselle, like a toddler being possessive over a favourite toy.

Say no, say no, say no, Libby chanted in her mind again and again.

But Giselle was suddenly smiling hugely, her hand on George's arm as she nodded. Libby watched as she waved goodbye to him, still smiling as if she had been given the best Christmas present ever.

Libby didn't need to see the huge inane grin on George's face as he watched her go to know what Giselle's answer had been. Feeling the tears that were threatening to spill over her eyes, she quickly pulled on her helmet, got on the bike and took off down the road. In her wing mirror, before she disappeared around the corner, she saw George staring after her in confusion, then sadly down at the spare helmet in his hand.

——

George paced the lounge, nervously. It was getting late now and he needed to speak to Libby about his big date tomorrow night. The Christmas ball, the music, the fairy lights, the Christmas decorations. It couldn't be more perfect. He had spent the whole afternoon up in Giselle's flat, talking with her, and she was ridiculously excited too. He hadn't seen Libby since she had taken off up the road. Obviously she was keen to try the Ducati out, but he hadn't seen her since. Now the excitement he had felt about his date had dwindled into full-blown panic.

He had thought about the disaster that had been his experience with Cerys and started getting scared. He had spent the last few hours studiously reading the homework Libby had given him. He picked his way through all the articles about how to please your woman, the articles on oral sex, and the step-by-step instructions for an array of sexual positions. But now he felt even worse than he did before. Sex had moved on a lot since his time with Josie; it was complicated, messy and a lot more daring than he was used to. He thought about what Libby had said, that she imagined that sex with him would be beautiful. It had given him such confidence to hear her say that. He just had to relax and do what came naturally. But the more he thought about sex, the more worried he became.

He was presuming that the date would even get that far. What if it didn't?

Just then, Libby pulled up on her bike outside. She took her helmet off and shook her hair out. Inappropriate images of her suddenly flooded his mind.

George's feelings for her had changed after that kiss. He still loved her, but now it was coupled with an all-consuming desire, a need for her, to have her. Whereas before he had always assumed that making love, kissing her, would never happen between him and Libby, now that they had, or nearly had, he wanted more. It was all he could think of now – that kiss in her bed the night before and how much he wanted it again. His memory of the night before was still woolly. He remembered finally finding the courage to tell her he wanted her, to make love to her. He remembered kissing her, holding her, touching her, trying to let her know how much she meant to him. And then he remembered her stopping him from taking it any further. He couldn't remember why, but it sure as hell hadn't been him who had stopped it. He wanted to tell her how he felt for her on the beach but the fact that she had stopped him making love to her filled him with doubt. She had stopped him for a reason. What if that reason was that she simply didn't return his feelings?

He quickly ran to the door. He had to talk to her. He and Giselle had this wonderful idea for his date and he had to make sure Libby would be happy with it. He was supposed to be taking Libby to the ball but he wanted to see if she would be OK with a last-minute change of plan.

'Hey…' George faltered slightly when he realised her face was blotchy as if she'd been crying. He took a step towards her. 'Where have you been?'

'I've been out on my bike, like you wanted me to. I didn't realise I had to keep you apprised of my every movement,' Libby snapped, which completely threw him.

'I've phoned you, you didn't answer.'

'My phone is in my flat.' She turned towards her front door.

'Are you OK?'

She turned back, her eyes flashing angrily. 'You're so fickle, George. You kiss me, you try to sleep with Cerys, and when that doesn't work, you try to sleep with me. Now you're going out with Giselle, and judging by the magazine you're holding with the top ten sex tips, you're probably going to try to shag her as well. Polly, I'm sure you could try her next, if Giselle doesn't work out for you. Sally, you told me you were in love with her a few months ago. But then you're a man, I should expect this from you, any hole's a goal, eh George?'

Libby stormed away from him and he stared after her for a second before he chased after her.

'Wait, wait, I don't understand. What's your problem?'

'I have a problem with you kissing me like... like I meant something last night, and then moving on to someone else today.' She stepped closer and jabbed a finger into his chest. 'I have a problem with you just using me for practice, refining your skills for someone better.'

'Libby... I...'

But she was already storming into her flat, slamming the door, and for the first time in six months he heard the flat door being locked behind her.

—

It had been a weird night and not at all what George had expected to happen when he had woken up with Libby in his arms that morning. Libby had refused to answer her door, and when he and Giselle had gone to the pub together, there had been many people who had given him evil stares for the entire night. In the end they had cut their evening short and decided to go back to his flat so they could talk some more over some hot chocolate.

He looked at Giselle as they walked back along the street. She had been lovely to talk to. He didn't know why he had been so scared to talk to her for the last week – she was easy-going, friendly, incredibly kind.

He let them into his flat. 'If you put the kettle on, I'll make a fire.'

Giselle moved ahead of him into the lounge. 'Oh.'

And even though he couldn't see what had made Giselle stop in the doorway, he knew it was Libby. He moved round Giselle and sure enough Libby was curled up on his sofa, fast asleep. She was wearing her pyjamas, and had probably sleepwalked into his flat and then drifted off into a deeper sleep when he wasn't there to take her back home.

'George, why is she asleep on your sofa?' Giselle asked.

'She sleepwalks, a lot. Sometimes she goes out on the street, sometimes she ends up in here.'

'Really?' She seemed genuinely intrigued by this. 'Does she just curl up on your sofa and go back to sleep?'

'No, sometimes she just stares into nothing; sometimes I can have actual conversations with her.'

'What do you talk about?'

'Oh, nothing sensible. The other day Clint Eastwood was buying her car.'

Giselle smiled, turning back to him. 'So she's quite intellectual when she's asleep then?'

He moved into the room. 'It's rare that she's just sleeping, that means she's gone past the sleepwalking stage and fallen back into a deeper sleep.'

'What do you do with her when you find her – isn't it danger-ous to wake her up?' She moved further into the lounge to look at Libby.

'Well, they say you shouldn't wake up sleepwalkers because it can confuse and scare them. When she's actually sleepwalking, I just take her back to her own bed; she's normally very compliant. When she's like this, she's probably safe to wake.' He moved towards Libby to shake her.

'Aw no leave her, George, it seems a shame to wake her. Look, let's leave this now, we can hardly carry on with our conversation while she's here. Come and see me tomorrow morning and we can chat more about it then.'

Giselle eyed Libby for a moment, then pulled the blanket off the back of the sofa and gently covered her with it.

'Goodnight, George.'

He bent his head to kiss her on the cheek. 'Thank you.'

Giselle smiled. 'My pleasure.'

As she left George turned his attention back to Libby who had quite clearly woken up, as she was glaring up at him. Had she seen him kiss Giselle? Where had all this anger suddenly come from? He had blurred the lines between him and Libby, and with the kisses, lying in bed with her, he had somehow hurt Libby too, which was the last thing he ever wanted to do.

Libby got up, quickly moving towards the door.

'Libby, wait, we need to talk.'

She turned back, wearily. 'What's there to talk about? You're with Giselle, the woman of your dreams.'

He faltered for a moment but then quickly pressed on.

'Listen, last night in bed, when I tried to sleep with you, you stopped me.'

Her eyes flared angrily. 'You think I stopped you because I didn't want you? I stopped you because I wanted our first time together to be beautiful, because a friendship as close as ours should have culminated in something wonderful, and not just a quick, easy, drunken shag. I stopped you because… I wanted you to make love to me because you loved me, not just because you were drunk and horny.'

She turned for the door again, but he was quicker, and slammed it before she could open it. She was facing away from him, his hands either side of her on the door. She was breathing heavily. Her fists were clenched but he could see goosebumps on the back of her neck as his warm breath touched her.

'Are you saying…' He swallowed. 'Are you saying you want me to make love to you?'

Libby turned back to him and then clearly regretted it as they were now standing very close. He couldn't move away from her, couldn't take his hands from either side of her body. She backed up against the door.

'No, you're with Giselle. You had your eureka moment today, when you realised you could do better than Cerys, and you said you were going to ask out the woman of your dreams. You chose Giselle, because she's beautiful, a woman you've known for a week. The woman of your dreams is not me, not good old Libby, your best friend for the last six months.'

'Hang on… I'm not… I thought…'

'What did you think, George? What were you thinking when you were kissing me so passionately in bed last night? What were you thinking when you came into my room, got into bed with me and told me you wanted me, that you wanted to make love to me? As the woman of your dreams is clearly not me, then when you said you wanted me, you didn't actually mean you loved me did you, you meant, "I want a shag, you'll do, in fact anything with a pulse will do right now."'

George swallowed, wondering how his lovely evening had ended so badly. 'That's not how it was at all.'

'I've booked my ticket to New York. I leave Christmas Day. It was cheaper if I flew out then rather than the start of January and as there was *nothing* here worth staying for there didn't seem any point in waiting around. I hope you get everything you ever wanted out of this thing with Giselle, but this time I won't be there to pick up the pieces if it goes wrong.'

He watched, too stunned to move or say anything, as everything he ever wanted walked out of his flat, and a few seconds later, he heard her own flat door lock as she closed it behind her.

CHAPTER 19

George came down the stairs from Giselle's flat feeling like he had run a marathon and it was still only ten o'clock in the morning.

He stopped suddenly halfway down the flight of stairs, staring in shock at the outside world that had transformed overnight into a sea of white that covered the beach with a thick blanket. How had he not noticed that before? He had barely slept the night before as he thought about Libby leaving. This morning he had woken determined to do something to stop it. He had to speak to Giselle about the ball and barely even given the outside world a glance. Proper snow in White Cliff Bay was almost unheard of. It had snowed before but nothing quite as spectacular as this. Normally, especially this close to Christmas, it would have filled him with pure delight. He would have dragged Libby down to the beach to make snowmen, but that wasn't going to happen today.

Suddenly Libby's flat door slammed open and she ran for the main door. Had she seen the snow and was running outside to enjoy it? But something about her urgency made him realise immediately that something was wrong.

'Lib?'

She glanced up at him, seeing him for the first time.

'George... shit, it's Kat...'

She ran out the main front door and he knew from her tone that something was terribly wrong. He ran out after her and Libby stopped on top of the steps, suddenly taking in the beauty of the snow scene in front of her.

'Shit, I can't get my car up to Two Hill Farm in this.'

George stared up the road towards the pub. There was a Land Rover parked outside loading chairs into the back.

'No, but I bet he could.' George pointed to the man, who looked vaguely familiar.

Libby didn't hesitate, she ran down the road towards the car. By the time George had caught up with her, she had already explained the problem to the man and he had agreed to help her. As the man turned, George realised it was the sickeningly good-looking bloke Libby had tripped over a few nights before.

'George, this is Henry, he says he'll give us a lift up there.'

Henry briefly shook George's hand and climbed in the driving seat. Libby got in the passenger side, leaving George to climb in the back, glowering at the back of Henry's head.

'I won't be able to wait with you I'm afraid, preparations for the ball have been thrown completely into disarray and I'm helping my girlfriend Penny with an emergency contingency plan.'

George stopped scowling. Henry had a girlfriend. This was the man that had nearly jumped in after Penny when she had fallen in the sea the other night. But then the scowl quickly came back on his face. Henry was right. The snow could ruin everything. His big plans for the ball could all become undone. He would have to come up with an emergency contingency plan of his own.

———

Libby watched Henry take the corners on the narrow road up to Two Hill Farm quickly, impressed with his handling of the ice and snow. Her heart was thundering against her chest. She felt sick, physically sick.

'What's happened?' George asked, leaning between the two seats.

'She's bleeding.' She glanced over at him, he looked pale.

'That's not good, is it?'

Libby shook her head.

'Where's Big Dave?'

'She sent him out to get chocolate milkshake, she's got a real dairy craving, and now she can't reach him on the phone.'

'Has an ambulance been called?'

'Yes, but, God, George, she sounded so scared, she said she was in so much pain, she was sobbing.'

'For God's sake, get there quickly,' George said to Henry and to Libby's surprise Henry put his foot down.

—

As the car skidded to a halt in the courtyard, George was already out the door. Libby stopped to talk to Henry for a second and George heard him say he was going to look for the ambulance and help them to get to the farm if he could, before Libby chased after George. They burst through the front door and up the stairs.

God, if anything happened to Kat or the baby, Big Dave would be inconsolable. Quite what he and Libby could do was another matter, but he was glad he could at least be here for her, for Big Dave.

'Kat?' he called, but Libby was already shoving past him to a door at the end of the landing. He quickly followed her.

Kat was lying on the bed, her face red and flustered, crying and writhing in pain.

Shit. He was way out of his depth here. The only thing he knew about first aid was the basics he learned in the Scouts about twenty years before.

Libby quickly knelt on the bed, holding her hand. Taking his knowledge of maternity care from TV and films, he quickly ran into the bathroom to get a wet facecloth to mop her brow.

He came back in and passed the facecloth to Libby, who looked at it in confusion and then duly mopped Kat's face.

'Libby, the baby's coming, but something's wrong, I can feel it,' Kat panted. 'We had sex the other day, what if... what if we hurt the baby?'

'It's OK, Kat, just try to stay calm, the paramedics are on their way, and Dave will be back soon,' Libby soothed.

'Where the bloody hell is he, I swear if I give birth to his baby and he's not here, I'll kill him, I'll fucking kill him,' Kat roared. George backed into the hall again, wondering if she would kill him just for being a man.

Fumbling in his pocket, he pulled out his phone and tried Dave's mobile for the third time, but as before it just went straight through to answer phone.

'Dave, for God's sake, man, get your arse back home now,' he growled into the phone, before taking a big breath and going back into the bedroom again.

Kat screamed, gripping Libby's hand so tightly it looked like she might have broken it, but though Libby grimaced in pain, she didn't relinquish her hold on Kat's hand.

'That's it, it's OK, just breathe, you're doing OK, you're going to be a wonderful mum, Kat, and your baby is going to be beautiful, just breathe,' Libby said.

She was so calm, so together, whilst George was panicking wildly. What if the baby came and there he and Libby were here? He couldn't deliver a baby, he didn't have the first clue about these things, other than what he had seen on TV and films, and there always seemed to be a lot of crying and screaming. What if something went wrong, what if he did something wrong?

He couldn't do this. He had nothing to offer here, he would be better off waiting downstairs. But as Libby looked round at him, he could see a real fear in her eyes and he knew he couldn't leave her.

Suddenly he heard the front door slam open, and from the footsteps that thundered up the stairs, he knew that it was Big Dave and that he'd got the previous messages that he and Libby had left for him.

Big Dave burst into the room and was at Kat's side instantly.

'Dave, oh God Dave, I love you, I love you so much,' Kat sobbed, reaching out her hand for him.

'I love you too, now let's deliver our baby.'

Kat beamed happily at him, but her face suddenly changed as she suffered another contraction and she screamed, squeezing both Dave and Libby's hands tightly.

'Hello?' called a voice from downstairs.

George quickly ran to the top of the stairs, and nearly wept with relief at the sight of the two men, dressed in the green of the paramedics' uniform, standing at the bottom.

'Up here, quick.'

The men hurried up the stairs, following him down the hall to the bedroom.

'OK,' said one of the men calmly, 'let's have some space in here, everyone out who isn't family.'

George watched Libby kiss Kat on the head, disentangle her hand from Kat's grasp, and then allow herself to be ushered out the door by one of the paramedics.

As the bedroom door closed, he realised that Libby was trembling.

'Shall I make a cup of tea?'

She nodded weakly, and he took her hand and led her down the stairs into the warmth of the kitchen. He made the tea and pushed the mug into her hands.

The voices and noises coming from directly above them were indistinct and not encouraging. There was a lot of screaming, shouting and loud bangs.

Libby stood up and started pacing, and he watched her progress across the kitchen floor.

'She'll be fine, Lib, so will the baby. The paramedics are here and Big Dave has delivered more baby animals in his life than I've had hot dinners.'

'Baby animals and babies are very different,' she mumbled, casting her eyes in the directions of the screams above her.

Suddenly there was a silence from above. A long deathly silence.

She ran out the kitchen and he followed her to the bottom of the stairs.

The silence dragged on and then suddenly it was broken with an ear-splitting cry, the cry of a baby with huge lungs.

George heard the bedroom door open.

'It's a boy,' Big Dave yelled down the stairs, over the noise of his firstborn. 'A bloody big healthy baby boy.'

George laughed and Libby, to his surprise, burst into tears. He quickly pulled her into his arms, and she cried against his chest, soaking his shirt with her tears.

———

At first, Libby had been too relieved about Kat and the baby to pay attention to what happened next. But just a few seconds after the announcement of the new arrival, she had found herself held tightly in George's arms, his fingers making soothing circles across her back. She wanted to cry forever if it meant he would hold her like that.

She looked up at him, and he smiled at her, taking her face in his hands. She closed her eyes as he wiped her tears away, but with his gentle touch, her heart exploded in her chest.

Suddenly aware of how close he was standing, how he was bound to feel her heartbeat, she stepped back, embarrassed.

'Come on then, you two, come and say hello to our son,' Big Dave called from the top of the stairs, and Libby nearly sighed with relief.

—

After hugs and kisses all round, after George and Libby had both held and cuddled baby Jake, they had left Big Dave and Kat to become acquainted with their son. The ambulance men had given them a lift part of the way and they had walked the rest, trudging through the still thick snow.

George walked into his lounge, and Libby followed him in.

'I feel so tired. Kat's the one that did all the hard work, but I'm knackered,' she said.

He nodded and threw himself down, sprawling out on his sofa. 'I know what you mean. Who would have thought standing and worrying could be so much hard work…'

To his utmost surprise, Libby, without a moment's hesitation, climbed onto the sofa and took her normal position of lying with her head on his chest.

It had been an automatic thing, almost instinctive. She hadn't thought about it, or asked him if it was OK, it was just this need to cuddle up to him. The angst of the previous few days was completely forgotten. For now at least.

He put his arm round her shoulders, as she shifted closer to him to get comfortable.

Her hand moved to the back of his neck, fingering his curls.

'Your hair's getting long,' she mumbled sleepily, into the side of his neck.

'Yeah I know, I'll have to get it cut soon.' That was another thing Cerys had brought up the other night, how tatty his hair was.

'I like it, it's wild and rugged and sexy.'

Right then and there, he vowed never to get it cut ever again. Reciprocating Libby's gesture, he stroked her hair. It was like satin.

He closed his eyes, feeling her breathing become deeper as he drifted off.

—

George woke later and his heart nearly ripped open at the feeling of having Libby in his arms, where she belonged. He couldn't let her leave.

Libby stirred slightly in his arms, pulling herself tighter against him, and opened her eyes blearily to look at him. He felt her sigh contentedly into the side of his neck.

'I'm sorry about… everything. Giselle and… everything I said,' Libby fumbled over her apology, though in reality she had nothing to be sorry for. 'I want you to be happy and—'

'Come to the ball with me tonight,' he blurted out.

She shook her head. 'You should go with Giselle, that's not fair on her to go with me.'

'You're leaving tomorrow. This will be our last night together.'

Libby didn't say anything as she clearly thought about it.

'Look, I'll even dance with you, you can't say fairer than that?'

Libby smiled weakly and finally nodded. 'OK.'

George had one more night with her and he had to make it count.

CHAPTER 20

George knocked on the door of Libby's flat, finding himself more nervous than he had ever been in his life. This night mattered and his other dates paled in significance. She opened the door wrapped up in a long black woollen coat and wellies. Her hair was swept up in a plait that circled her head like a halo. Her gorgeous green eyes were topped with sparkly emerald eye shadow. She appraised him in his tuxedo and her face split into a smile.

'You look fantastic, George.'

'So do you, really beautiful.'

She looked down at herself in confusion. 'I'm wearing a coat and wellies.'

'You've always looked beautiful to me.'

Her smile grew and she stepped forward to kiss him on the cheek. 'Giselle is a very lucky woman.'

George offered his arm and escorted her out. It wasn't a long walk up to the ball from where they lived, five minutes on a normal day, maybe slightly longer today because of the snow, but he had help for part of the journey.

Silver Cove beach glistened under its sparkling blanket as they walked along the deserted road towards the headland where the marquee was twinkling in the darkness. It was protected by the cliffs in its position nestled snugly halfway up the hill and with all the houses in complete darkness and even the pub closed for one night only, it was the only spark of light in the darkness, welcoming them in.

'Are you sure you don't want to take Giselle instead? It's not too late to change your mind.'

'I was never going out with Giselle.'

Libby looked at him in shock. 'But… what?'

George was silent as they started up the little path that led up the hill towards the marquee, which at some point had been cleared of most of the snow.

'But this is what we were practising for,' Libby pushed.

'We were practising to help me back into the world of dating again, but more than that, to help me feel confident in my own skin. We've done that. You've done that. Not only do I feel brave enough to date, but I feel for the first time that I'm ready for marriage again too.'

'So I don't understand why you didn't ask her out, she was the woman of your dreams.'

Libby was staring at him and he was thankful for that as she hadn't seen what was just ahead of them.

He gestured with his head, indicating the two reindeers and the sled that was waiting for them.

She turned and gasped, Giselle momentarily forgotten. 'Is this for us?'

George nodded and helped her aboard, covering them both with a thick blanket. A bottle of champagne and two flute glasses rested in a bucket of ice. He leaned forward and poured two glasses, handing one to Libby as the sled rocked gently into motion, sliding gracefully across the snow towards the marquee.

She stared at him in confusion as he settled himself back under the blanket. She hadn't touched the champagne.

'I should have told you yesterday on the beach but I wanted it to be special, I wanted to give you all the bells and whistles that you wanted and instead I ended up hurting you. I wanted the perfect end to our dates tonight, Lib.' He took a steadying sip of the champagne, the bubbles dancing on his tongue. 'Giselle isn't the woman of my dreams, you are. It's always been you, ever since the first moment I saw you. Libby Joseph, I love you.'

—

Libby stared at him in shock. The night sky made a stunning backdrop behind him, the stars twinkling down on them. The snow looked magical and she was on a sleigh pulled by two reindeer. It couldn't get any more sweepingly romantic than this. And her best friend was telling her that he loved her. This was everything she ever wanted. But none of it made sense.

'But… you never said anything before.'

'I didn't think you felt that way at all – you were leaving, what was the point?'

'But what about Cerys, how could you be with her when you were in love with me?'

'You were telling me my date with Cerys would be a good thing, that even if she wasn't the one I wanted to be with the rest of my life, it would be good to go on an actual date again. That confused the hell out of me. Surely you couldn't possibly have feelings for me if you were pushing me into the arms of another woman. But then that kiss…'

'I didn't mean it. I was in love with you, I was trying to be supportive. And then you went and kissed her and tried to have sex with her. It was only the sheer amount of alcohol you'd drunk that stopped that from happening.'

Libby was angry at him and she didn't know why. Hell, she did know why. They had wasted six months dancing around their emotions when they could have been together. He had hurt her by going out with other people when actually he was in love with her all this time.

'No, it wasn't the alcohol. I stopped her because I wanted to be with you, because if I couldn't have you then I didn't want anyone else. Don't you see, I couldn't ask you out because you were the only one that mattered?'

'I'm just the easy option, aren't I? There's no effort at all being involved with me. I'm the sweet but predictable taste of chocolate. You said so yourself.'

A polite cough from the driver of the sleigh reminded Libby that they weren't alone.

'White chocolate,' George corrected. 'My favourite thing in the whole world.'

Libby stalled.

'I don't want to be with you because you're the easy option. I want to be with you because I love you more than I've ever loved anyone. I love the way you dress, your quirky style. I love that you bite your lip when you think. I love that you have so much spirit, that you seem to grab life by the horns, that you will try anything. I love that you choose something different every time we go for an Indian. I love that you love the rain as much as the sun. I love that you ride a motorbike, I love that you love my mum. I love that you are the perfect height for me, just the right height to wrap my arms around you, that when you hug me, your mouth is level with my neck, and your breath on my neck is one of the best feelings in the world. I love that when I kiss you, it's like fireworks exploding in my heart, in my veins, I love the feel of your silky skin, I love the way you smell. I love you.'

Libby stared at him. 'But you asked out Giselle. I saw you ask her out. You went to the pub together last night. I saw you kiss her on the cheek.'

'No. I asked her to help me tonight with this. She makes sweets. I asked her for some fudge as I know it's your favourite thing and

I told her my plans for tonight and then she was helping me come up with some ideas. She was going to escort you to the ball and we had a big plan but most of it was ruined by the snow.'

He passed her a small gold box and she stared at it in confusion. In exasperation he opened it up for her and inside she could see several pieces of fudge.

'Some of these are rum and raisin, your favourite, some are cherry flavoured to remind you of our night at The Cherry Tree, some are champagne flavoured to mark our champagne picnic on the islands, some are mince pie flavoured to mark our third date making mince pies and… these are ice cream flavoured which was the closest I could get to something to represent our sledging date.'

Fireworks suddenly exploded in the night sky.

'They're for you,' George mumbled, thoroughly dejected now.

She looked up at the ribbons of gold scarlet and green as they sparkled and fizzed through the night sky.

Suddenly out of some nearby bushes leapt four men dressed in red and white stripy jackets and straw boater hats. They started singing a very strange, almost comical version of 'My Heart Will Go On' by Celine Dion, the song George always sang at the top of his lungs every time they watched *Titanic*. This is what they had joked about when she'd said she wanted the all-singing, all-dancing kind of love.

'Oh God, George, you've gone to so much trouble.'

The barbershop quartet started bobbing up and down as they walked alongside the sleigh, clicking their fingers. Libby wanted to laugh and cry all at once. This was utterly ridiculous. As they reached their crescendo one of them handed her a bouquet of flowers.

She should be throwing herself into George's arms with this wonderful declaration of love but her brain was still trying to process what had happened. They had been practising for Giselle and all this time George had been in love with her.

George was obviously disappointed with her reaction too.

The sleigh stopped round the back of the marquee right next to a huge ice carving of a diamond ring.

'I was going to ask you to marry me, but let's skip that part,' George said, getting out of the sleigh and walking off towards the entrance of the marquee.

Shit! Shit, shit, shit.

This wasn't the perfect date, this was the perfect proposal, and she had cocked it up spectacularly.

The driver of the sleigh turned to look at her in despair.

'If a man goes to all that trouble to ask me to marry him, I'd be saying yes and I'm a happily married man.'

'The man's an idiot,' Libby muttered, throwing the flowers and fudge to one side. Untangling herself from the blanket and passing the flute of untouched champagne to the driver, she raced after George to tell him that.

The ball wasn't what she expected. George had always told her it was a classy affair but it was charmingly sweet with a mix of different sized tables and chairs, oddly shaped table decorations, a buffet of sandwiches and cake and music playing from an iPod. But there was no time to think about any of that, she had to find George.

She cast her eyes around the marquee, spotting Amy being swung round the floor by Seb, who was staring at her as if she was the only woman in the world. She spotted Matt kissing Polly in a darkened corner, Judith dancing with George's Uncle Bob of all people. George's mum and dad were dancing too, Sally was chatting with Nick. Everyone seemed to be having a wonderful time. She spotted George by the bar looking absolutely gutted. Libby charged over to him.

'You're an idiot. You know that, don't you.'

George nodded then looked away. She grabbed his face and pulled him back to look at her.

'But I still love you, I think I always have, too. I don't know why it took all these dates for me to realise it. I think I was just good at suppressing it because you didn't feel the same way, because I was leaving and I never wanted to stay in one place, but you changed all that. You're the funniest, kindest, sweetest, most beautiful person I know and I love you, with everything I have.'

He stared at her in shock then pulled her in for the biggest hug, clinging on to her as he curled himself around her.

She hadn't found her home in White Cliff Bay, she had found her home with him and she was finally where she belonged.

He pulled away slightly. 'But you're leaving?'

Libby shook her head. 'Not any more. It was silly of me to leave because of you when I had already made up my mind to stay. I love it here but I love you more.'

He bent to kiss her and she held him tight against her, never wanting to let him go.

The heat of him and his wonderful tangy scent surrounded her. Flashes from the night they had kissed in her bed filled her mind and she suddenly wanted that more than anything.

She pulled away slightly and looked around the room. She loved these people and this town but she loved George more than anything else.

'Let's go home.'

His eyebrows shot up in surprise. 'But we've just got here. I promised you a dance.'

'I don't need any of this, the fireworks, the reindeer sleigh ride and the champagne. I just need you.'

He blinked in confusion.

'No more pretence, no more lies or confusion. The first time we can properly be together and we're surrounded by the whole town. Let's go home.'

His face cleared with understanding and he grabbed her hand and marched out. She giggled as she followed him.

As they broke into the cold night again, George picked up speed. He ran straight past the reindeer-led sleigh, obviously knowing the journey would be too slow, and across the path that led along the headland and down the hillside onto Silver Cove beach. He stopped to pull her into his arms and kissed her hard. It was everything it was meant to be, his taste, his smell, the way his tongue slid against hers was hugely erotic. God, she loved this man. She loved everything about him. And she was going to marry him. She let out a giggle of excitement against his lips.

He pulled back slightly. 'What?'

'I was just thinking how ridiculously in love I am with you.'

'That's good.' He was already pulling her along the beach towards their flats.

'When we get married, George, will we live at your place or mine?'

'Mine. It would take too long to move my huge collection of Christmas decorations to yours.'

'Fair point.'

They fell through the door of his flat, kissing and pulling at clothes. George's tuxedo jacket came off and George started tackling her coat in between desperate urgent kisses. He finally peeled it apart.

'Oh, nice dress,' he admired her green velvety halterneck affair.

'The back is better.'

He looked surprised. 'Why would you wear a dress that has a nicer back than the front?'

Libby laughed and shrugged out of her coat, then turned round so she was facing the wall. She heard a soft moan from George as he took in her completely backless dress.

His voice was coarse when he spoke. 'I see what you mean.' He bent over, planting a soft kiss at the very base of her spine as he trailed tiny kisses up her back, causing her whole body to erupt in goosebumps. He reached the base of her neck and undid the clasp that held the dress together.

She turned back and let the dress slither to the floor, so she was only standing in her tights, knickers and wellies. Damn it, there was nothing sexy about this and if she had thought there was going to be a chance of sex with the man she loved at the end of the night she would have thought more carefully about her underwear, maybe even worn stockings. But George seemed to not care about her tights and wellies as he moved back towards her, kissing her hard, pinning her to the wall with his weight, and she could feel how turned on he was.

He lifted her and she wrapped her legs around him as the kiss continued.

'Wait,' Libby giggled, utterly delighted with the way this evening had turned out. 'I'm still in my wellies. You can't make love to me in my wellies.'

'No, I guess not.' He carried her to the arm of the sofa and sat her down. He grabbed a welly and gave it a huge tug. It stayed resolutely on her foot. He yanked it some more and it came flying off, hitting one of the life-size deer in the face. 'Oops, sorry Bambi,' George muttered as he went for the other welly.

'You called the deer Bambi?'

He nodded.

'I frigging love you.'

He grinned, pulling the boot off carefully this time, then he slowly peeled down her knickers and tights until she was completely naked. He, frustratingly, was still completely dressed.

George stood back up and stared at her. When his hands returned to her waist they were shaking.

'How should we do this? We can go in the bedroom where it's more romantic, I could light some candles, play some music. What position would you like? We could do it against the wall or...' He trailed off as she caught his face in her hands.

'None of that stuff matters. I love you and there is not a single thing you could do now to make this more special. Everything about this is right because it's you.'

She slid his bow tie off his neck and started undoing the buttons of his shirt. He stalled her hand with his own but she gently removed it, placing kisses on his bare chest after she undid each button. She peeled his shirt open and trailed reverential fingers across his chest and stomach.

'I love you, every single inch of you, I promise you that.'

He stared at her for a moment, then he quickly grabbed her legs and rolled her backwards onto the sofa. She giggled as she landed on the soft cushions and he quickly climbed on top of her with a sudden confidence she had never seen in him before. He kissed her hard and she ran her fingers through his hair at the back of his neck.

He moved his hand between her legs, hitting the exact spot that made her weak with absolute precision. It took no time at all before she was hurtling over the edge, moaning his name against his lips. He didn't stop though, he kept touching and stroking as she trembled against him again and again.

Finally he knelt up and she was vaguely aware that he was grabbing a condom from the drawers on the nearby table and rolling it on.

He flashed her the biggest grin as he lifted her slightly and slid inside her. She groaned.

'Ten,' Libby said.

He frowned slightly and leaned over her, kissing her on the mouth as he moved against her.

'What?'

'This date is the most perfect date ever, you get ten out of ten.'

He smiled and kissed her again. With his hand at the small of her back he moved position slightly, hitting that sweet spot inside of her, making a tumble of inarticulate words burst from her throat.

'Let's see if we can make it eleven,' he whispered against her lips.

—

George woke the next day and moved to take his beautiful Libby in his arms, but to his surprise he was alone in his bed.

'Libby?' He sat up, but there was silence in his flat.

He looked around in confusion. The night before had been amazing. After they had made love, he had carried her, still clinging to him, through to the bedroom, where they had laid side by side, kissing each other for ages. He had kind of expected her to roll over and go to sleep as Josie used to. But they lay with their arms and legs entwined just kissing, until the moon had disappeared and the very first tinges of early morning light had started to appear. And then as he was stroking her arms, stroking her back, she had asked him to make love to her again. This time, he had made sure it was gentle and tender, without the urgency of the first time; they had taken their time to explore each other properly. He had made sure he kissed every single inch of her body. Making love to her then had been the single most beautiful moment of his life.

And after there had been more kissing, until she had eventually fallen asleep in his arms, with her mouth against his.

But then, in sleep, she had rolled over away from him and when he tried to pull her back into his arms, she had wriggled huffily out of his grasp. He had told himself that she was just dreaming, that she didn't know it was him, but now, waking up and finding her gone… something wasn't right.

He got up, pulled on a pair of shorts and padded across to her flat. She was in the bedroom; he could hear her on the phone as he walked in.

'Yes, it was lovely, Amy, the best sex I've ever had…yeah seriously. Look I have to go, I'll tell you all about it later, but I have to be out of here before he wakes up.'

George peered round the door and watched as Libby hurriedly shoved clothes into a suitcase. She quickly hung up the phone and stuffed a few more t-shirts into an already overflowing holdall.

His heart plummeted. Anger flooding through him, he pushed the door open and she spun around guiltily.

'Go where?' he said, surprised by how cold his voice was.

'Oh George, I thought you'd be asleep for hours yet—'

'I can't believe you. You're still leaving, after last night? If you don't know now that we were made for each other, that this kind of love comes round once in a lifetime, then there's nothing else I can do. If you leave now, I won't be here waiting for you to come back. I've done everything you asked, the reindeer sleigh, the champagne, the fireworks, the barbershop quartet. Damn it, I even bought you a ring, but it's not enough, is it?'

'You bought me a ring?' Her voice was quiet, hurt.

'Yes. It was your "one day before Christmas" present that I forgot to give you yesterday.' He was so angry that he took a step away from her, wanting to shake her so much.

'Were you planning on getting down on one knee and asking me to marry you, because if you were this is hardly the romantic setting I would hope for. Shouting at the woman you want to marry is not exactly conducive to a romantic engagement.'

'You'd love that, wouldn't you, for me to throw myself to my knees now and beg for your hand in marriage. Well you can sod off; I'm not humiliating myself any further for you.'

He turned and stormed out of her flat and back into his own. Though Libby was hot on his heels.

'Where's the ring?' she demanded.

'No, you're not having it. If you want to see how big the diamond is before you make your decision, you're going to be sorely disappointed. It doesn't even have a diamond.'

'Give me the bloody ring.'

He snatched up his trousers, grabbed the box from the pocket and passed it to her. 'Here take it, sell it for all I care.'

'George, you are the biggest idiot I have ever met. Do you honestly think after you made love to me so beautifully last night I could seriously go anywhere else but here? I was packing to come here. You said we would move in here. I wanted to move in whilst you slept, so that when you woke up my clothes would already be hanging next to yours in the wardrobe. Now, since you have no intention of going on one knee to ask me to marry you, I suppose it's down to me.'

To his great surprise, Libby dropped down on one knee and opened the box towards him.

'George, I love you, I will always love you, no matter how much of an idiot you are. Now… will you do me the extraordinary honour of marrying me?'

He quickly dropped to his knees in front of her. 'I thought that…'

'Yeah, well, you thought wrong,' she snapped, grabbing the ring from the box and forcing it onto his ring finger. 'There, we're engaged, and we're not having a long engagement either, I want to be married to you by the end of the year.'

He looked down at the gold ring, curved in gentle waves studded with tiny coloured stones in different shades of green, as it rested halfway up his finger.

'I think it might look better on you, Lib. Can I?'

She nodded reluctantly and he took it off. He took her hand, kissed it and then slid the ring gently onto her finger.

'When we tell the story of how we became engaged to our friends and family, maybe we could miss out the part where I was a stupid idiot.'

'Maybe,' Libby sniffed, trying to suppress the smile as she stared at the ring. 'Maybe when we got back yesterday from the ball, you dropped to your knees amongst the candles and flowers and asked me to marry you then, which of course I said yes to.'

George kissed her forehead. 'That sounds much better.'

He stood up and pulled her to her feet, though she couldn't take her eyes off the ring, which he took to be a good sign.

'It's beautiful, George,' she said quietly.

'Twenty shades of green,' he murmured.

'Even sprout?'

He smiled. 'Do you forgive me?'

She half scowled. 'Not yet. I might have to punish you, no sex for a month.'

He smirked. 'Happy Christmas, baby.'

She looked down at the ring box in her hand, and frowned. His heart leapt when he realised she'd seen the bit of paper stuck into the lid. She tucked her finger into the edge and prised it out.

Still scared that their engagement was built on quite shaky ground, he tried to take it off her.

'That's nothing, don't worry about it.'

She held the paper out of his reach. 'What is it?'

'It's silly, just… I did some rules for a perfect marriage, don't look at it now.'

Libby, stubborn as ever, unfolded the piece of paper with evident interest. He put his hand on the paper, covering the words. 'We can discuss terms, come up with an agreed set of rules between us, compromise on some, but rules one, four and ten are non-negotiable.'

She arched an eyebrow and he took his hand off so she could read it. He moved round behind her, holding her in his arms and reading it over her shoulder.

1. *Mr Donaldson will do ALL the cooking.*

He saw her smirk at this one.

2. *The Husband and Wife will partake in hot, passionate sex every day, without fail.*
3. *Every position in the Kama Sutra will be tried and tested, including the one with the pulley.*
4. *Absolute honesty at all times.*
5. *The Husband and Wife will live in a big house at the top of White Cliff Bay, overlooking the sea.*

Libby stopped reading at this one. 'No way, I'm not leaving Silver Cove beach; if you want a big house we'll have to buy one down here.'

'It's just that they rarely come up for sale down here, I thought we'd be more likely to get one in the main town.'

'We'll just have to wait until they do, I'm not moving, that's non-negotiable.'

He smiled. 'OK, keep reading.'

She returned her gaze to the list.

6. *The Husband and Wife will have three children, two girls and a boy, a dog called Sausage and a cat called Onion.*

'I prefer Bangers and Mash.'

'Fine, we're not going to argue over the intricacies, but Bangers is going to be a St Bernard or a Newfoundland.'

'Fine,' she said, shortly, though she leaned back into him as she looked back at the list.

7. *Every year we will add a new stamp to your passport.*
8. *The marriage must include silliness, practical jokes, daft conversations, anything that makes the other person laugh.*

'Get me a pen,' she ordered and, keeping one arm round her waist, he leaned back and grabbed one from the shelf. He passed it to her and he watched her scrawl a side note in her messy handwriting next to number 8.

'Practical jokes that scare the other person so much they knock themselves out are strictly prohibited.'

'Good point.'

9. *I will dance with you on our wedding day.*

He saw her swallow.

10. *I promise to hold you in sleep, keep you safe from harm whilst you dream. When you need to walk, in dreams or when you're awake, I will walk by your side. I promise that I will tell you I love you every day, wake you each morning kissing you from head to toe. I will support you, encourage you and laugh with you. And I will make it my mission in life to make you as completely and utterly happy as you make me.*

Libby folded the piece of paper, her hands shaking. She turned round in his arms and he was surprised to see tears in her eyes. 'I do love you.'

'I know. I've always loved you, Lib, always will.'

She smiled at him, and leaned up to kiss him. The kiss continued for some time, her hands in his hair, round his neck, stroking his bare back. And he was very surprised when he felt her undo his shorts and push them off his hips.

He pulled away. 'What about your terms, no sex for a month?'

'I've changed my mind, woman's prerogative.'

'Of course.' He quickly yanked her top off her and made quick work of the rest of her clothes, and she laughed at his impatience. 'Just in case you change it back again.'

She smiled as she took his hand and led him towards the bedroom.

'Now listen, when we made love, was it really the best sex you've ever had?' he asked.

She giggled with embarrassment. 'You heard that?'

He nodded.

'Yes it was, George, it was amazing.'

'The first time or the second time?'

'Both, absolutely both.'

He smiled, but then his smile fell. 'That's a shame, because that gives me a lot to live up to.'

She stopped next to the bed and rested her head on his chest. She looked up at him, as he pulled her tighter against him. 'It's only going to get better from here on in.'

'Maybe I should brush up on the Kama Sutra before we go any further.'

'If you think there's time,' she shrugged. 'But we're both already naked, what would you suggest I do with myself whilst you're doing your homework?'

He took her face in his hands and kissed her again. 'Maybe I'll brush up for next time.'

'That could be tricky – you do realise I'm not letting you out of bed for at least the next three days?'

'Excellent,' he grinned.

'Besides...' she lay down on the bed '...you already know my favourite position.'

He wracked his brains as he knelt on the bed, kissing her neck. The cobra? The elephant? The one with the pulley? 'What's that then?'

Libby smiled, pulling him down on top of her. 'The good old-fashioned missionary.'

He grinned as he kissed her. 'Thank goodness for that.'

Nash for the tireless promoting, tweeting and general cheerleading. Thank you to all the other wonderful people at Bookouture; Oliver Rhodes, the editing team and the wonderful designers who created this absolutely gorgeous cover.

To Oliver Mallinson and the RNLI for helping me with the details of the lifeboat rescue.

To the CASG, the best writing group in the world, you wonderful talented supportive bunch of authors, I feel very blessed to know you all, you guys are the very best.

To the wonderful Bookouture authors for all your encouragement and support.

And some other gorgeous people who have encouraged, supported, promoted, got excited or just listened; Rebecca Pugh, Lisa Dickenson, Sharon Wilden, Kelly Rufus, Simona Elena, Erin McEwan, Katey Beeden, Maryline, Jo Hughes, Dawn Crooks, Laura Delve, Jill Stratton, Tay Pickering, Emma Poulloura, Aga Klar, Catriona Merryweather, Lynsey James, Lindsay Hill, Ana, Alba Forcadell, Dawn Brierley, Sophie Hedley, Cesca Major, Rachael Lucas, Kat Black, Helen Redfern, Katy Gough, Emily Kerr, Jaimie Admans, Kate Gordon, Pernille Hughes, Louise Wykes, Paris Baker, Silke Auwers, The Blossom Twins, Daniel Riding, Pat Elliott, Shaun, Mark Rumsey, James Brown, Arron Davenport.

To all those involved in the blog tour. To anyone who has read my book and taken the time to tell me you've enjoyed it or wrote a review, thank you so much.

Thank you, I love you all.

ACKNOWLEDGEMENTS

To my family, my mom, my biggest fan, who reads every word I have written a hundred times over and loves it every single time, my dad, my brother Lee and my sister-in-law Julie, for your support, love, encouragement and endless excitement for my stories.

For my twinnie, the gorgeous Aven Ellis for just being my wonderful friend, for your endless support, for cheering me on and for keeping me entertained with wonderful stories and pictures of hot men. Although we have never met, you are my best friend and I love you dearly.

Huge thank you to my wonderful, incredible friends Kirsty Maclennan, Megan Milliken and Victoria Stone for the endless support and love. You are amazing.

To my friends Gareth and Mandie, for your support, patience and enthusiasm. My lovely friends Jac, Verity and Jodie who listen to me talk about my books endlessly and get excited about it every single time.

For Sharon Sant for just being there always and your wonderful friendship.

To my wonderful agent Madeleine Milburn for just been amazing and fighting my corner and for your unending patience with my constant questions.

To my editor Claire for helping to make this book so much better, for putting up with all my crazy throughout the whole process, for replying to every single email and for listening to me freak out with complete and utter patience. Thank you to Kim

LETTER FROM HOLLY

Thank you so much for reading *Snowflakes on Silver Cove*, I had so much fun creating this story and I hope you enjoyed reading it as much as I enjoyed writing it.

One of the best parts of writing comes from seeing the reaction from readers. Did it make you smile or laugh, did it make you cry, hopefully happy tears? Did you fall in love with George and Libby or Amy and Seb? Did you like the gorgeous town of White Cliff Bay? If you enjoyed the story, I would absolutely love it if you could leave a short review. Getting feedback from readers is amazing and it also helps to persuade other readers to pick up one of my books for the first time.

I have two books out this Christmas set in the town of White Cliff Bay, so if you enjoyed this book and haven't read *Christmas at Lilac Cottage* yet I hope you will love it too.

Thank you for reading and I hope you have a wonderful cosy Christmas.

Love Holly x

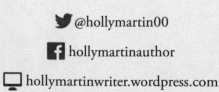

🐦 @hollymartin00

📘 hollymartinauthor

🖥 hollymartinwriter.wordpress.com